Paul Holbr

He currently spends ... days working at a secondary school in North Yorkshire, supporting the development of the next Great British generation and his nights plotting and planning the next Great British novel.

His second novel Domini Mortum, the sequel to Memento Mori is currently undergoing a crowdfunding campaign at Unbound.co uk. Please support it.

ISBN: 978-1530722679

© Paul Holbrook 2016
All rights reserved

**To Kathryn,
For being there**
x

Memento Mori

The Final Confessions of Sibelius Darke

By
Paul Holbrook

1
A Portrait

They called me a ghoul. They said that I preyed and profited on the misery of those lost within the depths of their suffering and grief. I was painted a demon, sent upon the world to revel in despair and gorge on the tears and woe of the piteous and broken.

Those that said this however; those who whispered to each other and crossed the road when I approached, those who spread malicious gossip and slander regarding the practices which took place within my studio; they were fools, simpletons, the weak and the narrow minded. They did not see the joy and comfort which my humble service provided to the families who approached me in distress.

I truly admit that there is truth in the fact that my futuristic operations caused some initial damage to the good name of Father's business, a business that both he and his father before him had spent many years building, turning it from a small service run by immigrants to a well-respected local mainstay. I am sure, and I reassured Father on many occasions, that this was because the people of the neighbourhood were yet to catch up with the times.

There were many professionals like me who plied their trade among the capitals of the continent, even one or two specialists elsewhere in London, who were well respected and sought after by those in high society. The only issue which I conceded with my work was in its location, based as it was in the heart of the poor Tower Hamlets area. The people there, although varied in their origin, had in common a superstitious and fearful nature when presented with an enterprise as new and 'odd' as mine.

When I established my business eight years ago through, I am ashamed to admit, funds provided to me through my assignations with sharpers and card folk, I saw it as an entity of the future. I was a spearhead, a brave and bold visionary bringing new technological advances to the people of this teeming metropolis.

Father took great convincing of this fact and held his reservations, however I did, through my work, provide the family business with some trade and I told Father that this mutually beneficial relationship would only continue to strengthen as my reputation grew.

The family who attended my small studio on the day that my terror began had used my services once before seven years ago. There were four of them back then; the father, the mother and the two children, one - a girl aged seven and the other, a new born boy. The father had written to me after being directed towards one of the advertisements which I placed on a regular basis in the Illustrated London News.

He stated, in a note delivered to me by messenger boy, that on becoming aware of the service I provided through contact at his club, he felt the need to arrange a meeting to discuss the best way of commemorating his family's situation. My attendance at his house would be required the following morning at 10 o'clock, prompt. The note gave details of his address along with strict instructions that he expected me not to divulge the nature of my visit to his staff on my arrival, they would be expecting a visitor on a matter of important business and that was all the information they required.

The boy waited silently on the other side of my desk, cap in hand as I composed a suitable reply stating that I found such a meeting and conditions agreeable and would attend his house as requested.

I recall that first meeting with great clarity. I had attended his house the following morning, bringing with me a few of the finer examples of my work to show the artistic merit of my profession and, of course, my own skill in such matters. I had rung the rear doorbell of their smart townhouse in Marylebone and to my great frustration found myself to be left waiting for nearly two full minutes.

When the door was finally opened it was not by a footman at all but by a girl who I assumed was the scullery maid. I tried not to show my obvious dismay at being greeted by such a low ranking member of the staff; however I have never been one who can display an innate ability to disguise my feelings, especially when these feelings are linked to disappointment. A girl of probably no more than twenty years, she behaved appropriately although I could sense a petulant edge hidden not far below the surface of her roughly scrubbed face.

As with many of the houses which I visited on such an occasion, I noted that all of the staff wore suitable livery for the circumstances, each with a wide piece of black cloth pinned to their right shirtsleeve as an armband.

"If you'd just like to wait here a moment sir, I will find the footman who will take you upstairs. Can I ask the purpose of your visit?"

"You cannot," I replied. "The master of the house is expecting me and that is enough." The girl looked rightfully scolded, although her eyes narrowed enough to let me know that she did not approve of my air of superiority - I gave it no attention.

The footman arrived, an elderly gentleman, who approached me with a respectful attitude which I found more fitting to the situation.

"Good morning, sir, I apologise for the delay and the inappropriate nature of your welcome to the house. Mr Earnshaw is expecting you; please follow me to the drawing room."

I followed the man up a flight of stairs at the end of the corridor and through to the hallway at the front of the house. He took my hat and coat and asked me to wait a short moment whilst he informed the master of the house that I had arrived. I took the time to admire the decoration of the hall, with its polished oaken staircase and sumptuous rug covering the floor. This was the kind of house that I aspired to live in one day. At twenty-eight, I still considered myself a young man and knew that, if I continued to follow the path that I had carved for myself, I would one day be in ownership of such a property, with all of the additional benefits that this entailed. My thoughts of future wealth were interrupted by the footman who came out of one of the large doors in the hall to tell me that I was to go through immediately.

I was led into a large well-furnished room where upon entering I took the opportunity to take in the décor. The room was busy but smart with beautifully maintained furniture throughout. I liked to observe each of the houses that I visited, so that I was able to mentally record the style and ornamentation. I would then make a point of writing down in my journal particular items so that when it came time to furnish my future house I would have already fully planned the layout of the rooms to the finest of details.

Charles Earnshaw, the master of the house was sat on the other side of the room at a pedestal desk, writing a letter when I entered.

"Mr Darke, sir," the footman announced and Mr Earnshaw waved him away continuing to write. I stood and waited for him to acknowledge my arrival, something which seemed to take an age. I had taken the initiative of carrying out some research on this gentleman the previous day, visiting a friend of mine, Stanley Hawkins, a carriage driver, who made it his business to continually scan the daily newspapers and keep a near perfect memory of who was who within London society.

Part of this I am sure was the fact that he liked to keep his beak in others affairs but, as a carriage driver it always paid to know who you may have riding with you.

Mr Charles Earnshaw was a scientist of some note, working in the field of medicine. He was a fellow at the King's College and specialised in neurology, which he studied under Jean-Martin Charcot at Pitié-Salpêtrière Hospital in Paris for seven years. His wife, a French woman twenty years his junior by the name of Jeanne Bouchard, was the fourth daughter of the eminent Paris physician Gerard Bouchard. Mr Earnshaw had a reputation as a generous and thoughtful man, often giving up his free time to provide advice and fundraising work for charities concerned with the secure aid of lunatics and the mentally unbalanced.

The price of this information was two quartems of gin. It was over the asking price given to me by Stanley, but it pays to keep a man like him close to you and feeling as though they are in your debt; one can never tell when his kind of knowledge may be useful to you in the future. Since my youth I had developed a series of connections and contact points, which were useful to know and have at my disposal for various services. Whether they be dockers and river workers for the occasional nod when I was looking for particular items of interest coming in, money-lenders for knowing who was up to their ears and looking for a bit of ready or a seamstress when a hasty bit of stitching or mending was required, something which was very handy in my profession.

I looked over at the mahogany and parcel gilt settee placed next to his desk and considered taking a seat to attract his attention. This could however be thought of as bad form so I decided upon a small cough just to clear the throat and remind him that I was there. It had the desired effect as, without looking up from his writing, he finally spoke.

"Mr Darke, you were recommended to me by a business associate of mine, Edward Belvoir, he said that you did some work for him last year when he found himself in a similar situation to my own."

"Yes I remember Mr Belvoir well; he was most pleased with the finished work. How is old Edward these days?"

"This is a business conversation, not an idle reminiscence." His voice was sharp and patronising. He had still not looked up from his papers.

"But of course, Mr Earnshaw," I agreed, deciding to keep it chipper and remain positive. "This is a serious enterprise," I continued, "However, please pass on my regards, I found him most agreeable, thoroughly nice."

He finally looked up from his desk, I would imagine more to press on with our meeting than to engage with me in an exchange of pleasant dialogue.

"Would you like to see some examples of my work, sir?" I asked. "I took the liberty of bringing a couple of pieces that I have completed recently. I have the commissioning gentlemen's acquiescence in these matters I can assure you."

I reached into my bag to withdraw the two items and handed them to him. He picked up his spectacles from the desk and put them on to aid his study. His eyes moved over them frantically as if searching for error or sign of impropriety. He would not find any, I was a master at my art and these two examples of my trade were among the best of my collection.

I chose this moment to point out the finer points, "If you look at the larger of the two I thi-." I was halted in mid-sentence by his hand, which he rose up without taking his eyes from my work.

I found his silence a little unnerving. Before me was a man not prone to genial conversation and friendly exchange, despite what I had been told by my contact. He had obviously gone through a grievous time of late, which I could understand;

it was part of my work to deal with those who had come upon a point in their lives which any person would dread. However, I found this type of abruptness a touch ungentlemanly and, had I not been able to see the wider picture and the potential benefits that a good new contact may bring, I would have taken my items and left Mr Earnshaw to wallow in his own misery.

When he finally spoke to break the stillness, the sound of his voice was slow and dry.

"Remarkable, really remarkable. When were these captured? ... I mean how long after? ..."

"Two days, sir. I am afraid that the very nature of my profession requires both speed and a calculated, high level of organisation." Finally a chance to give the patter. "I have my own premises in which I am able to complete a work, or, if you so desire I am able to come to you and work within your own home. Some of the families that I have completed commissions for think that the homely feel adds to the overall effect. I have seen the work of others in my field and I can say that you will find that there is no better in London than myself."

His eyes had still not looked up from their study but I could tell that I had him in my pocket now.

"Yes," he said, his voice sounding far away as if lost within the image in his gaze. "Yes, I can see that being in the home would create a better outcome," he finally looked up at me his eyes meeting mine. "My wife, you see ... she has not handled the situation well at all and I would not want her to travel across town at this time."

There it was, the deal was as good as done and, as usual, the hypnotic nature of my products had sold the idea to him.

"Very good, sir." I decided it was time to close the deal and put things into motion before he had a chance to back away. "I think you will find that you have made a wise choice today. Shall I return to-morrow with my equipment? The whole business should take no longer than an hour; I trust that you will make the arrangements for your family to be available?" I leant forward with my hand outstretched to take the pieces back. I had been in this situation before where a prospective client has been too mesmerised to settle matters.

"Mmm ..." he was still lost in thought, but quickly snapped out of it when I reached out to take back my work. "Oh yes of course. Shall we say eleven to-morrow morning? Come to the front door next time, I will tell Carter to expect you."

"Excellent. Excellent," I could not contain my happiness at the acquisition of this account. He watched me for a moment, his eyes narrowed as if trying to see the workings of my mind, it was a most uncomfortable instance, being examined as if a curiosity within a circus. "Would there be any other matters that you wish to discuss regarding to-morrow's appointment?" I asked, if only to break free from the scrutiny.

"Tell me, Mr Darke," his eyes did not move from my face as he spoke, "You strike me as an ambitious young man, is this all a great show for my benefit or are you as hungry for success as you would like me to believe?"

Whilst taken aback by the brutality of his question I smiled at his perception. I thought for a moment of the consequences of my answer before conceding to honesty.

"It is true, sir that I have a 'patter' and a facade that I like to employ upon meeting a prospective client for the first time, but I can assure you that I am as ravenous as I appear. Since an early age I have planned a path for myself, so far I have not wavered."

"And will you ... waver? What would it take to break this journey?"

I felt unnerved but answered in a confident manner anyway.

"Nothing, Mr Earnshaw, nothing will stop me from getting what I most desire. I mean to be a success in business and I mean to make that happen at all costs."

He continued to stare at me but did not respond, his face had taken on a serious and thoughtful provenance, which I found most patronising. I suddenly felt that the control of the situation had quickly been snatched from me and decided, wrongly or rightly, to take it back.

"If that is all, sir I will return to-morrow for our appointment." I took my work from his hands - perhaps a little too briskly. "I must leave now as I am a very busy man and there is another family awaiting my arrival." He nodded his approval and I took my leave.

The smile that I gave him as I left was well practised. Not smug or cheery but sympathetic with an air of a professional providing a service of extreme value. Inwardly however, I was leaping for joy, for not only had I gained a new client but my standing could only be improved by a contact so esteemed and well thought of. As I left his house, I knew that in some way this assignation would change the course of my life, my business and its rate of success.

I was correct of course. Mr Earnshaw was so pleased with the result of our appointment the following day that I received an embarrassment of further business through his personal recommendation and the wonderful spread of gossip in polite society. Thinking back to this first meeting made me realise just how much I had developed my trade since that day seven years ago. I felt as if I had come full circle as it were and wondered if the popularity of the service I provided would receive a further boost following our second meeting.

When I heard the carriage pull up outside I knew that he had arrived with his family for his latest appointment. I carefully returned the book I had been studying to my shelf and went down the stairs from my humble rooms to meet them at the door to the studio.

There were just the three of them this time; Mr Earnshaw, his wife and their daughter who was seven years older than when I had seen her last and was now around the age of fourteen. Two of Mr Earnshaw's staff accompanied them helping them through to the studio. I exchanged pleasantries with him and his wife before asking them to be seated on the far side of the room on a chez-lounge, which I had placed there earlier, surrounded by various pieces of set scenery such as a large house-plant and tall table. Their daughter, Marie, was seated between them and, once happy with the overall look of the piece, I retreated to my camera to begin.

I placed my head under the black cloth and looked through the viewfinder at the family. Although, I admit that I am an artist in my field, I have found that it often helps when I am presented with a family so attractive and so easy to capture as Mr Earnshaw and his family. The fact that the master of the house was such an affluent and influential figure was purely added icing on an already well-decorated cake.

My focus in this picture was, as always, the newly deceased figure, in this case the child, Marie. She had long, blonde hair woven into a plait and had been dressed in a pretty frock of deep red velvet which, I assumed, was either her or her mother's favourite as was often the case in the clothing worn by the passed family member for these pictures. She had such a clean face, unblemished by age or worry, perfect for portraiture and one which would have developed, if she had lived, into the visage of a beautiful young woman. I thought, as I often do at times like these, of the life that had been lost, of the husband who she had never met and the children whom she had never bore. These thoughts, when they came, did not fill me with sorrow or grief. A person in my profession or indeed any line of employment where the dead were involved could not let themselves be hindered by the sadness and grief which spilled forth from a family at this time. No, a person in my position had been hired for a purpose and it was to the benefit of the family and all involved if strict lines had been drawn between sympathy and professionalism.

I thought of my first commission with the family and the baby boy who had been the centre of the attention in that portrait. That child could have changed the world for the better; he could have been a great inventor or a medical man like his father. He could however, have become a tyrant, a man who beat his wife and children or even a murderer. This was the way of life; nature creates a path that we must follow and if that path is brief and ended shortly into its journey, then it was not a sane and temperate person who lingered on these futile dreams of what may have been. This lesson was taught to me by my grandfather, a man whose words and wisdom have influenced every part of my life.

"Please just hold that position," I said preparing to start the exposure. I stared at the family through the viewfinder, presented to me upside down. In the following moment however something happened which, whilst quite unexpected, sent a stuttering chill through me. I halted the procedure immediately and removed my head from beneath the cloth, staring at the girl.

"Is there something the matter, Darke?" Mr Earnshaw asked, a look of consternation spreading across his face as he noticed the intensity of my gaze. "What is the hold up?"

Surely I had been mistaken; surely my eyes had played a trick on me. I blinked rapidly twice and again stared hard at the daughter for a moment. Her face was unmoving, her eyes pale and rheumy. I reassured myself that it was a trick of the light.

"No hold up, sir. No problem at all," I replied, "I just wanted to make sure of a small matter before proceeding." I covered my head again and stared through the viewfinder, this time concentrating all of my attention on the dead girl hoping that it had been a mistake.

I found myself thoroughly displeased and fearful with my second view however, but removed the lens cover to start the procedure anyway. This was not an ordinary occurrence but I could not stop now. All I could do was hold onto my nerves and try to maintain some degree of composure underneath the cloth out of sight of the Earnshaw's. It would take approximately five minutes for the exposure to complete, and in this time, I could try to take in what I was seeing and make some kind of logical sense of it.

For here before me, through the viewfinder of my camera, I could see that the lips of the child appeared to be moving. They were moving in a repeating pattern as if saying the same word over and over. Whispered they were but becoming louder so that I could actually hear her voice. I squinted at her through the lens to try to see just what this word was, my eyes frantically reading the movement of her lips, my ears straining for a sound.

With a cold fear, which I had not felt since I was a child, the truth of this voice from the dead hit me. For as the sound of the girl's chant began to form within my ears, deadly recognition came. I knew the word.

It was a word from my childhood, a word which I hoped never to hear again. My heart seized as I listened to the lips of a dead fourteen year old girl as they continued to repeat;
"Surma."

2
MY DUAL EDUCATION

I feel that at this time I should provide to you, dear reader, something in the way of explanation as to why this word would fill me with so much affright, this being of course apart from the obvious reason that it was being spoken to me by a child nearly two days after her death. The answer is best expounded through some information regarding my background and childhood, a childhood which, both through birth and choice, has always been connected with death.

My father had been an undertaker, like his father before him. However, whilst learning the 'trade' as a boy working for father's business, I had always seen myself as a gentleman of the future. My role throughout most of my younger days was walking in front of the horse drawn hearse as it followed its usual route down Whitechapel High Street to St Mary Matfellon Church. I did this from the age of six until I reached ten years old, from then my younger brothers were deemed 'more angelic' due to their child-like faces and general sense of innocence.

As I got older and they took over my duties, I moved on to polishing the hearse carriage and caskets and caring for our horses. Following each service, it would be my responsibility to feed, rub down and stable the horses, something that I found quite abhorrent. I never had a love for animals in the way that other children often seem to, I saw them as base and stupid and the fact that they required so much attention was a drain on my valuable time.

I dreamt in those days, as many young boys do, of being a proper gent, well respected and a member of one the fine clubs up town, where I could spend my days sitting and sharing a glass with friends. My strategy for attaining this task though, bordered on the point of obsession. I did not attend a school as one would normally imagine a child of a moderately successful local businessman would, Father did not believe that I would ever learn anything of any note. Even when Christ Church School opened just around the corner from the funeral parlour when I was ten, Father disapproved of any education that I might have obtained there.

'You will learn what I think you need to know, boy,' he would tell me, 'mixing with the street filth will not provide a son of mine with the knowledge of how to properly provide undertaking services to the mourning families of this great city.'

That is not to say that I received no education, far from it. At an early age I was taught to read and write by Father and, I would envisage, I had a love of reading greater than any child for miles around. This would not be surprising though as most of the other children living locally were illiterate and quite uninterested in books. My desperation for books was enkindled and fed by literary works borrowed and sometimes given to Father from the more well-adjusted and educated families of the bereaved. This was sometimes as part payment for the services Father provided and because, as was often remarked;

'Your little boy is so adorable, the face of an angel and hair so blonde it is almost white'.

Far from being ridiculed by the other children of the area, my skill in reading was seen as a blessing by them as they would continually pester me to read stories to them. The source of these tales was not, however, in the novels and great works which I so vigorously absorbed at home, but more often it was to engross a collection of local nippers with the contents of the latest dreadfuls.

These pamphlets would be brought to me often after the boys had clubbed together to buy them or, I suspect, stolen them. With their garish and sensational accounts of gentleman criminals and murder most foul, I could see the fire of excitement light within the children's eyes and, I do admit, that I found myself not a little awed and excited by the nature of the penny dreadful's tales.

My education in the realities and horrors of life were provided for me through the environment in which I found myself. Over the years I had grown to know the cobbled streets surrounding the funeral parlour well, both during my working hours and in the evenings when Mother dragged me away from my books to run errands for her or in her words

'Hook it! Get out from under my feet and go bother someone else!'

Thinking back to those days, the thought that Mother saw me as trouble for her is quite incorrect as I was no more trouble to her than the mice that, although not invited, appeared to share our small lodgings based above the parlour.

During these moments let loose out in the wilds of the London street, I would scurry around the dark alleyways and narrow lanes, outwardly oblivious to the danger which presented itself to a small framed boy, wide eyed and soft of face. My inner thoughts however, were alert to all of the potential perils that could befall me and I knew that the combination of speed of foot and thought would be able to help me to avoid any undesirable predicaments.

On a daily basis I would visit the Ten Bells and other inns of the area to offer the drunks the job of mourning at a funeral for the payment of one penny per graveside appearance. Many of the more regular employees in this bizarre occupation would report to Mother at the back door of the parlour building on the morning of a proposed service, to collect a set of standard but vaguely respectable black apparel, which they would ensure remained loosely of clean appearance, from a distance at least. Following the service they would return to the parlour to receive payment of their miserably earned coin, first returning the mourning attire to the close inspection of Mother's interrogatory eye.

There were a number of these less reputable establishments which I made myself familiar with in those times when Mother expelled me from the safe security of the bedroom which I shared with my two younger brothers. The variety of the chores and errands which Mother, in her impatient wisdom and irate exasperation, would bestow upon my youthful form were wide ranging.

During one particular excursion into the depths of the lively streets and alleys that surrounded my home, I had been sent by Mother to recruit no less than a dozen souls to attend the funeral the next day of a local businessman. The word businessman I use in their loosest sense as he was in fact a local money lender who ran a dollyshop three doors down from Father's undertakers. The gentleman in question had preyed for many years on the poor and unfortunate to such a degree that news of his demise had been met throughout the drinking houses of the borough with a most raucous cheer and cries of pure joy that only the thought of freedom from debt can bring.

Edmund Crockleby was not a man renowned for his agreeable nature and kindness of spirit, in fact many stories were told, mostly following his death for fear of being refused credit, of the joy he would display as he revelled in the despair of those in need of his heinous services. Once money had been lent by him, a person was within a suffocating grasp from which they rarely escaped, such was the interest he charged and the unreasonable demands that he made on those whose names were scrawled in his black book.

Crockleby had been found dead at his lodgings by an associate of his, Bill Fletcher, a brute of a man well known for inflicting punishment beatings on Crockleby's late payers. Fletcher told the police that he had stopped around at his friend's rooms to invite him out for a small drink and had found his door open and Mr Crockleby lying on the floor beside his bed with his head stoved in and the bare wooden floor of his room covered in the red stuff. His belongings had been ransacked and it would seem that some items had been taken from a hidden area underneath a floorboard.

In the words of Inspector Stickett, who interviewed Fletcher as part of his investigation,

"Is Bill Fletcher a bruiser and a no good villain? Yes he is. Would I trust him with my family? No, I would not. But can I prove that he did batter Mr Crockleby to death? No, I have not seen the proof of this."

The culprit was never brought to justice, although it was noted in the weeks following the murder that old Bill was often seen about town flashing a fat wallet and wearing a fancy new suit. The fact that somebody had done away with Crockleby was a blessing both for the police, who had been seeking his downfall for a while, and also his poor debtors who suddenly found themselves with a clean slate, albeit a temporary one until the next undesirable with ready cash to lend, rose to the surface and 'helped them out'.

Crockleby was a villain and no mistake, but as well as this he was a bad man without a kind word for anyone, be they king or cripple, and despite being well known by every person in the manor, very few people felt bound to attend the service to commemorate his untimely passing. It was said that even members of his own family agreed to attend proceedings just so that they could see that he was put deep into the ground and the dirt was pressed down hard upon his grave.

As I toured the drinking holes on my usual route, I kept a keen eye out for the usual customers, those poor souls who spent their evenings sat in the corner. They nursed a nip, whilst carefully ensuring that the small amount of coins about their person lasted for cheap drink whilst still being able to afford enough for a small bite to soak it up and keep away the morning horrors. Some of them were professional mourners and could attend up to three funerals a day if they were blessed with enough unfortunate deaths in the vicinity. They of course had other revenue streams which they could access, occasional labour and errand running or working with the local girls to turn over a customer from out of the area. None however were as easy, or legal, as attending the service of some poor unfortunate soul who either nobody cared about or who had such a high opinion of themselves that they had prearranged their service to include hired 'sobbers'.

I knew each of my regulars by name and kept close with the bar-keeps who always told me where I could find suitable bodies for Mother, as the more the mourners earned the greater additional ready they would spend in their establishments. On the day of Crockleby's service I had been having particular trouble in finding more than a couple who could attend. This had filled me with confusion and worry. The confusion came through my wonder at where everyone had got to on this cold, wet Thursday afternoon. The worry pervaded from the thought of failing at my task and feeling the sharp disappointment of Mother, leaving me unable to sit comfortably for days.

As I entered the Two Brewers my confusion disappeared as I found, that a great many of the normals were holed up in there, merry as you like and drunk as a group of proverbial lords. It appeared that a great many of them were heavily into trouble with Mr Crockleby and following the news of his passing felt the need to commemorate the occasion with a service of their own. Needless to say that the offers of assistance in the hired mourner department were many indeed, in fact the opportunity to carry out this act gave them even greater pleasure as they knew that, in a reversal of fortune, Mr Crockleby would actually be paying *them* money, albeit from beyond the grave. Before leaving the establishment to tell Mother the glad news of my success in hiring I even enjoyed a couple of sips myself on my new employee's wallets.

It is my experiences in dealing with the downtrodden locals of the parish, which I look on most fondly of my childhood. However, even though I was young and entranced by the dangerous and exciting surrounding in which I grew up, I always kept within me a desire to move up in the world to bigger and better things.

Father had been disappointed by my apparent lack of enthusiasm for carrying on the family tradition, this disappointment was displayed however not through anger but sadness as, despite his sometimes stern nature, Father was warm and loving to my brothers and I and had dreamt of providing us with every security and protection for our future. When I had been born he had changed the name of his establishment to Edgar N. Darke and Son, in the firm and committed belief that I would naturally assume his role. This role involved continuing the business started by Grandfather when he had arrived in this country with his young family over fifty years ago.

My grandfather, Sibelius Johannes Dharkrot arrived in England after fleeing from our homeland following the Russian invasion in 1809. He had taken with him what he thought would be a comfortable amount of money to survive, but found that much of it was spent trying to escape the country and make his way across Sweden and Norway and boat passage across the North Sea. When he finally arrived in London his 'wealth' consisted of just enough money to buy a home and start a business. He altered the family name to ensure that the locals did not see him as an outsider. It is true that some of the ways of our family could be seen as odd, when compared to our east-end neighbours, but, as Father continued to press upon me throughout my youth,

"We have changed our name to fit in with the English, but within these walls we will continue to be proud of our heritage."

Within the house we spoke both Suomi and English, and although being born in this country and considering myself an Englishman, Father insisted that my two younger brothers, Johannes and Niko and I were fluent in both reading and writing in the language of our true homeland. Our favourite times as young boys were when we sat of an evening with Grandfather as he told us mythical tales of heroes and monsters, how the world was formed and how men learned the songs that gave them power and taught them skills.

For the benefit of my mother, who came from an English family, we contained our true language to specific times within the house for she had never managed, and Father said did not try, to learn the tongue of my father's ancestors. Mother's family were from the local area but we did not have any contact with them as they had not sanctioned her marriage to my father, who they thought of as 'foreign' even though he himself had been born in this country.

There is an old Finnish proverb that says, 'Father's goodness is higher than the mountains, Mother's goodness is deeper than the sea'. Of my father I would say that this was true as, despite being strict in his teaching of us and committed to ensuring that we were obedient, he did nothing other than look after our interests and give us the best education and care that he could provide. For Mother however the proverb could not be farther from the truth unless her goodness was so deep under the sea that it was undiscoverable. Mother, to the outside world, was an agreeable and good natured woman who provided an unenviable level of support to the family through the running of the home whilst her husband and boys worked, as well making available a small catering service to those that wished to employ her services for the pre or post-funeral gatherings. Her fare was nothing special, a few pastry goods and bread and soup, but this was often enough to lessen the burden on the families of the recently bereaved.

Within the home however, she was, to her husband, a nagging fishwife and to her sons a violent tyrant, willing to deliver a thrashing for the slightest of discrepancies in our behaviour. My brothers and I bore her vehemence well however, and took the beatings without a word of complaint. We each had learned early on that the smallest sign of rebellion or anger on our part would introduce the severest of behaviours from her including being locked in her kitchen cupboards for hours on end or, the most feared of her punishments, the use of a sad iron to deliver burns. The scars from these burns remained upon my legs and arms throughout my life, a constant reminder of the cruelty of life. Father watched her mete out her punishments with neither word nor action to stop her, even though I am sure he did not agree with the way in which she chose to teach us 'hard lessons' as she called them. For in truth, I knew that Father was as scared of being on the receiving end of her violent outbursts as his children were. I learnt his embarrassing truth during an incident thirteen years ago, which I will not relay at this time. After her death six years ago he appeared a much happier, more contented man, like one freed from an interminable hell from which there seemed to be no respite. For his lack of protection from my mother's violence, I showed him no ill will, for the love which he showed to my brothers and I through the time he spent teaching us as children was love enough to lessen the sting of mother's blows.

It was from Grandfather that I first remember hearing the word 'Surma'. I specifically remember when this was as it would have been the day prior to my eighth birthday and Father had told me that his plan to take me to the British Museum would have to be temporarily cancelled due to the requirement of his funeral services. Grandfather had been at the house and I had overheard him and Father discussing the deceased, a twelve-year-old boy from Spitalfields by the name of Harry White.

"The family wish the funeral to be as soon as possible," Father spoke in his usual quiet, deep tone. "I have told them that two day's time is the shortest notice that I can give to St Mary's, and that they are lucky at that."

Grandfather listened quietly, his face deadly serious as he nodded slowly. "What were the circumstances of the death?' He asked, 'why is there such a hurry?"

"There is not much left; they wish what remains of the boy to be put to rest as soon as possible."

"Not much left? Sorry business if you ask me. Give me an illness or a natural death any day. A brutal surma is never good, not for the family and not for the boy's soul."

The remains of the Harry White's body, it emerged as I continued to listen in on their conversation from behind the kitchen door, had been found at the rear of the market two days after his family had reported him missing. Large sections of the corpse had been removed including the boy's head. These missing parts would never be found and the child had only been identified by his father, a well-known local builder and joiner, due to a brown linen cap, found tucked in his trouser pocket, and a scar on his left forearm caused by a saw accident two years prior to his death.

I later learned from Father, after feigning fear of attack in the night that a man named Henry J. Holdsworth, a drayman from Bluegate Fields declaring himself to be the murderer of the child had been arrested after presenting himself at Holborn Police station. He claimed that the devil himself had spoken to him and had controlled his body into committing terrible attacks on at least three young boys (although the remains of only one had been found). He had, however due to a lack of any evidence and his obvious mental imbalance, been taken to a lunatic asylum on the outskirts of London, where he would never see the light of day again.

Grandfather told me and my brothers later that Surma was the Suomi word for 'kill' or more specifically it meant '*a kill*'. This was the first murder I had experienced with regard to Father's services, although I am sure that I had been protected by him in the past and there had been more.

Why then, you may ask, does this word bring me so much fear when it is a word used in my family's native Finland purely as a term for caused death? The cause of this fear that has plagued me since my childhood came from Father when he described the injuries suffered by the child.

"The boy," Father whispered to Grandfather in a voice filled with a faraway tone I had not heard from him, "was surman suuhun".

The next evening we were sat in front of the fire as we often did most nights to hear stories from the old country. Curiosity had driven me wild since overhearing the conversation and I decided to question Grandfather directly.

"But if surma means kill what does surman suuhun mean Grandfather?" I asked, "It doesn't make sense; I know that surman must be the past tense of surma and so means killed, but the word suuhun means mouth. Father said that the boy was 'killed in the mouth', where is the sense in this?"

"It is an old phrase, Sibelius, one that we pray that we do not have to utter too often." Grandfather leant forward in his chair so that his face was so close that I could feel his breath on my face, I could see the start of white whiskers protruding from his chin and his lips quivered as they spoke. "It means into the mouth of Surma. The child had suffered atrocious injuries as if he had been torn and devoured by Surma himself."

Niko, the youngest of my brothers, who was not yet three, huddled in close to me, his eyes widening at the thought of a child being eaten. I put my arm around him in an effort to reduce his fear but my inquisitive nature could not prevent me from asking a further question.

"What is Surma, Grandfather? Is it an animal?"

"Not an animal. No, it is neither man nor beast. Surma is the essence of death; a being filled with a never-ending hunger, who can sense the life within a person and will tear and rend them in such a way that they are unrecognisable. He has been described as resembling a dog, the largest that you have ever seen, with the tail of a snake and eyes that will freeze your soul. Only two men ever saw the Surma and lived, and that is the great Väinämöinen, the bard who I have told you tales of, although he never told of the shape of what he saw. The other was Lemminkäinen – and we all know what happened to him don't we boys?"

Niko shook in fear pressed his face into my chest and covered his ears remembering the story of the Swan of Tuonela. Johannes, who was only a year younger than I, sat wide eyed on Grandfather's knee. His face was impassive, but I could tell that he was trying very hard to be fearless in front of Grandfather. Johannes, I always felt, was the bravest of the three of us, because he had the greatest barriers to overcome, born as he was with a weakened constitution and constantly prone to illness.

"I believe, however," Grandfather continued, "that Surma is the embodiment of the fears within our hearts and as such will appear to each of us in the form of our greatest horror." My mind immediately raced, thinking of what I would see if I was unfortunate enough to come across Surma on a dark night. Images of wolves and bears with blood dripping from their glistening fangs shot into my mind. Niko let out a muffled cry and I pulled him closer in to me.

"Grandfather, I think that you should tell us a different story." My voice had taken on the tone of someone much older as I tried to brighten the mood for the benefit of my brothers. "Can you continue to tell us the story of the bard's journey to the north and how he caused Ilmarinen to create the Sampo?"

My Grandfather looked at me and our eyes met, he could see what I was attempting and smiled at me with his kind eyes.

"What a fine idea, Sibelius. Come Niko; bring your head out of your brother's chest so that I may tell you a lighter tale, one of music and the songs of power."

As the small boy stopped whimpering and emerged, I resolved to speak to Grandfather at another more expedient time. The thought of a mysterious beast wandering the streets of London and tearing small children to pieces, whilst creating fright within me, also caused a deep and gnawing hunger for more knowledge. From that day forward, I began an obsessive interest with the murderous entity spoken of in hushed and reverent tones and known to those from my family's part of the world as Surma.

Moreover, it is why I found myself sat in the mud, seven hours after hearing a dead child speak the beast's name, in the graveyard of St Mary's and as drunk as I had ever been in my life, talking to the spirit of Grandfather who had passed away ten years earlier.

3
THE PRINCESS ALICE

With the greatest of respect to my attacker, I really should have avoided the first blow. I can only blame the large amount of liquor which I had consumed over such a short space of time for the fact that I did not manage to evade the swinging fist which struck me hard on the left side of my head.

My supposed skill in dodging incoming assaults was, in fact, courtesy of dear Mother. Johannes, Niko and I developed an inbuilt ability to see where an attack may be coming from and, in the case of Mother, not duck to avoid it. Part of the harsh education, provided for us by her at a very early age, involved ensuring that any attempted assault reached its target with neither flinch or cower, the impertinence of causing her to miss would only bring further, more painful assails

The strike, delivered by my unseen attacker, was landed with ferocious strength, knocking me sideways, causing my legs to buckle. Before I had even hit the floor further blows rained down on my head and upper body, causing me to refrain from all thought of recovering and attempting to retaliate. Instead I decided to curl myself into as small a target as I could manage and see out the violence. Hard booted feet were employed to painful effect on my back before the attack finally subsided. As I counted the seconds following the final blow, I felt brave enough to lower my hands from my face and look up at my attacker. This, I decided later, was a foolish action and I should have remained motionless and protected. For as my head rose slightly and I tried to focus on the large man standing over me, he delivered one final punch to the side of my face which caused me to lose consciousness momentarily.

In the short time it took me to awaken from my enforced slumber, the man had searched my person for valuables and ran off down Commercial Street. I sat in the guttering outside the Alice and checked my pockets; I discovered that he had taken my pocket watch and wallet. My wallet contained very little in regard to any money, due to the furious level at which I had been drinking for the previous three hours. The silver watch, however, had been newly acquired the week earlier, costing £12 from Frodsham's of the Strand. The loss of this item, I will admit, affected me deeply in a way in which I could not have foretold, and I screamed obscenities at my now rapidly disappearing aggressor, words that I had rarely used in public since my days of mixing with the rougher side of my local neighbourhood. I was not particularly attached to the watch in any way, but I had bought it with the winnings of a card game and had decided that an item bought through luck would only prove to bring more good fortune. Sitting on the roadside, sore and dishevelled as I was, I certainly did not feel as though fortune's grace was shining upon me with a particularly bright lamp.

I dragged myself to my feet and began to walk, not to my apartments, but towards the direction of Whitechapel Road and St Mary's church. I had decided, through my inebriation, that it was time to visit a family member whose knowledge and opinion I valued most.

How did I get here? Just a few short hours ago I was at the crest of the world and continuing to rise. How did I in such a short time become drunken, beaten and without a farthing on my person? It had started, I supposed, when my appointment with Mr Earnshaw and his family finished that afternoon.

Mr Earnshaw, whilst appearing slightly concerned by the pallid nature of my features as I took the photograph, was very grateful for my services once again. I admit that I felt a degree of sadness when I waved goodbye to the two carriages taking the Earnshaws and their daughter away. However I am ashamed to say that my sorrow was only a small part for the bereaved family themselves and more so for myself as they had no other children and, unless an unfortunate illness or accident befell Mrs Earnshaw, this would be the end of my business dealings with this influential customer.

I tried to dismiss the word that I had heard the child speak as hallucinatory, and possibly the result of my busy schedule and recent lack of restful sleep, but it gnawed at my mind like the most voracious of rats, chewing its way in to my consciousness with terrible, unrelenting teeth. It was as if the mention of Surma and all that he represented was enough to claw and tear into my psyche, a murderous and damaging beast indeed.

As I closed and locked the door, I breathed a deep sigh, not of relief but of realisation that a long forgotten horror had returned to cleave my soul and tear at my nerves. I thought of changing my attire and going to the Dolorian club in Pall Mall. I had the pleasure of joining this club through invitation after carrying out commissions for a number of the members. Mr Earnshaw himself was a member, although I had not seen him there in the three months since I joined, I had been told that he had not attended much of late due to teaching commitments at King's College. However, I am sure that it was partly through his influence and position that I received the letter from the club's committee to inform me that I had been put forward for membership which would be decided by ballot. The annual fee of thirty-one guineas would be a struggle to maintain within the strict budget I had set myself, saving as I was for more auspicious apartments and studio space more central to the city. However, since such membership had been a dream of mine since childhood, I would ensure that the fee was paid even if it meant cutting back on my other expenses. It was clear to me that the kudos that membership of such an esteemed club could bring would only benefit my burgeoning business further. The disturbed nature of my mind, at this time however, brought about by my fearful vision of the child and the word that she had repeated, caused me to feel the need to drink in a way that would not be readily appreciated by the other gentlemen members of my club.

And so, with money in my wallet and grim determination, I headed to the Princess Alice on the corner of Wentworth Street and Commercial Street. It had been a regular haunt of mine in my younger days, before I started my business and began my move up in the world and into more refined social circles. I still had cause to visit on occasion and maintained a number of close associates therein, but my calls to this establishment were mainly for garnering information on potential customers or finding the whereabouts of the latest card and wheel games from my cabman contacts.

Normally when entering any of the local drinking establishments, my first action upon going through the doors, would be to scan the room for any familiar faces. Despite spending much of my youth frequenting the hostelries of the east end, either through family or other business, there were always those persons who were not aware of my local background and, through my dress and manner, saw me as an outsider and were notably suspicious. I did not let this dissuade me from visiting these inns when need arose as I felt confident in my ability to talk my way out of any situation and such confrontations with the drunken and unruly had not as yet led to any physical altercations. On that day however, I strode in ignoring the other patrons, my mind and focus entirely on the bar and the liquid salvation kept within.

I took a stool and motioned to a well built, middle aged man behind the bar that I required a drink. He strode over to where I sat, putting down a cloth which he had been using to wipe clean the bar top and reaching above the bar for an empty glass.

"You haven't shown your face in here for a long time, lad." He said, in a gruff but warm tone. "What kind of day has it been? What are you drinking?"

I smiled for the first time since the vision and took off my hat placing it upon the bar.

"Hullo, Tom. I'll have a beer for my thirst and a whisky for my temperament."

"That bad, eh?" Tom said drawing a large mug of beer and placing it in front of me on the bar. He then reached deep under the bar and pulled out a bottle which I knew he kept back only for my visits, keen as I was on this particular drink. Within seconds I had drained the beer and the contents of the smaller glass.

"Pour me another of each; I plan to stay a while yet." I said in a solemn manner. It was only after the first drinks had been taken that I cared to look around the bar area to see my fellow lushes. There were maybe half a dozen men, each of them sat by themselves and seemingly lost in barren thought. A sorry collection of sad looking souls, each carefully nursing drinks of various sizes and I thought how it would be possible to come into the Alice at any time and on any day and find these same men, or ones just like them, wasting what few shillings they had on a life in a darkened bar. Occasionally one of them would speak to another and a brief conversation would ensue, their words never lasted although this may be the only friendly conversation that they would have all day. I knew the names of a couple of the men; they had been hired sobbers, earning a small amount of coins to pay for their drinking life even twenty years ago. Some were over fifty years of age now and, whilst lucky to be alive though their destructive lifestyles, looked a great deal older than their years.

Tom had been the owner of the Alice for as long as I had known, taking on the establishment with his wife Beth as a young man. I remember most clearly the first day that I met them; I was nine years old and was, as usual before funeral services began, running errands for my parents. My particular task on this morning had been to visit the market on Commercial Street in order to purchase some cooking provisions for Mother and wax polish for Father, which doubtless would be given back to me so that I could ensure that the current stock of caskets were polished to perfection. I moved quickly through the crowds, head down and committed to completing my task in good time so that I would be able to return home to continue my reading with Father, which we did each day for one hour. Father had obtained a copy of the Kalevala, an epic poem which told the same stories from Finnish mythology which Grandfather had relayed to us since our earliest years. To find a copy of these stories in written form had caused me much excitement and only created a greater sense of awe regarding Grandfather. He could tell the stories so effortlessly and with such a sense of ancient magic, purely from memory, such was the tradition and commitment, long held within our people, to pass on these words through the generations.

As I skittled my way through the busy market I admit that my thoughts were far away, lost in dreams of Väinämöinen and Lemminkäinen, the great heroes of the tales whose search for knowledge and love led them to the ends of the earth and beyond into darker more dangerous realms. It was probably due to my wandering mind that I accidentally walked straight into a large man who had been carrying a wooden crate full of apples. The collision caused the crate to fall from his hands tumbling its contents onto the dirty, wet floor.

"I'm sorry, sir," I said immediately dropping to the floor in an attempt to pick up the unfortunate spillage. Despite my apology and display of assistance in restoring the fruit to the crate however, the man flew into a terrible rage, the like of which I had only seen exhibited by Mother before. Before I could put the first apple back into the crate the man had hit me, hard upon the back of my head.

"You stupid child," he screamed, "your clumsiness will ruin me, look at the mess you have made of my apples. They will all have to be washed before I can sell them and the delay will mean that I miss valuable time at the market!"

His fists rained down upon me and I found myself unable to escape from the attack, which continued as he called me a variety of names which my youthful ears, despite my street based education, had not heard and have rarely heard since. I tried to crawl away from the man, scuttling on all fours through the apples, straw and horse manure which littered the busy market street. The man continued to harangue me however, showing no signs of any loss to his rage. This was the first time I met Tom Finnan, as he, and no other person witnessing the assault, moved between myself and the brute who seemed intent on causing me irreversible harm by way of punishment.

Tom had always been a man who I had seen as large and powerful, even when I grew up and became taller than him. However, it was not his physical size that gave this impression, he was broad shouldered and muscular definitely, but he had an air of quiet strength about him, a slumbering sense of power which was clear through his manner and tone of voice. Over the years I have seen Tom stand toe to toe with drunken men twice his size who were full of rage and bluster. He had spoken to them in his firm resolute manner and through strength of word and the potential for action; he had immediately extinguished all craving for confrontation and violence within them.

This was the approach that he took with my attacker on that day, as he put himself between us and spoke to the man in a clear and measured manner. I cannot recall exactly what he said to the brute but within minutes Tom had helped me up and led me to the safety of the Princess Alice, leaving the large man scrabbling on the floor, picking up his wares and returning them to the crate, the fire in his face long gone, now replaced by guilt and not a small amount of fear.

"Beth, bring water and a cloth!" Tom shouted as we went through the doors, and then quieter to me, "We have an injured soldier to mend before he can go out on the battlefield again." He smiled at me with a warmth that I could not have expected from a man who I thought so initially strong. I had a cut above my left eye and my lip was swollen where I had hit the floor. My eyes were full of tears, which were held firmly in place so as not to let my saviour know how upset I had been by the beating.

When Beth appeared carrying a bowl, however, I almost felt glad that this terrible incident had happened to me, as she was, in the mind of a nine year old boy, the perfect epitome of beauty and grace. She was young, perhaps not yet twenty, and had such soft caring eyes that I immediately forgot my pain and woes and stared at her as though hypnotised. She cleaned the cuts upon my face and wiped away any sign of blood or tears as she spoke to me in soft tones, asking my name and where I lived. By the time she had finished Tom, Beth and I had become as good as friends and I found myself smiling and laughing in ways in which I could never imagine doing with my own parents. Beth was the antithesis of my own mother and, despite my smiles, I felt a deep sadness that I would have to return home eventually to further punishment and wounds from Mother for causing the poor man with the apple crate such a catastrophe.

Eventually I tore myself away from their company, thanking them for the care and assistance which they had bestowed upon me, and continued on my errands, racing out of the Princess Alice with new found warmth inside me. As I walked home my mind turned to Johannes who I thought of daily. He had not returned from running errands just over a year previously, after being sent out late by Father to the joiner, Albert Tunney's house to deliver a letter requesting two new caskets which had to be especially made and carved and not the usual type created by Father and Grandfather. Father had initially asked me to complete this task, but Johannes had begged him for the chance to help out. It was rare for Johannes to run errands due to his constant tiredness and poor constitution, but I know that he was desperate to help.

When he failed to return within the half hour, Father had left the house to find him. He did not return that evening and I remember lying in bed with Niko, the pair of us worrying about our brother and what had befallen him. When we woke the next morning and ran down to see my parents, we found them sat at the kitchen table. Father's face was ashen and colourless apart from red ringed eyes, Mother wore an expression that I had never seen her wear before, it was a mixture of grief and anger and, thinking back, I hope for Mother's sake, a touch of guilt. Father told us that Johannes had been hit by a carriage and had suffered terrible injuries. He had been taken to the infirmary but had been dead before he arrived, so great were his wounds. We sat as an injured family that morning, weeping and mourning the loss of our brother and son. Even Mother wept, and held Niko and I close. It is an eternal sadness held within me, that it took the death of my brother to cause Mother to show Niko or me any degree of love or affection. This period of 'love' from Mother did not last however and within days our lives returned to living in fear of her ire. Father would not allow Niko or I to see Johannes' body and say goodbye, he told us that it would do us more harm than good and that we should remember him how we last saw him. Happy but weak, warm but pale, our lost brother who had ascended to heaven.

When I returned to the parlour after leaving Tom and Beth, I did, as expected, take another beating from Mother, but somehow the strikes did not sting in the way they had before. I returned to the Alice whenever I had the opportunity and always received a grand welcome and a fuss from my new friends. To me, Tom and Beth were another sanctuary, other than within books, that I could escape to when I needed reminding that there was good in the world. This made the sadness all the greater when, two years after our first meeting, Beth was lost to us giving birth to their first child.

The loss I felt at her passing was as great as that which I felt for my brother and I did not think that I would ever recover from it. Even many years later, when looking at Tom, I could see a grief within his eyes that I recognised as also being within me. His was greater, of course, she was the love of his life and he never remarried or found another. The impression, which Beth made on me, however, a child with a deep need for maternal love, would never leave and would have a lasting effect. Their child survived, a girl who Tom named Bethany after his love. Tom's sister, Anne helped to raise her and she grew to be the image of the mother she never met, something which I know warmed Tom to see as she worked with him running the Princess Alice.

As I sat in the Alice, as a grown and visibly shaken man, drinking with a mission-like intent, I looked on Tom and his now grown up daughter. Rather than cheering me, as their company often did, I felt a self-destructive determination and continued to order more drinks.

Eventually, upon finding myself full of beer to the point of uncomfortable distension, my drinking moved on solely to the bottle which Tom kept under the bar. It would seem that with each glass however, rather than settling my mood and easing the fears for my sanity, I became progressively darker and more tenebrous. I paid less attention to my surroundings and began to stare broodingly at my reflection in the smoked mirror behind the bar. I would tell you, dear reader, that I looked pale, but that would not fully describe my appearance at this time. I have always been pale, sickly looking and on some occasions mistook for a sufferer of albinism, this look also assisted by my hair which was white-blonde to the point of powdered snow. On that day however, my slim, angular face took on a bilious look which I can only describe fully as that of someone who had come face to face with their own mortality, which, in part, I had.

I spent the majority of my days looking at the bodies of the recently passed, upside down through the viewfinder of my camera. Today death had looked back at me and had spoken the name of my childhood fear. 'Surma'. No amount of whisky could erase or even dull that name.

Tom, took notice of my seemingly irreversible blackness and made his way from the end of the bar, where he had been talking to Bethany to stand in the only spot at the bar which would obscure my view in the mirror. He leaned forward, and tried, as he often did, to shake me from my rancour and raise my spirits.

"When are you going to find a nice girl, Sibelius, get married, have a few nippers running around the house? A man needs to settle down sooner or later you know, and even one as ugly as you should be able to find a mule who'll have you."

Normally I would have been in more jovial mood and jested with him about marrying his daughter and becoming his son in law, but today my mood had been soured by my experience in the studio, today the drink made me bitter rather than sweet.

"My father once confided in me," I replied in a tone probably more angry than I ought to have shown, "in a brief moment of peace and freedom from the abusive, henpecking, harridan that he chose to spend his life with." I raised the glass to my lips and downed the contents, slamming the empty vessel hard down on the bar with a jolt which woke one of the sleeping drunks in the corner. "He told me that one day I would meet a woman, and that when I saw her the world would fall around her like a stack of cards, so that only she remained. He said that my life would feel as though it had been incomplete and irrelevant until that point, that I would gladly die to spend my last hours with her and I would cross the earth for one glimpse of her face. This was not conjecture, Father said, this was not something that may happen to me; it was fate, a certainty, an inescapable truth that I would never be able to shy away from. One day I would fall in love with the woman of my dreams and on that day I should remember my dear father's advice..." I paused for a moment and waved the empty glass a fraction, enough for Tom to realise that I wanted a refill. He reached under the bar for the near empty bottle, which had been almost full when I arrived two hours ago, and poured the golden liquid into my glass filling it to the brim.

I stood from my stool, swaying slightly as I did so.

"My father told me this...run boy, run away! Run as far away as possible, use carriage, boat or just your legs if you have to, but run, run away from that creature before you find yourself using words of stupidity and offering your future for a glimpse of her soft flesh. Because before you know it the beauty is a beast, you have a noose around your neck and a cage you call a home."

I lifted the refilled glass from the bar and raised it above my head, my voice had become loud and I had begun to slur my words.

"A man without a wife is like a field without a fence!" I shouted to the bar, and lowering my glass to my mouth, I drank my final drink of the evening. For in one swift motion, the drink had been downed and I fell backwards onto the floor.

Despite the weight of my fall, I did not, as is often the case in these matters, cause myself any major injury, apart from the denting of what little pride I felt in myself and the sudden urge to go outside the pub and purge my stomach. Tom and Bethany helped me to my feet and tried to get me to sit down in one of the stalls to sober a little but I was having none of it.

"Leave me, leave me!" I called and pushed away their arms, "Thank you for concern, but I know when it is time to go." I started to stagger towards the door in order to make my exit and stumbled slightly.

Tom made to catch me but there was no need I had regained my balance.

"Be careful, son." Tom said as I pushed open the door. "Sleep well and come to see me in the morning when you are better fettled, we will discuss your worries." I did not reply or even turn; I simply raised my hand in acknowledgement and stepped out into the evening air.

In my state of inebriation, I did not notice that I had been followed and did not expect the coming attack.

So now, bruised and bloodied the victim, both of an opportunist 'roller' and my own drinking, I found myself in the graveyard of St Mary Matfellon staring down at the graves of Grandfather and his wife, who I never met but heard many stories of. The graves were well kept; Father visited on a weekly basis and ensured that the stones were free of lichen and other blemishes, and that the grass covering them was trimmed to a finer degree than that which the warden would have the gardener keep.

Inscribed on Grandfather's headstone, in Suomi, were the words,

'*Oma maa mansikka Muu maa mustikka*',

This translates as 'Other land Blueberry Own land strawberry', an odd inscription indeed but one which summed up how Grandfather felt about being forced to leave the homeland which he longed to see again.

As I stared down at his resting place I saw, through the darkness, the beginnings of a weed growing in the centre of the grass in front of the headstone. I leaned forward to pluck it out and fell, striking my head on the stone - another swollen bruise to add to a long list acquired today. My vision swam now that I was prone and I felt the need to right myself in order to cease the spinning of the world, but found that I had neither the energy nor ability to regain my feet. I shuffled backwards slightly and managed to move myself into a sitting position leant against the headstone of Grandfather's neighbour. What a sorry turn of events this day had been and how quickly I had fallen into ignominy and self loathing.

"What are you doing, boy?" The voice came from above me. I looked up to see Grandfather, standing with his arms folded and a stern look upon his face. He wore his best suit and his white hair and beard were immaculately combed, I had never seen him look so smart. I did not act surprised, in fact, despite my earlier affright at the studio, I felt almost comforted by his company.

"I'm laying down, Grandfather. Laying down a hopeless drunkard. A drunkard without control of their legs." My eyes were struggling to stay open, despite the fact that I appeared to have received a visitation from the other side.

His face softened. "Are you sad? Have you lost a woman?" Grandfather's voice was soft and deep, how I always remembered it to be. He did not appear to be angry by the fact that I was not astonished at his appearance. His voice seemed full of care and worry at my descent.

"No, Grandfather. Although I wish that were the case." I shuffled slightly in the mud in an attempt to make myself more comfortable. "I do not have romantic issues and if I did then I would certainly not try to cure them by drinking myself into the grave, or even somebody else's grave." I laughed at my attempt at a joke but Grandfather did not laugh with me. He just stood, with a knowing smile.

"Do you not have a woman, surely even a boy as strange as you should be able to find a woman of some description?" His laughter although coming from beyond the grave was warm and full of life. "Even your father found himself someone, though God awful she was and I still wonder why he shackled himself to such a mare."

I found myself giggling along with him, dreaming of days spent enjoying his company. I missed Grandfather, his wisdom, his sense of family but most of all I missed his infectious humour. It was a trait that had been passed on to Niko, a charismatic something which made you want to be around them. Our laughter trailed away as the reason for my state of incompetent drunkenness returned to me. I looked up into his eyes, which smiled into mine.

"A dead girl spoke to me, Grandfather." I said with the sudden sadness which can overcome a drunk, "A child spoke to me from beyond the grave and I am afraid. God help me, a dead child."

"A dead, old man is speaking to you now, you do not appear to be running screaming from the graveyard." He laughed, "What did she say that brought you so much fear that you retreat into liquor?" I could tell that he was finding the sight of his grandson as drunk as a lord amusing. I was however about to remove the smile from his face.

"Surma, Grandfather. She said Surma but it was not just the word but her tone, it was ... foreboding, a warning that death is coming for me. A death so brutal that it brings coldness to my heart requiring liquor to warm it."

As I had thought, all sense of happiness fled from his face to be replaced by concern and fear. "Speak to your father, tell him what you told me," he said, his voice more serious than I had ever heard. "Tell your father what you have told me, he will not hold you in ridicule. And sober yourself for God's sake, boy. No solution was ever cured by viinas."

A sleepy smile spread across my bloodied face. "It was whisky, and I think that now I will sleep, Grandfather." I pulled the brim of my hat down, "Give my regards to the dead; I fear I shall be joining them soon for a party." My eyes could stay open no longer, and there, in a fog-filled graveyard surrounded by the bones of the dead, I slept.

4
Two Girls

I woke with the merciless daylight streaming in through the window of my bedroom. The light burned my eyes as if it had been cast by a thousand suns magnified with the aim of bringing about a blindness of white which coated my orbs in acid and scorched the day upon me. The groan I emitted, although voluntary, was produced with a volume which I did not know whether to blame on the pain, which seared through every part of my being, or the sensitivity of my ears. I dared myself to attempt to focus my vision and observe the state that I had awoken in and almost failed to achieve the bravery required to complete the task to any degree. I do admit a feeling of relief and gratitude, however that I appeared to have at least been successful in reaching some mark of comfort through my whole body's position on the bed.

I am ashamed to confess that this had not been a goal which I had always managed in the past and have awoken, on such sore mornings as these, in various states of undress and with varying success at reaching my mattress before the slumber of alcohol had cruelly stolen consciousness from me. On one occasion I discovered myself actually under the frame of the bed and staring at the unappealing sight of a full chamber pot not six inches away from my face. My only saving grace on that particular morning, a tainted grace though it was, was that I had managed to make use of the article and had not soiled my clothing.

As my eyes adjusted to the light which blazed a violent trail into my brain, I saw that the clock set on the table beside my bed gave the time as being shortly before seven in the morning. This provided me with a mixture of emotions both negative and positive. I found myself grateful for the fact that I had not lost the day, as I knew that I had an important new client coming to see me, but there was also a tinge of grief that my slumber had been disturbed as I would be troubled to sleep again now that I had awoken.

I rolled myself upright in a motion that was both pained but fluid. Various aspects of my body screamed in pain; from my face, which I remembered had been struck firmly a number of times, to my back and chest, which had borne the brunt of the booted feet of my attacker. All of these injuries would have caused the purest saint to curse and wail, however they were made worse still by the throbbing hammer in my head and the dry taste of bile which coated the inside of my mouth and had shrivelled my tongue into the shape and feel of a rough tree branch. I used every effort that my body could muster to swing my legs over the side of the bed and stand. The room swam slightly, but I managed through brute concentration to maintain my balance and totter, as one might imagine a small child taking their first steps, over to the wash basin where thankfully I found a jug of water. Banishing all thought of how long this water had stood there I lifted the jug to my lips and drank deeply. Rather than washing the foul taste from my mouth, the first touch of liquid upon my tongue and upper palate felt as though it had reactivated an ancient evil, pure poison with a hint of whisky, sent to choke all life from my veins whilst causing the pit of my stomach to fight anxiously against its arrival. In an instant I had regurgitated the fluid into the washbasin, but rather than causing me further distress, the action seemed to clear my head somewhat as if my body had made steady progress in its attempt to return some degree of balance to my wellbeing. I shuffled to my kitchen area and, finding a cup from the cupboard and turning on my tap, poured myself a cleaner, more refreshing brew of Adam's ale.

I may have spent more than half an hour slowly rehydrating my wracked, near dead corpse whilst sitting and staring out of the window onto the waking street below. I thought of the previous day and of how it had started so brightly but had disintegrated into a messy heap, unrecognisable from the type of behaviours and experience that I would normally espouse to. Of course I had been on the wrong side of the demon drink before, in fact, it is something which I always enjoyed. For me and the strictness of my childhood in terms of what I had been allowed to get away with, there was something of a freedom contained within the shallow end of a good bottle. The freeing of my mind and the tight boundaries which I had, in pursuit of my dreams of a better life shackled myself within, was a requirement for the goodness of my soul and the keeping of what thin sanity I had.

The strangest parts of my recollections however, were how they seemed to be so clear. I remembered every part of my time in the Alice with perfect clarity; from the misery and morbidity of my thoughts to the words I had spoken to Tom and the conversation with my dead grandfather, which I decided was the result of alcohol and not of any type of supernatural experience. Yes, I had been spoken to by a recently dead child, but somehow I found this to be in some ways possible. The thought however that I had received a visitation, whilst drunk, from someone who had been dead for the last ten years, was beyond any sense or logic. As I thought of the day I had experienced I found that laid before me, in horrific detail, was each small minutiae of my drunken interlude.

Each part except one.

I had no recollection of how I managed to find my way home to bed, my last memory was of telling Grandfather that I needed to sleep and closing my eyes, and then nothing. The journey from the graveyard to my studio and lodgings was not a long one, it would have taken no longer than five minutes, but it had been erased from my memory, a victim of the poison I had put into my body with such fervour.

When I felt that I had recovered to a suitable enough degree to cope with getting on with the day at hand, I stood in front of the mirror in my bedroom and surveyed the damage that had been inflicted upon me by the roller outside the pub. I was not as horrific an image as I had expected, or felt. I had bruising to the left side of my face and my eye on that side had closed slightly. There was a tear on my right cheek and a mark in the shape of the ring which had been adorning the hand that had been so roughly driven into my face. I thought, with a small degree of ironic humour, that for one so desperate for money that they would beat it out of a stranger, that he was not so poor as to not own any form of jewellery, although the item would probably have been the spoils of some previous assault on the drunk and unfortunate. My mind turned to thoughts of my Frodsham's watch and the humour that I felt evaporated to be replaced by anger and grief at its loss.

My face inspected, I slowly lifted my shirt over my head so that I could witness the damage done to me by those hard boots, which he had used to such destructive effect about my body. I was red and sore with the beginnings of the blueness which signified the stamp of bruising about me. My chest, on the right side felt particularly sore and I wondered whether there had been any fracturing of the ribs, such was the pain I felt upon breathing in. As self-pity and disappointment at my luck began to drag my mood down even further into a deep lake of dark gloom, I was disturbed from my inspection by the sound of someone rapping loudly on my door downstairs. I pulled a clean, folded shirt out of my drawer unit and made my way down the stairwell, whilst putting it on.

I opened the door to find Bethany standing there in the grey morning drizzle. The shock which my face showed at her appearance on my step, however, was not due to the surprise I felt at seeing her so early in the morning, moreover, I am ashamed to admit that on first seeing her face I took her for her mother, dead some seventeen years since. The thought that it was Tom's wife Beth, who had visited me that morning, although shocking, sent sudden and temporary warmth throughout my body, which made me forget all of the pain and woes, which I had inflicted upon myself. The sight of a person I thought dead would have been lunacy for me to imagine twenty-four hours ago but my recent experiences with the deceased had inured me to such impossibilities.

Despite my obvious wonder at her appearance, Bethany's face was an odd combination of relief that I was alive, and rage and annoyance at the behaviour which she had last seen me performing in her establishment. That much was clear from the look in her eyes. My initial warmth at the mistaken identity was quickly replaced by a glow of a different kind as I blushed in shame at her wordless admonishment.

"Bethany," I said, my voice cracking slightly both in embarrassment and as a result of the soreness which permeated my body. "I er ... didn't expect to see you ... here. Come in out of the rain, come in please do."

"I shall not stay," she snapped, bustling through the doorway past me. "I am only here because Dad asked me too and because of my care for your brother. Rose is waiting outside for me, some people have better things to do than waste the morning with sore heads!"

I closed the door after her and followed dutifully as she strode into my ground floor studio with some purpose. "You have a job on today I see," she glanced at the backdrop and items positioned in the studio ready for the client who would be attending this afternoon. "I hope that you are up to it, and not too worse for wear." There was a hint of reprimand in her voice which was not suitably disguised by any show of concern for my wellbeing.

"I am feeling fine this morning," I lied, "Never felt better, although I do admit to possibly drinking a little too hard yesterday." I ventured to add the touch of a smile to my words in the hope that a show of humour would help to lessen the obvious disappointment which she felt.

"A little too hard?" she replied, "Dad was worried sick about you last night, he even came here when the pub shut to see if you were still alive. Someone had come through the door after you left and said that some drunken toff had got a kicking and he feared that it was you." Her eyes examined the cuts and bruising to my face and my nearly closed eye. "You are lucky to be alive, you know that don't you?"

The shame of the worry I had caused Tom and, although she would hate to admit it, Bethany, filled my face. I looked to the ground in an attempt to avoid her steely glare.

"Yes, I may have had a little altercation with a gentleman in the street." I mumbled but then decided that bluster was the best way to continue this conversation. "He asked me the time, and when I pulled out my pocket watch we had a fiery discussion regarding its worth. He agreed to take it to a jeweller to have it valued." Her expression had not changed, the hard stare remained and I felt thoroughly on the back foot, she certainly was developing into a woman who should be reckoned with. I decided that the only safe course of action would be to attempt a complete change of subject.

"Will you be seeing Niko today? I have not seen him for a few days, how are the wedding plans going? The lad won't tell me anything about them." The mention of my brother's name brought the first signs of a thaw to her face.

"I plan to visit Niko this afternoon; I shall be at the market with Rose first. Niko has asked that I visit him after this as he tells me that there is good news." The thaw had well and truly set in now and the ice of winter had turned into a spring bloom, such was the brightness of her countenance. Once again, I found myself looking at her and seeing her mother reflected in her, from the dark curls of her hair to the way that her skin seemed to glow with a warmth and softness which pervaded the world around her. Niko was indeed a lucky man to have won such a heart, despite everything I had said in the Princess Alice the night before regarding marriage.

"Do you think that he has finalised your plans?" I asked, not a little mesmerised by the joy which had come over her face.

"I hope so, it has been two months since he proposed to me and nothing would make me happier than to become his wife." Knowing Niko as I did, I knew that he returned the feelings, they had been inseparable for the last year and I knew that Tom and Father approved also. It was a good match.

"If I know my brother as I think I do, he will have been thinking of nothing else. You mean everything to him and he is only capable of thinking of one thing at a time." I laughed.

However in my moment of triumph, I ruined any chance of making Bethany forget her disappointment in me. For as I became animated in my happiness for the young couple, my body decided to remind me of the sore ribs which had been kicked so hard the previous evening. As I winced in pain Bethany's face hardened.

"Go to visit Dad later on, he worries about you." She said, the coldness returning to her voice. She strode from the room, turning as she reached the doorway, "We all do, although I often wonder why." Her eyes dropped and she left me burning in the fire of my guilt.

The door slammed as she left, a final indication of her annoyance, and I resolved to visit Tom later and apologise to him. He had always been a good friend and I hated the thought of adding to his worries. I would go to the Princess Alice, but not to drink. My first stop after my photographic assignment however, would be to Father's. For although I remained firm in my belief that I had imagined the discussion with Grandfather, to share my torment would be the best option and Father would be sensible enough to provide me with sane advice. First however,

I had a rather special appointment to prepare for, and so, with the bite of Bethany's words still adding an internal pain to my bodily aches, I set about preparing the studio for a most peculiar client.

Shortly before midday, I stood on the street as two carriages arrived outside my doors. The first was a small hackney, from which stepped two men in brown suits and bowler hats. One of the men was much broader than the other and a good head higher, and I thought that, had they not been so well dressed, I would have sworn that their normal employment would be as enforcers of some kind. Between them, they carried a large trunk, which I assumed would be filled with clothing props or other items required for the photograph. The other carriage was a hearse pulled by two well-bred horses. The casket held within would contain the centrepiece for today's photographic assignment.

"I trust you are Mr Darke, Sir?" the smaller of the two men asked as they approached the doors. I nodded and held them open, so that they could go through to the studio. "My name is Dawes, sir and this is my colleague Mr Soames. We have been sent by His Lordship, delivering a package that we are to return to him later this afternoon."

"Yes, come this way," I said motioning towards the studio which they entered placing the trunk on the floor. "I trust everything that I need is contained within?" I asked pointing at the dark wooden box.

"Yes, sir, His Lordship, said everything you needed would be found in this trunk, as per his instructions, which he has given to you previously. There will be just one other item which my friend and I will fetch from the other carriage. It wouldn't be much good without her, would it?" They walked back out to the street, Dawes laughing and slapping his large colleague on the shoulder.

I allowed myself a smile, which reminded me, with a small stabbing pain, that my face carried bruising. He was right though, without the girl in the box it would indeed be a wasted afternoon. As usual with any new appointment of mine, I had gone through the process of gathering background information through my normal sources. Apart from a natural curiosity, it paid to know who you were dealing with when it came to matters of death. Today's assignment had filled me with particular interest.

Annie Lowther was an actress on the up. From lowly beginnings in the small music halls she had been fortunate enough to meet some very influential people and rose quickly appearing at The Canterbury and The Middlesex, where she became the darling of the crowds. She had higher dreams though and wished to become an actress, spending her spare moments perfecting some of the most famous female roles. She had appeared in some small productions and, regarding her talents as an actress the initial reviews were very favourable. It was predicted that she would have been one of the greatest actresses of our age, if she had not suffered an unfortunate accident involving a large set of stairs and the badly stitched hem of an expensive dress. Oh how they wept in the bars of Shaftesbury Avenue when they heard the news,

"Our little dove has flown, stolen from us by the fickle hand of fate, torn from the prospect of a life of fame and fortune, forever to live in our memories."

The truth behind her demise was, however, a much more unfortunate and seedy story. She had been first sighted by Lord William Falconer when just seventeen years of age and appearing in an unpublicised role at a local brothel.

He had been mesmerised by the simple beauty of this young waif who came from such sad beginnings. The daughter of a local abbess, she had never met her father, truth be told her mother had only met him twice, once when he had come to her abode one night as a young street girl, carrying a terrible collection of expensive liquor and opium and the second time when he returned for another piece of her and had been informed that he had placed a very potentially expensive bun in a cheap but operational oven. The woman finding, herself with an ever expanding midsection, lost herself in dreams of being taken from her poor lodgings by this mystery man and would find herself content in the life of a respectable lady, happily married to a rich man who loved her and her baby. This was not to be the case, however as the man told her in a most direct of terms, that this would never be the case and that she should,

"Get rid, as soon as possible".

The mystery man must have had some degree of morality about him, either that or he was terrified by the thought of scandal, because he gave the woman a large sum of money to end the pregnancy and keep her silence. She was a smart woman however and, rather than carrying out his wishes, she had kept the child and the money so that she would be able to start a 'business' of her own.

The baby, Annie, had been born and was raised within the confines of this den of inequity. Her mother, rather than seeing the good fortune that Annie had brought about, resented her, reminding the abbess, as she did, of the man who abandoned her. This resentment saw her put Annie 'to work' as soon as she was old enough to turn a man's head and make her mother some coin. Unfortunately for young Annie, there were men who visited her home for whom the only thought of age was whether it was not yet double figures. This was the terrible life which Annie Lowther, future star of the west end stage, endured until Lord Falconer visited her establishment one evening and 'saved' her from her mother. This salvation, as had been the case throughout her short life was sealed with a cash payment. Her mother sold her.

She had been set up in apartments, financed by Falconer, and provided with all the means necessary for her to attain her dream of performing on the stage. Falconer's idea, it is said, was that she could have a little career in the theatre whilst ensuring that she was suitably grateful to him and showed her gratitude as and when he demanded it. What the philanthropist Lord neglected to consider however were her natural talents and charisma when treading the boards. Her star rose over the London sky and, rather than playing a small but happy part in the dramatic arts, she soon became the 'bright new maid of the music halls'. Falconer, distressed by her sudden fame and high ideals threatened to bring her down unless she slowed in her rise to the top, but this butterfly was not for hiding and, as a result of believing the critics words, she developed even greater dreams of becoming a true theatre actress. The flight of her success however, was dealt a disastrous blow when the accident clipped her wings to a mortal extent.

Hushed rumours of a violent argument, fed by the drunken rage of her benefactor Lord, now wracked with guilt and grief, remained unproven and I wondered, as her casket was unloaded from the hearse, whether Falconer made a habit of killing those who did not obey him.

Dawes and Soames entered the studio, carrying the casket containing the unfortunate girl and I began to wonder if I would be forced to witness another talking corpse through my lens this afternoon. If this was to be the case, it would be better if these men were not present. I decided to find out tapping the large man on the shoulder as he passed me.

"Mr Soames, I am afraid I may be over an hour with my task, do you care to wait here or will you return later?" They placed the casket on the floor next to the camera and Soames turned to me smiling but not speaking. "Well?" I said.

"He don't speak no more, sir." Dawes said, motioning to the larger man with his thumb. "Poor old Mr Soames here can't, on account of his accident. He had a previous engagement with a knife." Soames smiled at me and motioned with his finger to a large star shaped scar on the left side of his throat. "He shouldn't have survived really, lucky he was, I never saw so much blood as what came out of my good friend here."

Mr Soames grinned in a way which told me that this was a routine which they were used to performing for anyone new that they met.

"Four inch blade what did it, I was surprised not to see it come out the other side." Laughed Dawes and his large friend smiled and shook in a silent display of laughter. "I saved him I did," Dawes continued the patter, "left the blade in there and stopped the blood coming out with a handkerchief I had in my pocket." His eyes studied my face looking for any sign of shock or horror. He saw none. "Lucky we were near the Belgrave on Gloucester Street so we rushed him right in and found a doctor. Saved his life but lost his voice he did." He looked at me again, waiting for a reaction. It was clear that they were not going anywhere until they had completed telling the story and I decided to press him to continue.

"That is a fascinating story, Mr Dawes. How lucky he is to have a friend like you around to save him. Did they catch the man that did it?"

"Well it's a funny thing that, Mr Darke, very funny indeed because you see it was me. I stuck the knife in him." This time my shock was difficult to hide and I supposed later that this was the effect that the story received each time the tale was told and was a daily source of entertainment to them. Shocking or not however, I needed them to leave so that I could proceed with whatever strange experience the afternoon held for me.

"So you are saying that you stabbed your friend in the throat and then saved him from dying? I must say Mr Dawes that Mr Soames and yourself are very surprising characters indeed. How did you come to stab him?"

"Well it was his own fault, Mr Darke. You see we were playing a game of cards and he cheated me, I knew he had and he has since admitted it, haven't you Will?" He looked to the larger man who smiled and nodded at me. "I didn't mean him no great harm, I was aiming for his cheek, thought I'd give him something to remember not to cheat his friend in future, but he moved you see, and bang! There it went, right into his throat, claret everywhere and a right mess on the card table. Still he won't forget it now will he? At least some good came of it and he's never cheated in a game of cards since, have you?" Mr Soames shook his head; the smile had faded from his face.

"It looks like you've just come back from the wars, if you don't mind me saying. I hope the other fella looks worse." Dawes continued and I smiled in return, I was not about to say how I sustained my injuries and let these men know that I was an easy mark. Dawes noted my lack of response and saw it as a sign that I wanted to start my work. "Anyway, we won't take up any more of your precious time, Mr Darke. We will return for her at three this afternoon if that's convenient for you. We will be taking our lunch at the pub on the corner."

"Very well," I replied and led them to the door. I watched them as Dawes told the carriage drivers of their plans and told them to meet back outside the studio in three hours. They wandered down Osborn Street, side by side towards Whitechapel Road, and I decided that if I ever needed anybody stabbing, that I would do no better than to call on those gentlemen. I went back inside closing and locking the doors behind me and walked to the casket, removing its lid.

There is certainly no doubting that, when alive, Annie would have been a beautiful sight to behold. Even in death, and with the benefit of rouge and other makeup, she retained some allure. In spite of my knowledge regarding her background and upbringing I could fully understand how a gentleman such as William Falconer could become obsessed by her simple beauty.

I spent the next half an hour preparing the room with the items which Falconer had sent in the trunk; stage props such as a vase and jewellery and clothing for Annie, before taking Annie from the casket and sitting her on the lounge settee where she would be photographed. As someone who had been surrounded by the dead since a babe, the thought of handling a dead body and even dressing one held no sense of fear or oddity to me. I have always believed that the body is just a shell we inhabit, an item of clothing if you will, and when a person's life has ended the shell is abandoned, empty.

Once happy with her reclined position, I moved towards my camera and mentally prepared myself for what awaited me through the lens. As expected when I looked through the viewfinder at the corpse, she seemed to have life breathed into her as she turned her face towards me and spoke, her eyes firmly fixed upon the lens of the camera.

"My lord, I have remembrances of yours, that I have longed long to re-deliver," her voice was ethereal and a marked improvement to the more aggressive chanting of the child who spoke to me the day before. I had heard this line before somewhere, a distant spark of recognition firing at the back of my troubled mind. As I continued to watch her she spoke again.

"My lord?"

My fear of the speaking cadaver grew as I realised that this recently deceased girl appeared to actually be expecting something in the way of a response from me. I removed my head from the cloth covering the camera and found, as I knew that I would, an inanimate body, devoid of all life and, of course, unspeaking. I returned to my viewing position to see again the slightly more life filled version of Annie Lowther, who, although sat in the same repose, smiled sweetly at the camera waiting for some kind of sign that I had heard her voice.

"My Lord?" Her tone was becoming more insistent, with a desperate edge as if panic was beginning to ensue.

My voice returned her salutation, although it quavered slightly, unused as I was to conversing with the dead.

"Good day, my lady. What remembrance is it that you have? Do you have some news of Surma, is he coming for me?"

An expression of confusion came over her pale, dead face. Her eyes narrowed as if the concept of talking to the living were as alien to her as my own experience.

"What means your lordship?" she asked

"Surma, I need to know if he is coming, if he is already here. Tell me what you know of the gatekeeper." Her face remained filled with confusion and I decided to try another tack. "My lady, what is it that you have to tell me?"

Quite unexpectedly, Annie moved from the position she had been placed in and stood, her legs appeared unsteady, as a newborn lamb. Gaining her balance she stepped dreamily to the other side of the studio, her fingers brushing against the painted backdrop in an inquisitive manner as if seeing the world for the first time. I moved my camera so as to keep the dead woman within the view of my lens as I feared that if she were to move completely out of the camera's view that our strange liaison would be brought to an abrupt halt. I admit that I began to shake at the fact that she was now mobile, how could I trust the dead? What if she were to attack me? I controlled my nerves and continued to watch her.

She began to speak again, her voice far away and wistful,

"White his shroud as the mountain snow. O my lord, my lord, I have been so affrighted!" She raised her hands to her mouth in an almost theatrical manner and I had the briefest of thoughts that I was glad that I had never seen Miss Lowther on stage when she had been alive. For if this was the type of line delivery that she made a habit of producing, quite how someone could bear to put themselves through two hours of this type of performance would require a level of stamina and patience which I could not profess to. She picked up a small ornament on the mantle of the fireplace and continued. "As if he had been loosed out of hell. To speak of horrors- he comes before me." She had obviously decided to speak to me in riddles, something that I abhorred and I felt my hackles rising.

"Who is he?" I asked. "What horrors are to come?"

"My lord, I do not know, but truly I do fear it" As she spoke I noticed that apart from her eyes, which were glazed and milky, she would appear to be as alive as I. As she spoke she looked down at the long white dress that she wore. Her small hands played with the cloth swaying it from side to side over her feet. She appeared lost in thought, preoccupied by some madness brought on by her death.

"Annie," I said in an attempt to break her from the daze in which she seemed glued. "Annie, is he coming to bring death, am I in danger of any kind?" She looked up staring at the lens of the camera.

"I do not know the Annie of whom you speak; I fear that you have mistaken me my lord." Her face looked almost apologetic and I began to wonder if the body of Annie was being used as some kind of vessel to portend doom to me. This thought was fleeting however as the truth of the matter finally struck me. This was indeed Annie but the words that she spoke were of Ophelia, the character who she had been rehearsing for when her accident happened and who Lord Falconer had wished her to be dressed as for the photograph.

"Ophelia?" I asked, although I felt a fool for doing so. She smiled in recognition. "Ophelia, what is the danger that you speak? Who is it that you think is coming?"

"I think nothing, my lord." She spoke with a sadness, as if she knew that her time back in the living world was soon to end. In a sudden change of mood she cried out and dropped to her knees, her voice full of anguish and terror. "O, help him, you sweet heavens! No, no, he is dead; Go to thy deathbed."

Her head dropped and she became filled with wracking sobs, as if all of the woes of the world were upon her. She had truly been filled with the madness of the character she thought herself to be. I tried for a final time to obtain some kind of information from her and thought to myself, with a morbid humour, that if this poor girl was the best that the dead could do, by way of a messenger, then they would never make me understand their warning. It would seem that my alcohol poisoned state had drained the patience from me, even when being spoken to from the other side.

"My Lady, tell me who is dead, whose deathbed should I visit? Tell me something of worth for pity's sake."

"His beard was as white as snow, all flaxen was his poll. He is gone, he is gone, and we cast away moan. God 'a'mercy on his soul! And of all Christian souls, I pray God. God b' wi' you."

It was obviously no good; this poor dead girl would not get her message to me. With a frustrated sigh I withdrew my head from the cloth and looked across the studio at the dead girl stiffly sat on the settee where she had been before her ghostly wanderings. Without returning to look at her through the viewfinder I went to the darkroom and withdrew a plate from its silver bath. After loading it into the camera, I pointed the lens at her and glanced through it just long enough to hear her last words to me.

"I was pushed you know." Her face was full of sadness at the memory. It was as I had feared but I could not do anything about it. What would I say? That the dead girl told me that it was murder and not an accident. I withdrew my head from the cloth and started the exposure, I had no wish to engage in further dialogue, there would be no reason.

I hoped that if these conversations with the dead were to continue that I would be visited by someone with a little sense and the ability to help me understand the oncoming danger, and that I would not be burdened with the troubles of the recently passed. I was still no clearer as to the meaning of these warnings. Grandfather was right I should visit Father and ask his advice.

I took the plate to my darkroom where I completed the exposure using a developing bath before fixing the image with potassium cyanide and hanging it to dry. Without looking at the time, I left the dead girl where she sat and went upstairs to my apartments where I washed and changed, a process which was as much to make me feel better than to make my appearance look less coarse. I was disturbed in my ablutions by a sharp knocking at the door downstairs and I realised that it must be Dawes and Soames, returned for the girl.

Once I had ensured that both she and the contents of the chest were re-secured in their boxes, I waved both gentlemen, whom were both a great deal merrier for their lunch, off and watched the carriages as they headed off on their way back to the affluent, and murderous, Lord Falconer.

The experience with the actress, rather than creating distress within me, as the child had done the day previously, filled my mind and heart with a sense of frustration and bizarre humour that I did not expect to feel. It was with this warm sense of absurdity inside and a smile worn on the outer, that I locked the doors to my studio behind me and set off towards Whitechapel Road to visit my father and brother. Although I may have had news to impart that I had communicated with the dead and the discussion would be serious, the day's events had, in a strange way, lightened my mood and put a spring in my step. Hopefully all of my future communications with the dead would be as free of terror and as oddly amusing.

5
THREE BOYS

It was obvious, even to someone who had never set eyes on us before, that we were brothers. Each of us had piercing blue eyes, an unruly mop of hair so blonde that it could be described as white and the same lean, angular frames, although we were of course different sizes.

We shared many things between us however, apart from our similar looks. Firstly there was our bedroom, a small room on the uppermost floor of the house which was just large enough to fit the bunk bed and single bed where we slept. Both of these beds were built by Grandfather and Father who were skilled carpenters, a requisite required of them in their line of work as they had always built caskets, which they were able to offer families of the recently deceased. Father told us that by making their own coffins and offering them directly to families they were cutting out the 'man in the middle', something that I of course understand now but at the time was a useless phrase which I did not try to comprehend. As a result of this more direct approach they were able to absolve any additional costs charged by an external carpenter, something which helped to make us the undertaker of choice in an area where few people had the money to pay for an extravagant funeral service.

On days when no services were being held Johannes, Niko and I would sit on the side bench of Grandfather's workshop and watch them work together sawing, planing and sanding the wood which would make up the panels of the caskets. When this preparation work was complete we would gaze in amazement as they created the intricate wood joints and pin these panels together. This part of the process never ceased to hold our full attention as Father would explain to us the type of joint that he would be using and its benefits. I am sure that he would use a different variety of joints not so much because they were required but because it was part of our education, as his father had provided for him when he was a boy. My father was the only surviving child of his family as his three brothers and two sisters had died during the cholera outbreak in 1831 which also claimed his mother. Father, who was only seven at the time, lived through it and, until he met and married my mother in 1845, he lived alone with Grandfather dutifully learning the family trade. The bond which they developed, during those years alone with each other, was as strong as I have ever known between father and son, something, which I truly admit, created a sense of jealousy within me as their closeness transcended words or actions. Sometimes only a short look between them would say more than a thousand words to each other, a trait which my brothers and I found almost unnervingly telepathic.

Our fascination with watching them about their work would grow to obsessive levels as we would stare avidly at their actions, making the same arm movements ourselves and desperately trying to memorise each tiny element, in preparation for the day when we were older and would be working in this same workshop together. Occasionally one of them would invite us to help him, a great honour indeed, mostly with sanding or varnishing where there was little chance of us causing any permanent damage.

Apart from Grandfather's stories by the fire, this time spent watching our working elders was some of the happiest we spent together as brothers. One possible reason for this was our love for Father and Grandfather and because it provided us with precious respite from the constant anger and potential violence of my mother. Time spent in the workshop, according to Mother, meant "My time for peace from the troubles and misery of men", and she would take the time to get on either with her baking in the kitchen or washing of clothes. The "peace from men's troubles" had only been replaced by other furies of hell sent to test her undying patience as we would often hear her shouting and swearing at the oven which burnt her bread or the mangle which tore the clothing creating further work for her. Safely protected from her ire, through the fact that it was furiously directed elsewhere, we would giggle and snort at each hurled curse, something made even funnier by watching Father and Grandfather's expressions and knowing looks towards each other. It would seem that they also enjoyed the opportunity to feel free of her vitriol within the safety of male company.

After Johannes' death we continued to have these carpentry sessions but his absence weighed heavy and was always felt. A lot of the jovial humour was gone from Father, and Niko would always sit as close as he possibly could to me almost as if he felt that if I moved out of arm's reach I would be lost like our dear brother. In all respects Niko and I became closer after being reduced to a pair, we became more appreciative of each other and, despite my sometime annoyance at his constant shadowing, we rarely fought as brothers do. Even many years later and as young men we would not forget Johannes and would often drink a toast to him if out together or remind each other of the fun times that we had as a giggling trio.

A second thing that we all shared was our fascination with the tales told to us by Grandfather and also Father but to a lesser extent. We felt as if we had ownership of our heroes. They were ours to talk about and dream of, ours to pretend to be when we played in the small yard at the back of the house. The other children in the area did not know of them and many could not even say the names of Väinämöinen and Lemminkäinen. We saw this as further proof that the tales were ours and ours alone. It would seem, when we played, that there were no bad roles to be played, unless of course one of us had to play a female part, which we avoided if at all possible. Each of the three of us were pleased to have the opportunity to be the brave and wise bard Väinämöinen or the daring and reckless Lemminkäinen. We even relished the chance to be Surma himself, the gatekeeper of Tuonela, the land of the dead. A beast tasked by the God Ukko with ensuring that those who had crossed the border into the underworld never return and were torn and devoured for their attempts.

Only Väinämöinen and Lemminkäinen ever survived their meetings with Surma, Väinämöinen used his wits to fool the beast into letting him through. Lemminkäinen was not so fortunate, when he visited Tuonela to carry out one of the tasks set by Louhi, the Queen of the north whose daughter he wished to marry, he was bitten by a poisonous snake and his body fell into Tuonela's river where it was dashed to pieces by the rocks below the water. His distraught mother searched the river, dredging and collecting all of the parts of him and sewing him together again. Even then he was not returned to life however, his body was whole again but his mind was lost, an empty shell without a soul. His mother, in a final desperate attempt to recover her son, sent a bee to the halls of Ukko himself to bring back a drop of honey as ointment. This powerful magic worked and Lemminkäinen was revived but never returned to his reckless ways and lived out his life as a humble, god fearing man.

I remember one particular day in my childhood, a few weeks before Johanne's fatal accident. It was shortly after Grandfather had first told us about Surma and how he guarded the gates to the underworld, devouring all those who tried to return to the world of life. As the eldest I decided which parts we would be playing, I decided that Johannes would be Väinämöinen; they were similar in many ways. Both used their wits and intelligence to their greatest benefit. Johannes, with the weakness in his body which hindered a great deal of physical activity, became reliant on his mind, his reading even more voracious than mine. However, whilst I revelled in novels and tales of bravery and death, my brother preferred books of the non-fiction variety. I have never known anyone other than my brother who could sit quite happily reading an encyclopaedia, working his way through the alphabet and absorbing the information like the largest of sponges. His knowledge of the world, although learnt only from books and very rarely through personal experience was, for a seven year old boy, greater even than learned men who I know now. Of the three of us Johannes was the eyes, he saw the world and understood it, maybe this is why he always had a sense of sadness about him.

Niko would be Lemminkäinen; both were brave to the point of recklessness, full of life and warm-hearted. Niko was a sensitive soul, able to pick up on people's feelings more adeptly than Johannes or I and willing to do anything to brighten a mood and improve the suffering of those in distress. Sometimes this meant acting the fool, which often led to trouble or accidents, both of which he laughed off as if without a care. Of the three of us he was the heart, feeling for us and bringing life to our little group.

This left the role of Surma to me. Strangely enough, and trust me dear reader I have been called strange and many similar things in the past, I coveted the role of Surma as my own. The thought of the power of this terrible beast, of the fear and awe which he inspired was attractive to me, even though in life I have never consciously attempted to terrify anyone. As the largest of the three of us I felt that it was fitting that I towered over my brothers as a terrible monster committed to devouring them, something which I acted out with great relish, especially when pretending to tear Niko into tiny pieces and which brought fits of giggles to my youngest sibling.

There was also something else which made the character of the beast so interesting to me. I always felt that there was a degree of sadness to him, as I feel that sadness and hurt within people is the cause of most, supposedly evil, behaviours. I often wondered why Surma had been given the unenviable task of guarding the gates of the underworld. Had he committed some ancient wrongdoing and been given the undertaking as an eternal punishment by a greater power? Were the souls of those attempting to return to the living world his only sustenance and as such forced to commit such atrocities through hunger? These were just some of the questions which I pondered and constantly plagued Grandfather with. For his part, Grandfather would never be drawn on such questions and would only say that he felt that, although horrific in his actions, Surma played a vital part in the balance of the world. The dead should not normally return; man cannot live forever and should acknowledge his fate and follow the path provided for him. This was an idea which I, of course, agreed with in principle if only because it kept my family in business. If Johannes were the eyes and Niko the heart, then I feel that I was the mind; always thinking, introspective, self conscious and touched with nerves that sent me from thrilling, endless energy to destructive morbidity.

On this particular afternoon Father and Mother were engaged in the provision of a wake held for Miss Henrietta Frankish, a lady of local repute and ancient age who had been a towering figure in Bishopsgate for nearly fifty years. Born to the East London Union Workhouse at Dunning's Alley, her mother, allegedly a disinherited lady made pregnant by her father's valet, died during childbirth leaving her to the custodial care of the parish. Throughout her hard childhood she was known, in the workhouse, as a girl whose enthusiasm and commitment to toil of any description made her a valuable asset to the institution.

At the age of twelve Miss Frankish was taken on, for a fee of course paid to the local church fund, by no less than Mr. James Haskell owner of Haskell's Tobacco, one of the largest importers and producers of fine smoking goods. She was initially employed as a ladies maid for Mr Haskell's wife but soon after displaying her aptitude for business, through discussions with her lady employer, was given a role in Haskell's shipping affairs from their United States tobacco producers in Virginia, where she moved to and lived for nearly ten years. Her role within Mr Haskell's enterprise, being not just a woman but a woman of poor beginnings, was frowned upon by many in the business world. Rumours spread of how a woman such as she could reach such giddy heights and been given so much responsibility, many of which threatened scandal to Mr Haskell and his lady wife. Although they vociferously denied any wrongdoing or disrepute, they did eventually buckle to popular thought and removed Miss Frankish from her position. Henrietta disappeared from public life in an instant and moved back to Bishopsgate where, with new found and unsubstantiated funds she opened a small tobacco shop, selling pipes, tobacco and other smoking paraphernalia. Never married, she continued to run this establishment until a ripe old age indeed, becoming well loved and respected in the area as a donator of funds to local poor charities.

Miss Frankish dropped dead in her shop, keeling over, by all accounts, during a fit of laughter after telling a tale to a customer of a ladies maid who enjoyed the affections of both her master and his lady wife. Henrietta Frankish, whilst known for such coarse humour, had finally had the last laugh. A great, hearty chuckle which killed her with a smile on her face. She left ownership of her shop and the remains of her estate, minus the cost of her funeral and a large street party, to charity. The final beautiful act of a well-loved and grand lady.

The street party was catered for, in part, by Mother, a cause of much aggravation and anger to her whilst preparing the food. Her curses and violent outbursts towards inanimate objects under her control set my brothers and me into a furious bout of giggling as we sat, out of earshot and striking distance, in the yard.

Father and Mother were attending the wake and had left us under the charge of Grandfather who was sat, as was his habit, in front of the fireplace dozing.

"Out of my way Surma! I am Väinämöinen the bard, and I wish to return to the world of the living!" Johannes faced up to me his hands on his hips and as bolstered as he could make himself. Niko snorted from the other side of the yard, finding his older brother's attempt at acting amusing.

I stood over him, trying to put on my most terrifying face and speaking in a low growl.

"No man may pass me; all who try will face my wrath and be devoured!" My attempt at portraying terror in the extreme had some effect on him as he visibly shrank back from me and I continued to growl, a low guttural sound which owed more to Grandfather's description of Surma as some kind of giant wolf-like creature. My own view was of a ghostly, wraith devouring souls by sucking the life from them and tearing what remained to shreds. The wolf creature however was a particular fear of Johannes and I decided to use it to full effect. It worked, maybe he saw something in my eyes but, although playing, I was trying my hardest to appear frightening to the seven year old. For a moment we stood, face to face, monster and prey, the only sound a rumble created in my throat. I could see his eyes trying to read mine, a slight tinge of desperation as he searched for a sign that this was still a game.

The moment was broken by Niko, who suddenly laughed out loud, causing Johannes and I to remember where we were and what we were doing. Johannes began to smile, a nervous crack across his face which sought some kind of response from me. I toyed with the idea of holding my position and continuing to scare my brother. The pose felt somehow good inside me, the reaction that I had got was as gratifying as it was surprising.

"Sib?" Johannes quietly said, his eyes beginning to fill with a watery glaze. The realism of the moment suddenly became clear to me. Despite enjoying the ability to create fear, I had no wish to reduce my dear brother to tears through my action. I let him know this with a wink, a small sign that was not seen by Niko. A small sign of relief shot through Johannes face, he knew what I was planning to do.

Niko stood up and began to approach us, he had sensed that there was upset in the air and tried once again to break the moment and return us to our game.

"Sib, Johannes? What's going on? Have we stopped the game?"

As he stepped ever closer I made my move and suddenly turned growling at him.

"Now, reckless Lemminkäinen! It is your turn to be torn into tiny pieces!" I shouted, raising my arms and extending my fingers into talons ready to rend him. Niko screamed with joy and began to run but he was too close and I leapt on him, tickling with my talons.

Our play descended into rolling around on the floor with a mixture of growls and giggles. Even Johannes, who was normally kept out of our roughhousing games, joined in screaming and jumping onto my back. The noise of our chaos had grown too great though and we were interrupted by Grandfather who appeared at the back door of the parlour, bleary eyed and face of thunder.

"Can an old man not get a moments peace in this house? Stop this fighting at once!" he shouted, but seeing the happiness on the faces of his grandsons as they played together his face softened and the smile, which suited his face so well, soon returned.

"Grandfather, help us. Niko and I are being eaten by Surma!" Johannes cried, and in that moment Sibelius the elder decided to turn from old man to playful boy again as he raised his arms above his head and bellowed;

"I am the great god Ukko; I am here to save you brave warriors!" He jumped among us with an agility which was past his years and he probably regretted later and for the next twenty minutes he joined in our games, making us the happiest boys in the world. The thought of that day never failed to bring a smile to my face.

Many years later, two weeks before the dead had started to talk to me in fact; I sat with Niko and Father over dinner at their house and we reminisced about that afternoon and shared loving memories of Johannes and Grandfather.

"So, Sibelius, how is business?" Niko leant forward refilling my wine glass. I had an early start to-morrow and had probably drunk too much already, but my brother knew my weaknesses and, as such, knew that I would not refuse.

"It's steady, Nik. I cannot complain, things have been a little sparse of late but there are a few things in the diary which could turn out to be very lucrative indeed. You should come along one day; see how the modern businessman sets about earning good money." Niko and I laughed but Father was more serious.

"You do know that there is enough work here, Sib?" he said with a look of concern in his eyes. "The sad fact of the matter is that there is more than enough death around here to keep the three of us busy, Nik and I have had to turn down customers and send them down the road to Woodrow's."

George Woodrow ran the Undertakers on Leman Road and had long been a friendly competitor of Father's. It had not always been this way. Ten years ago when they first started their business, my parents had been concerned that we would lose custom, especially since I, as a headstrong eighteen year old, had recently told my father that I wished to start out on my own. Mother showed her disapproval, but the time when she would have responded with more than just a sharp word had long since gone. I had grown too tall and she had begun to shrink into the beginnings of an old woman. This was the reason that she did not raise her hand to me anymore, that and the confrontation between us three years earlier.

Mr Woodrow had called around a week before he opened. He wanted to introduce himself and discuss ways in which both businesses could work together to ensure that competition was not a problem. Unfortunately for him, and for all of us, Father was out at the sawmill arranging his next delivery of wood for casket building. I am sure, knowing Father as I do, that he would have been agreeable to such a discussion. However, poor George had the pleasure of meeting Mother instead, and she was in a particularly foul mood. Woodrow left our parlour that day with, what mother called, "A right good flea in his ear". Relations between the two business' remained sour until after Mother's passing four years later, for which Father, in a display of bridge building and good nature, asked Mr Woodrow to arrange the funeral. George and Father had been firm friends ever since.

"Thank you for the offer, Father but I have no need of extra work." I took a sip of the wine. "Unlike Niko and yourself, I don't need to work daily to earn enough to survive. I have savings and I do not exactly lead an extravagant lifestyle."

"Apart from your membership of a gentleman's club uptown of course," Niko cut in, with a wry smile on his face. "Not all of us can afford to mix with the upper classes, Sib; I'm surprised that you still have the inclination to be seen with the hoi polloi."

"Dear brother, there is nothing that would keep me away from your enlightening company. How could I ever survive the endless dull conversations with Lords and Gentlemen without the occasional thrilling conversation with you about the cost of pine and the erratic bowel movements of your horse? I pray for the day when you marry Bethany and find some other dire subjects of conversation, like babies or housework. My God, do I not pity the poor girl for being forced to live with you though." Niko's smile remained despite the playful insult and I could see his mind working frantically to come up with a suitable response. Our Father smiled as he watched his two remaining sons banter and spar. He reached over and clasped my hand as it rested on the table.

"With all seriousness, Sibelius, I know that I have had my reservations about your business ventures in the past and I have made my thoughts on your love of gambling well known, but I need you to know that I am proud of you. We both are. I sometimes wish that I had been brave enough to strike out on my own as a young man, I didn't of course but I take great pleasure in watching you thrive in your independence. Your Grandfather would be proud also."

I felt a gnawing lump in my gut and my eyes began to itch somewhat. It took me a moment but I realised that Father's words had struck something within me and made me feel emotional. This was not a normal position for me to find myself in as I had always found difficulty in showing emotions of any kind. I put this inurement down to my attendance at so many funerals in my life and keeping control when surrounded by so many people displaying their grief. This theory did not stand too much examination, however, as Niko had always been victim to such public displays of tearfulness and affectation. I saw Niko studying me now as I carefully raised a hand to my face and wiped the bottom of each eye with a finger.

"Sibelius Darke, do I detect tears in those cold, dry eyes? Father I do believe you have achieved the impossible." He broke into a laugh which Father echoed, but rather than feeling aggrieved by my brother's words, I felt a well of emotion which thankfully I managed to control somewhat and disguise with laughter of my own.

Father's words reminded me of the phrase that Grandfather would often remind us of as children; 'a child is like an axe; even if it hurts, you still carry them on your shoulders.' No matter how old or independent we became, Father would always see us as boys, his boys. In that one moment I felt as safe and at home as I had ever felt with my family and my only regret was that Johannes did not survive to grow up with us and share this happy meal.

Despite the gnawing worry which I now felt, after my incidents with the dead child and actress, my mind was relatively content in dwelling on these happier memories of fraternal fellowship and family love, as I crossed the Whitechapel Road with a spring in my step and approached Darke and Sons Funeral Services. The main door at the front would be closed, there were no funerals today and I knew that Father and Niko had planned to spend the best part of the day in the workshop. When Niko had told me of their plans I do admit a pang of jealousy and regret that I had, in effect, removed myself from this part of my family's life by setting out on my own. I walked down the alley at the side of the building, expecting to hear the sounds of their toil, but found that all was silent. They may have finished early for the day but it was not yet four o'clock and I had never known Father, despite is advancing years, to call a premature halt to a day's work. As I turned the corner at the end of the building I saw that the large sliding workshop door was shut and locked, maybe they were out, called short to a potential new appointment. It was then that I noticed the back door to the parlour was ajar.

For some reason I suddenly thought of Grandfather again, stood in this same doorway, bleary eyed and watching three boys rolling around in the yard, screaming and laughing, enjoying life as brothers. Johannes was gone, but at least I still had Nik.

"Niko? Father? Are you there?" I called as I pushed the door open gently.

Whatever light heartedness and peace I had felt on the short walk over from my studio vanished in an instant, when my eyes came upon the scene in the back hall by the staircase.

For there, hung by their ankles and torn to pieces, were the bloody corpses of my poor dear father and what I assumed to be Niko. I could not tell in that first instance because of the fact that his head had been removed at the neck. A head that I looked down and saw at my feet, his blue eyes, that had once been so full of life and laughter, stared in cold terror and his mouth was agape, stuck forever in a silent scream.

The sound I made was loud and primal.

6
THE SCENE OF MY DOWNFALL

"Exsanguination, Mr Darke. I trust that being an intelligent man, you are aware of the word and what it means?"

Inspector Frederick Draper eyed me suspiciously, as you would a child who had been caught in the pantry. Though no more than ten years older than me, I felt that his tone was patronising in the extreme, and I took an instant dislike to the man. He was thin to the point of skeletal, his skin appeared to have been stretched across his sharp cheekbones giving his head an angular quality which was topped with a slicked layer of red hair scraped across, concealing a bald pate beneath. Draper was a good six inches taller than me, and this only added to the air of self confident superiority which flowed from him.

Stood behind him was his sergeant, a heavy-set man in a green checked suit, someone who could be described as a thug at best. I had seen his type before, if he had not been a police sergeant he would have made an excellent enforcer, (which I assumed he was for the inspector). I had no doubt that he enjoyed the more physical elements of his job and that his heart leapt when someone resisted arrest. He would not have had the intelligence to progress any higher than the role in which he now found himself, and would see out his career, threatening and beating anyone whom his boss saw as suspicious. His close-set eyes never left my face and I wondered if he had even blinked since entering the room.

As I replied to the question, my instant dislike of Draper was barely contained within my voice.

"I know what the word means, Inspector, but I have never seen it carried out on a man." The thought of Father and Niko, hung from the landing railings and bleeding out onto the floor put a rock into my throat. "Believe me when I tell you that to see it is disturbing, but to see it when carried out on the only two surviving members of my family, then it will be a wonder if I ever sleep soundly again without the reoccurring image thrusting itself into my mind."

I had been held in this room for the last forty five minutes, most of the time left alone with men observing me through the windowed pane of the office door. Draper had entered ten minutes ago to question me and I did not care for the direction that our conversation was heading.

"I understand that you have a job to do, Inspector Draper," I continued, "but today I have lost a part of me that I will never recover, no man should see what I have seen today, and the fact that it was my father and only brother makes it worse a hundredfold. I would be grateful if we could conclude this discussion while I try to come to terms with the horror of it and be allowed to grieve in peace."

"I'm afraid that the law cannot allow for grief when there is murder being made." The firmness in the Inspector's face showed no sign of fading.

"Well it should, I will answer your questions, cold and immaterial that they are, but I will not be held accountable for the deaths of the two people left in the world that I had any love for." I was beginning to grow exasperated with the way that this man seemed determined to tear me apart.

There was not a flicker of sympathy shown in Draper's face throughout my plea for time and dignity; however, I am sure that I saw the smallest glimmer of a poorly hid smirk from the ape stood behind him.

I am not a man known for my bravery or willingness to engage in physical violence. At that moment however, I would have had no hesitation in attempting to strike the smirking fool where he stood, no matter what his size, had I not been housed in a room at Leman Road police station with a barrier of at least twenty policemen between myself and the outer door. I was, as

Draper had said, an intelligent man and I was fully aware of the brevity of my situation and place which I currently held in the list of potential suspects in the murder of my family. My greatest hope lay within my love for Father and Niko, and the knowledge that I had nothing to do with the grisly scene I had discovered upon entering the back door of their house.

"When did you last see your Father and Brother?" He asked, staring at the notepad in his hand.

"Please do not tell me that you think I am responsible for this?" I almost laughed at his supposition. "They were my only family! What good would it do me to kill them? Ask anyone in the area who knows us. We are close, Inspector, as close as fathers, sons and brothers could ever be. I did not do this thing and I do not know who did!"

The urge to scream at the man was strong within me. I was aware that he would be trying to do his job, but there seemed to be no degree of understanding within him that this could be the worst day of my life. I had always been accused of being cold in the past but I felt as if I had met my match with this man. I had not met him before this terrible day, but I had heard mention of him. It paid to know who was who in the local police especially when, like me, it was necessary to stray to the other side of the law to obtain certain items of use to my business such as chemicals for use in the development process or even, on occasion, camera equipment which may have come from unknowing sources.

Frederick Draper had recently moved back in the area after a secondment to the City of London police where he had been working within a team specialising in fraud. Before joining the police he had aspired to be an accountant, being adept at figures, his father, however had been one of the first of Robert Peel's constables when the force was formed in 1829. He had remained on the force rising to the role of inspector and, wishing to start a family tradition and unbeknown to young Frederick, had submitted an application to Scotland Yard on his son's behalf. The younger Draper had acceded to his father's wishes and, like his father, had risen through the ranks at a rate which, to the observations of an outsider, would seem suspiciously nepotistic, as he was the son of a senior member of the force. The very nature of the man, upon my first impressions, gave me the feeling that he would feel more at home when surrounded by accounting ledgers; he did not feel any comfort in dealing with people on any level.

"You have not answered my question, Mr Darke, and so I shall ask it of you again. When did you last see your Father and Brother?"

"Last week, on Thursday, if it is that important to you, Inspector. I came over for dinner with them, as I do every week. I have told you, we are a close family and never had even the slightest cross word between us, not since Mother was alive anyway. I loved my Father and Niko as much as I could love anybody on this earth, and I could not conceive in the slightest why I, or anyone, would be driven to commit such a crime towards them."

"So could you tell me where you were between the hours of seven o'clock yesterday evening and six o'clock this morning?"

"I was in the Princess Alice; I spent the better part of the afternoon there in the company of the Landlord Tom Finnan and his daughter Bethany. They are good friends and were soon to be family, Niko was engaged …" I paused, and for the first time since finding the bodies, I thought of poor Bethany and the distress she would feel when she found out her fiancé's fate. At that moment the tears came, the tears for my father and brother, the tears for Bethany and the loss of the life she had looked forward to and the tears for me, left alone without the comfort and stability which Father had always given me without question.

The Inspector seemed uncomfortable by my display of grief and looked towards the floor rather than looking at me and seeing the tears of a grown man. In some distant part of me his discomfort was pleasing and I hoped that it would deter him from any further questioning. He waited patiently however and a small cough made me realise that he would not be swayed by my emotions and required me to continue answering his enquiries. Realising that I must continue I spoke again.

"I left The Princess Alice at around eight o'clock, I briefly visited my grandfathers grave at St Mary Matfellon's and returned home to sleep." The last part was a lie, as I had no idea of how and when I had returned home. A thought tickled the back of my mind. I had no memories of the time between the cemetery and waking up – How had I got home?

"...and can anyone provide an alibi for your whereabouts after you returned home?"

"Of course not. I live alone."

"Did anyone see you leave the public house, Mr Darke?"

"Yes, lots of people saw me leaving!" I snapped. "Tom Finnan, Bethany Finnan, a collection of drunkards inside the pub at the time and the thieving bastard who beat me and stole my pocket watch as soon as I had got outside!" The anger which I displayed was as much a part of my continued annoyance at losing my watch as it was at my irritation with Draper.

"Is that where you received the injuries to your face then?"

"Yes, I don't think he would have been able to influence me to part with the watch through the use of persuasive language and charm, I doubt that he is able to call on either. He relied on the use of fists and feet, Inspector. It is not just my face you know, I am covered in bruising if you do not believe me." I stood and started to lift my shirt to show the injuries I had sustained. Draper, however, had no wish to see them, raising his hand in objection.

At that moment I heard a familiar voice from the other room. Tom had arrived and was arguing with the policemen, telling them that they had no right to detain me any longer. The disturbance caused Draper to turn and nod to his Sergeant to open the door. As he did so Tom came through into the room, his face full of a fury which I had never seen exhibited by him before.

"Inspector, you have no right to keep this man." He said. "Can you not see that he is distraught? He has lost his only family and if that was not enough, he was the man who discovered them. Can you not leave him to his grief?"

Tom's angry tone carried no weight with the Inspector, who shocked me by becoming even stiffer in his posture than before.

"It is because of Mr Darke's discovery that I am talking to him, sir. Is it not strange that the man who discovered the murder has no proof of his whereabouts when the killing occurred?"

"He may not himself have proof, sir, but I can vouch for the man." said Tom, softening his face and returning to his usual more relaxed tone. "He was as drunk as I have ever seen a man, and after leaving my pub, he returned a half hour later wanting more drink. I refused his demands and took him home myself, ensuring that he was asleep in his own bed before leaving him. The next person to see him was my daughter, just a few hours later, when she woke him to check that he was suitably recovered." Tom was a marvel at making men feel comfortable in his presence and it seemed that, despite his coldness, even Draper was not immune to his calm, reassuring manner. As he spoke Tom stepped forward and placed his hand on the Inspector's arm. The Inspector did not flinch away. "You must believe me, Inspector Draper, when I tell you that I left Sibelius in his apartments, he was unconscious from drink and would have been unable to stand, let alone commit the grievous murder of two men."

Draper appeared to have been set off balance by the intervention of the charming landlord, and in that moment, I knew that Tom had the man's confidence and would save me from the injustices of the police.

"Very well," the Inspector said, "you may go Mr Darke, but be assured that I will come calling on you again before this investigation is done and the murderer found."

I stood up and started to make my way towards Tom and the door, but Draper held out an arm to stop me.

"Before you leave though, Darke, I will say this. I believe that this is not the first work carried out by this killer. Some boys have disappeared from the area over the last few weeks, and we have found the remains of two of them. They were not displayed as your family members were, but the wounds were of a similar nature." His eyes fixed mine with a stare which brought a lump of guilt from somewhere within me. "Be aware, sir, that I will use every tool at my disposal to bring in this killer and your name is known to me."

"Of course, Inspector." I said trying to hide the fear within my voice. "I wish you every success in your hunt. I pray that this murderer of my family be found and brought to justice as much as you do. Good day, sir."

As we left the station and stepped into the street outside, the relief within was evident and I breathed in the air of freedom, full of the rank stink of London though it was.

"Thank you, Tom. I am in your debt as ever." I forced a smile which, although meant, felt painful under the circumstances. "I would not expect anyone to lie for me as you did and I pray that your words do not come back to haunt you in the future. That man is a heartless monster and he will stop at nothing to see someone hang for this crime whether they be the killer or not."

Tom put his arm around me in support,

"I know that you did not do this thing, Sibelius. I know you better than you know yourself and there is not a hint of murder within you."

Tom did indeed know me well, but even I would stake my life upon the actions that I could carry out whilst drunk. Surely any man would be capable of murder if put into the right circumstances, many a murder had been committed by the drunk – Who was to say that I was any different? – But my own family? Could I have done this? If only I could clear my mind and recover those few hours lost to me, then I would be as sure as Tom was regarding my innocence.

"I am glad that at least one person believes in me, Tom. How did poor Beth take the news?" Since remembering the girl during my questioning, her face had been a constant in my mind as I worried for her wellbeing. In terms of closeness to my murdered family, only she would feel the pain as great as I.

"She is not good, Sib." He said, a sorrowful look in his face. "She went to her charity work after leaving you this morning, distributing food to the street children and helping at the orphanage. When I heard the news, I ran to find her before she found out from anybody else, found her in the laundry at the orphanage on St Mark's I did, took her home and broke it to her. You would have thought that I'd killed her stone dead there and then, the shock that was in her face. She never said a word, just tears."

"Where is she now, Tom? Don't tell me you left her alone to come and find me?"

"No, of course not, Sib. I left her with Anne, shut away in her bedroom, crying her heart out, I've not seen her like this before. That brother of yours was her life you know. I ... I don't know what to say to her." Tom seemed as uncomfortable as I when dealing with matters of emotion. For many years he had been strong, with regard to the loss of his wife, but now with the prospect of discussing the death of a loved one with his daughter he seemed quite weak and fearful. "Will you come and see her, Sibelius? Will you come to speak to her? This tragedy has given you much in common and I think that you may find comfort with each other."

I stiffened; the thought of sharing my grief with anyone made me feel a little liverish. I was already ashamed of my tearful outburst with the Inspector, but to engage in some kind of weeping duet would be more than my battered ego could bear. That is not to say that I did not feel a shared pity with Bethany, I did, and within a small part of me, I would have quite happily gone to her and offered condolence. The truth of the matter was that I was weary. Waking feeling crapulous this morning seemed like so many lifetimes ago, and I wanted nothing more than to retire to my rooms and be alone, left to sleep and sob, to suffer by myself. I tempered the response somewhat to prevent any hurt towards Tom or Bethany.

"I will visit Bethany, please assure her of this. Tell her I will visit her to-morrow when I am rested and of a more stable mind. For now, my friend, the time is late and I will go home and see you to-morrow." I shook his hand, thanked him for his timing and rescue, promising to come to the Alice in the morning.

As I walked the remainder of the journey back to my rooms, I cursed myself for the lie.

The depth of my grief was overwhelming. I had always prided myself on having an arrogant level of self-belief and independence, borne of an inherent desire to be my own man, to create a life for myself founded on my own design.

I had in the past, and not in cruelty, cursed my family's oversight and judgement. The pressure of growing up within a family business could be suffocating, being told how your life has been set before your birth can be crippling to the soul. Father had always ensured that his feelings were known with regard to my individuality of spirit and had made an example of Niko, always making a point of stating how good it was that one of his boys wished to remain safe within the family business. Now I found myself without any close family ties, rather than feeling freed to blossom, I felt hollowness inside caused by the loss of those who I felt most near.

For the next week I cancelled all of my appointments and remained within my apartments, festering in my own grief and self pity. The tears, which I had restrained, poured from me in wracking sobs combined with fits of terrible anger which caused me to lash out at my surrounding belongings, hurling chairs and tearing pictures from my walls. I sat surrounded by the broken remains of my life which, through my fury, had taken physical as well as mental form. I ignored the constant rapping at my door and the calls to my window from Tom shouting at me to come out to see him. I could not bear to see anyone at this time, even Tom and Bethany who were the closest thing to a family that I had left. I knew that Bethany's grief for the death of Niko would be great also and knew that I did not have the strength of character or the words to comfort her at this time. Thankfully, I also did not have any further communications with the police during my self-inflicted isolation, the thought of meeting with Draper when in such a weakened state filled me with horror.

I do not know how long I would have stayed entombed in my apartments, hardly eating or drinking, wallowing in my own filth and anguish, but I was finally disturbed one morning when I found myself opening the raft of notes and letters which had been put through my door. Contained within this pile of letters of commiseration and sorrow was an envelope bearing the name of Father's solicitor, Harrowman's. I opened it and found a covering letter from Charles Harrowman, explaining that Father's estate would be resolved once the police had completed their investigations into his death. However, they had instruction from Father to hand on a personal letter to Niko and I on his passing. Mr Harrowman stated that he did not know the contents of the letter but had been assured by Father that it was not related to his last will and testament in any form.

I looked at the sealed envelope which was addressed to Niko and I in Father's own hand. I stared at the script for a while, wondering whether to open it at once or save it until a time when I felt mentally strong enough to deal with the contents. Despite my fear, a combination of curiosity and a desire to be near to Father caused me to tear open the seal and read.

31st March 1872

My Dear Boys,

I have made arrangements with the solicitors to execute the terms of my last will and testament, but I also wished to send you a different message, something more personal and unsullied by the dust and formality of the legal environment.

I have never been a brave man; I admit this to you as it is something which I came to terms with very early in my life. This lack of will on my part has led to many regrets and disappointments which I will not burden you with fully, but I wish to take this opportunity, albeit as a coward and through a letter given to you upon my death, to apologise for two particular items of which I have kept from you in life.

Firstly, there is the issue of your mother. I apologise for not being brave enough to protect you from her anger and the terrible acts of violence which I know she inflicted upon you. I should have drawn the line and stood firm, acting as a shield for the fury which she constantly aimed at you both, but I did not and this is to my eternal shame. I ask however, that you try not to hold too much hate in your hearts for her actions. I cannot condone her behaviour fully, but you must understand the hurt which was burned within her. She lost the family she loved when we became betrothed and was forced, as a result of her unplanned pregnancy, to marry a man who she did not really know and ultimately did not love. In a short period of time she lost her parents and her siblings, cast out of their loving home because of her relations with someone who they saw as an unworthy immigrant. She was immediately lost, alone and hurting. This hurt caused her to resent the union and, as a result, resent the fruits of that union, our three beautiful, innocent boys.

My second great regret, I kept from you purposely when you were children and couldn't bear to tell you when you grew older as I had no wish to taint your memories. It is regarding your brother and the manner of his death. I recall this most clearly as if it happened only last week, this is not only because of the events of the day but also because it has been constantly in my thoughts every day since its occurrence.

I remember feeling so much pride when Johannes came to me that evening and begged me to let him run an errand for the first time. As you know he was not the strongest boy in terms of stamina and strength and so had never been given the opportunity to show his usefulness in to the family business, apart from walking ahead of the hearse on short journeys. Initially, despite my pride, I was of a mind to refuse his offer of help and rely, as I usually did on you, Sibelius. However, something within me had enough voice to make the decision to give the boy a chance, it was not far to Albert Dunning's house and Johannes would be back within twenty minutes.

To see the joy within his face when I agreed was a blessing to me that I still cling to, even to this day, and I chanced a dream of my three boys, all grown up and working together and keeping the family business going for years to come. I gave him the note and told him to take his time and not run, the air in the streets at night was not good and he often suffered from problems with breathing when trying to exert himself too much. He promised this to me and said with words which ring through my head daily;

"Do not worry, Father. I will be back before you can blink and make you proud of me, I promise."

I watched him as he wandered off into the early evening light and kept my eyes on him until he turned the corner. A small part of me felt the need to follow him, and it is to my eternal sorrow that I did not listen to my heart and keep Johannes within sight.

I spent the next twenty minutes sitting nervously at the table in the parlour, my eyes alternately switching from the door to clock, picturing in my mind where he would be on his journey. When he did not return within the expected time, I thought to run from the house and find him, but again, I resisted the feelings of my heart and decided to give him the chance to complete this errand on his own.

After half an hour had passed my anxiety had grown too great and, shouting to your Mother that I was going out to find him, I left our house by the back door and ran off up the street towards Tunney's house. I found the short journey there to be fraught and filled with anxiety, my eyes constantly scanned the streets as I ran, looking down alleyways with desperation growing within me. By the time I had reached Albert's house I had convinced myself that Johannes would be inside, sat talking with Albert's wife telling them how proud he was of himself for running errands for me. I rapped on the door, shouting out for them to hurry and answer. The door finally opened and Albert's wife Maeve was stood with a look of alarm on her face. She asked what the problem was and whether Johannes had forgotten something.

In that moment I realised that my worst fears could be true. 'Especially when she told me that he had left her door not five minutes prior to me. I felt the bitter sting of bile in my throat, I should never have let him out on his own, he was not strong like you, Sibelius or as quick as you, Niko. I knew that the streets were dangerous but I always trusted that you could get yourself out of any trouble if it came for you. Johannes did not have the strength to fight his way out of difficulty.

'I thanked Maeve as I ran off. My legs felt weak with dread, a sickness bit into the pit of my stomach, but despite my terrible fright I headed back the way I had came, determined to search out each alleyway and snicket in the hunt for my lost boy. With each minute that passed, the dread grew within me and I hoped that when I finally found him that it would not be too late for me to stop whatever terrible act he was undergoing.

I found myself running up Church Lane towards Whitechapel Road, the thought in my mind that maybe Johannes had decided to take a short cut and risk the darker streets in order to get home quicker. The light was beginning to fade into a chill darkness, made even more threatening by the area and I stopped at each dank alley that ran off of the lane, staring hard into the gloom and shouting Johannes' name in the hope that he would hear me. As I approached Whitechapel Road I came to the final passage which ran behind a disused building which, until the last couple of months had been the refuge of many homeless and sorry souls. They had been cast out when a boot maker had bought the building and started renovation work, gutting most of the inside of the structure. The passageway was almost filled with wood and building debris, thrown by the contractors into the alley for later disposal. Despite the piles of wreckage a slim path was still in place through to the end of the passage.

As I looked into the alleyway, I could make out a crouched figure in the distance with his back to me among the piles of rubbish and I thought to call out but something within me held my tongue silent and instead I silently approached the hunched figure, trying desperately to see what they were doing through the gloom. The darkness seemed to clear as I got within twelve yards and it was then that I saw a child's arm lying on the floor. The realisation of what the man was doing struck me and I found myself shouting; no words came from my lips, just an incomprehensible howl of horror and anger.

Hearing my noise the man turned to face me and I saw that the worst fears which I had for my child had been realised, for the man's face was covered in blood, and, beneath a pair of eyes which glowed white in the dark, was a red maw hanging from which was a lump of my son's flesh. In that briefest of moments I looked from the face of this creature to the body at his feet and saw our dear Johannes, his throat torn wide open and his pale, dead eyes staring into the abyss. I found myself quickly grabbing at a lump of splintered wood which lay amongst the rubbish by my side.

Without an ounce of fear for my own safety in my heart I launched myself at the beast, swinging my makeshift weapon with as much force as I could muster. My speed must have been great because the creature did not have a chance to react or avoid my first blow which struck him full in the face knocking him to the floor. I did not stop in my attack however and continued to strike at the beast, my frenzy so intense that I gave no chance for retaliation. Again and again I brought the wood down on his head and I do not feel that I would have stopped had it not been for the strange and frightening sight which then met my eyes.

As I brought the wood down upon the head of this vile and horrific man, something happened to his form. It was as if there were two identities inhabiting the same body as his face flickered and changed rapidly, switching from the face of a man close to death, to that of a pale demon with bright white glowing eyes and a mouth which seemed almost too large for its head and filled with row upon row of tiny razor sharp teeth.

The sight before me made me falter in my attack, as I blinked hard wondering whether my mind, incensed with fury and bloodlust, was tricking me into seeing some kind of visual illusion, unreal and separate from reality. As I watched in a state of sudden stupor this pale demonic figure appeared to be attempting to tear itself free of the now crumpled form of the man, almost, I thought as I stared at its ghostly shape, as if in fear.

My mind reeled with the scene before me and, in a matter of moments; I wrestled with the thought that maybe the supernatural vision in front of me was actually real and that I was close to killing the being. In a snap I shook myself from my trance and threw myself at the twin-being, bringing down the wood onto its body with more force than before.

The demon's attempts to free itself from the form of the man became furious and desperate and, as my frenzied assail continued, it finally drew clear of the unconscious body, rising up into the air with an almost ghostly, ethereal quality. As it rose the beast looked down on me and looking into my eyes gave a final howling scream and shot upwards out of the passageway and into the sky.

I stood over the body of the man I had killed, which lay next to the remains of my dear son Johannes. The poor boy had gone from this world, viciously torn from his family by a hellish beast which inhabited a man. Weeping, I gathered up the broken body of your brother and, wrapping him in my coat, carried him home.

Your mother was distraught when I returned home holding the corpse of her child, I began to explain what had happened but thought it too strange for her to believe, and so, I gave the lie that he had been hit by a carriage, the same lie which I told everyone except for your grandfather.

I sat and cried in my father's arms that night and recounted the ghostly horror which I had experienced and which had taken our Johannes from us. Your grandfather, believed me without question saying,

"There are things on this earth, Edgar, that we cannot attempt to comprehend. That thing that you saw has visited this world before and been cast away by one such as you. It has ran away to the underworld to recover and will await a time when it will have another opportunity to return with its hunger for flesh and its thirst for death. Today, as Väinämöinen once did, you faced Surma and survived. He is gone and now we must put him aside and grieve for our lost boy."

I later heard that a heavily beaten man by the name of Henry J Holdsworth had presented himself at Holborn police station, confessing to be a killer of children and on hearing this news I knew that I had not killed the man in the alley but that he had recovered with memories of his awful crimes. I held this man no malice as he was not in control of his actions. He was controlled by another and the other had left this world.

I am sorry that I kept this truth from you, I had been meaning to tell you when you were grown but, I did not want to taint your happy memories of your brother with the stain of Surma and the curse he brings with him. There are things in this life which we are ignorant of, and, for the most part this is a kindness by which our world is blessed. However I now impart this knowledge upon you in the hope that you will understand the circumstances of your brother's death and forgive me for my lie.

I only hope that the words which I have written will give you a small level of comfort in a time when you feel that you have been left alone. You are not alone, my boys, as you have each other. I was not fortunate enough for my brothers, or my sisters for that matter, to live long enough for me to develop the kind of bond and friendship which I have seen grow between you since you were children. Despite my pride and love for you however, there has always been sadness within my heart that dear Johannes did not join you in the journey into manhood, but as your Grandfather has never relented in telling me,

"Johannes met his time."

I have worked all of my life for this family of ours, and it is my sincerest hope that you are left in comfortable positions with the prospects of happy and loving lives with families of your own. I could not have wished for two more well-rounded boys, and I ask that you remember me with fondness from time to time and tell your children of our family.

Your Father
Edgar Sebastian Darke

As I closed the letter I felt that my mind had been opened. This was the coming death of which the deceased had tried to warn me. This revealed the killer of Father and Niko, a demonic entity had returned to this world with a hunger for life, but had also sought and gained his revenge. I wiped the tears from my face and stood from my desk walking to the window of my study which over looked the bustling street below.

Surma was alive and inhabiting some poor puppet to undertake its will. Could I surely say that this puppet was not I? What better way to exact revenge upon your enemy than to have his loved one carry out the crime?

The beast was killing children and had taken my family from me through an act of retribution. How it had returned I did not know, but I resolved to hunt down the beast and drive it from this earth as my father had done before me. With grim determination I decided that to find this creature I would require more information about it and how it took possession of physical form. The greatest way of achieving this would be to speak to one who knew only too well.

My journey would take me face to face with Henry J. Holdsworth, my brother's killer.

7
Appointments and Bridges

It would seem that my destiny was being controlled by messages from the dead. Firstly, there had been the young girl, warning me of Surma's coming; this recently deceased child had scared me beyond belief through her monotonous yet chilling drawl. Then the alcohol created apparition of my dead Grandfather had directed me towards the sage advice of my father. This had been closely followed by the dead music hall actress telling me, in her own garbled, riddle-like way, that a man with a snow white beard had been killed. If it had stopped there I would have taken it for my own inner madness, surfacing to create fear and irrationality in my usually well ordered and perfectly controlled life. However, when I then received a letter, from the said white bearded man, I decided that perhaps I was not entirely on the road to lunacy and should start to attempt to regain control of my life through actions, which did not entail the drinking of whisky.

It was, therefore, the receipt of a letter from beyond the grave that spurred me into decisive actions, which would enable me to take a firm and steady grasp on destiny. The first of these actions was to wash the stink of self-pity and doubt from me and garb myself in my finest robes of self-esteem and inner belief. Which particular clothes these were did not really matter, it was the manner in which they were worn and the posture of the frame inside them that counted, and so it was that I drew myself a bath and scrubbed away my grief and odour with a stiff brush and soap. Suitably cleaner I dressed in a new set of clothes, for the first time since locking myself away, and set out of the house to the barbers on Colchester Street for a shave and haircut.

I had a number of objectives which I wished to achieve before the end of the day, following my ablutions. The first of these would be to stop at Father's house and attempt to gain access. The main reason for this was to revisit the place that gave me such great shock before. I wished to enter in a more settled state of mind and try to take in what had happened and look for anything out of place, any clues which would be known to me, who knew the property but may pass by the eye of the police inspectors without so much as a second glance. The final reason was to find and secure a certain object which I felt that I would need before the end of this terrible saga.

Once this task was complete I would have to put myself through the fearful chore of going to The Princess Alice to face Tom and, more importantly, Bethany. This more than any other objective of the day was the one which brought me most trepidation and discomfort. I am not a man who is known to be free with his emotions, more so than most men and the thought of placing myself in the most awkward but necessary situations brought about a feeling within me akin to nausea.

As I stepped out of my house I saw that standing on the opposite side of the road, in the same position occupied all week by his colleagues, was a policeman. I had noted their constant presence during my self-inflicted isolation; it was not hard to miss, even in my frantic state of grief and inner turmoil.

On most days it was young uniformed officers who took on the unenviable duty of leaning against a lamp post with their eyes on my front door but I had noted that on two occasions during the week it had been Draper's bull of a sergeant and even the Inspector himself had even made an appearance. I made no effort to hide myself from sight by keeping away from the windows, but did nothing to acknowledge the fact that I was obviously under some kind of close watch whilst the investigation into Father and Niko's murder continued. Of course, the police had not realised that the upper rooms of my apartments, which I used mainly as storage areas for my photographic equipment, contained access to the roof of my building and as a consequence an unobserved route away from my spectators if I required.

The policeman observing me on the day of my first excursion outdoors was a young man who looked new to the force and not too long away from his mother's arms. The shock on his face when I emerged from my doorway and turned to lock my door was as great as had ever been seen on a man and the sheer blunt panic which followed, as he attempted to shadow me down the street whilst attempting to decipher just what he had to do in this situation, caused me no end of inner humour, a welcome return to some kind of normality for me, for which I was grateful.

As I strolled away from my apartments Osborn Street to the barbers I took occasion to glance backwards at regular intervals to check that he was still following me and to force the poor boy into numerous uncomfortable attempts at looking casual. This game kept me amused during my walk and also helped me to avoid the staring and finger pointing which ensued as I passed locals who did not normally grant me as much as a second look. Despite the multitude of inhabitants in this area, Whitechapel was a tight, and some might say claustrophobic community, where one person's life could never stay completely private no matter how hidden they tried to keep it. The fact that my family had recently been slaughtered like cattle and hung as if in an abattoir, meant that my life was now public property and the gossips and tattlers could revel in my misfortune and spread slander and malicious rumour regarding my innocence in the matter.

I reached Humbolt's on Colchester Street and took note of the young officer taking up a post on the other side of the street, whilst desperately looking for another policeman so as to be able to pass on news of my sudden appearance.

Charlie Humbolt smiled as I entered, it was not a smile soaked in pleasure but rather one of sympathy and happiness at the sight of me. Charlie had been a friend for many years. Distantly related on Mother's side, he was the only member of Mother's family who was willing to speak to our family. As a drinking partner and confidante of Father, my brothers and I often spent time with Uncle Charlie, helping him in the barbers when Mother needed us out from under her feet. A large bald man, he was always seemed to have a smile close to hand, and his shop was a welcome friendly refuge from Mother's spite.

"Sib," he half whispered, with open arms. "I am glad to see you, my son. I heard that you had shut yourself away from the world. I thought to call on you but knew that you would reappear when you were ready. I am so sorry, boy; we have all lost good friends and family through this murder."

"Thank you, Charlie." I said awkwardly stepping into his embrace. I fought back a reoccurrence of any emotion by slapping him strongly on the back. "I had some time to myself to grieve, but Father would not want my life to fall apart, he would need me to carry on."

"I hear that you were questioned by the police, they don't believe that you were responsible do they?"

"I am not sure, as you can see from across the road I have a constant shadow. There are those, even within the police, who like to assume that the simple answer is the truth. I intend to find the killer though, Charlie, even if the police do not."

"Have you not heard, Sib? There's been another murder, two nights ago, in Sheppy Yard. A child, no older than six I believe. Torn to shreds he was, draped over the steps of the laundry, one of his arms missing. They say there were bite marks on the child's body."

"It is a horrible business to be sure. But I have been under constant surveillance for over a week, they must know that it was not me, why do they still follow?"

"I am not sure, but I have had dealings with this Draper chap before and he is meticulous to the point of obsession. If you are within his sights, Sibelius, then beware, he will not stray from a scent." He turned the barber's chair towards me and gestured to it. "Anyways, I trust you are not just visiting me on a social call. You look like a street beggar. Take a seat so that I may take a razor to you."

I sat and smiled, drawing a hand across the rough, pale stubble on my chin. Charlie knew that I had never been a friend to facial hair of any form, maybe some type of rebellion against Father and Grandfather, both of whom were the owners of full beards. Even Niko had taken to growing a moustache which, although giving him the appearance of a more mature man, I felt looked ridiculous.

I spent an hour in the company of Charlie Humbolt, during which we reminisced about happier times and days spent in the barber's with Niko, laughing and making conversation with Charlie's customers, who were always pleased to see us.

As I prepared to leave the shop I took one final check in the mirror. Charlie had, as always made a good job of the shave and had trimmed my hair by a short amount also. He knew not to take too much of my white hair, as he was well aware that it was my one point of vanity, to which I constantly tended.

"It would seem that your young friend has been granted some reinforcements," laughed Charlie

I looked out of the window to the other side of the road; the boy policeman had been joined by Draper's sergeant who now stood with his hands on his hips staring at me. I smiled and waved at him and he struggled to contain his obvious anger, responding to me by pointing a finger. I could almost hear the low growl. The brute seemed to given up the pretence of keeping their shadowing a secret and I pitied the man for trying such an obvious ploy to rile me.

"You want to watch him, Sib. Abe Thomas has a reputation for acting outside of the law when it comes to making a point with those that anger him."

"Do not worry for me, Charlie. I would wager my wits against his strength on any day of the week, he is no more than a common thug and holds no fear over me."

I paid Charlie and promised to let him know when the funerals of Father and Niko would be. Their home would be the next stop on my day's journey as I wished to gain access to Father's bedroom, where I knew he kept a pistol. If only he had carried it with him on the night of his visit by Surma then he and Niko may still be alive. Stepping onto the street, I made a point of grinning in the direction of Sergeant Thomas, an act which he made a pitiful job of ignoring. Shouting goodbye to Charlie, I closed the door behind me and set off towards Whitechapel Road and Father's home, closely followed by an infuriated police sergeant.

When I reached the parlour I found that it was still cordoned off and had a police guard stood at the alleyway leading down the side of the property. I approached him.

"Good morning, Constable. I am Sibelius Darke; this property belonged to my father Edgar Darke. He and my brother Nikolas were murdered here a week ago."

"I know who you are," he replied. Only his lips moved, the rest of his body remained motionless and impeding.

"I have need to access the property; there are items within which I require in order to begin settling my Father's affairs." I began to walk down the alley, "If I could just ent..." The officer stepped to his left, halting my progress.

"No one is to enter these premises unless given permission by Inspector Draper; this is a crime scene and as such restricted to members of the police force and named others only. No other person is to enter, not family and most definitely not you."

"But this is my Father's house, is there no way in which I can just bob in to collect these books? They are of no import to the police investigation." The sentinel did not move or even begin to acknowledge my question. I observed the number on his collar and stepped backwards in an attempt to try another ploy. "Well Constable ... 237H, I have found you most unhelpful and will be saying as such to Inspector Draper when I see him shortly."

I saw the flicker of a smile come across the constable's face, this was not the kind of response I had expected. It was as I turned to leave the scene that I found myself facing a broad chin, whose owner briskly placed large bear-like hands upon my shoulders. My young police shadow stood behind Sergeant Thomas, leering in a most self congratulatory way. Thomas smiled as he spoke to me.

"Mr Darke, I hope you were not in the business of trying to intimidate one of my constables. That would be a terrible mistake upon your part, and one which you would regret for a very long time, sir." It would seem that I had placed myself in a situation of some danger and I cursed my idiotic overconfidence.

"Sergeant, how nice it is to see you again, I would ask if you were well but I have noted that you seem to be a picture of health." I stepped backwards only to find that Constable 237H had blocked my retreat. "I was just explaining to the Constable here, that there are a couple of items within the property of my fathers that I needed sight of, in order to assist in the settling of his affairs."

"I would expect nothing less of Stanley," he said motioning to the young constable. "What might these items would be, Mr Darke? Perhaps if you told me what they were and where I could find them I could retrieve them for you." It would seem that Thomas was not as stupid as he looked.

"It is his appointments and contact books," I lied. "I wish to pass them on to George Woodrow, the owner of the funeral service on Leman Road. Father and he shared business from time to time and were great friends; he would have wanted to pass on his custom to old George. I am also planning to ask Mr

Woodrow to arrange the services for my dead family, when their bodies are released, of course. You don't happen to know when that will be by any chance do you?" The smug look which came over the ox-like sergeant told me that he believed my lie.

"The investigation is on-going, Mr Darke, and I would be unable to tell you when the bodies will be available for burial. Please feel free to come down to the station and discuss the matter with the Inspector if you wish. But for now, I am afraid that the items you require are also part of the investigation and unavailable. I will of course let you have them once the killer is found." His smile was as pleasing to me as it was him. Unfortunately I did not hide my happiness as well as I should and I suddenly found myself lifted from my feet by the collar and in closer proximity to Thomas' broad face than I would have liked.

"Listen carefully," he spat each word with spite and threat. "Your conceit offends me and I am not a man to offend, Darke." I did not need any further persuading, but being the oaf he was he did not realise this and continued, "The Inspector is a good man, he has marked you as trouble and will not rest until he has you down. He will see to your end through the book. I on the other hand am not as rigid, and so I will tell you this." I felt myself being lifted higher and he swung me hard letting go so that I crashed into the wall, knocking free any wind left in my body. He stepped towards me and leaned down, his face, once again pressed close to mine. "The longer it takes for the Inspector to nail you, the closer you will come to feeling my justice. Now leave here and do not return. You are being watched." He stood upright, taking a hold of the scruff of my collar and pulling me with him. "Now then, sir. If that is all, you may carry on with your day. I will see you ... soon."

Suitably threatened, I straightened my jacket and, giving a final meek smile to the group of now laughing policemen, set off on way towards my next port of call. As I walked down

Whitechapel road towards Commercial Street, I attempted to regain a little composure. Looking over my shoulder, I saw that my shadow had resumed his duty, however this constant companion had now taken on a more sinister edge and I no longer saw the young boy in the uniform as a figure of fun.

As I made my way towards my final destination of the day, I checked my watch. The action depressed me as I had been forced to resort to using my old pocket watch, a present from Father and inscribed on the back with the message;

'Isoja kaloja kannattaa pyytää vaikkei saisikaan'.

In seeing this phrase, I realised then how much Father was proud of me and how I should have cherished his pride rather than just expecting and disregarding it. The message translated as 'Big fish are worth fishing even if you don't catch one'.

I stopped at the corner of Commercial Street and Wentworth Street and stepped up to the door pausing for a moment. From inside, I could hear the rough rumble of conversation and smelled the stale odour of alcohol. Even though I had not had a drink for over a week, the scent made me retch slightly as it hit my nose, reminding me of the heights, or rather depths, that my binge reached the last time that I crossed this threshold. There would be no drink for me on this day, however. My mind needed to be clear for the coming hunt. I pushed open the door feeling the warmth and noise of the Princess Alice wash over me like an unwanted, but necessary, rain shower.

I do admit to some fear as I approached the bar and waited for Tom to become aware of my presence. Cold and arrogant I may be, but I had never hidden from the friendship of Tom Finnan before and the thought that I had in some way damaged our relationship through my isolation, left me a little on edge. It was not just this though that brought me shame and embarrassment; it was the fact that I had abandoned Bethany in her grief. What must she think of me, that I would refuse to come to see her when she needed to share her sorrow the most?

Tom stood at the other end of the bar talking quietly to a customer. I shifted a stool to sit down and the unintentional sound of its legs scraping the wooden floor alerted him to my presence. There was an initial glint of happiness in his eyes, which he quickly quashed and, excusing himself from the customer, walked over to where I sat.

"Does the life of a hermit not suit, Sibelius? Have you finally need for the company of those that care?" His face was sad, a sure sign that I had angered the man. I looked into his eyes but found that I struggled to make any kind of eye contact and constantly felt the need to look at my hands on the bar or anywhere but at his disappointment.

"I apologise, Tom. I have been a self-pitying fool." I mumbled, finding an odd fascination in my thumbnail. Tom slowly reached over the bar, placing his hand over mine and covering the object of my interest. The action brought about a choking sensation which I was becoming tired of feeling in recent days. "I ... I just needed," I concentrated hard to give my words an unbroken roundness. "I needed some time to myself. Some time to purge the demons inside me." I dared to look up and saw that Tom's face continued to look sad; I saw, however, an edge of sympathy touching his eyes which gave me the strength to continue. "I am a private soul, Tom, and there are some things that I do not want anyone, not even one as close as you, to see of me."

There was a silence between us but it was in no way awkward. I was sorry that I had hidden from Tom, but I would do it again if the circumstances required it. Tom finally spoke.

"I do understand, Sib. You took yourself away to deal with your grief and it has obviously worked for you as you look well and ready to tackle the world. For Bethany though ..." He drifted off.

"How is she, Tom? Does she understand why I haven't been to see her?"

"Bethany is still a child, Sib. She does not have the experience or the tools to deal with things the way you do. She has been lost to me this past week as you have. Hardly eating, drinking minimally and she will not speak of her own accord. It is hard to see that in your child, Sibelius. It is hard to feel so helpless."

I straightened my back and smiled at him, I had been so self-absorbed in my own pity that I failed to think of the effect that this terror would have upon my dearest friend.

"I have been awoken from my gloom, dear Tom. I feel grief and loss at the deaths of my family, but I have found a purpose which has dragged me from my pit of depression. I am a changed man and I will take my change and use it to bring poor Bethany as far from her misery as she can go. I will go and speak to her, if you wish. Is she up in her room? May I go up?"

Tom's face visibly brightened with my display of swelled confidence and bravado. A warmth came to his cheeks and, still holding on to my hands, shook them with vigour and the thought of hope for his child.

"Yes, yes, by all means go to her. You may be shocked at her appearance but please do not let that sway you from your task. She will be gladdened to see you so well and this may then rouse her also." I stood from my stool and started to make for the door which led to the upper rooms of the pub, but Tom suddenly stopped me. "Tell me though, Sib. What is this purpose that has caused this sudden change in you? What thought can have had such a happy effect?"

"It is not a happy thought, Tom. I mean to hunt the killer. I mean to find him and I mean to kill him before he steals from another family." And with those words I started through the door and up to Bethany's room before Tom forced me to say any more on the matter.

I walked slowly up the stairs. Seeing Tom had been difficult and I had dreaded it, but seeing Bethany for the first time since Niko's death brought about a crippling fear within me and would be the hardest test of my new found resolve. The accumulation of having to discuss emotional and heart rending issues, combined with the fact that these discussions would take place between myself and a young woman, made this something which I knew would be most uncomfortable to undergo.

As I reached the top of the staircase I saw Bethany's Aunt, Anne, coming out of her room. Anne, an older woman, far greater in age than her brother Tom, had never married and had devoted the past seventeen years of her life to helping Tom to raise his daughter. She had moved into the pub when Bethany was born and had been ever present in her life since.

Anne smiled as she saw me and held out her arms inviting me into her embrace. Despite the fact that I was fond of Anne and felt a great respect for the time and effort she had put into playing mother to Beth, I never relished her frequent displays of affection which often came in the form of a hug which drew me into the generous folds of her large frame. In all honesty, I have never been fond of physical contact with others of any description. I find tactile people cloying, and struggle to hide the tenseness and displeasure in contact which I deem to be overly intimate and inappropriate.

I withstood Anne's constrictive attentions in manner which I felt was accepting but not reciprocated, although I am glad that, during the clench, the poor woman could not see my face.

"My poor, poor boy," she breathed. "Such a tragedy for us all, but more so for you and my Beth. I hear that you spent time alone to burn your grief? I suppose each of us has our own way of tackling such misfortune."

I extricated myself from her gasp.

"Yes, Anne, it is indeed a horrible time for us and I have struggled to come to terms with it all. As you say though, I have spent time grieving and in the depths. However I now find myself with the required fire and energy to venture out and take control of the matter." I placed my hands on her shoulders, more to be able to hold her at arm's length than to invite further affections. "I have come to see Bethany, if that is convenient for her. Tell me; is she awake and able to receive visitors?"

Her face looked heavy with sadness. "Awake? Yes. But I fear that she would not make great company for any person to visit, other than you. She has asked after you daily, and her worry at the lack of news regarding your well-being has only added to her woes. I told her that you would come when you are ready and I am happy to see you arrive. The sight of your face will do more to cheer her than you could know."

"And I will do my best to bring her back to some kind of normality, Anne, although I am not one known for my skill in comforting people."

Anne looked slightly quizzical, "You should not put yourself down, Sibelius Darke. I have known you since you were young and I have always felt you to be full of warmth for others, some of the time it takes a little coaxing out of that cold façade, but it is in there, trust me."

"You are kind indeed, and you never fail to see the best in people, Anne. Be assured that I will always come to you when I am in need of seeing myself in a brighter light."

Against all of my natural instincts, I drew her to me and planted a kiss upon her cheek, making her blush. The action made me shiver inside, but I felt that it was the right thing to do. Without another word, she scuttled off down the stairs, stopping briefly at the bottom to look up and smile at me before disappearing into the bar.

I approached Bethany's bedroom door and knocked gently upon it. There was no response and so I knocked again but a little firmer this time. A voice came from within the room.

"Leave me be, Anne. I have told you that I am tired today and have no wish to eat at the moment."

I thought to leave, it would be the easiest thing to do and I could go about the business of finding my family's killer with a clear mind and without the nagging emotion of dealing with a teary-eyed young girl. Better judgement overtook me however.

"Bethany, it is Sib. I have come to see you; there are words that we must share, words that may help us to heal our pain." I knew that I was being over sentimental, but she was a woman and I knew that this kind of talk would be more appealing to her. There was a tumbling noise from inside the room followed by footsteps and the door opened.

I expected her to look terrible; to wear the heavily baggaged eyes of one who does not sleep, to be pale and sickly looking like a person who has not seen the sun through being locked away, to look drawn and weak as if starving themselves of food and water through the melancholy of the grieving soul. In truth however, my first sight of Bethany Finnan as she opened the door to her bedroom was of a beautiful girl, filled with the joy of life and wearing a smile as warm and welcoming as any I had seen from a young lady. Of course, I knew that the smile that she wore was held carefully in place and created for my benefit, but if anything, this made the sight of her even more pleasing to me.

"Sibelius, thank you for coming to see me. Are you well?"

"As well as can be expected, Beth, I have suffered, as have we all, because of this. But I have dragged my sorry soul from my malaise enough to try to get on. My first thoughts, of course, were to come to see you."

She stood and stared at me for a second, not saying anything maintaining her smile, her eyes were glistening slightly, as if on the verge of tears. The moment, although brief, became slightly uncomfortable for me, and I suddenly felt the need to break the silence.

"So, Tom says that you have locked yourself away, this will not do, young lady. We will have to see you out of this room and becoming social again." The change in my attitude was intentional, as I felt that I had maybe overdone the sentimentality of my tone and caused her to become too emotional. I had come to try to bring her around and get her out of the same hole that I had been in, softness and tears were not the way to achieve this.

She opened her bedroom door a little wider and without a word began to step forward out of her room, forcing me backwards into the hallway.

"Shall we go into the kitchen?" she said walking away from me down the hall. "It is a more appropriate place for conversation than my bedroom doorway, and there are seats where we may sit and talk some more."

I stood for a few moments watching her disappear into a room at the end of the hall before following without a word. As I entered the kitchen I found her sat at the table, motioning to the chair opposite her as an indication that I should sit. This was not what I had in mind, I had imagined finding a weeping wreck who would sob and wail until I left. She was, however, calm, composed and it seemed pleased to see me. I took the offered seat.

"So tell me, Sib," she said her eyes staring hard into mine, a gaze which I felt unable to break. "Did you kill them? I have heard that you are a suspect. I have even been visited by a police inspector who asked many questions about you and your relationship with Niko."

I paused for a moment before answering, mainly because my mind was racing because of the thought of Draper being here and spreading malicious suspicions about me. I finally managed to break her gaze and looked down at the table to my hands.

"Of course I did not kill them, Beth, and I would hope that you would have told the police the same thing. You know how close I was to Nik, and Father for that matter. We have never had a cross word, you know this."

The smile returned to her face and she reached across the table, taking my hands into her own.

"Of course that is what I told the Inspector. I just wanted to hear it from your lips. I am not a liar, Sibelius, but I know how to spot one. I needed to erase any lingering doubt that remained in me, and you have done that."

I breathed a visible sigh of relief although I do not know why; maybe it was the knowing that someone believed in me, maybe it was to assuage some deep inner guilt that I felt for some reason. Whatever it was, I immediately relaxed in her presence.

"The Inspector has me a marked man, Beth. There are police outside my door and within 20 yards of me at all times. They watch for me to make a mistake and give them the proof they need to take me in, but they will find none. I know of my innocence and I am angered that they waste their time and resources. I mean to find the killer though, Beth. I mean to find the hole in which he lurks and kill him for myself. For all of us."

Her smile had faded, replaced with the serious determination which I had become accustomed to since she were a small girl. Her delicate hands, still holding mine had tensed when I mentioned killing the murderer.

"How may I help you, Sib. Tell me what I can do to bring this man down?"

I had not expected this reaction from her, but at that moment I had an idea of how her assistance could prove conducive to the next part of my plan.

"There are two matters which you may be able to help with actually, Bethany." I said releasing my hands from her grasp and immediately enclosing hers in my own. Her hands were warm and soft. It was my turn to smile, as I told her of a task that she could perform for me, before telling her to come to my apartments at nine o'clock the following morning, dressed in her finest clothes and prepared to be out for the day.

We spent another half an hour talking, our conversation turning to pleasant reminiscence regarding Niko. Our talk however was not morose, but joyful as we shared happier memories. When I was assured that she was suitably stirred into a return to positivity and action, I said my farewells and left her to prepare for the first task which I had given. I stopped in the bar downstairs and saw Tom, who I spoke to briefly, telling him that I had found Bethany to be on a steady path of return and that she had agreed to accompany me out the following day, if Tom gave his blessing for this.

The relief on Tom's face was palpable, and I was pleased with my afternoon's work, staying for a short while to force down a small beer as a sign, to Tom, of my recovery.

My planned tasks completed for the day, although with some difficulty, I returned to my rooms to prepare myself for the following day. I would be catching the morning train from King's Cross to New Southgate and Colney Hatch Station, whereupon Bethany and I would be visiting the Second County Middlesex Asylum for a luncheon date with Mr. Henry J. Holdsworth.

8
LUNCHEON AT THE ASYLUM

We boarded a train the following morning at King's Cross. Bethany had never travelled by train before and I spent the journey in secret happiness as I witnessed her wonderment and childlike excitement at the experience. She of course tried to hide the extent of the joy which she felt in boarding the train, but knowing her as I did I was reminded that, at seventeen, she was still only a child within despite her sometimes hardened exterior and efforts to act older than her years.

We were alone in our compartment and she sat opposite me for the duration of the journey staring out of the window and attempting to fully take in the sights of London which passed gently by to the sound of the soft roll of the engine and the rhythmic bounce of the wheels along the track.

She had arrived at my rooms at nine thirty as planned, dressed in an olive green long dress and tailored jacket, a present from Anne the previous year and meant to be brought out only on special occasions. Atop her head she wore a small hat attached with a long pin which had a small fringe of black netting which partially covered her face. Her hair, normally worn long and tied into a bunch at the back was worn up, her auburn curls confined and controlled by an array of clips and pins. I admit that when I opened the door to her and ushered her in that I was quite shocked at her appearance, I knew her to be a girl of pleasant features, something which I always attributed to the looks inherited from her mother, but the sight which met me that morning was a surprise which I found quite appealing (something which I of course attempted to keep well hidden from her). I invited her in and looked across the road before closing the door behind her. A policeman stood at the other side observing her arrival and making a note in his pad.

Bethany had been successful in the first task which I had set her the previous day. She had come from Father's parlour where she had fluttered eyelashes and provided flattery to the young constable on duty, actions which enabled her to enter the building and collect 'personal items' of hers which were under the ownership of Niko and which she wanted returning. There were, of course, no such items but she had managed to find and bring to me Father's revolver and a small supply of ammunition. Once the pistol had been handed over I gave her a small sum of money and told her to use it to take a carriage to King's Cross where I would meet her in one hour.

Bethany had left me then, an action which I ensured was seen and noted by my watchman, and I had made my way upstairs where I secreted the pistol in a place where no officer searching my rooms would find it. I made a final check through the window to see that the policeman was still in place and then made my way up to the roof of the building and along the route which would take me across the rooftops to a place where I could return to the streets unnoticed and onwards to the train station to meet my accomplice.

As we sat together, watching the streets of London disappear and become transformed into the first signs of the countryside, we amused ourselves with happy talk. Our conversation, of course, concerned my lost brother, but we steered away from the grisly nature of his death and instead kept our thoughts to tales of happier times we had spent together. As we reminisced in comfortable banter I became aware that we were both smiling and laughing together, something which a week prior to our trip I would never have contemplated ever happening again. This thought, at first, stung me with a pang of guilt at our lack of solemnity, but I brushed this aside, making the decision to enjoy such company and happiness when I could.

The path upon which I now found myself, was a potentially fatal one, I should take pleasure in these moments as they may be scarce in coming. As with many instances in life, I remembered the words of Grandfather as he imparted one of his old Finnish sayings on us as children, 'Life is uncertain, so eat your desert first'. I had taken his words to heart on this sunny morning and looked to enjoying the moments of happiness when they could be found, and as such I found that on our journey a smile was never far from my face. I think the company helped.

"You should smile more often, Sib." Beth said in a pause between stories. "That harsh crack of a mouth suits it well and it does your eyes good to brighten so." I found a rush of colour coming to my cheeks, unused as I was to compliments of any kind. I avoided further embarrassment by reverting to the diversionary tactics which I held so dear as a tool.

"I'm afraid, Bethany, that happy brightness is not part of my image. I would hate to disappoint my many admirers by changing a style which it has taken many years to perfect." My words were said however, with such a smile intact which she returned and for a moment there was a silence in which I realised just how difficult I found it to make eye contact with the girl.

Bethany broke the calm, something which I felt initially grateful for as it would save my further blushes. Her words, however, brought another jagged stick with which to taunt me.

"Why have you never married, Sibelius? I have never known you to court a lady in all the time that I have known you, which, I suppose, is all my life. Has there never been anyone to catch your eye? I cannot believe that you are such a solitary man."

I did not answer at once, for, in truth, I was at a loss to be able to put such a response into to some semblance of understandable English. It was not a subject which I had any history of discussing with anyone, other than myself within my own mind. Whenever Father or Niko would pose the question I would always be able to deflect their probing through some humorous aside. When questioned by Bethany however, I did not feel fully able to distract her. Whether this was because of an inability to speak or an unwillingness to lie to her, I did not know. Whatever the reason, I gave some serious thought to the answer before speaking.

"It is not that my eye is unable to be caught, Beth. But rather it seems that I find myself without the necessary skills to be able to develop such a gaze into achievable words and actions." I stumbled over my words somewhat, partly in trying to make Bethany understand but also as a prime example of the impairment through which I suffered. "To be honest with you, women are a mind-damaging mystery to me. They are a breed apart and one that I rarely find comfort with. This is not to say that I am immune to their charms, quite the opposite, in fact. I am able to acknowledge beauty and fair manner of ladies when they cross my path. I just ..."

The words came to me but got stuck in my throat like a spiked ball of shame, desperate not to be revealed. I fell silent and looked down to my shoes, allowing the moment to thankfully die. I had said more about my inner feelings than I had meant to and more than I had ever expressed to anyone before. In the silence I pondered why Bethany had brought this out of me and why at this time. She must have seen my discomfort and did not try to press the point any further.

The silence between us continued, but I found that it did not lie awkwardly upon me and I hoped that Beth felt the same. I dared to look up to her face and found that she had returned to gazing out of the window of our compartment, trying to take in and remember as much of the passing vista as possible. I felt grateful that I had not revealed myself any further. The closeness which I came to speaking the truth, was, in a strange way both comforting and the cause of some consternation to me, and I felt a wave of emotion building within. This was a common feeling to me in times of private inner stress, but one which I worked hard to keep to myself. I prayed inside for the journey to end and felt grateful when I saw Alexandra Palace out of the window and knew that our station was drawing near.

We stepped off of the train at New Southgate and Colney Hatch station just before noon, and followed a group of fellow disembarkers out of the station and through a set of large black, iron gates into the grounds of The Second Middlesex County Lunatic Asylum

The Asylum itself was a wondrous spectacle. As large a building as either I or Bethany had ever seen before, stretching away into the distance to an end point which was obscured by trees. It was two stories high, with taller tower-like points along its length and at its centre a large pillared building upon which sat a dome. The beautifully maintained grounds surrounding the asylum were green and pleasant, dotted with trees, bushes and flowering beds, and pathed throughout with benches at various points of natural beauty. I wondered how this building could have been created as a place of lunacy and not some exquisite country home for some member of the aristocracy. It had been built some twenty six years earlier, the first stone being laid by Prince Albert. I had seen pictures of the building in the past but never quite realised its size and magnificence before this day. All together it housed over two thousand sufferers of madness and delusion and I wondered if the majority of these poor souls had come to this place of their own accord or been brought and secured against their will.

As we walked through the grounds to the central building Bethany took my arm and we walked in quiet comfort together, trying to take in the delicate surroundings before we entered the asylum itself. We spoke of our plans after entering and I reassured her that I would ensure her safety at all times and that if at any time she wished to leave then we would do so.

We stepped through the large central doors beneath the dome and found ourselves in a large high ceilinged atrium. The room was beautifully decorated and large paintings hung on the walls, further giving a sense that one had entered a stately home rather than a place of insanity. At the far end of the room was a desk manned by a small hunched man who sat writing with a quill in a large leather bound book which was almost the size of his desk. As we approached him, he did not look up but continued in his task, which I could see, now close, to be an admissions book. We stopped at the desk and I coughed gently to gain his attention. He looked up unspeaking.

"Good Morning to you, sir." I said. "My wife and I have come to visit a relative who currently resides within this grand establishment." The small man continued to stare at me unblinking for a moment and I wondered if he were hard of hearing. I decided to speak a little louder. "Good Mo..."

"Name!" He barked, still unblinking.

"My name is Shakew..."

"Name of Patient!" He interrupted and I now knew that he was not deaf but merely rude.

"Henry J. Holdsworth." I replied, at which point he began turning back the pages of the large book until he reached the pages marked 'H'. As a photographer I spend a large amount of time looking at the world upside down, I remember, when I invested in my first camera, being often confused and disorientated by this strange view of the world. Over time however, it began to feel natural and it was with my trained eye that I made a note of the writing next to Holdsworth's name in the book. He had been admitted on 12th August 1857, transported by officers from Holborn police station and was currently housed in Ward 5. A large red note next to his entry read 'NOT FOR RELEASE'. It would seem that this man was as dangerous as I had expected.

"Secure wing. No visitors." The old man snapped closing the book and dipping his quill into an ink pot. For him our discussion was clearly over. For me, however, it was most definitely not.

"Excuse me, but my wife and I have travelled a very long distance to visit Mr Holdsworth, and I will not be dissuaded from my task by a desk clerk!" My firm tone brought him to attention once more and he shook off his quill before placing it carefully on the desk before him.

With some degree of aggression, the hunched man rang a bell on his desk and after a few moments the inner doors to the hospital opened and through them came a man who can only be described as quite the largest person who I had ever laid eyes on. As he came through the doorway, the top of his head narrowly missed the architrave, despite it being nearly seven feet in height.

Bethany gave an audible gasp, as on first impressions this man would have scared most people who he came into contact with. He was not just tall but broad also, twice as wide as I, with long muscular arms which strained the stitching of his blue jacket and hung at his side like weighty pendulums swinging as he walked. His head was hairless and his brow appeared to extend outward over his eyes, putting in my mind the image of a gorilla which I had seen stuffed and exhibited in the Natural History departments of the British Museum the year before.

"Barney!" The hunchback barked. "Take these people to see the Medical Superintendent straight away. Tell Mr Stourbridge that they wish to see Henry Holdsworth." The large man did not respond but smiled at me weakly and beckoned for Bethany and I to follow him through the doors

As we stepped through I received my second moment of awe at the building which we had entered. For, as I looked to my left, all I could see was one corridor which flew off into the distance before me, there seemed no end to it. I turned around to look to the right and was confronted by its mirror image. We had entered the asylum at its centre and were stood in the middle of the longest tunnel I had ever witnessed, each side stretching away into an indefinable point. I knew of course from my view of the outside of the edifice that this corridor did not actually carry on into infinity and did in fact have an end point at each side of the building. To be stood in this corridor's very heart however, it seemed that the corridor itself was a living breathing tube, a piece of architecture which was in itself cause to make those who found themselves within it begin to doubt their own semblance of reality. The thoughts and experience of those who did in fact have hallucinatory experiences, were quite beyond my reckoning but I began to suspect that the very design of this monument to madness was geared to making those within it fear for their own sanity be they crazed or not.

I realised that Bethany and I had halted our steps as soon as we had stepped into the tube and that Beth had been as amazed and aghast as I at its magnificent lunacy. I felt her hand touch mine at our sides, as if reaching out for a piece of something physical which she knew to be real. I stretched out my fingers and dared to take her hand in my own, for strength of companionship if nothing else. I was shaken from my stupor by the large attendant who spoke.

"Scary is it not, sir. I remember my own thoughts when I was introduced to the hospital as a young boy of fifteen." His voice suited his size, the low growl of a mountainous bear.

"It is a sight beyond reckoning," I replied, trying to wrestle my gaze from the hypnotic drag of the tunnel. "Shall we move on?"

"Of course, sir." He rumbled and I detected a note of humour in his reply, as if he took pleasure in drawing the innocent into the realms of madness. He lumbered onwards taking us away from the corridor and towards a large set of dark oaken wooden doors. A brass sign screwed to the door told us that it was the office of the Medical Superintendent. The large man approached the door with some reverence and tapped gently with his huge paw, an action which belied his size.

"Come!" called a voice from inside and the doors were opened by Barney who stepped inside closing them behind him and shutting Bethany and I out.

We heard muffled voices from inside the office, the low growling thunder of the attendant followed by a higher more distinct voice. After a brief discussion Barney opened the doors again and ushered Bethany and I inside. We stepped into the office and were greeted by a thin middle-aged man, who had stood from his seat at a large highly polished desk and made his way over to the door to shake my hand and spoke;

"Good morning, sir. Thank you for waiting so patiently. Barney wait outside please and I will call when our guests are ready to leave." The huge man nodded silently and backed out of the doors again closing them gently.

I studied the superintendent closely. He seemed a nervous, fidgety type, constantly on edge with a tenseness in his thin shoulders which caused them to sit higher than is normal. Balanced below the bridge of his nose he wore small round silver spectacles which appeared so dusty that I wondered if anyone would be able to see anything at all out of them. His hair was greyed and neatly combed across his head and on his cheeks he wore a large set of whiskers which appeared wild and covered the majority of his face.

"I understand that you wish to visit one of our patients? Mr Holdsworth is it? Yes, Yes … Can I ask the nature of your visit?" He gestured to the chairs in front of his desk and quickly edged back around to the other side and retook his seat.

"Of course, sir. My name is Bernard Shakewell-Young, and this is my wife Isabelle. I have recently returned to the country from the Punjab following the death of my father who was the Chief Commissioner to the Lieutenant Governor of the province. I have returned to London to start a new life and have set about tracking down my family here. I have found however that I have a dearth of contactable relations, my family being wholly based in the colonies, and to date the only person that I have been able to find who is referenced in my Father's papers is his distant cousin Henry. It was quite a surprise to me, however to find that he was a resident of your fine hospital."

His face twitched nervously, much like a squirrel.

"Believe me, sir there are those within our world who require the secure protection of facilities such as ours. For the safety of us all." His fingers tapped the arms of his chair as he spoke. "Many times I have tried to get him transferred to the hospital at Crowthorne because of this."

"Crowthorne? What is at Crowthorne? And why would this be more suitable?"

"There is a specialist facility at Crowthorne, which I feel is more fitting for his needs. I trust that you are aware of the circumstances which brought Mr Holdsworth to us?"

"Why no, sir. I am not." I played the ignorant, innocence card to the best of my ability. "This is my first visit to London for over twenty years. I was only a small child when my mother took me to the furthest reaches of the empire. I was never told of his fate. Is he truly crazed?"

"I'm afraid he surely is afflicted with a serious degree of mental instability." He looked at Bethany as if in fear of speaking before her.

"Please Mr Stourbridge do not hold back in telling me the truth in front of my wife. We have come from a harsh brutal world and there is not much that will cause her terror." Perfectly on cue, Bethany smiled sweetly at the man, as a sign that I spoke for her. Her behaviour so far during this trip had both pleased and surprised me as I could not remember a time where she had managed to hold her tongue and remain subservient to anyone before. As an actress she played her part beautifully.

Stourbridge continued to eye her for a brief moment and then continued.

"Mr Holdsworth took himself to the police and confessed to the brutal murder and cannibalism of three young boys. He was clear in his speech and gave full descriptions of each of the killings. However the reason that he gave for these murders gave the officers cause to believe that he was not sane of mind. He stated that he had been possessed by an unearthly being who craved the flesh of children, he raved and shouted, screamed and bellowed that the beast was abounds and that it could return to him at any time."

Whilst Stourbridge spoke, Bethany continued in her role, giving gasps of shock and horror at the most opportune moments, even withdrawing a lace handkerchief from her sleeve and holding it to her mouth to accentuate the revulsion.

I stared at the superintendent in disbelief.

"I am sorry, Mr Stourbridge. Are you telling me that Holdsworth is a child killer? Did he really commit these crimes?"

Stourbridge sat forwards in his chair so as to ensure that I fully understood him. His voice lowered somewhat and his tone became deadly serious. "The police did not think so, sir. No, not at all. They said that there was no evidence found except for part of one boy's body which turned up a good mile away from where Holdsworth said it would be. A Chief Inspector from Scotland Yard itself, George Atterbury, intervened in the case, saying that he was a lunatic but a harmless one and that there was no link between him and any crime. He was sent here for moral treatment and recuperation."

"But he has been here for twenty years, is there no sign of recovery? If you say that he is no risk to anyone then where is the sense in keeping him?"

"It is not I who say that he is harmless. No, sir. In fact I believe him to be a most devious and dangerous man. He remains as resolute, regarding his crimes, as he was on the first day that he arrived here. So much so that it is my personal feeling that there is truth to his tales." He tapped his fingers nervously on the edge of his desk. "I do not include his claim of possession, however, as this is clearly madness, but I believe that he may have killed those boys as he said he did and many more besides.

I have entreated the commissioners to move him to the Crowthorne site, but they say that there has been no evidence of murder and as such he is just a delusional fool. The fact that he remains here under our care is as much due to his desire to remain caged as it is my fear for the poor children of London."

"Well, I thank you for your honesty Mr Stourbridge." I said, trying to move the conversation along. "Now, I would be grateful if you could just have us taken to him so that I might see for myself and give him news of the family."

Stourbridge leant back in his chair studying me. It was clear to me that he wished to exert his authority in this situation and ensure that any element of help that he was able to give would have to be drawn slowly from him on his terms. Finally he spoke;

"You were of course told at the front desk that any visitations to those on our more secure wings were not permitted due to the patient's thin grip on their more base emotions." He tried hard not to show the smile that was brimming within him, and I knew at that point that I had lost my chance. I had been brought to him for sport and nothing else.

"I am sorry to have wasted your time, Mr Shakewell-Young but I cannot permit any visitors to him at this time. In my view he is volatile and dangerous and I would not want to put any members of the public at risk, no matter who they are. You are welcome of course to stay for one of our special luncheons. We hold these events regularly and they have become quite 'the thing' amongst the ladies and gentlemen of London. I am sure your lady wife will find it most enlightening." He gestured towards Bethany, who stared at him most defiantly. "You are lucky to be here today I have been assured that there will be quite a spectacle."

My mind flashed a hundred different thoughts in the space of a moment as I thought of my next move. It was clear that Superintendent had no intention of allowing us to see Holdsworth and that it would be foolish to try to change his mind on the matter. I would need to employ more discreet tactics to achieve my goal. I stood and shook his outstretched hand thanking him again for his time, and Beth and I were led by the large attendant down the long corridor to the end of the building. As we reached the end of the corridor we were met by two sets of doors. Barney pointed towards the set on our left.

"Ward 5 is that way. That's where he stays, your friend." And he giggled to himself as he opened the doors on the opposite side of the corridor. We passed through them and found ourselves outside in sunshine again in, what appeared to be, a small amphitheatre.

"Help yourself to a drink and take a seat anywhere you like." The attendant snorted and as he stepped into the sunlight I could see the sheen of sweat upon his puffed face. His eyes remained downwards at all times avoiding looking at either Bethany or I. It was clear that he had spent too long in the company of lunacy and did not spend much time talking with regular people and I hazarded a thought that perhaps he had once been on the other side of the ward door.

We took our seats on the fourth row from the back. The air was full of the busy chatter of the assembled crowd, well-tailored gentlemen and perfectly dressed ladies awaited the show, holding small linen umbrellas over their heads to shade them from the mid-afternoon sun. Although we were high in the stands we had a perfect view of the scene below.

At the foot of the seating area was a well swept stone floor and behind this a building some twenty yards across which was bricked on three sides and held iron bars at the front. It was, to all intents and purposes a cage, a locked enclosure which would not have seemed out of place had it been in the centre of a zoological gardens. One side of the building was attached to the main structure of the hospital and I could see from my seat that there was an adjoining door. The 'cage' was empty at present and I suddenly realised just what this 'spectacle' described by the Superintendent was going to be. I glanced quickly to my left and saw that Bethany had reached the same epiphany, as a sadness had come across her face which spoke volumes to me.

A small man, dressed in the blue cotton attire of the hospital orderlies, stepped into the cleared area in front of the cage and, after coughing loudly to gain the attention of the audience, began to speak in a loud faux-gentrified manner.

"Ladies and Gentlemen, Welcome to today's luncheon entertainment." There was a small ripple of polite applause from those looking down on him. "Today, for your delectation and wonder, we have trawled through this fine establishment to bring you the very maddest of the mad, the cream of London's lunatics, the wild and the weird, the incredulous and the insane."

The man began to step backwards waving his right arm in introduction.

"First today I give Nathaniel the pony boy!" Within the cage the adjoining door opened and a dishevelled man was pushed through into the eyes of the waiting throng. The sight of him drew gasps from the audience, as he was quite the most disturbing human being that they, or I for that matter, had ever seen. His body was that of a normal man, a little bent and twisted in places but a man nonetheless. His head however was misshapen to such an alarming degree that if I had only seen it alone I would have doubted that it was a man at all. The skull was malformed to such a degree in its lower part, the bottom jaw protruded to an animalistic extent met on the upper of the mouth by equally protrusive nose and cheeks. I could not believe what I was witnessing because this man-thing more closely resembled a horse in the shape and size of its head.

He shuffled slowly into the centre of the cage as the gasps and giggles of the crowd continued. Bethany and I were silent but all the same neither of us could take our eyes from the man within the bars. He stood for a moment before slowly turning in a full rotation and I found myself realising that for this poor creature, today's show was a regular event and one which he was often forced into.

The man in blue approached the bars of the cage and tapped sharply on them twice making the poor beast jump in fright. It was obviously a cue as the so called 'pony boy' began to skip around the cage in a trotting type motion, much to the amusement of those around Bethany and I.

The announcer moved again to the middle of the dusty area in front of the cage.

"...and next, here's one for the gentlemen in the audience, a real beauty fellas. We present Olive the 'Hag of the Hatch'!"

The side door opened once more and a woman entered. She was elderly, with a wild mass of grey hair which sat on top of a heavily wrinkled and haggard face. She strode into the cage as if she were a member of the royal court. Her head held high and a wide smile upon her face. She wore a grey dress which ended just below her knees and revealed heavily veined and dirty lower legs which ended in bare feet. As she strode to the centre of the cage, she looked out through the bars into the audience and began waving to one of the gentlemen sat in the first row. This brought gales of laughter from all around, a noise which intensified as she began fluttering what was left of her eyelashes and blowing kisses at him whilst stroking the sides of her body.

The look of horror which was set firm upon Beth's face was, for me, the most disturbing part of our luncheon appointment and I felt a harrowing guilt at bringing such a young woman to witness such a scene. Tears welled in her eyes as she looked down on those poor souls caged below her and put on display for our 'entertainment'. She had seen her good share of the bitter ignorance and petty cruelty of people growing up in 'The Alice' but nothing on this scale. However I think that it was the laughter and jollity of our fellow spectators which provided dear Bethany with the greater share of her sorrow.

The announcer continued.

"How about that then ladies? Olive is certainly a beautiful woman, is she not? Hold on to your beaus or she'll steal them from you!" The laughter continued, growing even louder when one man in the audience stood up and blew a kiss down to the cage. "Steady now gents, steady yourselves!" called the small man. "We have more to come, plenty more to see before the shows over. In fact, here is the next one. Boys! Can you send out the beast?!"

The side door opened once more and the crowd fell silent as a loud screaming sound was heard. Nothing came through the door however and the screams turned to growling shouts and there was the sound of a scuffle. Suddenly a leg was seen poking through the door closely followed by the rest of the body of a well-built man. His face was bearded and his toothless mouth howled as he was pushed into the cage by hands and batons. As he got through the door it was quickly slammed shut behind him and he continued to howl and rage, running around the cage, shaking the bars and pushing the deformed boy and the old woman over in the process. The woman started screaming herself and sat hunched on the floor, rocking violently.

The sight of this brought a deep sadness to me, something which was not felt by the so called gentry around me. I looked down to Beth's hand which shook upon the green painted wooden seating, her grip upon the edge of the seat was so tight with tension that I thought that she would tear a chunk of wood off, such was her hold. Even though the hand was gloved I knew that her knuckles were white bone beneath. Cautiously I placed my own hand upon hers, not in a display of affection but more to let her know that I felt and shared the anger and sadness which befell her, and which she was trying so hard to hide from the outside world. I wondered if she would recoil from my touch, however I found that the comfort of my hand over hers caused some slight abatement in the tension within her fingers. I looked to her face in the hope of seeing some respite for her from the revulsion which she obviously felt and she tore her eyes from the wretched lunatics before us and hazarded a quick glance at me.

"Why ... Why do they ... do this?" she stammered her voice quiet and seemingly at breaking point. "How can this be right?"

"I am sorry, Bethany." I whispered, "You should not have been exposed to this and I think it is time we took our leave from this place." My hand still held hers and I dared to make the gentle touch firmer to show my understanding of her affright.

"Animals... just animals." She said and I knew of whom she spoke. To my surprise her gloved hand released its hold of the seating and turned upwards clasping my hand gently. "Let us go, Sib. Please."

She made to stand, but I quickly stopped her. "Bethany, I have one more favour to ask of you today. Do you feel able to travel back alone?" I kept my voice low and my lips motionless. "I still mean to see my man here today and do not intend to be dissuaded by the Superintendent's attempts to confound and deny us. I will give you money enough for your train ticket and a hackney from King's Cross to Whitechapel."

The announcer below was introducing another helpless victim to the fray, but neither Bethany nor I looked downwards again.

"Do you really believe he can help us?" Beth asked. "What if it is true what we were told? He may be nothing more than a raging lunatic with no sense of what is real and what is not."

"I cannot let this go, Beth. Come let us walk towards the exit and from there we will part. I promise to come to you as soon as I return and tell you of the meeting." We both stood and, making our apologies to the enraptured fools beside us, we walked towards the gate leading to the gardens at the front of the building leaving the cruel circus behind. Once at the gate I turned to Bethany, who seemed relieved to have left the spectacle, "Thank you, Miss Finnan. We shall speak soon."

She gave a sly smile in return, "Be careful Mr. Darke. They are all mad in there, you know, and none more than those in charge." I gave a small chuckle and, with a final gentle squeeze of her hand, we separated and I made my way along the wall of the building to a small entrance door. I tested the handle and found it to be open.

Taking one last look at the disappearing figure of Bethany as she made her way towards the gates of the hospital I stepped inside. I had underestimated her before today; it was not a mistake I would make again.'

Inside the door I found myself in darkness, full of the smell of damp and human detritus. Coming from the bright sunshine, it took my eyes a few moments to adjust, but slowly I began to make out the walls of a corridor. I took a few tentative steps forward, desperate to be as quiet as possible. I had an image in my mind of where Ward 5 was, in relation to my current position and hoped that I could find its entrance and once there find an attendant willing to facilitate a meeting with Holdsworth. I had brought money with me for just this type of occasion and knew that the moral fortitude of the working man could easily be tested by the right amount of notes and coins.

I scaled my way along the corridor until I came to a corner. Peering around I saw that the next corridor was slightly better lit and had a number of doorways along either side. I could hear the muffled sound of voices from afar and decided that the best way to continue my exploration was to walk down the corridor and ask directions from any person willing to listen. I could then feign innocence through being lost or even pretend to be a visiting doctor. Whichever of these seemed most appropriate, I felt confident in my ability to play this card.

I strode forwards purposefully and decided that I quite enjoyed this type of cloak and dagger work, it stirred the blood and gave life a sense of immediacy and threat which was actually quite enlivening. As is often the case when feeling emboldened and full of confidence, however, this was of course the time when things tend to go most awfully wrong and this was certainly a perfect example of this type of occurrence.

For as I walked past one of the doorways, it quickly opened and a large blue sleeved arm reached out, grabbing me by the collar of my jacket. As I was hauled towards the door and into the darkness beyond, a huge hand clamped over my mouth as I tried to shout.

I had been taken. It would seem that my game of spies was up.

9
THE KILLER OF HARRY WHITE

My scream was muffled against the broad pad of flesh that pressed into my face. I tried to struggle but found that the hand, and the arm across my chest, made any type of escape impossible.

"Calm yourself, Mister. I don't want to have to hurt you to shut you up, but I will if you bring attention to us, so help me I will." I recognised the voice of Barney, the bear of an attendant and knew then that I had no hope of wrestling myself away from the tight hold that the monster had on me. Now that I was in close proximity to the man I found that the odour from his body was almost as overpowering as his size.

I ceased my struggling and tried as hard as I could to relax my body to demonstrate to this muscular beast that I had calmed enough for him to release his crushing hold upon me. He appeared to take the hint and slowly began to free me from his grip. As his hand came away from my mouth I decided to try to explain myself to him.

"It is not how it looks. I merely wished to see my family..." my confession however was short lived as once again the hand clamped itself over my face.

"Hold your tongue, sir," he hissed in my ear. "I know not who you are, and in truth I care not. But you have caused something of a concerning stir amongst my superiors with your questions and requests today.

"No one has ever wished to see Mr Holdsworth in twenty years and that is how he would prefer it. We speak together, he and I, we speak together a lot. And the one thing that he always asks is whether he is asked for, whether anyone has come to see him. It is a concern for him, a great concern that there are those that wish to get to him. So I will ask you a question and you will tell me the truth. Lie to me and I will snap this here neck of yours as easy as a stick. Do I have your understanding on this or do I have to crack it a little first?"

My head was loose enough within his violent embrace to give a nod of assent although if he could have just looked into my wide eyes he would have known that I was in no mood for having my neck snapped.

"What is your name, and what is your business with Henry?" His warm, fetid breath spread over my face as he spoke. "Speak no lie or it will be worse for you." He loosened his hand over my mouth again bidding me to tell.

"My name," I began, "is Sibelius Darke and I am the brother of the last boy, killed by Holdsworth." I saw no reason to continue with any contrivance with this monster. My task was too important for me to end up dead in an abandoned room in the dark reaches of a lunatic asylum. "I have come to talk to him of his claims of possession as I fear that the spirit which controlled him then has returned to plague the city."

Barney did not release his grip on me immediately, I could almost hear the cogs and wheels of his mind whirring as he decided whether to kill me or not. His thoughts may have only lasted for a short time, but to me the wait for a response was interminable. Finally his grip loosened somewhat, although I remained within his grasp.

"You will wait here, while I speak to him." He swung me around so that I faced him; the sight of the huge man was terrifying to me now, I was at the mercy of this behemoth. "If he wishes to speak I will come for you and you will have your time to speak." He continued, "If he fears you however, I will return to end you."

He threw me into the corner of the room and it was at this point that I saw that I had been brought into a disused cell; its walls marked with the scratches of many an abandoned inmate. Barney turned to leave and stepped through the door.

"One more thing!" I called after him, "Tell him that it was my father who beat him nearly to death and who freed him from the demon. He will know then that I speak the truth." He did not reply but closed the door, leaving me alone in there. I heard the clunk of a lock and I knew that I was trapped like a rat, at the cruel mercies of an overgrown imbecile and a crazed child murderer. It would seem that fate had long since left me to fall headlong into whatever earthly hell and damnation that could come my way.

I do not know how long it was that I waited in that darkened cell, and the thought that I may have been deceived by the attendant into becoming his very own inmate crossed my mind more than once. I had pulled my watch out of my pocket and tried to make out the position of the hands but the darkness was too great and the time remained a mystery to me.

The cell stank. It was empty but I was sure from the strong odour that it had been used as a privy and this thought ensured that I endured my entombment stood upright and did not attempt to seat myself. As the time continued to pass, my fear of being abandoned began to grow ever greater and I found myself wondering what I would do if he did not return. There was no window or potential exit of any kind except for the door.

Solitary, darkened confinement was an experience which I had grown used to as a child. Mother would often throw us into the small kitchen cupboard, which she kept empty and ready for use at any time that we were in the house. It had a thick wooden door to which Father had attached a pair of large iron deadbolts. These had been installed originally for the security of foodstuffs which she did not want my brothers and I to have access to. To this end, one of the deadbolts had been fitted at the top of the door and remained out of reach to us, until Niko and I had reached our teenage years, by which time Mother had developed other punishments more suited to older boys, such as belt beatings and the loss of bedding.

I remember quite clearly sitting in the dusty hole accompanied only by the spiders which Mother refused to clear out of the cupboard and which I remained unnaturally scared of into my adult years. Niko and I would speak of how we imagined that she brought flies, caught from around the house, to the cupboard, adding them to the webs to ensure that the eight-legged beasts of the cupboard grew to as large a size as possible. Despite the darkness in the cupboard and my fear of my arachnid companions, I bore my times of imprisonment bravely. I would close my eyes tightly shut and try to dream myself away to a different place where my brothers and I could be free to play all day and where mothers did not hate their children.

As I stood in the cell I thought about the last time that Mother had tried to bully and oppress Niko or I. I was fifteen years old, Niko twelve, and the pair of us had shared a day together at Grandfather's small house in Plumbers Row, helping him to move his bedroom to the downstairs parlour. His legs had grown weak following an illness earlier in the year and the effort of climbing the staircase to his bed had become too much for him.

Despite his increasing frailty, Grandfather had retained his humour and love of storytelling and Niko and I had spent an enjoyable day in his company, reliving the tales of Kalevala, which we had loved when we were younger, and to which Grandfather now gave a darker, sinister and more adult tone. We had returned home in the late afternoon after leaving Grandfather asleep on his newly moved bed, with supper on the table waiting for him when he awoke. Niko and I were in high spirits on the walk home, laughing and cajoling each other and thoroughly enjoying each other's company. We more or less fell in through the door when we arrived home.

The sight that met us had a very sobering effect as we found Father, his left eye red and swollen sat at the kitchen table with his hands on top of his head, Mother stood over him, fist raised and seemingly ready to continue. As they saw us, Father looked deeply ashamed and Mother immediately turned her attentions towards us. She was obviously in the middle of a furious rage which she had not fully vented upon Father and had found two further potential victims who were smaller and easier to frighten.

"What is the meaning of this laughter and hilarity?!" she bellowed, swinging her fist towards the head of Niko who cowered away from her, causing her to miss. "Come here when I hit you, boy!" she shouted advancing on the now shaking child who knew that he would have to stand still and take the punishment.

In that moment something happened within me. Whether it was because I had grown a lot in the previous six months and was now taller than her, or just the culmination of years of abuse and torture from this wicked woman, I had seen and felt enough. As she swung for a second time at Niko I stepped into her path so that the blow struck my shoulder.

The force of her fist was hard but I did not flinch or move when she hit me. I gave her no sign at all of any hurt and I turned to face her making myself as upright as I could so that I looked down upon her furious face. I set myself with steely determination and, although not speaking, gave Mother a look which told her that I was not afraid. She did not take the hint.

"Oh, you want some as well do you?" she spat, "I'll strike you as easy as I like, and then we'll see who's in charge around here." She swung her arm again, her cruel knuckles aimed for my cheek. It did not arrive. As the fist neared me I raised my left arm and blocked her blow, her wrist hitting my forearm hard, hard enough to hurt her. The shock in her face caused me much inner joy although I kept it hidden. Father had stood up now and was watching my defiance.

"You devil!" She shouted. "You evil little cur, try to hurt me will you?" She swung again, this time I blocked the blow with ease and caught her wrist in my hand. The fear in her face was immediate and I decided that the time was right to press the point. Still holding her wrist I raised my arm so that it was hard for her to get close to me with her other hand or wriggle free.

"This ends today, Mother." I said in as calm a voice as I could manage. She cried out, a weak wailing sound like a stray cat caught in the jaws of a dog. "This ends." I continued. Father and Niko remained silent but I could sense a change in the room. "For years we have taken your beatings, your burns, your tortures, but today this ends. I will not take another of your blows and neither will Niko or Father. The next time you strike at us I will strike you back and I will have fifteen year's worth of anger within me behind my fist." I raised my arm even higher so that she was stretched out in front of me. The fire of anger was gone from her eyes replaced by fear and age.

From that day forwards Mother never struck or punished me again, and to the best of my knowledge this also applied to Father and Niko. Her spell was broken and she no longer held fear over us. She would still shout and scream, curse and swear, but there was no threat of violence behind her words. I never forgave her for the pains that she caused me, but I did not look back on my youth and see a vision of terror and fright, rather I saw her as a thing that should be pitied. She was a weak being, who used violence on others as a way of tempering the hate which burned within her.

My thoughts were interrupted by the sound of steps approaching the door and a key turning in the lock. I stood against the wall in a pathetic attempt at staying in the darkness and out of sight. Barney blocked out what light there was coming through the doorway and spoke.

"He is waiting for you." he said, "here, put these on." and he threw me a set of ill-fitting attendant clothing which I placed over my suit.

The journey through the dimly lit corridors seemed to take an age and I was sure that I would never be able to remember my way out of this accursed building again without help. After ten minutes of walking in silence through the maze, occasionally retreating into a room to avoid the attentions of other attendants we finally reached our destination.

The door was no different to any other that we had passed on our journey apart from the paint flaked sign which stated in bold lettering 'Ward 5'. This was the ward which the superintendent had spoken of, the secure place where those deemed most dangerous were kept. Barney withdrew a large key ring from his trouser pocket and selected a wide iron ring from his collection. He turned the key in the lock and we entered a corridor, some forty feet long with five doors on either side. Slowly we walked to the end; I heard the sound of laughter and tears coming from the rooms as we passed. Finally at the last door on the left we stopped and he unlocked the door.

"You will not have long. I will patrol the near corridors and keep watch for others coming," he said opening the door and gesturing me inside.

As I moved cautiously into the man's cell and peered through the gloom to the figure hunched in the corner I felt a sense of fear at what type of beast I might find here. This was a man, after all, who had hunted small defenceless children, tearing their bodies and rending them unrecognisable from human form. This was a man who had sunk his teeth into their pale flesh who had sated his hunger on the raw, blood soaked pieces of what had once been a living breathing child. I had come to terms with the fact that he had been possessed by a demonic soul, driven to fulfil these terrible acts by a force out of his control, but there was a part of me still which wondered whether he had enjoyed the horror which he had undertaken, whether he joined in the blood lust and felt power from the act of murder.

The stench in the room was overpowering and I fought every urge within me to retch and gag. My work was too important to fall prey to such a matter however and I wiped the tears forming in my eyes and concentrated on the figure awaiting me.

Holdsworth was a large man, that much I could tell from his shadowy presence at the back of the room, as he seemingly cowered away from the light coming from the open metal door of his holding place, his knees brought up and his head bowed and hidden. I moved into the room a little further, starting a little when Barney made a noise behind me, bringing in a wooden chair from the corridor outside. I took the seat from him and positioned it by the side of the cot bed upon which Holdsworth curled. I heard the door lock behind me and knew that I would be trapped in here until Barney returned.

Despite his size I could see that Holdsworth was malnourished. I could clearly see the angular shape of his bones jutting out of his shoulders and elbows as he covered himself from me. His head was bald and bore scars upon it. From my knowledge of the treatment of the patients within this building I knew that these would have been caused from being struck. These were not small scars; they looked as though they had been deep wounds, gouges which would have seen infection and decay. I noted from his forearms that there were similar marks, defensive wounds caused by arms thrown up above the head to prevent more grievous injury.

"Good evening, Mr Holdsworth." I intoned tensely, "I am Sibelius Darke and I would have you tell me about your time as a killer of children."

He looked up at me, his eyes becoming visible over his forearms. I noted that they were milky in their tone, such as a blind man may have, and I wondered if this was caused by years of darkened isolation and little exposure to natural light. He squinted in my direction as if trying to make out the face of the person speaking to him, there was obviously some sight left in the man. He observed me closely, studying my face as if attempting to see into my mind. Finally he spoke,

"I hear you attended the show." He said in a half whisper, "Tell me, what did you think of it? Was it a glorious spectacle? Did you laugh and bleat with the rest of the sheep?"

He remained half hidden behind his arms, his body pushed back into the darkness of the corner as far as he could fit.

"I thought it a horrible thing, sir." I replied in truth. "I see no joy in exposing a person's madness and misgivings to the world. I left before it was done."

His arms dropped slightly and the skin where there would have been eyebrows lifted in enquiry.

"I left, you say? I left? Were you not with a young girl?" The bridge of his nose now showed and I could tell that it had been broken on more than one occasion in the past, crooked as it was like a bending road down his face. "Barney tells me she was a pretty thing, soft skin and auburn hair, young and tender. Tell me, is she yours? Yours to play with?"

I could just make out the tips of the corners of his mouth, and I could tell he was smiling broadly, hoping for some kind of perverse and depraved gain from my answer. I would not be providing such.

"I will not speak of her to you, as she is not of your concern." I replied sitting back in the chair and folding my arms. The smile did not fade from his face, but I felt that my reply caused it to serve a different purpose. His knees lowered as did his arms and finally I could see, in full, the man who I was speaking to. His face was terribly scarred, and pale, so pale that his skin seemed almost translucent. For twenty years this man had lived in shadow, out of the glare of natural light and out of the sight of the world. He stared at me hard and I could see that I had made the right impression on this man, despite his level of sanity.

"You are a man of principle," he said, his voice clear and solid. "Despite the fact that I would love to hear of her, I will respect your wish and press you no more, except to ask, did she enjoy the show?"

"She did not, she found it abhorrent."

"Then she is also principled and with true morals, not those forced upon us. I was a part of the show once you know. I was forced to take part in the lunchtime entertainments. Hit with sticks and dragged before the baying crowd. Just the once, did they let me perform my act. It was not ... popular.

"I defecated onto the floor of the stage. Oh how the ladies cried in horror and tried to shield their eyes." He chuckled to himself, a deep throaty sound like the grating of a washboard. "Shielding the eyes did not protect one poor girl though; no she was not saved from the act. The attendants ran in to the cage to try to drag me away but not before I had scooped up my waste and flung it through the bars and into her pretty face."

He threw his arms up in the air as he spoke re-enacting the incident with pure joy in his mind and losing himself in the moment. Laughing loudly, his mouth opening wide so that I could see the few broken teeth which remained within it, the sound of his humour became more crazed as it continued and he leapt to his feet on the bed and danced.

When I thought he could get no louder the crescendo ended as he suddenly realised the noise that he was making. His laughter quietened and stopped as his mind continued to reminisce on the memory and he sat down on the cot again, the darkness returning to his face.

"I took a beating for that; a hard lengthy bout of moral re-education, but it was a thrashing I would have again and again to see the looks on the faces of the so called gentry. Every stick, fist and boot which struck me following my extrication from the stage was happily taken as payment for such a beautiful act." He appeared to be staring into the distance although his focus was the grey wall opposite and I attempted to pull him back to reality and the purpose of my visit.

"We need to speak of your past; it is of great import to me."

"Were you sent by the club?" he asked in a matter of fact kind of way.

"Club? I do not know what you mean. Which club do you mean?"

His grin widened and he looked to the ceiling.

"I cannot speak of the powers that control our worlds, Mr Darke. Our lives are ruled by others and we are low beings, pawns in their game. Our will is lost and our fates are sealed. It is a failure in our thinking to try to break the spell." His words became a mutter as he seemed to fade from reality once again. It would seem that I would have a job to keep the man's feet on the ground and extricate any sense from his madness.

"I do not understand, Mr Holdsworth, but I do not need to. I am the brother of the last child you tore and the son of the man who ended your killing. I wish to know more of the demon who took you, the beast who controlled such vile actions. What circumstances turned a drayman to a child murderer?" I leaned forward trying to gain eye contact and rein him to me so that he may speak sense. He met my gaze and answered.

"I do not know the date that the beast came upon me but my fate was sealed when I drew the straw at the brewery yard. It was an onerous task delivering to these premises. Other draymen told of a cold sense of fear when entering, a chill which froze the marrow and caused them to flee in haste once the delivery was made." He continued to meet my gaze and I felt that I could almost be talking to one devoid of madness such was the normality of his voice. "As a young man, new to the job, I thought it a lark, some kind of ruse to scare the new boys and cause merriment to the men. They told me that it was a place of horror and that, although deliveries were rarely required, it had become the norm among the regular workers to leave the barrels and bottles at the cellar doors not daring to enter."

I thought to take out my notebook and record his tale, but I felt drawn in by his broken eyes and caught by his words.

"I had not been on the job for long on the day when they brought out the straws and gathered next to the delivery cart. I joined in their game, thinking it fun, oh how I regret that now. When the straws were drawn, mine was not the shortest, that fate belonged to the man to my left. He had been at the brewery longer than I and, although he had never visited the place before, he had truly believed the tales of fear and threat which had been told." Holdsworth winced as he recalled the memory, as if it caused him physical pain. "When he held that small blade of hay in his hand it was as if he had been frozen to stone, a look of terror and foreboding chiselled into his face. But still I thought it a ruse, and, being a foolhardy and brash young man I snatched it from his hand. 'Here,' I called, 'Let me have the job, you cowardly fool. I do not scare easy and I think that you take me for a callow child, which I am not!' Oh, how I bragged and strutted around the yard, ignoring the warnings of the men, casting away their advice as if it useless and untrue. Stupid boy, arrogant child! Deserving of his fate!"

The wildness had returned to his face, which he struggled to control. But control it he did although the effort forced a tear to his eye. "I arrived at the site of my delivery with a smile on my face and a sense of power that I had seen through my co-workers joke and come to this place without fear or trepidation. I admit that the club itself was a somewhat doom laden building, tall and narrow as it was and constructed from bricks so grey that one would mistake them for black. The windows were small; some round, others thin to the point of looking like arrow slots in an old castle. I noted the wooden cellar doors, painted black and sealed shut with a large padlock. The delivery that I had on my cart was small, two barrels of Brandy, one of rum and I thought of how my fellow workers would leave their cargo at the cellar doors ring the bell of the door and leave as quickly as their horse would take them. I briefly considered doing the same but my curiousness and idiocy prevailed and I climbed the steps to the large red painted door and pulled the bell. Stupidity ... idiocy ... foolishness beyond belief ..."

He had returned to his self-muttering and now began a rocking motion which reminded me of a toy horse, back and forth he went, cursing himself both inwardly and outwardly with an anger so great that I thought that he may begin to cause himself physical harm should it continue to escalate.

"Sir," I called insistently. "Sir! Please continue with your story. Our time is brief and you have yet to reach a stage which would provide me with any information of worth." I reached out in an attempt to stop him from rocking so and bring him back to the moment and his tale. At the touch of my hand upon his leg he flinched with an action so severe that I thought that he would force himself through the wall behind him if he had the power. This initial scare however brought him forth from his meanderings and he continued.

"I pulled the bell – Stupid! – and waited for the door to be answered – Fool! When it opened I was met by a small man of Chinese persuasion dressed in the livery of a butler of sorts, his clothes however made of the finest black silk. He was a good head shorter than I and wore his long greased hair in a plait.

"'You bring the delivery,' he said, his voice low and steady, his eyes not meeting mine. 'Please step inside briefly, the club secretary wishes to give you a message regarding our account.' I though this a little odd, although I had been given notes for my employers before to deliver from our customers but, cap in hand I entered that accursed building – Idiocy! – And waited in the hallway. At the servant's invitation I took a seat in the long regal hallway and even took a cup of the murky green tinted filth that he claimed was tea, awaiting his return. I sat in that chair with a smug, self-satisfied smile on my face – Dolt and Idiot! – The day had been hot and, despite a suspiciousness of the fluid, I downed the contents of the cup in one - drained it. It was bitter and cold but I think there was a respite from my thirst. I say I think because I can remember no more of the visit and awoke within my own rooms that evening with no knowledge of how I had returned.

"The following day I went to work as normal and apologised for my actions the previous day, thinking that I had abandoned my cart and gone home straight from the club."

The silence within Holdsworth's cell was threatening as he paused in his words. Despite my interest in his story, the man had still not told me anything of his time as a murderer, and I had begun to feel impatient for some information of note.

"The boss looked at me strange, though, when I begged to keep my job. 'What are you on about, Henry, you stupid boy. You returned here in the early afternoon all your deliveries complete, I have never known a job done so quick and well. I gave you a tuppence bonus and sent you home.' The boss's words confused me, but this is where it started. The killings."

He paused momentarily, clenching his hands into pale fists before resuming his story.

"I never really knew what I did; to me the deaths were like dreams, coming to me in the night as I slept. I dreamt I was a wolf, hunting my prey, bringing down helpless deer to feed my hunger and fulfil my longing. I did not know that I was hunting children; I had no memory of the truth of it all. I would feel tired and ache throughout the day and would return to my room to sleep when the workday was complete. There were differences in my behaviour though, noticeable changes. I was not hungry and the taste or even thought of food made me retch, I felt full to bust but began wasting away, and then there was the blood. I would wake up with blood on my face and on my hands, not knowing where it came from. On one occasion I awoke at dawn laid in an alleyway, on another I was on the rooftops curled up at the base of a chimney pipe.

"I assumed that I had some kind of sickness," he laughed aloud, "I even thought that I was losing my mind, falling prey to madness." This thought gave Holdsworth great amusement and he again faltered from his story, giggling wildly and muttering to himself until I coughed aloud and he remembered that I was there and that he was telling me his tale.

"Barney says it was your father that beat me with a stick, that evening. That your father discovered me hunched over the corpse of your brother and feasting on his flesh –ah the joy of the taste! He was a soft one, your brother. He saved me, the man with the stick, saved me from the demon controlling my nights, saved me from my double life. It was only as I neared death that I knew what I'd become. I felt the power within me, a power so beautiful, so strong. In those few moments I was both disgusted by my actions but joyful of the feeling of the power I had displayed, a feeling that could I feel beginning to drain from me, as the beast began releasing me from his bonds. He was running from my body to prevent being trapped within a dead vessel. If I were to die, he would be trapped within my corpse for eternity, never freed, chained within a dead man. I shared these thoughts and I knew his fears, he would leave me for another, move from me to your father if he could – lucky man!, but your father did not come close enough, close enough for me and my friend to touch him, to pass on my curse, my love. And so the demon inside me left, fled back to his dark place, back to his guardian task, to lick his wounds and wait for another chance at life ... at bringing death."

He paused and looked up to the ceiling of his cell, squeezing his eyes shut as hard as he could, a grimace stretching his round face. In the partial light his face looked almost demonic and could be taken for one of great joy; a broad smile of ecstasy etched within his features. As I studied him though for those few seconds before he continued however, I only saw agony, self-contempt and deep mental pain, this was a man who had hated himself for over twenty years, abhorred by his own actions.

"When the beast departed I felt his loss, I felt as though a part of me had died – wicked! -and, although it is a cause of great shame to me, I felt a loss at the thrill of the hunt and the joy of the kill. Following my beating I fell into unconsciousness, soaked in mine and your brother's blood. Your father must have thought me dead – cruel devil, should have died! But when I finally awoke, I knew the full terror of the crimes I had committed, I had memory of each of the children I had killed and devoured, I knew what I had done. I was too cowardly to take my own life, and so I took myself to the police and handed myself in, claiming guilt for my crimes and asking for the noose."

"The actions of a man good at heart." I said, "You cannot think yourself as bad if you acted so?"

"You know nothing, boy!" He screamed, spittle flying from his lips and onto my face as I jumped backwards into my seat. "I handed myself in because I wanted the rope. I wanted to hang as a killer of children, to be cast as evil and to be accursed in death to hell. I did this because the draw of the club was too great; the temptation to return and take on the beast's cowl was strong within me. Better to be dead and cursed for eternity than to continue." He drew in a long breath; I heard a wheezing in his chest and a crackle in his throat. "They said they did not believe me, said that I could not have carried out these crimes. The more I told them of the beast, the more lunacy they said they saw within me, but I know their game. They watch me still, watch and wait for the time when I can be reunited again, joined and freed to continue their work. This is what I fear and this is why I pray for death."

"And you think that it was at this 'club' that the demon was entered into your body?" I cut in. "Do you remember nothing from your time there?"

"I remember some things." He said his voice distant. The pain within his face continued and I could see the conflict within him as he wrestled with his love of the demon and his self-hatred. "I have thought hard over this in my long time within this cell. Sometimes within dreams I see things that are familiar to me but I know not if they are just my foolish mind playing cruel tricks. I see hooded men, sickle signs and an altar of stone, no real memory however."

Suddenly there was the sound of clattering outside the cell door. Holdsworth visibly jumped and shrank back into the corner expecting the worst. The door flew open and Barney burst in, his face red with sweat and a panicked look in his eyes.

"They're coming … down the main corridor … they know you're here, we must run!"

Holdsworth shrank further into the darkness of the corner and began to rock violently again muttering to himself in words that I could not understand. The large hand of the attendant grasped my collar and pulled me to my feet.

"Move, man, move!" he hissed angry at my lack of movement. He pulled me backwards towards the door as I tried to continue my questioning of the now near hysterical Holdsworth.

"Where was it?" I shouted, "What was the name of the club? I must know." But Holdsworth did not respond, he seemed lost to logical thought or conversation now.

"You must go now!" The attendant growled. "If they catch you, they will kill you or worse!" Barney dragged me from the cell and pushed me down towards the bottom end of the corridor opposite to the end which we had arrived from. For the first time I could hear the footsteps of approaching men, coming from the other side of the doorway. There was a jangle of keys and the barking of voices getting louder as they made their way down the long corridor towards the entrance to Ward 5.

"The club!" I shouted back through the Holdsworth's door. "You must tell me what the club is called!" Barney pulled me further away and began to close the door on Holdsworth. The door to the cell slammed shut and the large attendant locked the cell, but I was determined and would not let it end like this. I fought my way out of Barney's grasp to run back to the door. "The club!" I shouted through the small grill, "what was it called?" I saw the seated figure of Henry J. Holdsworth in the darkened corner of the room. He looked up at me for the final time, his eyes full of fear and despair.

"Sorrows." He said quietly, "We called it The Club of Sorrows."

The collar of my shirt was grabbed roughly by Barney and he heaved me away from the cell and down the corridor. I struggled to keep my feet on the floor and help with any kind of movement as he essentially carried me away from the secure wing and back through endless corridors. All the while we heard the sound of running feet and the shouts of men as they chased us through the asylum.

Through the endless corridors we rushed, Barney heading the way, an unstoppable hulk of a man, dragging me, a waif in comparison, wheezing and puffed through the exertion of running. Although relatively physically fit, I have never had cause to run any distance since childhood and I was shocked at how much the effort of sprinting now burned my legs and strained my heart, the thumping sound in my ears drowning out my heavy breathing.

The crashing feet of the chasing men spurred me onwards, however and I was grateful for the large attendant's knowledge of these darkened winding corridors. Once or twice, where the floor was wet, I lost my footing and was hauled upright and pulled further into the darkness. The effort was beginning to weigh heavy upon me now and I found the breath to call to Barney.

"I cannot go on further. We must stop soon, how much longer must we run?" There must have been sure sense of desperation in my voice as Barney slammed to a halt as the corridor came to a section much like a crossroads, dividing off into three possible directions.

"Take the left corridor," he said his voice low and commanding. "Keep on this route until you reach a dead end with two doors. Take the door to the right it will lead you outside at the end of the west wing. Follow the gravelled path to an iron gate, from there you are free of the grounds and can bide your time until the first trains leave for London in the morning. I will cover your tracks. Now go!"

"I go," I wheezed. "But promise me, Barney. If he says any more to you about his crimes, you will come to me, Sibelius Darke; my studios are in Osborn Street just off of Whitechapel Road. You will be rewarded for any information."

He nodded his assent and threw me down the corridor with such weight that my legs struggled to keep up with the rest of my body. I was tired, more tired than I had ever been in my life, but I ran through the pain and I ran hard to escape this terrible building.

Barney had obviously kept to his word as soon I could no longer hear the sound of chasing men behind me. I followed his instructions and with great relief reached the final door at the end of the wing which took me out into the cold night air. The chill hit my lungs as I breathed deeply to try to regain composure and energy to continue in my escape, and its bite caused me to vomit, throwing clear the small amount of food that I had consumed earlier in the day. It was raining, a heavy but steady fall which seemed to soak my clothes within moments. I raised my face to the downpour and allowed the rain to cool the heat, which had developed through my exertion. Pulling my handkerchief clear of my pocket to wipe clear my eyes I continued to run. The grounds were pitch black, but I was led by the sound of the gravel under my boots to the surrounding wall of the asylum and to the wrought iron gate which led to my freedom from this place of madness.

Throwing open the gate I ran onwards into a wooded area and there I stopped to gain my bearings and decide upon my next course of action. I had come out of the asylum's grounds at completely the wrong end of where I needed to be to journey home, and so, at a steadier pace and keeping the wall of the asylum to my left I made my way back towards the east of the building and the train station.

The journey took twenty minutes or more in the dark and I finally reached the edge of the woods, which overlooked the station. I sheltered from the rain within some bushes which I hoped would also keep me hidden from any giving chase and made myself as comfortable as possible, although both tired and wet through. I waited there until daylight broke and the first trains coming through to King's Cross ran when I headed back to Whitechapel and my studio, filled with a greater knowledge of the task ahead of me and with a grim determination to see this terrible business to its deathly end.

10
The Witness and the Watcher

My mood was stern and determined in the days following my escape from the asylum. I had returned to my rooms through the rooftop entrance and, following a change of clothes, had taken myself straight to my bed. I was cold and damp from my night in the rain soaked woods and needed to recover from my lack of sleep. My tiredness must have been dire as I ended up losing the rest of that day and night, although when I finally did wake I seemed to feel just as lethargic.

The police presence outside of my rooms continued, although I am sure that the allocated constables must have become very bored by their task, as, according to their knowledge, I had not left my house for three days. I hoped that this supposed lack of activity on my part would mean that the continual examination into my affairs by the police would soon abate.

I had not yet met again with Bethany, although she had apparently visited my studio on the day after our visit whilst I slept and had, at some point, passed a note through my door.

Dear Sibelius,

I came to visit this morning but there was no reply. I am hoping that you are well and that you have returned intact from our visit yesterday. I admit that I felt some worry regarding your wellbeing after I had left and boarded the train. I even considered returning, although I do not know what I would have done to aid the situation. Dad is pleased that I appear to have lifted from my gloom, I told him that we had journeyed out of London to the countryside and that we had enjoyed a pleasant day. I do not know how I could ever start to explain to him exactly where we had gone and the terrible and strange things that we witnessed.

Please come to see me at the earliest possible time following your return, I would be very interested to know the results of your investigations and the sight of you will ease my concerns for your safety.

I have decided to return to my charity work in the area, much to Dad's relief. It is a comfort for him to have the impression that things are returning to some normality. I will however make myself available to give my assistance if you require it.

Be safe
Beth

The discovery of Bethany's letter gave me reassurance. I had been concerned regarding her welfare after sending her, a young girl unused to life outside of a few streets of London, to journey alone back to her father. I also felt terrible guilt for exposing her to the horrors of the asylum that we had witnessed. The images which I had seen had become imprinted in my mind and I felt they would never truly leave me. Their effect on a girl, no more than a child in terms of age and experience troubled me and I wished to see her again to ensure her mental wellbeing. That said, I had been impressed by her composure throughout the day, she had carried herself in a manner far beyond her years, especially when asked to pose as my spouse, not a role I would ever recommend to anyone.

There were a couple of other written messages which had been passed through my door which I decided to give attention to before venturing out to the 'The Princess Alice' and disclosing to Bethany the next stage of our investigations. I took these messages up to my study where, after checking out of the window, to see that my police watch was still in place, I sat at my desk and saw to my affairs.

There were two messages of note; one from George Woodrow informing me that he had been in contact with the police who had informed him that Father and Niko's body's would soon be released for burial. Their return to me would play a vital part in the next stage of my plan to track down and exact revenge on their murderer. I had decided that if I were to be hounded by the dead through the lens of my camera, that I should use this to my advantage and, through the pretext of a memorial photograph, converse with my recently deceased relatives. Even if they were unable to identify their killer, at least I would have the opportunity to bid them a fond farewell.

The second message was from a gentleman named Benjamin Peckard, who had recently suffered the loss of both his wife and the new-born child during the delivery process. Mr Peckard, a young lawyer from a distinguished legal family, wished me to send a message to him, at my earliest convenience, regarding the availability to record their passing with a memorial photograph. He had heard about my service through Lord Faulkner, who his family's law firm represented and who had spoken of my discretion and quality of service most highly. If I would be able to perform this service for him at his Knightsbridge home within the next two days, he wished me to contact him immediately.

It is in the nature of my work that such assignments are presented to me at short notice. Families, despite wishing to have their loved one's demise recorded for posterity, also had the pressing concern of internment to deal with and often I would lose business if I did not keep an ordered diary with room for manoeuvre and flexibility.

I wrote a short letter of reply agreeing to take the commission and told him that I would come to his residence in two days' time at three in the afternoon. I asked that he arrange to have the bodies available and the setting, where he wished to have the memory recorded, prepared. This type of pre-planning on the commissioning individual's part often made the process of photographing their deceased a much quicker, discreet and less painful experience.

After placing the appointment in my diary, I prepared myself to find a delivery boy to give the letter to and stop in at Woodrow's for a discussion with George before visiting Bethany. After dressing myself appropriately and ensuring that I looked smart enough for tackling the outside world, I opened my doors and stepped out into the busy street, straight into Inspector Frederick Draper.

He was accompanied by his ever present shadow, Sergeant Thomas and, looking across the street, I noted that my officer on watch for the morning had now departed. Draper was smartly dressed in a suit of woven Donegal tweed. The suit, which was tan in colour, struck an immediate chord with me as I had been meaning to order something of a similar nature for myself. My suit however, would be Harris Tweed, in my mind a distinguished and refined weave, much more suited to the circles in which I had until recently hoped to mix in. Those days of expanding business and ever growing reputation seemed so far away now.

"Mr Darke, I would see you for a short time if feasible." He announced, in a much more polite and friendly tone than I had experienced on our last meeting.

I thought to delay him and continue on my business but, thinking on George Woodrow's note, I invited him in to my studio. "Of course, Inspector always pleased to help, I am afraid I have become a bit of a recluse of late and have caused many hours of boredom for your most attentive constables." He smiled slightly and I realised that this was the first sign of any kind of emotion I had seen in the man. He stepped over the threshold turning as he did so and raising his hand to his sergeant.

"I don't think that there will be any need for you to accompany me inside, Abe." He said blocking Sergeant Thomas' entry into my studio. "I shall only be with Mr Darke for a short time, and will not require any assistance. Wait here for me."

Abe Thomas' face was the perfect example of restrained fury, red with rage and embarrassment but controlled enough not to cause any offence to his senior. I took the opportunity to give the good sergeant my sweetest smile before closing the door on him. As I turned into the hallway I saw that Draper was making his way along the corridor and looked to start climbing the stairs to my private rooms.

"Please, Inspector," I called, not wanting him to pry any further into my life. "There is room and chairs in my studio we may speak there if you wish." I gestured to the door on the right hand side of the corridor, which led to my photographic rooms.

"Of course." He replied, opening the door and stepping inside. He looked around the room as he entered his eyes taking in the camera equipment set up on tripods and the collection of sets and scenery which I kept available for my work. "When I first heard that you had remained in the family's business of death services, I assumed that you were a funeral director like your father and brother. I must admit I received quite a shock when I was told that you photograph the recently deceased."

"It is not a normal business," I admitted offering the inspector a chair by the window where I had a small table set up. This area of the studio was often where I met prospective clients when they visited me in person. It was here that I provided them with my best sales chatter, and a mask which I was able to wear when required. "My father had a little difficulty with the concept at first, but once he saw that there was a market for it, he gave me his full support."

"Forgive me for my inquisitiveness, I suppose it is the nature of my employment, but how do you actually photograph the ... er clients. Are they, forgive my vulgarity, in a box?"

I laughed aloud at this idea. "Good lord no, sir. That would not do at all. No, the service I provide is to give a memento of life as near to life as is possible. My clients are the families of the deceased not the deceased themselves and the pictures that I create are of the recently passed as if alive and sat in the frame looking down on their grieving loved ones. Would you like some tea? Or I think I have some coffee if you prefer."

Draper waved his hand. "No thank you, Mr Darke. As I told my Sergeant, I have limited time and I am sure that you have your daily affairs to attend to." I noticed that he continued to scan the room, studying each facet and intricacy laid around the studio as if it were an environment completely alien to him. "So the deceased," he pushed onwards, "they are recorded in a photograph on their own, in a setting decided by their grieving families?"

"Sometimes it is this way," I replied. "It very much depends on the needs and wishes of the departed's family. Sometimes those that have passed are recorded on their own, but more often than not it is a family portrait, such as would be kept were the person still living."

There was a shock in his eyes at this revelation, something which I must say that I enjoyed as well as finding somewhat charming. The idea of what is normal within one person's range of thought can scarcely be believed by one such as me. I have, what I like to think of as, the good fortune to see the multitude of oddness and peculiarity which goes on behind the closed doors, even of those such houses that the pedestrian from the outside would think of as 'well to do' or 'decent and upstanding'. As I believe I have mentioned it is the discretion that I show in my dealings with those that commission my work which, holds me in such high regard by those that have contracted my services. I learned early on in my days as a budding photographer, offering distinct and individual studies of the human form, that a broad minded view was required if I were to establish myself as the type of professional whose name was passed on to those who may be partial or in need of my service.

"So a family may gather with the dead person at the centre, posed as if still living?" Draper asked, the height of his eyebrows a sure sign that he was learning something through our conversation.

"Well of course," I replied. "There is often a requirement for some element of make-up and tending to the appearance of the person. Why in one case I was charged with the almost impossible task of conjuring a family style portrait which included a father who had lost a large part of the right side of his face through a machinery accident. The use of lighting, posing of the subject and some garden scenery solved that problem. I have a copy of that particular print if you would like to see it?"

I could see that the deep yearning for enlightenment was fighting a heavy battle within him but he declined.

"I am sure that it would be a fascinating scene to study." The war within him won by reason and task. "I feel however that I have allowed myself to become strayed from the path on which I set out on this morning, engaging though I find the subject of your work to be. I have come to inform you that you will no longer be observed by my officers and that the bodies of your family will be released when requested."

I demonstrated relief, although it was, thanks to the nod from old George, the news that I had been expecting. As I felt that I had crossed a threshold with the Inspector I decide to press the matter further.

"Why, I am most grateful to you for this news, Inspector, and would ask that their bodies are sent to George Woodrow for the funeral arrangements. The coroner will have the address details. Tell me has something happened to bring about such a change?"

"There has indeed, Mr Darke. There has indeed" His hand rose to his mouth and long fingers smoothed his moustache as he spoke. "Unfortunately, there has been further loss of life of a similar nature to that which befell your own dear family. Loss of life of the most grievous kind and happening whilst, as you were well aware, you have been under the observation of my fine officers."

I felt humility and guilt within his voice, as if his notions and ideas of responsibilities for these murders had been proven to be so very wrong, combined with the thought that his 'fine officers' may have been better placed and directed in search of a killer on the streets rather than a grieving man who remained within his home for days on end. Of course I knew that this had not been the case and that I had led them a dance through the rooftop exit of my building, but I was not about to start being truthful with the man.

"I am sorry to hear that there have been further outrages, Inspector. Tell me are you any nearer to finding the man behind them?"

"Solid clues are scant." He said spreading his hands wide. "These murders happened just last night and my men are still hard at work at the scene. The modus operandi or cause of death that the murderer employs is consistent throughout, as there is no evidence of any weapons used other than the hands and, dare I say, teeth of the killer. It is sufficient for me to say that at this moment we are dealing with a crazed abomination and I fear for the safety of any soul braving the streets of this area alone after dark."

"Indeed," I returned, "Indeed. And, may I ask, have there been no sightings?"

"Well, it is interesting that you say that, Mr Darke, as we have the beginnings of a description thanks to the assistance of the person who discovered the last poor soul who fell victim. It would seem that she disturbed the killer before he had finished his business and has been able to provide some elements of aid. Nothing that is of any use to anyone but the police, I can assure you."

He obviously had no intention of revealing what these clues were and I made a note to myself mentally to find out more about the mystery witness and to find out what exactly they had said. There was a moments silence as he made his point.

"You have an interesting life, Mr Darke. Not one which I think I would enjoy, I see enough death in my work as it is, but most interesting nonetheless." He stood and straightened his jacket. "I must attend to my duties now, but I am sure that I will be in touch when we finally have the killer within our grasp."

I stood and outstretched my hand. "I thank you for your time, sir, and would be grateful for further news when you receive it." I knew that he had no intention of sharing information with me but I felt that the request was worth a try. He did not respond and began to walk towards the door.

"I can see myself out, Mr Darke." He said turning as he reached the doorway

"Goodbye, Inspector." I said and I followed him into the hallway to make sure that he left. As the door closed behind him I walked back into the studio to watch him walk away down the street accompanied by Sergeant Thomas and decided that my own investigation should continue in earnest now.

After waiting for ten minutes to ensure that the Inspector and his dog were out of the vicinity, and checking out of the windows to see that my police presence had truly gone, I left the studio and headed down the road. My first stop would be Leman

Road and George Woodrow's parlour, to arrange for the bodies of my family to be brought to my studio, the following afternoon so that I may be able to photograph them.

George was most pleased to see me and said that he would gladly receive the bodies when they were sent to him. His face however showed a little concern when I asked for them to be sent to my studio so that I may photograph them, he never really understood the nature or benefits of my work.

It was when I asked him if he knew anything of the previous night's murder that his eyes lit up and he excitedly imparted the news. He told me that a friend of his had arrived at the scene shortly after the police. The friend, Vance Crocker, was a well-known gossip and tittle-tattler, always able to tell the willing ear the latest news. I tended to use him as a point of information when all other avenues failed, as he had a habit for exaggeration and sensationalism. Vance had been most pleased with himself for being in the right place at the right time, as it were. This type of first-hand knowledge would be invaluable to him and would give him fuel to burn in terms of being respected as the person in the know. According to Vance, the story is as follows:

James Flint, an older boy of perhaps fourteen years, was a renowned thief and snakesman. Well known to the local police, he had spent many a night in the cells at Holborn station, but had never had an accusation or conviction stick with any real relish. This freedom from gaol or the noose was attributed by many to his apparent friendship with Hubert Redditch, a local and well respected man of law who always seemed to be on hand to post bail monies and provide legal representation for the lad. Time and again Mr Redditch appeared to fight most voraciously in Flint's defence claiming that he suffered from a broken childhood, and was the physical proof of the society's treatment of the working classes. That such vehement struggles should be undertaken by such a highly thought of solicitor were not as much a surprise to the on-looking public as the continued leniency of the judges hearing the evidence against Flint, which was often as clear and damning as could be provided.

Rumours abounded of certain payments and favours granted to these high men of the courts, although this talk did not have any proof behind it and was never spoken aloud to those in authority. More steadfast gossip however concerning the depth of the relationship between Flint and Redditch was common knowledge and even talk of certain 'favours' given to Redditch by his ward and further talk of these favours being recorded photographically was often the talk of the local pubs and drinking houses. It was only the continual threat that these images would find their way into the hands of Mrs Redditch that kept little James out of the hands of the law.

These past indiscretions and their recording on photographic plate were however, something that he did not need rely on for a living. A tall, skinny youth, he would often be seen during the day wandering the streets in search of men with fat pockets ripe for dipping. It was not for pick-pocketing that he was well known to the police for however. Being slim as he was and due to his former life as a small wretch working the chimneys of central and west London, James had a natural and well-practiced skill at squeezing himself through the tightest of spaces. This talent came in particularly useful for his night-time occupation of house burglary, something which he had acquired a taste for as a sweep's apprentice. Both his day and night occupations and the success he achieved at them, made him popular with the fences and less reputable pawn brokers in the area. He was never short of a shilling or two and had begun to develop his own gang of street boys all of whom saw him as a role model.

Mary Tanner, a local prostitute, discovered a shadowy figure crouched over Flint's half-eaten corpse as she descended some steps in an alleyway off Hope Street, near to where she lived, as she made her way home from a 'hard night's work'. She was, by all accounts drunk and the shock of her discovery caused her to the misfortune of falling down the remaining steps and into the body of Flint. Her state of inebriation and the lack of street lighting in such an area did not prevent her from realising what it actually was that she had fallen into. For as she fell and landed in the bloody remains, she reached out to grab something to help her up and found herself holding a forearm, complete with the nimble hand of a pickpocket. Her screams could be heard three streets away, it was not long before a small crowd, and two members of the local police joined her. She claimed to have cried with joy when the police came to her aid, although it was said that if they had arrived any earlier they would have found her, soaked through with his blood and rifling through the pockets of what was left of the young lad.

The constables attending the scene of the murder immediately recognised the mutilated boy, as they had enjoyed the pleasure of his company at their cells on numerous occasions. Bartholomew Weeks, the senior of the two men was said to have remarked how he knew that it was the Flint lad because;

"Even in a state of death, the lad had ruddy cheeks and the smirk of a villain who was used to getting one over on the police."

Inspector Fred Draper visited the scene within the following hour and was overheard to state that;

"The manner of the boy's death and the state of his body bear many similarities to previous murders. This added to the fact that it would appear that Flint's head has been torn completely from the rest of his body, through no other weapon other than the hands of the assailant, would also link the killing to another open case involving a father and son recently butchered."

I went from George's parlour on to 'The Alice'. I wished to see Bethany and I wished to inform her of the results of my discussion with Mr Holdsworth and to share the next stages of my investigations with her. I had decided to make her a full partner in my quest whilst sat in the wet undergrowth outside the asylum awaiting the opening of the train station. Her conduct and composure in the performance as my alleged wife, as well as the understanding which we shared regarding the death of our loved ones made me feel that I was able to trust her. I had thought of including her father in this 'circle of knowledge' but felt that the time was not yet right for this. In truth, I was a little apprehensive of discussing my encounters with the dead or the supposition that the murders were caused by a demonic possession. The fear that others may question my sanity would only cause disruption to the task in hand.

I sat in the pub, on the stool which I could have probably claimed for my own, waiting for Tom to take over from his barmaid and start to tend the bar. He had been out when I arrived, taking Bethany to meet a friend so that she may restart her charitable duties visiting the poor children of the area. Tom had arrived back a half hour earlier but gone straight upstairs to speak to Anne and let her know that her niece was safe and back into her normal routine, something which Anne would be greatly pleased to hear.

I had nursed the same beer since my arrival over an hour ago, the thought of drinking with any kind of purpose still a sickening thought. I was considering going home when Tom appeared from the door at the end of the bar.

"Sib, how are you?" he said reaching under the bar for a glass and pouring himself a beer. "Do you want another? Bethany tells me you had quite a day out."

A wave of panic ran through me. "She told you where we went?"

"Not exactly, she said that you took her to a stately home outside London and you spent the day wandering the gardens, you had said that the house belonged to a friend of yours. You really are a dark horse, Sib. I never knew you mixed with the upper classes. Now, how about that beer?"

I felt able to breathe again and felt even more secure in sharing my plans with Bethany later. I forced a convincing laugh.

"You would be surprised who I have been mixing with of late, Tom." This was a statement that held more truth than I had planned. "I shall not take another drink, I have work today I find that beer makes it far too easy to delay and defer. I hear Bethany is out feeding the street kids, do you know when she will be back? I would like to speak to her if I could."

"I expect her back within the hour. She is with her friend Rose, who has promised me that she will keep the closest of eyes on her." He looked at me inquisitively, "What are the pair of you up to?"

"Nothing suspicious, Tom I can assure you. I am simply trying to plan for Niko and Father's funeral," The lie came naturally from me, and I wondered later whether I was becoming too adept at devising falsehoods. "I have been to see George Woodrow," I continued, "Father and Niko's bodies have been released to him and I am planning for the funeral. I wished to include Bethany in the planning, if you saw it fit."

"I see, of course, of course. If she is happy to do so." he replied, obviously not expecting as serious an answer from me. "It is good that she seems to be addressing Nik's death now. In those days before you came to visit her I admit I was worried that she had lost all hope completely, but there is something about her now, as if she has a purpose of some kind. Whatever it is you have done, I am grateful."

I was not sure exactly what I had actually done, other than providing her with the opportunity to assist me. The fact that she had shown such a change of attitude in her behaviour and shade in her countenance was something, which I could only take partial responsibility for. I do admit, however that I had found her assistance so far to be as much as a driving factor behind my enthusiasm and perseverance as anything that came from me internally.

I spent the next hour in the company of Tom; talking of local gossip and discussing my lack of plans for Father's parlour and business. Although usually quick to perceive an opportunity for making additional income I had not yet given any thought to what to do with the property. I was sure that I did not wish to return there, as I had already decided long ago that my next move would be to a location more central to the city, but any thought of sale or lease of the building was far from my mind at present.

Eventually our conversation turned to death. He had heard news of the Hope Street murder but could shed no further light on the manner of the boy's death or the description given by Mary Tanner and could add nothing more to what had come from the loud and much used mouth of Vance Crocker. It would seem that if I wished to know any more information which would lead to the killer I would have to hear it from Mary herself.

When Bethany finally entered the pub, it was nearly six o'clock and I had begun to give up hope of seeing her, coming to the conclusion that I would have to hunt down the unfortunate Miss Tanner by myself. As she walked through the wood and glass door, she sighted me sat at the bar in discussion with her father. Her face broke into a wide smile as she approached.

"I was just beginning to think that you would not be returning to-night." I said, standing from my stool. "Please tell me that you have not overfed the urchins too much. They will start to expect you to wait on them hand and foot, you know."

"I could never over feed them," she smiled. "There is not enough food in the whole of London that would begin to tackle the hunger that they are forced to abide. I hope that I have not kept you too long in the company of Dad. He can be a terrible bore."

I looked to Tom, and reached over the bar to slap him on the back.

"I would never tire of speaking to your father, Bethany Finnan, and your cruelty to him is a demonstration of the goodness within his soul that he is able to bear the likes of you for a daughter." Tom laughed and wandered to the other end of the bar to serve someone, muttering to himself about disrespectful children. As soon as his back was turned and he moved out of earshot, Bethany came close to me and whispered in my ear.

"I have been worried about you, Sib. You must tell me what happened to you in that terrible place. I have been out of my mind with fear."

Beth's closeness was a shock to me although, I should admit, not one which was uncomfortable. I laid my hand on her arm and spoke, my voice low.

"There is much I must tell you, Beth. This is not the time or place, however. I would ask that you come out with me this evening. We have a person to find and the search will give me the opportunity to tell you all. Are you able to come out with me? I promise that it will not be anywhere near as disturbing as our last outing."

"Of course, I would be available. Shall we go now?" her voice seemed eager, almost insistent. "I will only have to let Dad know, he will be fine if I am in your company."

I agreed and, after providing assurances to Tom that we would not be out too late, we left 'The Alice' and headed out on a tour of the drinking houses of Whitechapel. As we walked out of the door I looked back at Tom behind the bar. He gave me a warm smile and mouthed the words 'Thank you.'

As soon as the 'Alice's' door closed behind us Beth excitedly pulled on my arm demanding to know what happened. Her behaviour was like one would imagine an over eager puppy to be when their master finally returns home. I bade her to calm down so that I may tell her my news.

"It would seem, Bethany," I intoned keeping my voice as low as possible so as not to attract the attention of those passing by in the street. "That Mr Holdsworth feels that there are forces at work here, the murder of our loved ones are similar in act to those which he claims to have committed."

"How did you find him?" She asked. "Was he truly crazed and wild?"

"I fear that the state of his mind was disturbed somewhat. There is no doubting that he suffers from some kind of lunacy but, I felt that there was some truth and sanity to what he said."

"But he did commit the murders as he claimed?"

"Yes I believe he did, but there was more to his story than initially meets the eye. I think that there is an element of control over him by powers beyond any normal man understands and that these same powers have returned to bring death and murder." I stopped walking and looked at her in the eyes. "I will be placing my trust in you, Bethany, and there are things that I will tell you and things that I may say, that you will find strange and fearful." I reached out and held her hands within mine. "I care for you as I would care for any member of my family, and I want you to know that if you do not wish to continue with this task, then I am willing to continue alone." She stared into my eyes for a moment, before frowning.

"Stupid man." Her voice had an anger to it although I judged it more to be patronisation. "There is no way on this earth that I would let this continue without me. I am invaluable to you in this and I will prove it to be so." She smiled and we continued our walk. "So tell me. Where are we going?"

"I am sorry to say that I am taking you on a tour of the pubs and drinking establishments of the area. We are looking for the woman who claims to have seen the murderer about his business last night."

"You mean Mary Tanner?" she said, in a matter of fact way which made me stop my stride once again.

"Yes." I struggled to contain my shock. "How did you ..?"

"I am not deaf, Sib," she laughed, "and I have been hearing of nothing else all day. Murder and death makes people talk. The streets are full of the stories of how Mary fell and landed on the dead boy. Come with me, Mr Darke, I will take you to her." I joined in her laughter and we continued our walk heading in the direction of 'The Two Brewers'.

As we walked into the pub, it was plain to see that Mary was enjoying her moment of fame. She was easily identifiable, sat on a table in the corner surrounded by a small crowd, all hanging on her every word. Bethany smiled at me knowingly; it was just as she had predicted, Mary was regaling to all who would hear her of the 'pale beast who fed on children's flesh', whilst happily accepting the drinks being bought for her which she claimed she required for her nerves.

There was a booth by the window free and Bethany went to sit down after telling me that she only wanted water to drink. As the daughter of a landlord she claimed to have seen the best and worst of people who had taken too much, and did not wish to show these sides of herself to all and sundry. She was not an aggressive abstainer though and never tried to push her own moral laws on others. As she told Niko, Father and I once over dinner,

"Drunkards have given me too much laughter and entertainment over the years, but I prefer to be the audience rather than the fool on stage."

I bought myself a beer and took our drinks over to the booth where I sat next to her.

"We shall wait until the clamouring masses die down and we have the opportunity to speak to her more privately." I said in a low voice, "for now, I am afraid you must put up with me alone."

"That is not the hardship that you claim it to be, although it can be a test of nerves and patience. Now, tell me do you have money with you?" I thought for a moment about the contents of my wallet, I did not wish to take it out of my jacket pocket and start counting large notes in front of some of the less reputable patrons.

"I have means enough to buy the information if you think it will be necessary to do so."

"Knowing Mary as I do, I think that you will need to be free with your expenses if you wish to hear anything not already told." Bethany stood and walked over to where Mary held court. She made her way to Mary's side and, holding her hand over her mouth, bent down to whisper something in her ear. Upon hearing what Beth had to say, Mary looked over at me and laughed. She muttered something back to Beth and although I do not know exactly what was said I would wager that it were coarse, as Bethany immediately burst into laughter and went very red in her cheeks.

I shared her embarrassment, feeling the colour rising within me also. Wishing to extricate myself from the situation, I looked around and noticed that I was being watched by a tall bearded man at the bar. He did not look like a policeman, but I could not discount the idea that Draper was still having me followed. My eyes dropped down towards my drink and avoided any further eye contact with either Mary or the watcher. When I finally looked up, I saw that both Bethany and Mary were sat opposite me, both smiling at my discomfort.

"Yes, I can see what you mean about him. Beth," Mary Squawked. "Easy to shame and fun to tease. Just like a little boy." I cleared my throat at her directness and tried to take control of the situation.

"I understand that you witnessed a murder this morning, Miss Tanner, and I would like to know the details of this if you could. I am not the police but have an interest in the killing and would pay for your assistance in my inquiries."

She giggled at this. "Oh, then I am full of information should the money be right. It was as I came down the steps to my lodgings that I first heard a noise from the cobbles below." It was plain to see that this was not the first time she had performed this story today and would probably be performing it many times more as long as the drinks came to her. "It was like the sound of a large dog tearing at a bone. As I got nearer, that was when I saw it ... it was a man, as normal as any other, scruffily dressed and feeding on that poor boy's body."

"When you say, normal as any other," I stepped in. "Can you not give me more information on the character?"

She was obviously put out by my interruption and shot me a hard glare before continuing.

"When he heard me coming he looked up at me. I couldn't see his face too clear, but he had glowing white eyes and was pale, like a ghost. His skin was whiter than a bed sheet and his mouth was red and wet where his terrible teeth had torn at the flesh of that poor boy. He wore a white shirt which was open to his stomach and there was a marking on his chest like a star. He growled at me then, he did, and ran off, quicker than I have ever seen a man run; springing away like a wild dog, into the darkness."

I raised my hand and stopped her again, "The Star?" I asked. "What did it look like?"

She shrugged, "It was just a star, that's what I told the Inspector. He never offered to pay for my information though. He might have heard more if he had." I removed a hand from my pocket and placed a one pound note on the table before me. The sight of it made her smile.

"Very pretty," she said. "But I think that what I have to say may be worth more to those that wants to hear it." I stared at her facial expression and made a mental note to try to replicate it next time I played cards. She would have made a most excellent match for anyone at the gaming table.

I removed my hand and reached into my pocket again before placing a further two pounds on the table. The widening of Mary's eyes told me that I had reached and possibly exceeded her expectations. I also noted that the bearded man at the bar had moved and was now sat in the next booth. I ignored his presence and continued.

"Now, perhaps this amount will allow your memory to be taken to last night in the alleyway. Miss Tanner, I would be grateful if you could provide further information on the detail of the star that you saw."

"Well, of course." she beamed, reaching out her hands across the table to take the notes from me. They did note move from my grasp however, as my fingers remained firm in their hold. I do not know which look I preferred at this point, it could have been the shock and disappointment worn by Mary as the notes did not come her way, or the smile which shone across Bethany's face as she realised that I was not to be taken for fool completely.

"Be warned." said I, keeping my voice as solemn in its tone as I could manage. "I am not some mark to be taken for his money with no return. I will gladly give you these notes, Mary, but should the words that you speak next prove to be positive in their assistance to me there will be a further three more coming your way soon after." There was further show of disbelief on

Mary's face, as I am sure that she expected a threat rather than the offer of further reward. This incredulity turned to a wide smile though as I loosened my finger's grip on the money allowing her to take it and put it within a hidden pocket in the shoulder of her dress. She leant forward so that only Bethany and I could hear her.

"The star on his chest was topped with a crown and there were numbers in its centre." My ears pricked at this statement and I found myself leaning closer so that her next words were heard most clearly. "The numbers were four and two. They do not mean anything to me, but I am sure that in the right hands, this information would be useful."

I sat back and smiled, something, which I admit; my facial muscles were unused to, but a smile nonetheless.

When I heard these details, I felt sure that the following afternoon's photographic appointment with the bodies of my Father and brother would give me all the final clues I required to be able to hunt down the killer. Father had always been a particularly observant man and I hoped that he would be able to fill in the missing pieces of the profile, which I was beginning to form within my mind.

"Mary," I whispered. "If you were not so drunk and me so shy, I would lean across this table and kiss you." This comment made her giggle like a young maid and she stood.

"I will expect those other notes in good time then?" she asked as she went to leave.

"I will deliver them myself, when I attain my goal." I said, and watched as she made her way back to her table a happier, wealthier woman.

"Does your smug exterior bode well for our investigation, Sibelius?" Beth asked, an edge of excitement in her voice.

"It does, Beth. It does." I lifted my glass and drained the beer which, while not being the best of drinks, slipped down with ease. "Finish your drink and I will take you back to your father while the hour is still early."

"But you have not yet told me the full story of the asylum yesterday! You promise much but deliver nothing by way of knowledge." Beth snapped in exasperation.

"Patience, Bethany. Let me get you home and I will tell you all, and much more besides, to-morrow morning. Come to my studio before lunch and I will widen your knowledge before we have a family reunion in the afternoon."

"Family reunion?" she asked loudly and I saw the bearded man in the booth glance over. I motioned to Bethany to be quiet, stood and held out my hand, before leading her past him. As we passed, I looked down and noted that he had hardly touched his drink. As we stepped out of the doors into the cold, evening air I pulled Bethany close and bade her take my arm. "I promise you." I whispered. "You will know more than you want to by the end of to-morrow. I will hold nothing back."

Her lips parted as if to ask further questions but she stopped herself and we walked in comfortable silence back to her father and the safety of her home. There I spoke my goodbyes to her with reassuring oaths that the next day would bring answers. I strode home with purpose, noting that the new shadow which I had gained remained within sight of me whenever I looked over my shoulder.

It mattered not to me that Draper had lied, I would go home to rest and prepare myself to be reunited with my loved ones, if only for a short time.

11
Saying Goodbye

The day that Grandfather died was the saddest day of my life. I never wept so many tears and sobbed or as hard as I did on that dark September evening. To those that said that I was devoid of any sense of emotion or feeling, I would say that you do not know me and you did not see the wracking howls which came forth from me as I knelt by the deathbed of the person who I loved most in the world.

He had been growing steadily weaker for a number of weeks but, in the summer of 1867, it seemed that his downturn accelerated at an alarming pace. His ability to move around the house slowed, his appetite grew poor and, worst of all, his memory began to fail him.

I spent many hours in his company in those last dark days, assisting him to walk when he felt able, or just sitting by his side and trying to keep his mind active, his memories intact. It felt as if I was not just losing him, as I knew that his end was near, but I was losing my link to a magical world of stories, where heroes fought evil queens and where gods and immortals ruled justly and with wisdom. This alternate place, where Grandfather had taken me since I was old enough to understand his tales, was now a stark contrast to the world in which I now found myself. The harsh reality of life in Whitechapel with all of its filth and brutality was a sobering draught to take, after a childhood where I believed every story that this gentle and wise man told me.

On the morning of his death we all knew that this would be his time of passing, and that by the next day he would be gone from our lives in the physical sense and remain only as a sweet memory for us to talk about and remember. Even Mother was quiet and restrained that day, not raising her voice to any of us and silently carrying on with her chores whilst Father, Niko and I spent our last hours with him. He told us many stories before he left that day, stories which we had heard before countless times over. Some however, appearing through the thick fog that was now his memory, we had never heard him speak of before and this made his imminent demise even more painful, as we wondered how many tales still to tell would be lost to us that day.

The story I remember most clearly was not new but a tale that had always held particular poignancy and meaning to me. It was the tale which both Niko and I loved him to tell us the most. Even though it held no great adventure or action. It was Niko who asked him to tell it to us one last time as he lay in his bed slowly failing. The story was to be, and fittingly so, Grandfather's last.

His voice, though weak and faltering, was as deep as it always was whenever he told us a tale. Father, Niko and I sat at his side while he recounted to us the story of the Swan of Tuonela.

"Lemminkäinen travelled north to Pohjola, a desolate and desperate place, barren and frozen with harsh sweeping winds and grey skies which made you believe that you had wandered into the underworld. Lemminkäinen bore these lands though, fighting the wind ever northwards to reach his goal. He ventured forwards towards the mountain within which the Queen of Pohjola resided.

"Louhi was a potent and compelling woman, an enchantress of many dark and awful powers, who ruled this bleak land with a cruel, hard heart which caused her subjects to fear her but also to promise to love and revere her. They called her the Witch Queen, a title that she did not attempt to disavow, and the tales were many of her destruction and treachery to those who dared to disobey or disrespect her. She was said to be able to change shape, to take the form of others both human and animal, and it was through this deceit that many of her enemies or those that spoke against her met their end. It was told that she was the most beautiful and seductive of women, although only her most trusted subjects were kept near enough to witness this. She lured powerful warriors to her and enticed them into her bed to provide her with daughters. Once used, these warriors were discarded; broken husks of what they once were, drained of their souls and sucked dry of their wits.

"It was of her many daughters that she was most proud and that she gave what little love she had in her heart. All of the princesses were beauteous and blessed with heavenly looks. Many a brave man had travelled to Pohjola to seek the hand of one of the daughters of Louhi, but few succeeded. To win the slender hand of one of the maidens of Pohjola the suitor must first complete a task set by the Queen herself. Each task was carefully devised to be almost impossible to achieve, and even if the potential husband came close to completing a task, Louhi would often use her magic to ensure that the attempt ended in failure.

"Strong was Lemminkäinen, strong of body but also strong within his heart. He was brave beyond compare, although this bravery was often mixed with a reckless nature which would bring him into great peril and terrible danger. Lemminkäinen had heard of the daughters of Louhi and wanted one for his own to be his wife. The idea of having to complete a near impossible task, made even more difficult by the treachery of the Queen ensured that he was filled with much greater enthusiasm, for he was confident of his strength and was not in fear of any form of test. He walked, through the ice and the snow, through the deadly landscape that made up the land of Pohjola towards the mountain where the Queen awaited with her daughters. After many weeks of hard terrain he finally reached his goal, the mountain at the top of the world, the place where Ilmarinen the blacksmith had forged the magical Sampo, the all powerful instrument of the gods, which could create and rule time itself, and which turned continuously to craft the ages.

"When Lemminkäinen entered the doors of the mountain and stepped into the halls of Louhi's palace he was met with the respect and esteem that the Queen gave to all potential suitors who braved her lands to ask for the hand of her daughters. Louhi was glad when suitors came as it gave her entertainment to tease, to play and to destroy those piteous fools lured to her walls by dreams of beauty. When brave Lemminkäinen saw the daughters of Louhi, he was not disappointed, a multitude of fair princesses stood before him and, despite each maiden's beauty he chose the daughter whom he wished to marry.

"Louhi smiled when she saw his choice, for she had devised a most difficult task for the man who would bid to win her. Louhi told Lemminkäinen to journey to Tuonela, the underworld, where he would find, gliding around the island of the dead, a swan. Lemminkäinen's task was simple, take the life of the swan, and return to Pohjola with its lifeless body. The warrior was pleased with this task for there was no better bowman in the whole of the Kalevala.

"When he reached the banks of the Tuonela River he saw the black swan, his quarry, floating peacefully, moving with grace and beauty in the water between the land of Kalevala and the underworld, the place where the dead reside and stay forever, prevented from leaving by the dreaded beast Surma. Lemminkäinen took the longbow off his back and notched an arrow, drawing the swan into his sights. As he pulled back on the bow's string however, he heard the sound of singing, a haunting wordless song which told him of love and adoration, of heartache and the troubles of human existence. The song was sung by the swan itself and, as the tears began to sting Lemminkäinen's eyes, he faltered in his task, unable to loose the arrow and end the sound of the beautiful swan.

"Across the waters in the underworld, Tuoni the Lord of Tuonela saw the young warrior on the banks of Kalevala, his bow set to kill this beautiful being which inhabited the waters around his island. In fury, he released a water snake which swam across the river and onto the banks of Kalevala biting Lemminkäinen as he sat bow in hand. The water snake's poison was strong and, dropping his bow, brave Lemminkäinen's heart stopped beating and he fell into the waters of the Tuonela. There, within the water, his body was dashed against the rocks and torn into a thousand pieces, scattered in the current and sinking to the river bed.

"It was only through the love and commitment of his mother that Lemminkäinen was returned. She heard of his fate and travelled to Tuonela to retrieve him. She dredged the waters and brought forth the shattered bones and ripped sinew, sewing his skin together and singing the ancient songs of healing. Even with the most powerful of magical songs, however the corpse of the young warrior was devoid of all life, a hollow shell without soul or mind. And so the mother of Lemminkäinen sent a bee to the great halls of Ukko to fetch a drop of honey that would return her beloved son to life.

"Lemminkäinen awoke but was not the same reckless and foolhardy warrior that he was before travelling to Pohjola. He lived out the rest of his days a broken man, forever haunted by the song of the Swan of Tuonela."

There were tears in all of our eyes as Grandfather reached the end of the tale. The tears were not for poor Lemminkäinen, nor were they for the sadness of the story. The salt water which ran from each of our eyes was for our Grandfather, for so many years the head of our family and the beacon of strength and happiness in an unforgiving and cruel world.

We sat in silence for a while. Grandfather had closed his eyes and his breath had become ragged and restless. Niko and I looked to Father for reassurance that this was not to be the end of our most loved, but Father was unable to provide that for us. For in truth, he himself was losing the one constant that had been there for him throughout his life, the wise and kind man who had brought him up alone when the rest of their family were lost.

In those last moments Grandfather spoke to each of us in turn. To Niko he said to be strong and to grow well and find happiness in the world, for there was happiness to be found in even the darkest of places. To Father he told him to be there for his sons and to protect them with all the strength in his body, for children are a blessing and will carry the love and the stories of their families with them through the generations.

To me, his words were a riddle, one which I have struggled to understand and has been the cause of many choices that I have made in my life, choices which I have since regretted.

"When the time comes for you, Sibelius." He whispered in little more than a cracked wisp. "Do not falter in your task as Lemminkäinen once did. Block your ears to the sweet sound of the swan; do not listen to the song that will break your heart, for it will not help you in your task."

Grandfather's hand stiffened at this point enclosing mine. He held my hand so tight that had it been at any other time it would have felt as though the bones in my fingers were about to break. This was the strength of his love though, a love that was leaving. The warmth within him flowed into me and it felt as if my eyes were going to explode, such was the pressure within them.

At that moment, I felt as if my heart had stopped and it seemed as though all time had frozen within the room. It had not, and it was not my heart that had stopped beating. Time moved onwards taking Grandfather away from us. Away from me. My life until this point, though hard, had been filled with the love of this dear man who had taught me so much and I knew, that now that he had gone, a piece of me taken with him.

I do not know why I thought of Grandfather's final tale whilst I sat at my desk and waited for the knocking at my door which would signal the arrival of Bethany. Although I thought of him every day, I did not often think of his dying day, as the memory was too painful to continually relive.

I had spent the morning, sorting the many files in my study. Within each file were written notes on countless numbers of people, the amalgamation of each of the background stories that I had made and kept. What some would see as an obsessive act, was a vital tool for investigating and preparing me for business interactions. I made it a ritual to research each person that I came into contact with, through discussions and bribery with hackney drivers, barmaids, servants and associates. I did not feel comfortable attending a meeting if I did not know as much about a person's life as I could find out. Kept within the shelves of my study were the life stories, secrets and rumours of lords and ladies, drunkards and whores. In the wrong hands the information that I kept could shame and destroy, but to me they were the tools I needed. Indeed, such was their power that I had left instructions for Tom that upon my death he was to ensure that they would be burned and lost to anyone other than me.

A rapping sound from the bottom of the stairs told me that Bethany had arrived and I skipped down them to let her in. As I opened the door to her she pushed her way inside with some force, barging me out of the way and shutting the door behind her.

"Sibelius!" she gasped. "I have been followed here by a large and most frightening man. He made no secret of his task; he did not stray from within twenty feet of me since I left home. Why are the police interested in me?"

I took her hand and led her into the studio where I went to the window, moving the curtain to look out across the street. There, stood next to the bearded man who had trailed me back from 'The Brewers' last night, was a tall, smartly dressed man who bore a large scar down the left hand side of his face. His arms were long and heavy and ended with hands which when fisted would probably be good substitutes for mallets. I could see why Beth would be in such fear, as the sight of him made me feel quite unnerved.

"Come, take a seat, Beth." I said, sitting her down on the long sofa in the corner of the room. "I was followed home from the pub last night and I can only assume that they are the police, although they look different from any officers of the law who I have seen before. You will have been followed because I have been in your company, and for that I am sorry." I glanced again out of the window and saw that they were talking animatedly, obviously discussing Bethany and I.

"You are safe with me for now," I soothed, "and I will come up with a plan to protect you before you leave here. For now I have much to tell you, some of it will shock you and some you may feel is pure fantasy, but I can assure you that I will only speak the truth."

She seemed calmed somewhat by my words and appeared to relax in my presence.

"I have been wondering all evening about what you have planned today, Sibelius. You must tell me as well as letting me know everything that you know about the murders."

Her face was a stone block, her eyes hardened on to me. There would be no more attempts at delaying telling her the full story; I could not put it off any longer. Sitting by her side, I took her hands within my own.

"My dear Bethany," I began, although I did not know what words would soon be leaving my lips. "I will tell you things now that you will find hard to believe, such is their oddness and lack of connection with any kind of normality." There was no movement on her face, and so I decided to be a bit more brutal in my warnings. "I may make you begin to doubt my sanity, and you may be scared by what I say, but I can assure you that, terrible though it is, everything that I say is true." I looked to her again and still saw no sign of fear or worry.

And so I told her all, I told her about the dead girl and of how she warned me of Surma. I told her who Surma was and how this was all linked to Finnish folklore and tales told to me by Grandfather when we were children. I showed her the letter from Father detailing the death of Johannes and of how he saw the beast fleeing from Holdsworth's body. In all of the time I spoke to her she listened attentively and quietly, not saying a word, not questioning the bizarreness of it all and not showing any sign of disbelief. As I finished I looked to her, searching for some kind of sign that she believed me and that she did not think me a madman, raving and paranoid, claiming to be able to commune with the dead through the lens of my camera. Finally she spoke;

"You can be quite the storyteller when you wish, Sib." she said, a smile forming on her face. "But a convincing one, nonetheless."

"Then you believe me?" I asked, feeling happier that I had told somebody the truth of it all at last.

"I believe a large part of it, Sibelius. I believe that there is a crazed killer, taking the lives of children and I believe that this man, whoever he is may be possessed or controlled in some way."

"...and my conversations with the dead?" I pressed

"I believe in ghosts, I believe that there are things about our world that we do not understand, but the thought of you speaking to dead children through your camera is probably a step too far for my imagination." My face dropped. I tried to hide my feelings and, to be truthful, Bethany trusted in my story much more than many others would. She could see my disappointment.

"Oh, Sibelius. This does not mean that I think of you as some kind of lunatic, moreover, I think you are one of the sanest people that I have ever met. Your moods can be extreme in their limits though, Sib. You have to remember that I have known you all of my life, I have known you to be dark and sullen to the point of ignorance, fleeting quickly to being excitable and as full of life as a child. These past few weeks have been an awful test for all of us, and no more so than for you. We have all had a terrible shock and we all find our own way of dealing with such situations. I think that these …meetings with those who have passed are just how you have seen best to manage."

I laughed aloud at her most heartfelt speech. Her level of understanding was a blessing, in that she had accepted so much more than I had expected of her. It would seem that this young lady would continue to amaze and delight me on a regular basis.

"My dear Bethany," I coughed, trying to contain my joy somewhat. "To know that you are with me on this and that you even begin to believe such random ideas, gives me more hope for our success in our task than I have ever had before. To any other person in the world I would be called a madman and taken to that awful place that we visited not three days ago. There I would spend my days being taken by the attendants to perform in a cage for those ghouls and harridans who pose as members of polite society." I could tell that the memory of that experience still held some pain for Bethany as she winced at the thought of me locked in a cage like an exhibit in a freak show. She did not yet share my humour of the situation in which I could have found myself and so I decided not to press the point any further. I clasped her hands firmly and with warmth.

"Beth, if the only doubt that you have about my experiences over the past few weeks are the fact that I can converse with the dead through my camera, then I am pleased beyond compare and hope to be able to remedy the situation this very day."

Almost perfectly on cue there was a knock at the door in the hallway and I looked out of the window to see that George Woodrow and his assistant had arrived in their carriage with the subjects of my afternoon's photography session. I leapt to my feet.

"Bethany," I smiled my voice full of nervous excitement. "I ask you to trust me and my actions for just a little longer and you will see for yourself just how crazed I really am." The look on her face was one of polite and graceful bemusement, but she was smiling at me and I found myself meeting her gaze with my own and stopping for a brief but precious moment. "Bear with me, Beth. Bear with me!" I called as I left the studio and went to answer the door.

I could see from Bethany's face as we brought the two caskets into the room that she had deduced what was going to take place. She stood nervously as the boxes were placed carefully on the floor. After assuring George and his apprentice that I would be able to manage with the moving and placement of the bodies by myself, I led them to the door, asking that they return in two hours to collect them. After agreeing that the following Tuesday would be a suitable day for which to carry out the burial, George left to speak to St Mary's and make the necessary arrangements. Father had long since set aside space for us next to Grandfather, Johannes and Mother. Their placement being one benefit of being in the trade and knowing the right people.

"If you would prefer not to be here during this I would understand," I said, motioning towards the caskets within which my family were held. "I know that you have always been tolerant of my business, but that it is something which you do not fully understand. Within these wooden shrouds are my Father and our dear Niko, if the sight of them would bring you pain then I would not be offended if you wished to leave." I approached her, taking hold of both of her hands and looking her in the eye. "I thought, perhaps with all the sensibilities of an uncouth man, that you would wish to say goodbye."

Her hands shook within my own, but her jaw remained firm as she answered.

"I am strong enough to see him, Sib, and I thank you for the thought. Please let us do this so that we can move them swiftly to find peace." I am not sure if she fully realised that if things continued as I predicted she would actually be able to speak to Niko, rather than to his inanimate body. I continued anyway, unscrewing the lid of the nearest coffin to me and pulling it away.

Bethany let out a small gasp and I quickly turned to see if she was still comfortable with the process. Without a word she waved me on and I looked down into the box before me. There, laying cold before me, was my father. His eyes closed and his face serene. There had been a small amount of makeup put on him at Woodrow's, probably by George's wife, as this was her area of expertise. His white beard was trimmed and neat, his hair combed neatly across his head and held in place with a discreetly hidden metal clip. He wore his best black suit with a pale blue silk necktie, placed with care around his collar. To the casual observer he would have looked like a man of advancing years who had been asleep, and I was thankful for the effort which George had obviously made for his friend, creating such a peaceful image for me to see.

Crouching down, I placed my hands underneath Father's shoulders and knees slowly lifting him out of the casket. Despite my slim demeanour, I always ensured that I retained the strength necessary to be able to lift the dead weight of a body and Father's was by no means the heaviest that I had lifted. I carried him over to the sofa which I had placed on the other side of the studio opposite my camera. Once there, I placed him in a sitting position, using well placed cushions to ensure that he stayed upright. Placing a short rod down the back of his collar, I tied a piece of string around his neck to keep his head upright. I had undergone this procedure countless times in the past with members of other people's family, but it was only now, when in close contact with this man who I had known and loved for all of my life, did I appreciate the indignity of it. My last act was to open his eyes.

Of all the parts of my work this was the moment that I usually felt any type of emotion. The body can be dressed, painted and positioned, to imitate life as easy as it would be to mould clay, but the eyes could never lie, they took on a milky sheen that prevented them from showing any light of life. As I looked into Father's eyes momentarily, I felt a surge of tears rushing towards my own and I forced myself to look away, lest I broke down into sobbing which would make me unable to continue. Control and fortitude were the words which revolved through my mind, as I held myself in check and continued my preparations.

With Father in place, I approached the dwelling of Niko and began the task of unscrewing the lid. Panicked thought ran through my head, as I remembered the last time that I had seen him. Strung up by his ankles, his throat ripped and torn, his head separated from the rest of his body. I silently prayed that George had taken as much care with the reconstruction of my brother as he had done with Father. As I pulled the lid aside I could see that my worries were unfounded as my poor younger brother's face came into view. I heard a little noise from behind me and glanced back to see Bethany, her hand covering her mouth, seating herself so as not to fall to the floor.

As with Father, the Woodrow's had managed a sterling job of returning my brother to some semblance of normality. His eyes were closed in sleep and his skin, although pale, was as smooth and unworried as porcelain. He wore a high necked shirt underneath a brown woollen suit and, on closer inspection; I could see that the height of the collar was intentional to cover up a countless number of small stitches which held his head in place. This needlework, I knew, was completed by George Woodrow himself and I silently thanked him for the time and concentration that he must have put into this job, considering they had only taken ownership of the bodies the previous evening.

As I lifted my baby brother out of the coffin, I was amazed by just how light he was, my mind was taken back to the many rides on my back which he enjoyed when we were children, his happy smiling face full of laughter and light. I positioned him next to Father and, with a little more care than I had with Father for fear of tearing any stitching; I ensured that his head remained upright and that his newly opened eyes were looking towards the camera.

There they sat; the last two members of my family, dressed in their finest clothes and awaiting the camera. I admit to a great deal of fear and trepidation at this point, fear of starting the process, fear of facing my family again, of hearing of their murder, but most of all fear of saying goodbye to them for the last time.

I walked to the other side of the room and slowly took a seat next to Beth for a moment. To take stock of the process and to look to the state of her emotions and her control over her grief. We did not look at each other, but sat side by side gazing upon our loved ones.

"Are you managing with this, Beth?"
"I am."
"... and do you wish me to continue?"
"I do."
"Then I shall start."

I stood and walked to the tripod which held my camera and, carefully placing my head under the cloth, I looked through the viewfinder.

As I expected Father and Niko were sat, as alive and breathing as I remembered them the last time I saw them before their murder. Their features were pallid; their eyes slightly glazed but Mr Woodrow had done a wonderful job of making them presentable for photography. I felt tears in my eyes at the sight of them so apparently healthy and alive, but I fought them back. I did not know how long we had together and there was business to discuss.

"Hello, Father. Hello, Nik. I would say 'how are you?', but I think that may be in bad taste." Father looked overwhelmed to hear my voice.

"Sib," gasped Father. "How is it that I can see and hear you? What kind of magic is this?"

"I do not know, Father." I said. "It is beyond my reckoning. However I am glad to have the chance to speak to you one more time."

Niko, seeing Bethany sat behind me, suddenly burst into life, his milky eyes on the edge of tears at being reunited with his fiancé.

"Beth!" he called out. Standing and walking forwards, "Beth, I am sorry. I'm sorry that I have left you." His voice sounded slightly strangled and I wondered if this was an after effect of having his throat torn from him during his murder.

"She cannot hear you, Nik." I halted him in his advance. "To her you are an inanimate corpse sat on a chair, and I appear to be speaking to myself. I will let you speak to her in a moment, but first there are pressing matters to attend to. I need to know the cause of your murder; I need to know who did this to you."

"Of course, dear brother." His voice solemn and serious. "I will try to remain patient, but I need to ask of you. Will you care for her and look after her for me. It is painful to see her again so sad and lost, more painful than death itself."

"You know that she is most dear to me, Nik. Now please, Father. Would you tell me what happened?"

Niko took his seat again and Father began his tale of their death.

"I cannot tell you much about the man who killed us as it was so quick. I was in my bed when I heard a sound coming from downstairs. I lit a candle and went out onto the hall landing and that is when he came at me from the dark of the stairs. He was so quick, so strong, Sib. He moved liked an animal rather than a man, he was well built possibly a military man of some kind by the way he held himself. I knew who it was the moment that I saw him however, I had seen him before on the day that poor Johannes died. Surma has been summoned to the world of the living once again, Sibelius. This is a terrible thing, yes, but worse is to come. They may have set loose a killing machine onto the streets of London but I fear that this is not their final aim, there is a larger goal, one most terrifying and dangerous."

"What is it, Father and who is the source of this terror?"

"That I do not know, Sib, but if the underworld has no gatekeeper, what is to stop the dead from returning to the world of the living? Who is there to prevent those who refuse to take their place in Tuonela from returning? How long however, before those in Tuonela realise that there is no gaoler? Once the truth is found out, the light of life will draw them back like a moth to a candle and the dead will storm back to earth, they will not be able to control themselves. This is what the fools who summoned Surma mean to achieve. Hell on earth, the end of days and apocalypse."

"But who would do such a thing, Father?"

"I do not know, Sib, I truly don't. After Johanne's death I told your Grandfather what I saw, how the beast left the body at the point of death and fled back to Tuonela. We hunted for those responsible but could not get close to Henry Holdsworth to ask where it came from. Whoever they are, they have friends in high places, son. The police kept the murders quiet and the doctors shut Holdsworth away in an asylum, claiming that he was disturbed and that the murders were all part of some elaborate paranoid fantasy. We knew the truth but were unable to act, and now they have begun their quest again."

"I have seen Holdsworth, Father." I indicated. "I went to the asylum where he is kept. He told me of how the beast came to him and mentioned somewhere called 'The Club of Sorrows'. Tell me have you ever heard of such a place?"

"I know nothing of any club of that name, but I did not ever mix in the kind of social circles where gentlemen friends were members of such clubs. I would have thought that it would have been within your area of knowledge, not mine."

"Since speaking to the man I have thought of nothing else, Father. There is not a club in London, renowned or otherwise that I have not heard of. It galls me to think that there is one that lies secret."

Father found this amusing, "Ah, the great Sibelius Darke, flummoxed by a riddle which he should answer without thought. Think on, son. Think on, the answer is within that head of yours somewhere." He stood and opened his arms to me. "If only I could hold you for a last time, Sibelius. It should be a man's right to hug his son and wish him goodbye before he leaves the world, although I am grateful for this opportunity to speak. Come, I fear we must let the young lovers say their piece. We will not speak again, son, but know that we will be thinking of you wherever our spirits alight. Find our killer. Stop the soldier."

"Goodbye, Father. Goodbye Niko," I said choking slightly on the words, "I am missing you." And with that I withdrew my head from the cloth, Father's final words ringing in my ears.

I looked to where they sat, once again dead and cold, lost to me forever. I turned to Bethany who stood by the window watching me.

"So, Beth. Do you believe me now?"

"I don't know, Sib. To me you just seemed to be talking to yourself, a one way conversation with someone you believed to be answering you."

I suspected that this would have been the case, and so I beckoned her over and asked her to place her head under the cloth and look upon Niko and Father through the viewfinder. She did this without question, and as her gaze presumably fell upon them, alive and mobile, she let out a gasp of shock and began a tearful conversation with the man who she loved and who she had planned to marry.

I shall not tell the words which she spoke, for they were private and between her and Niko. They have no place in my story and shall remain forever hers. For twenty minutes I listened to her words, though. Such sad tenderness I cannot begin to understand, as I have never experienced the kind of love and togetherness which they were lucky enough to share between them. Finally, after saying her final goodbyes, she removed her head from the cloth, her face flushed and her eyes red with anguish. A strange sense of relief washed over me as I finally knew that she believed and that it was not just some crazed fantasy of mine, created from madness.

A look of grim determination was set into Bethany's face and she wiped her eyes with her handkerchief and steadied herself.

"Tell me then, Sibelius, What is our next step?" she said in a controlled and level voice.

"I think that for the moment we should divide our efforts and go out seeking information. We have all the details that we need to track down the killer. It is just about asking the right people the right questions."

"What do you mean all the details?"

"There is good reason why I was so happy with the detail that Mary gave us in the Two Brewers last night and Father has just confirmed my suspicions to me. The tattoo that she saw on his chest; the star with the crown and the number forty two, it is a military insignia. Our killer is an ex-military man, a member of the Black Watch and a veteran of Ordashu, I would wager."

"Sibelius, I am lost, how do you know such things?"

"After speaking to Mary last night, I set out early this morning before you arrived and went to see an associate of mine, Stanley Hawkins, a hackney driver who is ex-military himself. From the description that Mary gave I knew that it was a military badge and I knew already that it is the fashion of many soldiers to have their regiment's insignia tattooed onto their arms or chest. It is a sign of their pride, as well as being a way of identifying them should they fall in battle. The star with a crown and the number forty two at the centre stands for the Forty-Second Regiment of Foot, many of whom, Stanley tells me, had the tattoo inscribed on their chest rather than arms due to a nasty rumour regarding the Ashanti's predilection for severing the limbs and head of any of their enemy who fall or are captured in battle. I am informed that the last Ashanti battle that this regiment took part in was at Ordashu three years ago, hence my theory on an ex-serviceman. A man like that should be known to someone, so I think we should ask around and try to get a name."

"I shall ask this evening, if he isn't known to the regulars in the Alice then the street kids may have heard something."

"Good, I shall also start to spread the word and a little cash to see if it loosens lips a little. Promise me though, Beth. If you hear anything that could be of use to us then tell me at once. Do not attempt to tackle him alone. Remember he is a killer and he would have no hesitation in attacking you." I smiled at her to soften the warning a little. "I promised my brother that I would care and look out for you, Bethany Finnan. Caring is not a task that comes naturally to me, but keeping promises is."

"There is more to you than you like to let show, Sib," she said with the most delicate of smiles. "And you may find that if you let go of your hardened shroud a little, that you would yourself see this. Niko told me to make a promise also, and that was to see you safe and happy. So it would seem that our departed loved one has tied us together. Let us keep our promises shall we?"

I laughed at this, firstly from the thought of my brother scheming from beyond the grave to keep us safe, but also because I knew, deep inside me, that no matter how hard we looked out for each other, that the death and heartache had not yet ended, and that it would be all too likely that I for one would not survive. My one true wish however, would be to protect Bethany to the best of my abilities and if this meant giving myself to save her then I would do so in a heartbeat.

"Come then, my unavoidable partner," I declared, holding firm to the mask of happiness and confidence which I was bound to present to her. "Let me take you home to your father so that we may be freed to continue our investigations apart for this evening. I will, of course, be visiting you so that we are able to compare the results of our findings and hopefully have a name and address in common. Only then should we attempt to tackle the situation directly. Are we clear?"

She nodded her assent and watched patiently as I returned Father and Niko to their caskets.

After George and his apprentice came to collect them later that afternoon, we made our way out of the studio. As we strode out into the street, I noted that our large shadows had deserted us for now. I could tell, without a word being spoken between us, that Beth had realised this also and we found ourselves moving, at pace, back to the safety of 'The Alice' before they resumed their duties. There reaching, I spent a short while speaking to Tom and others in the bar over a couple of glasses before heading outwards, into the wilds of the east end, to begin the search for a local veteran of 'The Black Watch'.

As I pondered upon my route for the evening, a similar feeling of excitement and energy filled me, as I skipped down Commercial Street, to that which I had felt when creeping into the asylum through the rear entrance not three days earlier. The thought that I was involved in some kind of 'adventure in detection' gave me strutting confidence and a self-important air that far outweighed any fear of what might be to come.

I should, however, have borne in mind the situation which this puffed up sense of worth and enthusiasm had taken me into when at the asylum. For, as is often the case when one feels that they have clambered to the top of the heap, life, in all of its wicked irony has the unnerving knack of picking you up by the collar and throwing you headlong to the bottom once again.

And so it was that I found myself, within a matter of seconds, swaggering with an inflated sense of ego and nervous energy one moment, and feeling the hard pointed barrel of a pistol in the small of my back the next. Such ignominious humour was something to which I should now have come to expect, as I was led forcibly into a waiting carriage and brought face to face with someone who I really did not anticipate seeing again.

12
A Carriage to Despair

The idea of death is something which I have always held a pragmatic and unspiritual approach to, that is, of course, until I first started communing with those recently deceased through the medium of the camera lens. For as long as I could remember, I had been surrounded by dead people. To me they were just things, hollow shells and barren husks once able to think talk and walk and caused, through ill health, accident or other reasons, to no longer function. I reached this conclusion as a child, from intensive studying of medical books brought to me by Father and visits, as part of the day-to-day running of the funeral service to the infirmary and its morgue. To me, man was simply a collection of working parts, liable to damage or breakage and causing, on a regular basis, the death of the individual.

The inevitability of one's passing is something that I have always been very comfortable with and I can never remember have any kind of internal battle where I wondered about our existence, our purpose or what the meaning of our placement upon this world is. To me, a man could drive himself to insanity toiling with the wherewithal of our role within the universe. This kind of ludicrous contemplation is not for me and never has been. Men like me are driven to get on and get ahead in the world and any thoughts of position and status should be limited to the here, the now and the immediate future, and not drowning in doom laden thoughts of inescapable death and the unavoidable cessation of life.

Despite my love of Grandfather's stories of ancient heroes, powerful and wise gods and different planes of existence, I knew, within my mind that these were stories, nothing more. They were tales created by men to explain the unexplainable, to satisfy their need to know what death meant and to provide the unsure and the anxious that there is a point to it all and that there is a better place for us all to move on to, if we only have faith.

I did not have faith in any god, in spite of the fact that many of my childhood years were spent in and around churches and in the company of those for whom religion was not just an answer to their questions, but the basis for all of the thoughts and actions within their desperate lives. I prided myself on believing in a scientific and realistic point of view. There was no afterlife or better place to go to, we were born, we lived and we died, the end. This maxim, by which I measured all of my beliefs, was simple, straightforward and left no room for thoughts of a great creator or a spiritual journey. That is not to say that I begrudged or looked down from a high place upon others for whom religious belief and the love of some omnipotent being was the core upon which they based their lives. If these thoughts gave them, happiness and helped them to sleep at night, then who was I to belittle them?

I am reminded of the story of John Hamersley, a man for whom religion and the word of the lord was a rod by which he ruled over his large and, for the most part, feral family. Living in three rooms of a large tenement block on Crispin Street near to the market, John had fifteen children of varying ages from new-born to eighteen years old. The supposed mother of the children, Jane Hamersley had spent nearly twenty years of her life carrying unborn babies whilst raising new-borns. Also living in the house were two other women, whose names were never made common knowledge, who assisted Jane in her child rearing, household and wifely duties. Rumours abound regarding the extent of these lodging women's duties to John, although this was never proven.

John Hamersley was well known throughout the local area as a coster; he would be seen and heard pushing his handcart through the street selling the fruit and vegetables that he acquired from Spitalfields early every morning. As a seller of goods he was known as one who was good to those truly in need but sharp and clever with those who he saw as having 'too much ready' and not enough sense. Popular with the other costers he was often looked to as a leader when trouble came to them, and was well known for the charm of his speech as well as the strength of his arm when need arose.

Within his home however he was truly the master of his clan. His 'wifeys' were subservient and dutiful, and his children lived in fear of his anger when the word of God came to his lips. Those children who did not show the proper respect to their father's ways would receive punishments of the most brutal and often odd manner. Sometimes he would eject them from the house to live on the streets for days at a time, even those as young as five or six. This he said would teach them the ways of the world and what it meant to be lucky enough to have a home to live in. Boys would be forced to wear their sister's clothing and answer to names like 'Annabel' or 'Grace', this he said would teach them what it meant to be a man and to cherish this responsibility.

The most fearful time in those poor children's lives though were when God spoke directly to them through their father's mouth. This could happen at any time and would be signalled by John Hamersley violently shaking and screaming, raising his hands above his head and calling out the words,

'This is the voice of the Lord your master!'

The 'Lord' gave many commands during these times of possession and control of John Hamersley. Sometimes he would order the whole family to follow him into the streets where they would walk for miles barefoot, because 'The Lord' had blessed them with a vision that through the penance of pain and blisters they would be rewarded with bountiful riches and excellent fortune.

Mr Hamersley's end came most unfortunately however when one of his visions caused him to demonstrate to his ungrateful family the terrors of the fires of hell. The ensuing blaze destroyed much of the tenement building where they and many other families lived with the loss of over forty lives including two of his 'wives', most of his children and members of four other neighbouring families. Only John Hamersley, the youngest of his lodging ladies and a nine year old daughter survived the blaze, and were last seen heading out of London to find a new life 'closer to God in the countryside.'

It is stories such as these, and there are many, which I heard as a young boy from children in the area and the patrons of the many drinking houses which I visited as part of my parent's chores, that gave me such a lack of respect and love for any kind of religiousness. The idea of God and the belief in spirituality and a meaning to our sorry existence are a madness, created by man to give meaning to our lives and to enable some to commit lunacy in the pursuit of power over others and dominion over the weak minded and desperate.

Although the events which I experienced with the recently passed had not changed my views on religion and the religious, I had been forced to concede that there may be elements of our existence and a greater depth to the thought of a life after the physical which I had never previously given credence to.

My mind had been full of these thoughts as I wandered back to my studios after taking Bethany home. I had been lost in contemplation, wondering, quite apart from the on-going issue of murder and coming apocalypse, just how the planet worked and whether there was such a thing as a life after death, be it in some other form other than the physical one which we experience in this world. It was because of this lack of awareness of the world around me that I did not notice the return of the two large men who had been watching Bethany and I and who came upon me as I neared the door of my lodgings. In fact, it was not until I felt a hard object press into my side and looked down to see that there was a pistol held to me, that I realised that there was anything out of the ordinary at all. Of course, my mind was immediately brought back to the present time by this sight, but by then I was being led to a carriage at the side of the street, where the door was opened for me and I was ushered inside accompanied by my large, newly acquired companions.

The carriage hurtled through the streets, its wheels rattling off the cobbles, I could not see, from the position in which I been forced, where we were heading, but I knew that at that moment it did not really matter. I was helpless, stuck on a seat, wedged between the two brutes that had dragged me into the carriage and opposite me was sat a man who, not two weeks ago, I had photographed with his recently deceased daughter.

Charles Earnshaw was dressed in a long-tailed suit of black with a white tie; a top hat sat upon the seat next to him and he looked as if he was dressed for some kind of formal function. He wore a smile as he looked at me over his silver thin rimmed glasses, the type of expression one would wear when looking at a dear friend or associate, someone whom one was fond of. I found this odd, as the manner in which I had been treated, and the force which was being put on me by the large men on either side of me, would not have been amiss had I been someone who he thought of as a dreadful enemy.

"What is the meaning of this?" I protested, "What right have you to take me by force?"

Earnshaw continued to smile, holding his hand up to his mouth like one would do when perusing a curiosity. His face turned to the window of the carriage and he stared out into the city beyond.

"Do you not love London, Mr Darke?" He said, his gaze remaining on the view from his window. "Do you not see it as the greatest city in the world? I did, once a long time ago before the streets filled with the hungry and the depraved. Before the world's detritus flooded in and the greed filled rich turned it into an industrial factory."

"It is progress, sir." I cut in, "It is the way that the world is developing and it is making our country great." He ignored me and continued.

"Do you see the smoke that pours from the chimneys into our air, Mr Darke? Do you even know what they are manufacturing? They are manufacturing poor people, Darke; they are creating an impoverished underclass to act as drone slaves to do their bidding." He turned his head and looked me in the eye. "Come now, you are an intelligent and well-read man, you must have read some Engels in your time, The English money-monger is treating the working man with contempt, they are oppressing the working classes of Britain are they not?"

"I have read his work, Mr Earnshaw, and I see some sense in his rhetoric, but are you not one of the opposing Middle Classes? Do you not live in an expensive Marylebone townhouse, with servants and other members of the working classes bowing and scraping to you?"

He laughed at this statement, a low throaty chuckle which filled the carriage.

"I do indeed, Darke, I do indeed, but I have not always been this way. I came from poor beginnings you know. I have fought to get where I am today and fought for a purpose. I lived in Paris years ago, Mr Darke. Did you know this?"

"I did."

"Of course you did, you are a stickler for information gathering and knowledge, your study is filled with endless notes on those within society."

He noted my shock that he knew this and smiled. He, or associates of his, had obviously been to my building and searched my belongings. I tried to keep my discomfort at this to a minimum as he continued.

"When I heard of your little library of lives I was a little confused. You see, I found you to be a contradiction. Everything that I have heard of you has told me that you are a gambling man, Mr Darke, that you are no stranger to the gaming tables and that you have managed to fund your lifestyle through the attainment of winnings. But a gambling man with such an intense obsession with knowledge and forethought? It did not sit right within my mind at first. However, it became clear to me that I had heard wrong. You are no gambler, you have never gambled in your life. Each action that you take, whether in business or in the gaming hall, has been carefully researched, you only place your stake if the odds are in your favour."

He paused for a second; letting his words settle within my ears. "We are similar you and I, Mr Darke, we have a lot in common. We have a drive to succeed and a thirst for knowledge, which brings me back to Paris and my youth.

"I learnt a lot in Paris, a lot about what happens to the ruling classes when they oppress those below them. Do not get me wrong, Mr Darke, I am not sympathetic to the cause of the common man, in fact I truly believe that there is an order to things, an order which needs to be maintained. Oppression through work and poverty is not the way to achieve this, not at all. It is fear that brings control, fear of the unknown, fear of death and the protection of a greater power.

"Do you know what a rat will do when it is cornered at the end of an alleyway, Mr Darke? It will fight whatever it is faced with, whatever the object in its path. It is not fear that forces the rat to act this way however, it is defiance and anger, a desire to break free from the restraints placed upon it. People are the same you know. When the working classes feel that they are shackled and downtrodden, they will rise up and fight their oppressors, they will sound a war cry that will resound throughout the land and bring war to the palaces of their oppressors. I brought this knowledge with me back to London and found a group of gentlemen who shared my view that the world is heading in the wrong direction. We have seen into the future and it not a place where we wish to send our families. I am talking about revolution and it is this which we mean to stop, we are doing this for Britain and the Empire. We are, of course, in the early stages of our operation, which brings me to the reason for our impromptu meeting.

"We have business to discuss, Mr Darke, business of a most important kind. It seems you have been involving yourself in detection and investigation. You have made industry in the uncovering of this foul killer that walks our streets at night."

"I have a personal interest in it, yes." I answered. "He was responsible for the death of my father and brother and so I see it as my right to find the man and bring him to justice."

Earnshaw laughed a little, a sound echoed by those beside me. It was a belittling sound, designed to make me feel ignorant and dumb.

"Do you think you have the means to do this, Darke? Are you some kind of brave defender of the poor, the saviour of children that nobody cares for?"

"I do not have any pretensions of this kind, sir, but I do know evil when I see it and I do know that it will prosper when it is unopposed."

Earnshaw interlocked his fingers and placed them on his knee. I could tell that he had no wish to start debating differing ideas of evil with me and he continued to try to turn the conversation to my investigations.

"So you could tell me who this terrible killer is if I asked you?"

"No, but I could tell you about him, if I felt inclined. I could tell you the type of man that he was and where he has been and who are behind his actions. I have built a shadow of the man in my mind and it is only a matter of time before I track him down."

"Ah, yes. Such good information you have found. The paranoid fantasies of a declared lunatic and a description gleaned from a drunken whore who you paid to speak. I am impressed with your skill in detection. It is a wonder that you have never attempted to employ your sharp mind to aid the police in the past. Maybe you could have even joined the force, you surely would have made inspector by now. You could have given Fred Draper a run for his money." His tone was patronising, so laced with sarcasm and acidity that, although not a violent man, I am sure that I would have quite happily struck him about the face if I had been able to move my arms.

"I do not feel that everything that Holdsworth said was fantasy. In fact I mean to prove him right and bring down whatever putrid organisation is behind this operation. An organisation, which I now know, you are a part of. Tell me, do you seek to bring about this new order by the senseless slaughter of homeless children?"

"As I have told you this is just the first stage in the process, a test if you will, before we unleash a greater terror. We are in the business of long term planning, Mr Darke, and change will not come overnight. Steadily our actions will increase in size and ever greater will grow the terror of the underclasses. When the masses are so terrorised that they beg for redemption and pray to be saved from the horrors of the night, they will find that we are only happy to provide such."

I laughed aloud at the twisted logic of this supposition and wondered to myself how the men whom I thought were intelligent and wise could act as such dolts, encased within their feelings of superiority over the normal man to such an extent that they thought that they could herd them like sheep towards a pen of their making.

"I think that you underestimate the wit and will of the normal man, Mr Earnshaw. He is not for moulding to the will of a handful of jumped up middle class braggarts." The smile was wide on my face now as I realised the extent of the delusions within Earnshaw and his associates. "Did you believe that summoning a demon from the underworld would save the world? I say that you are meddling in the supernatural to meet your ends and that you're meddling will only lead to your own death. You took an innocent man and filled him with the spirit of a voracious killer, he survived the experience and the beast abandoned him. You failed before and now you have tried and will fail again. Your mistake was letting Holdsworth live, he has given me the information that I need to bring this to an end."

Earnshaw sniffed haughtily at my impudence, I could see that he was entranced by his black misconceptions and would never see the folly of it all.

"I'm afraid there has been a terrible incident with Mr Holdsworth in the asylum." He said, the hint of a dark smile appearing on his face. "I only heard of it as I am on the institution's board and I spend a lot of my spare time there helping those of a delicate mental disposition. It would seem that a cruel killer took Holdsworth's life last night, someone who had been employed to care and look after him. I think you know the attendant in question; you met him during your visit, a brute by the name of Barney Foulkes. It would seem this beast's vile anger knew no bounds; he slaughtered Mr Holdsworth in a most terrible way, his limbs torn from him and his internal organs pulled free from his body. The medical examiner who studied the dead man thinks that the killing took place over a number of hours and that Holdsworth did not die until the very end. How cruel and imaginative some people can be in the ways that they choose to take the life of another, you would be amazed, really you would. Foulkes, of course, is a danger to others and has been sent to Crowthorne, he is quite insane, and I do not know how the asylum had not noticed it before.

"The business involving your family was unfortunate and could not be avoided. Your father knew too much from our previous attempt at change. Your brother had to be taken as there could be no witness. You on the other hand are a different prospect. You are a businessman and you know that in business there are those who succeed and those who fail. Do not be a failure, Mr Darke. You are only still living because I have spoken for you. There are those who would have had you killed as you lay drunk and beaten in the gutter outside 'The Princess Alice' two weeks ago. You will be glad to know that the man who took advantage of your inebriation and jumped you was taken care of."

He reached into his pocket and withdrew his hand, within which was my Frodsham's watch. The silver chain sparkled as the watch hung down and turned slowly. I stared at it for a moment, this was obviously some type of bartering ploy devised to buy my silence and end my investigations into the murders.

"Think of it as a sign of good faith, Mr Darke. We are returning your watch to you and can promise many other treasures. A man such as you with your drive and ambition would do well with us and you could find yourself very well rewarded for aiding us in our work. I have watched you for some time now, Darke; I have watched you develop into an individual with promising elements. Who do you think it was that arranged for your invitation to the club? You suit us, Sibelius and I think you find that we share many qualities with you. If only you could see past the matter of your family's death. I thought you a more practical man who would be able to see the larger possibilities available to men like us in life."

My mind was suddenly filled with clarity and I cursed myself for the fool that I was. The Dolorian Club, of course, my stupidity astounded me and I cursed the single mindedness which had closed my thoughts and blocked the most obvious answer from my view. Dolorian was linked to the Latin 'Dolor' meaning grief, suffering, pain and ... sorrow. The Club of Sorrows, the very club which Henry Holdsworth visited on the day that the creature took hold of his body, was that which I was a member of, bade without solicitation, and invited by the man sitting opposite me.

I reached out to grab the watch, but found myself held on each side as Earnshaw snatched it away, moving it out of my reach. Seeing my frustration he slowly moved his hand forwards so that I was able hold the watch within my hand. The silver felt cold but comforting on my palm, the memory of its weight and worth flooding back to me. Not its value in cash though, but the fact that it was a sign or moving forward in the world, of having ambition and achieving success through hard work and intelligence. Such ideas now seemingly lost to me.

"I could never be a part of this," I barked, "You are obviously not the judge of character that you think, sir, although I concede that neither am I, for I thought better of you."

"Life is full of little disappointments, Sibelius, and I am afraid that if you will not join us then this is how you will be remembered by me. Now, Mr Darke, do I have your agreement that you will cease in your asking of questions and uncovering of secrets? I have stood for you on this matter. I am all that stands between you and my colleagues and it is not only you that I protect, it is those who you love and hold dear also. Think of Miss Finnan and her dear father, would you wish to be the cause of harm because of something that you have done?"

"You would not dare to harm them in my name, surely?"

"No, of course I would not, Sibelius." He leant forwards placing his hand sensitively on my knee. His tone was fatherly and soft, reassuring and kind. "I am the friendly, social face of those who I work for, the acceptable face if you will. But there are more forces at work than just I, Sibelius, and I could not bear to think of the terrible things that these people would do if they wished to indirectly bring you harm through those that you care for."

"I always thought of you as a man to be respected, Mr Earnshaw."

"You will find that I am."

"Everything I had ever heard told me that you were a kind and thoughtful member of society."

"Again, this is true of me."

"I think you are mistaken. It would seem that you are none of these things however. You have a dark heart and a cruel mind and I would never fall into line with one such as you no matter what threats you utter or what foul deeds are committed by your instruction."

"I am saddened that you feel this way, Sibelius, really I am. I could have made you a part of this and you would have achieved all of the things that you have yearned for since your childhood." His face had softened and I could see his disappointment that he had obviously failed in his attempt. "I cannot argue with your principles," he continued, "you want so much to be the hero and you would forsake the riches and power that I offer to achieve this." He looked down at the knee of his trousers and brushed away an imperceptible fleck of dust. "You will not be that hero though, Mr Darke," he continued, "in fact there is little doubt that your story will end in failure and your piteous demise. However, I feel that you must suffer more grievous loss before your time is finished, and so I think I will let you out of the carriage and leave you to battle some more demons. I doubt that we will meet again, but if we do I think that I shall find you a different man, beaten, lost and praying for redemption. There will be none, goodbye."

The horses had not slowed in the slightest and continued their fervent gallop as the carriage door was opened and I was thrown with great menace out onto the cobbled streets. I hit the ground hard, trying to roll as best I could to cushion the impact, but being flung from a fast moving carriage is not an experience which I would recommend for those wishing to avoid soreness and bruising, and I count myself as lucky that I did not break my shoulder, such was the force by which it struck the hard stone.

I came to a stop at the feet of a large lady who looked down at me in disbelief. I am sure that it is not a common occurrence to walk down the street only to be halted by the body of a tall, white haired man who has been thrown from a moving carriage.

"My apologies, dear lady." I winced as I tried to get to my feet. "I appear to have lost my ride, small altercation with a friend."

The lady scowled at me, the shake of her head causing her jowls to shake loosely.

"Choose your friends more wisely," she spat and continued on her journey, her capacious skirts swishing into my face as she bundled me out of the way, sending me sprawling to the floor once more.

How unwittingly true her words were, though. For in my blind drive to reach the upper echelons of society it would seem that I had wandered unknowingly into a nest of vipers; malevolent and evil, preying upon the piteous and the poor.

I looked around me, scanning for a sign of something familiar. The sight of the buildings told me that I was no longer in the east end of London; the houses were too large and clean. The air felt different somehow, there were two strong smells battling for the attention of my senses and I quickly worked out what they were, as I looked up to the sky and saw one building overshadowing the rest. The odours were of the Thames, a smell which was unmistakable to any Londoner, and the powerful scent of hops. Looking down the street I could see the large wrought iron gates of the Barclays Brewery and I knew at once that I had travelled over the river by the Southwark Bridge and had been dumped in Bridge Street.

I estimated that I had been in the carriage for a little short of half an hour and, knowing where I was now, thought that it would take me at least an hour to walk back to the relative safety of Whitechapel. The fumes from a brewery are, I am aware, not the type of odour which many people find agreeable, I however found it a comforting smell, I found its sweetness warming and soothing like some long forgotten memory of a happier time. I inhaled deeply as I passed the gates; all too aware that as I approached the river a new type of odour would fill my senses and sting my eyes.

I crossed Southwark Bridge with my breath held as much as I could, the effluence of the water was overpowering in high summer and, although I was no stranger to the thick stale waft of London at its worst, it was something that I had always known and I was grateful that I did not live nearer to the river.

Back onto the northerly part of the city again I made my way to Cannon Street following it to its easterly conclusion around the bend until I reached Fenchurch Street. From there the road would be straight and lead me back through Aldgate to home again. My first stop however would be to The Princess Alice. Earnshaw's words had unsettled me greatly and I wished to cast my eyes over Tom and Beth to ensure that they were still safe. Although this terror had visited me uninvited, the thought that my actions had brought about the threat of harm to those whom I cared for created a knot of guilt which tore at my chest.

I purposefully strode back to more recognisable and homely pastures thinking on Earnshaw's words. For all of his madness and paranoia, I could see some shred of sense. I did not necessarily agree with this sense, but I could see how this twisted view of the next stage in the world's journey would scare someone such as him. Where he saw a pathway to hell and destruction and the end of humanity however, I had always seen progress and enlightenment and a growth in man's control of the world. The grand city which towered over me as I made my way back to Whitechapel was, to my mind, the greatest in the world. Of course there was poverty and depravation; it had always been there however. Earnshaw's concerns had been raised, I felt, by the number of people that now populated the city and its surroundings. Where some saw a burgeoning workforce ready to help to take our country into the next century as the world leader in trade and industry, he saw a swelling mob of malcontents, stirred into revolutionary action by talk of oppression and subjugation. It was true that in the past fifty years the number of people living in the capital had increased more than threefold to almost four million. Many of these people had come to the city from the countryside to find work in the factories and, of course, this meant that living conditions were crowded and that, for most members of the working classes, times were hard. I had no doubt in my mind though, that the end result to this increase in industry and city dwelling population would be nothing other than an boost to our a standing in the world. People would suffer in the pursuit of this but that was the way of things. There are winners and there are losers and until recently I had always thought that I would end up on the victorious side.

These thoughts filled my mind for the whole of the journey home. I cursed my predicament but a small part of me felt some comfort in the fact that I now knew the enemy in my midst and had started to form the beginnings of a plan to ensure that once the killer had been vanquished, there would be no repeat of this horror.

As I finally turned the corner into Commercial Street and made my way to the corner of Wentworth Street, I saw the doors of The Princess Alice beckoning me in. I could hear the noise and bustle coming from inside, something, which due to my increasing headache through the formulation of plans, I did not relish experiencing. I needed to see both Bethany and Tom for myself however, if only to reassure myself of their safety and to warn them against the threatening actions of the members of the Dolorian Club and their associates. I had decided, on my journey back, that the time had long since past when I should bring Tom into the fold and make him aware of the danger which he and his daughter faced. I loved and respected the man too much to lie to him any longer.

I pulled on the door handles and the noise increased dramatically. Stepping inside I saw that the pub was full and that Tom and Sylvie, his barmaid, were busy trying to keep up with the constant stream of demands for drink which seemed to be coming at them from all sides. Despite the rush and the hurry Tom noticed my arrival and nodded to me smiling,

"Give me five minutes," he mouthed, nudging Sylvie and telling her to make sure that a drink was poured for me. I bustled my way to the end of the bar and, grabbing a nearby stool, I took a seat just as a full pint pot was placed on the bar for me.

"Is Beth upstairs, Sylvie?" I asked as she went to walk back to the middle of the drunken throng at the bar.

"No, she went out earlier with her friend, Rose. She said something about going to find some man called Arthur something ... Dowley ... Downer, something like that anyway. She had been talking to Jed Barrow asking him lots of questions and she got excited by what Jed told her, said she had found who she was looking for, strange if you ask me. Anyways, she told Tom that she was going out with Rose, said that she would be back to-night before it got too late."

My heart was filled with a mixture of elation and fear. Bethany had obviously managed to track down our killer based on the clues that I had given her, but had stupidly gone after him herself. My fear for her safety was deafening, she had put herself in harm's way, facing a murderer possessed with an ancient demon and filled with the desire to kill whoever got in their way.

"Do you know where it was that she went?" I asked, hoping that she had overheard an address.

"No, not really. Shadwell way maybe."

I shuddered a little despite growing up in an area of London where some would dare not tread after dark; Shadwell had a reputation which made even the roughest of blackguards wince. Up until recent years, police were known to avoid the area for fear of violence and attack. It was said that there was a bounty on the heads of certain police officers and that anyone known to have caused a member of the law damage or injury, would be able to have many an evening of drunken revelry without having to put their hand in their pocket.

In a moment I made up my mind regarding my next move, and calling out to Tom to tell him that I would return later, I ran from the pub and onwards home to retrieve Father's pistol from the hidden ledge in the chimney breast in my bedroom. Filling my overcoat pocket with shells, I shut the door behind me and went to search for Bethany, hoping that I reached her before she found her man.

As I walked at pace down Commercial Road, I became aware that there seemed to be a growing group of people heading in the same direction as me. This slowly pricked my nerves somewhat as I had seen this type of behaviour before and it usually happened when word had spread of an accident or some other type of incident, which so often draws a crowd. My stride quickened by the step and soon I found myself running blindly in the direction that the others seemed to be going, pushing my way through the mob as they made their way forward to a point further up the road. Deep within me I knew that Bethany was at the heart of this disturbance somehow and my hand remained in the pocket of my coat firmly gripping the butt of the pistol within it, tensing as I ran. Odd words came to my ears, words which only served to increase the tension and fear within me. Words such as 'murder' and 'killing', reverberated within my head causing me to hasten in the pace of my step to almost running speed. The noise of a loud whistle sounded behind me and the crowds parted to let a police carriage through.

Through the dimly lit street, I scanned the faces of the growing crowds, searching for anyone familiar who could tell me what was going on. In the darkness however the faces seemed to blend together, making everyone look the same, a mob of sorts, all stumbling forward, eyes alert, each looking for the first sign that something had happened.

As I neared Arbour Square however, it was not my eyes which gave me the indication of the disturbance, it was my ears. I heard the loud, screeching sobs and screams, which I recognised as belonging to that of Rose Utterson, friend of Bethany. Between her sobs and screams of woe she cried the same name over and over.

"Beth!"

13
THE LONGEST NIGHT

I never get angry.

It is not that I do not feel anger in any way, I do, it is just that I experience difficulties expressing any feelings of frustration tempered rage of the same type which I often see others sharing. The feelings are there; the upset, the tension, the urge to explode and vent at the subject of my ire, but I cannot seem to bring it out into the open, to release the burning demon within me.

As children, Niko, with all of his devilish ingenuity, and before his death even Johannes, normally so kind and thoughtful, would see fit to test the limits of my patience and fortitude. They would tease and they would taunt, nip and niggle, behave in the most aggravating and unsettling of manners to try to see my darker side.

Inside I would be a blazing fire, all crackle and spit, a tumultuous furnace stoked high with vehemence and malcontent. The blood would rush to my face and fists in an effort to bring energy and life to violent and furious action. My legs would tense and cramp to the point of pain in their shaking stiffness, preparing to spring into me through the roof in a volatile arc of screaming fury. The knots would form within me and would tear at my insides, ripping and feasting with such relish that I feared that I would be torn inside out by the force. This powerful energy would eat away at my good nature to create a disagreeable and potentially violent monster which, for some reason, would remain chained internally. A devil within, hidden through reasons unknown to me.

Sometimes I would pretend to be angry as a way of trying to accede to their demands to see the beast. I would shout and bawl, threaten and push, but there was no anger in my actions, in fact it was more act than action. The bile within me kept its place and remained inactive; the wrath remained, trapped within a glass bell jar inside the pit of my stomach.

Grandfather, who noted my brothers' games and watched them try to draw out my anger, sat me down one day and told me that the road which my mind had taken me was a road to ill feeling and despair.

"It is no good to keep such things within yourself, Sibelius." He would say, his voice urging me to release the creature. "The energy used to create such a monster inside never dies silently, and if you do not unlock its cage it will reach through the bars and claw at you from the inside. Such beasts must cause damage and horror and if they are not let out into the world then they will destroy no other quarry than you. The damage and horror will come to you only and lead to hate and violence of the most terrible kind, the kind that you aim at yourself."

Although his words made sense to me I felt unable to act on them. It was beyond me, and the doubt and self-hatred did indeed grow and fester, leaving me a piteous figure full of loneliness and despair. At these times I wished to bring myself harm, to take the burden that I placed upon the world away. I wished to retract myself from the lives of those that surrounded me, a sweet but small blessing; a final act of kindness on my part to those that I held dear. I even tried to act on it on some occasions, but my failure to complete my goal only added to the self-loathing. I learned over time, and through hard lessons, that these moments pass. They were transitory instances which left as quickly as they arrived, sending me spiralling into mile high ecstasies, proving to me that I have once again survived myself and had worth and purpose.

These dramatic switches between the depths and heights of my personality were something which, I knew, I would always be a victim of. It would seem that I was destined to live with the curse of an unsure mind.

As I ran with the growing mob through the dark and grimy streets, dodging through the crowds, my blood racing through my veins, I felt pure anger firing within me as close to emerging as it had ever been in my life. There was hatred in my heart for Earnshaw and his threats, there was hatred in my heart for the black society of which he, and unwittingly I, was a part of, but most of all there was hatred in my heart, for myself. I hated myself with a passion for dragging Bethany into this and by doing so bringing murder to her.

As I approached Arbour Square the crowd thickened, held back by a line of policemen desperately trying to keep the area clear of the baying throng. The voice of Rose could still be heard over the chatter and bark of those around, and it was towards her that I headed. I pushed and bustled my way through, drawing looks of anger and aggravation, as well as curses and threats from some. The wracking sobs and howls from the young woman acted as the beacon towards which I was pulled.

As I finally reached the edge of the crowd, I could see Rose knelt on the floor in the distance, holding Bethany in her arms and calling her name over and over. My way however was blocked by a line of young policeman who were trying their best to keep the growing mass of onlookers at bay. I tried to push through but my shoulder was held by one of them.

"I'm sorry, sir, you can go no further. There has been murder committed here to-night and this area is not for the likes of you."

"But that is my fiancé laying there!" I shouted, the lie coming easy to me. "Please I must go to her. Rose! ... Rose!" I called to Beth's friend who looked up and saw me standing with the policeman and desperately trying to get through.

"Sib!" she cried. 'Oh, Sib, look what he's done to her, look what he's done to our girl."

At this the policeman acceded to my requests and let me through. I ran to Rose's side, falling to the floor beside her and grabbing Beth in my arms.

She still breathed.

"I told her not to go," Rose wept. "I told her it would be dangerous and that we should fetch a policeman but she never listened to me, stubborn girl. She never listened."

I looked down into Bethany's face. Although pale, I could see that she still lived but was unconscious to the world. Her breathing was ragged and the lids of her eyes flickered, but she was by all accounts physically unharmed and asleep in my arms. I held her close to my chest, thankful that she was still alive and that I had not been the cause of her death. Her body felt small and light against mine, she was so young, still a child. What had I been thinking drawing her into this terror?

At that moment I heard the sound of hooves on cobble and looked up to see that a carriage had arrived bearing Inspector Draper. The horses were having trouble getting through the crowds and, seeing the delay, I saw my chance and looked to Rose.

"Listen to me, Rose." I spoke in a low whisper so as not to be heard by the police around us. "There is an Inspector coming to us now, before he arrives I want you to tell me what happened here to-night. Who did this? Tell me everything."

Rose's eyes were wide with terror as she quickly recounted to me the events of the evening.

"Beth and I were in the Alice earlier and she told me that she had to go out to Shadwell, said it was something to do with the man who killed Niko. She seemed very excited and said that she had to go now, but I wouldn't let her, I said that it was dangerous and that she was stupid. When she wouldn't listen to me I said I'd go with her and that the first policeman I saw, I would tell what she was doing. She said we were going to find a man called Arthur Downing, she said he lived on Love Lane opposite the Alms houses. Well we went there and we found the address where this man lived, some small lodgings for dock workers. I told her then that we should go to the police, but she never listened, she said that she had to make sure that it was him, so she knocked on doors asking if anyone knew where Arthur Downing lived, said she was his sister. When they pointed out his door she told me to fetch the police, and that she would wait there and follow him if he left. God help me I left her, I left her with a killer, God help me" She fell into sobs once more. Tears of guilt and woe ran down her face. "I came back with a policeman but she was gone, it was only when I heard the screams that we ran here and found her, out of her senses, talking about demons and murder. There's a boy over there ripped to shreds, she must have seen it all and tried to stop him."

I heard a noise and looking up I could see that the carriage had now made its way through the crowd and the door had opened. Draper was stepping out of it and looking towards Rose and I knelt on the floor.

"The address, Rose." I hissed. "I need the address, tell me now and I will finish this."

Draper was now making his way towards us, Sergeant Thomas in tow behind him, the expression on Thomas's face told me that he had seen me and that he was not at all happy.

"The address, Rose. Love Lane, what was the number?" I grabbed her arm, squeezing it tightly to pull her out of her stupor. Finally she answered.

"12," she muttered. "Top floor. The room with the green door."

"Mr Darke! What are you doing here?" The voice of Draper told me that he had arrived. "This is a scene of murder, what place have you in it?" I stood to face him.

"This girl was the fiancée of my murdered brother," I said. "I followed the crowds and found her here."

Thomas scowled at me from over the Inspector's shoulder.

"You need to leave right now, you have no business here!" He growled, his face full of anger.

"Please Sergeant, I will deal with this," Draper reprimanded. "He is right of course though, Darke. This is a police matter. I thank you for looking after the girl, but you need to allow us to manage the scene. We will look after her from here."

"Very well," I muttered, trying to withhold my relief at the excuse to leave. "Please have someone fetch her father though, His name is Tom Finnan, and he is the owner of The Princess Alice."

"I know the man," said Draper, "and I will have him informed and brought to her."

A policeman came over and took hold of Rose, bringing her to her feet as another knelt to take Beth. Seeing my chance I stepped away from the scene.

"Please look after her, Inspector." I called as I moved off. "She is dear to me. Most dear."

And with that I made my exit towards the crowds again to the south of the square. As the crowd thinned I began to pick up my pace and began to run, entering Devonport Street at great pace. There would only be a small amount of time before Draper also found out the address from Rose, and I hoped beyond hope within my heart that Downing had returned to the address and that I could get to him before the police.

For a street with such a soft sounding name, Love Lane was the most desperate of places. It had originally been called

Cut-Throat Lane and looking at it, in the cloying blackness of the night, it would seem that this title was probably more apt. There were a few people on the streets; many of them dock workers, full of drink, meandering back to the tenements where rooms were rented for those who only wished a bed to sleep in and not a home.

On the opposite side of the street to the tenements were Captain Carr's Alms houses, a place where the poor and destitute, unfortunate and cursed came to the bottom of their own particular barrel. Whilst I had sympathy with their turmoil I was fully aware of the ways in which some of these people saw fit to help make ends meet, and so I kept the pistol in my pocket within my reach as I had heard tell of many a person who had come to an end in these streets.

I felt a nervous energy within me as I readied myself to face this killer of children and my family. I had not really given thought until this moment regarding whether I would actually be able to pull the trigger and end the life of another man. Of course he was a killer and as such he deserved to be stopped, but a part of me was reminded that this was a normal man who had been trapped, drugged and filled with the spirit of a demon from the underworld; a beast with an insatiable thirst for the flesh of the young. Whether he be truly innocent inside however, this must be ended to-night and I would not see another man imprisoned as a lunatic for actions out of his control. I resolved within myself to carry out my own act of murder as a way of freeing him from the beast and ending his misery.

I approached the steps to number 12 Love Lane, and quickly withdrew the weapon for a final check that it was loaded and ready to be fired when needed. Each of the chambers was filled and I could feel the weight of the other shells within my pocket, although I hoped that my aim would be true and that just the one would be enough.

The main door to the tenement building was not locked and I opened it stepping inside. The hallway was dark; the only light being that which came through the door from the gas lamps outside. I could make out a battered wooden staircase ten yards ahead of me and by the side of this was a small white-painted ledge with a collection of wide candles in a variety of heights and a sealed metal box which I found to contain loose matches. Choosing a candle of generous size, I struck one of the matches against the rough section of sand paper stuck to the lid of the box. The white phosphorous blazed into life and I quickly held the match to the wick of the candle, an action which caused the hallway to light to a degree. With my way forward now shown to me, I started slowly making my way up the stairs, ensuring that I held on to the roughly painted banister on one side. Looking at the state of the stairs and the rotten repair of the boards and risers, I had decided that the banisters, despite being loose in places, may be a point of salvation from potential accident.

The stairway was silent as I crept up a stair at a time, I was aware that the slightest creak or moan of worn wood beneath my feet could make Downing aware that someone was climbing the stair and ruin the element of surprise so instrumental in the achievement of my goal. I prayed that the green door to his room was as decrepit and weak as the rest of the tenement as I would have to force it open in order to get to my man and carry out my dark deed.

The candlelight's flicker threw strange shapes and shadows upon the walls and floor, giving the impression that they were alive with movement. Occasionally I would start when the glow fell on a bundle of rags upon the floor or, in one startling instance on the second floor, a rat which scuttled away further into the darkness out of the light's reach.

The stairs groaned under my weight at a couple of junctures, but I simply paused long enough to let the cry of the wood disappear into the blackness, before carrying on towards my goal.

Finally, upon reaching the top of the staircase, I spied the door within which I hoped to find the killer of my family and so many poor unfortunate children. The green paint which covered it was flaked in places, showing chipped and damp looking wood underneath. The door was shut but was ill fitting to the frame and as such I could tell that it would not be a difficult task to put through. I put my head to the door gently, listening for any sound coming from within. All that could be heard was a deep rhythmic creaking, such as would be made by a person rocking in a chair over a loose floorboard. I wondered what could be making the sound but decided that it was foolish of me to worry about such things; the noise was a sign that the room was occupied. Slowly, and with great care, I withdrew the pistol from my pocket and pulled back on the hammer above the grip, its click deafening in the still of the moment. I braced myself, leaning my shoulder forward and preparing to charge at the wood.

In that short moment I tried to foresee the scene, how it would happen and what action I would take. I would break through the door and find Downing sat in a rocking chair by the window. He would look to me, his mouth and chin covered in the blood of the child he had just slaughtered and attempted to eat. I would raise the gun level to my shoulder and pull the trigger, the bullet leaving the barrel of the pistol and finding its mark in the centre of his forehead with such great force and magnitude that, when it left at the rear, it would create a hole large enough for a man to put his fist into. The soft, wet expulsion which would fly from the exit would create a bloom of red upon the back of the chair and the wall behind him, more vibrant and expressive than the most beautiful of roses.

Holding the pistol steady in my hand, I paused momentarily. Was I ready to kill a man? Did I have the inner strength to look a man in the eye and end his life? Now would be the time that I would find out. I lowered my shoulder and charged at the doorway.

The constitution of the door did not fully measure up to the levels of security which I had trusted it to have and, as a result, I flew through the door with greater haste than I had foreseen. This speed of entry, however, did not stop me from seeing the shape of the man who I had come to kill in front of me. Raising the pistol and pointing it at him, I quickly pulled the trigger, the loud report of the gun thundering in the small room.

I should at this point reveal, and it may come as no surprise, to you, that I have never fired a pistol of any description before. The whole act did not sit comfortably with me and, as I fired my first ever shot, I soon learned that there were basic and fundamental qualities which the wielder of such a weapon should possess and use if the purpose of employing the gun is to meet its full potential. The most obvious of these is, of course, the importance of keeping one's eyes open when aiming the weapon and not just pointing the barrel and shooting in a blind and haphazard fashion. I learnt this lesson quickly as I opened my eyes to find that I had missed Downing altogether and instead managed to make a fair attempt at killing a section of wall more than a foot to the right of him.

The sound of the slow rhythmic groan of wood echoed through the room and, as I saw the scene that met me, I discovered that there was indeed no rocking chair in the room. In fact there was no furniture of any kind in the room other than a battered wooden bed covered over with a woollen blanket of deep grey and the remnants of a torn sheet.

Downing was also not stood, sat or even laying in the room. He was swinging from a rafter in the ceiling, hanged with the plaited strips torn from the filthy sheet tight around his neck, its constriction making a deep purpling mark upon his throat. The man was quite dead and, judging by the small movement of his swing, only recently so. The low painful sound of the wooden rafter groaning under his weight cut through the silence which now seemed absolute following the report of the pistol's discharge.

His face was not one that I expected to see of a hanged man, not that I had ever seen one before. For although his neck was quite obviously snapped, his expression was not one of abject horror and painful death, but rather of placidity and paleness that would not have been unusual to see on any other body where the deceased had died in their sleep. There was blood surrounding the man's mouth and stubbled chin, but I took this to be the blood of the child, whom he had killed in Arbour Square, as it was dried and dark in colour. On closer inspection I saw that Downing appeared to be crying tears of his own blood, their bright red tracks scoring an indelible path down his pallid cheeks. How apt, I thought that a man possessed and controlled into murdering children should now appear, hanging from a self-inflicted death with bloody tears of remorse upon his face.

His shirt was unbuttoned to his navel and, although his chest was also covered in the splatter of blood so dark it was almost black in colour, I could make out the military tattoo, made up of a crowned star with the number forty-two at the centre on his chest, which told me that I had indeed found the killer.

I thought of Holdsworth's words. Of how he had contemplated suicide but did not have the bravery to carry out the act, instead handing himself over to the police. Perhaps Downing, being a soldier, had the courage within him to carry out the act that Holdsworth could not. Whatever the truth of it, there was no need for me to commit a murder myself to-night.

I heard the noise of a commotion in the street outside coming through the cracked window on the other side of the room and I knew that the sound of my pistol would have alerted those near to an altercation of some kind. I decided that since

Downing had done my job for me that I should make my exit from the building at the earliest opportunity and, taking one final look at the dead man hanging from the ceiling by his neck, I left the room pulling the door closed behind me.

As I began to descend the stairs I could hear people entering the building on the ground floor. I could not be caught in the building lest my continued presence at murder scenes be seen as some kind of unwarranted link to the murders. This of course was true, but I felt that any further attention on me may take away from the fact that the true killer had indeed ended his life.

As the sound of footsteps of the stairs below me began, I saw that there was a small window with a latch upon the landing on which I stood. I approached it and, using the handle of the pistol to break the lock holding the latch. I pulled up the lower sash and carefully manoeuvred myself out onto the ledge. There I made use of a drainage pipe running down the wall from the roof above to make my descent to the alleyway at the back of the building below.

I stepped out of the alleyway, emerging at the end of Love Lane, and heard a policeman's whistle sounding from the inside of Number 12; obviously the body had been discovered. It would not be long before more officers of the law arrived and a link would be made to the murder in Arbour Square.

My primary concern at this point however, was for the safety and wellbeing of Bethany, and so it was with utmost urgency that, with my head down to avoid recognition, I hurried back to The Alice so that I may find news of her.

As I approached the pub I noticed that it was closed and there were no lights showing in the downstairs of the building. I looked at my watch and noted that it was shortly after midnight, it was most odd for the place to be shut so early as, even though Tom kept to stricter times than most in the area, it was rare for there not to be any late stragglers in the pub at this time of night. This was most worrying to me and I wondered whether Beth had been brought back here or had been taken to the local infirmary. Looking up I could see that there was a solitary light glowing from the room which I recognised as Bethany's. I approached the door and began hammering on it.

"Tom!" I called, "Tom! It is Sib! Let me in!"

At first there was no response, very soon I could see the faint glimmer of a candle light approaching the doors.

"We're closed, go away," came the voice, which I recognised to be Anne.

"Anne, it is Sibelius, Sibelius Darke! Is Bethany here? I heard what had happened. If she is here I must see her."

I could almost feel the sense of relief coming from Anne as she struggled to unlock the bolts on the doors to let me in. Before I could speak another word, a clutching hand was attached to my arm and I was pulled in off the street.

"Oh, Sib, Sib. What a terrible business. We have lost our little girl."

"She is...dead?" I cried in shock.

"No, not dead but I fear she has lost her mind, that her soul has been taken from her. Please come upstairs and see her for yourself, Tom will be so pleased to see you, I have not seen him like this since her mother died."

I took the stairs three at a time in my haste to see her and hurried into the room where I found Tom kneeling by the bedside, holding her unmoving hand and silently sobbing.

Bethany was laid on the top of the bed, rigid in position with her arms by her sides. Her eyes were open but did not move upon my entry to the room, they stared upwards towards some indistinct spot on the ceiling and immediately I understood

Anne's words. For it seemed that, if it had not been for the gentle rise and fall of her chest, that anyone seeing her would claim her to be as dead as anyone who I had photographed or seen throughout my life.

I quietly approached Tom and laid my hand upon his shoulder, he did not look up but spoke, his words a wavering crack upon the silence of the room.

"What has happened to her, Sib? What has happened to my little girl? The police brought her to me like this. She has not spoken or responded to either Anne or I, she just stares into the distance. Is she truly lost to us? What did she see?"

"I do not know, Tom," I lied. "I found her like this with Rose but was sent away by the police who were at the scene. Has she not said a word to you?"

"No, it is as if she is in a trance; she will not answer anything of me."

"Do you mind if I try to speak to her?" I asked.

"Of course, you may have more luck; it was you who pulled from her troubled misery when Niko died, perhaps she will wake for you." He stood and made space for me at her side. I took his position, kneeling by her and holding onto her hand. Her face was so still, but even though there was no emotion shown, it did not appear that she was in any way at peace.

"Beth," I called to her gently, "Beth it is Sibelius, you are safe now, safe at home." There was no movement and I knew then that her mind had been lost. Whatever she had seen when she had disturbed Downing had unhinged her. I thought of Father's letter to me and of how he described seeing Surma in the face of Henry Holdsworth. If Bethany had seen something similar as well as observing the half eaten remains of a child, then I would be sure that it could cause such extreme shock and hysteria which could separate this poor girl from the world around her.

The guilt within me boiled, creating an inner turmoil that I was sure would explode in anger at any time. For the sake of Tom and the girl lain in front of me however, I managed, as always, to keep the rage and disgust within. It was a full but tightly stoppered bottle, ready to poison me at some point of isolation in the future and drag me into the depths of self-loathing and despair.

I remained by her side for some time, with Tom sat in the doorway behind me. In the silence I thought of this sweet girl and of how I had known her since she was a babe, brought into the world at the expense of her mother's life. I remembered how I had watched her grow, from a funny and lively little girl to confident and outspoken young woman, and my heart was filled with sorrow. Sorrow for her loss of my brother who would have been such a good husband to her, sorrow that I had lost her just as I had begun to spend time and appreciate her, and finally sorrow for the misery and madness which I had brought upon her through involving her in this whole sorry business.

I do not know how long I sat by her side looking at her face, time did not seem to have any meaning any more, there was nowhere else to get to nothing else was as important to me as the wellbeing of Bethany Finnan.

We were disturbed in our silent thoughts by a pounding on the door downstairs. The noise shook me into instant alertness and edge. Muffled shouts came from the other side of the door and Tom stood, running down the stairs. The doors were answered and I could hear a discussion ensue between Tom and another man. The detail of their words were unclear but one word rang through to me immediately bringing a sense of worry and concern.

"Police."

As quickly as I could I pulled the pistol and shells from my pocket. If the police were here and downstairs I did not wish to be found with a loaded weapon in my possession. Apologising in a hushed whisper to the catatonic girl on the bed, I lifted the corner of her mattress and placed the revolver as far underneath as I could manage. Reaching again into my pocket, I found the last of the shells just as the heavy footfalls of boots echoed on the stairs. I threw the shells under the bed as quickly as I could and retook the hand of Bethany, closing my eyes and feigning prayer.

"Mr Darke," came the voice of Abe Thomas, "what a pleasant surprise to find you here. I have been to your abode and found it unattended, so I thought to check in on young Miss Finnan. It would seem that fortune is smiling on me as Inspector Draper is keen to speak with you regarding the events of earlier this evening. He would like your views on the incident."

I could see from the smile on his face that he would be more than willing to take me by force if I gave the slightest move to resist. I decided to play along, I was confident of my ability to see my way safely through any kind of interrogation.

"Of course," I replied. "I would be happy to help the good Inspector with any information that I have. I am not sure, however, how I can begin to aid him." I turned to Tom. "I will return as soon as I am able, to watch over her once more."

The carriage ride to Leman Road, although short, was silent and uncomfortable. Sergeant Thomas did not take his eyes off of me for a moment and I could see the desire within him to strike me given the chance. I tried to ignore his angry stare and look out of the window of the carriage, but there was nothing to see but the darkness of Whitechapel rushing past, black and forbidding.

On arrival at the Station I was led straight to the office of Draper and told to wait. The Inspector was currently interviewing witnesses related to another incident in the area earlier this evening and would be with me shortly.

I sat and observed the office surroundings. As I had expected it was kept in a most orderly and neat manner, each particular item on his desk clearly had its place and I hazarded a guess that I could take a rule to the placement of them and find that they were equally spaced to within an eighth of an inch. I wondered how a man who was so infinitely particular with the smallest of details in his office could find the time to investigate such important and critical issues as murder. Surely he either did not sleep very much or had a mind so ordered and clear as to allow every minute of his day for the pursuit of his obsessions. This was obviously, where the accountant within him still resided. It was as I contemplated the essence of the man that I found myself drifting away into the half-sleep of one who had been awake for an inordinately long period of time. My eyes struggled to stay open and, despite my surroundings, I dropped off to sleep in the chair.

"Good evening, Mr Darke!" The sound of Draper's voice dragged me from my slumber in the most startling of manners and it was only through quick reflexes that I managed not to fall from my seat. His voice was aggravatingly happy in its temper, and the fact that he had woken me only served to add to my annoyance at the man. He noted my alarm and annoyance with the most boyish of giggles and took a seat on the chair on the opposite side of the desk.

"I trust that I have not prevented you from having a good night's sleep," he smiled, "but I felt that it was really very important to see you as soon as possible. I would not like to let important events that you may have been party to fall from your memory."

"Of course, Inspector," I said struggling through my stupor to remain civil with the man. "You know that I am always happy to help in your investigations, although I admit I find the time a little out of the ordinary."

He continued to smile at me, an act, which I noted, made his skin stretch over the sharp points of his cheekbones and I wondered if his grin were to broaden further whether they would indeed break through.

"I understand that my sergeant found you at the bedside of Miss Finnan, it was most worrying the state in which she was found earlier. Tell me, before my carriage arrived in Arbour Square, did Miss Finnan speak at all? Did she mention what she had seen? Did she give a description of her attacker?"

"No, I am afraid not, Inspector. When I arrived she was unconscious and as unspeaking as you will find her now. I fear the worst for her, really I do."

"And her friend, Miss …" he paused momentarily studying the notes on his desk. "Miss Utterson. Did you speak to her at all? Did she say anything of note?"

"Again I am afraid that I cannot really help you, sir." I remarked. "Rose, Miss Utterson was quite distraught and hysterical, it was a wonder that she was able to speak at all."

Draper looked on me suspiciously and, pulling open one of the drawers in his desk he withdrew a pipe and a small tin of tobacco which he then endeavoured to fill and light.

"That is such a shame, Mr Darke. Are you aware of an incident which involved a person in Love Lane shortly after the discovery of Miss Finnan?"

"I am not."

"And can you tell me if you have ever heard of or met a man named Arthur Downing, a dock worker from the area?"

"Downing … mm," I feigned thought and attempts at memory. "No I cannot say that I have. That is to say that if I ever met the man I did not know his name."

Draper looked at his notes again, his lips moving as he read them to himself. He paused once or twice as he read to look up at me; he appeared confused by something. Finally, he stopped and placed the notes on his desk.

"Apparently this evening a man of your height and with blonde almost white hair was seen running away from the Love Lane area," he paused in an attempt to gauge my reaction before continuing. "This was shortly after the sound of gunfire in one of the tenement buildings. On inspection of the building, my officers found a man; Arthur Downing, hanged in his rooms and covered in blood. Blood that was not his own. It is my belief that this man is the same person who Miss Finnan encountered and who is the killer of your family members, as well as some boys from the area. Are you sure that this man seen fleeing was not you, sir?"

"I am quite sure, Inspector Draper. After leaving Arbour Square I headed straight home and remained there until my concern for Miss Finnan's welfare became too great for me to bear. That is when I went to the Princess Alice to see her."

"Are you telling me, sir that you did not visit Love Lane earlier this evening and enter the property of Mr Arthur Downing?"

"I did not, Inspector." I repeated. "After leaving Beth's side in Arbour Square, upon *your* instruction, I returned home to my rooms on Osborn Street. There I thought to take to my bed so distraught was I at the events of the evening. I found, however, that I could not sleep for worry over the health and wellbeing of Miss Finnan, and so I took myself to The Princess Alice, where Sergeant Thomas found me."

He eyed me for a moment and, for an instance that dragged like a full lifetime and more, I felt transparent to his gaze. I concentrated on my breathing, ensuring that each breath was measured and controlled and that such scrutiny would not accentuate any physical misgivings.

"Tell me again, Mr Darke. Before this evening, had you ever heard of the name Arthur Downing?"

With a steadiness which surprised even me, I replied.

"I can say with all honesty, Inspector Draper, that before hearing his name upon your own lips I would never have any given mention of it a second thought." His eyes continued to bore into me.

"You seem very calm, it is not usual for one held by the police to behave so."

"That is because I am sure of my own innocence in this matter. If there is any semblance of excitement about me, Inspector it is because you have told me that the vicious murderer of my dear family members has met his end. My only regret is that he did not live to see the full force of the law meted out to him. I am grateful for the news that you have brought me, but it is indeed news, I have no knowledge of this man."

He sat back in his chair and folded his arms, smiling at me. There was a distant twinkle in his eyes and I sat for a while meeting his gaze. His fingers drummed upon his arm and I could sense that he was on the verge of making a decision. Finally he spoke.

"Then it would seem that I have no further need for you, Mr Darke. You may go."

I looked at the man in shock; surely my lies had not worked on such a shrewd mind?

"Truly?" I asked, attempting to disguise my amazement.

"Of course," he replied, smiling warmly. "I apologise for detaining you in such a way. This is a night where we should be celebrating the end of a most foul and murderous spree. Please, let me hold you no longer."

The streets were empty and, though it was still dark, I knew that dawn's light would soon be beginning to brighten the dirty streets as I came through the doorway of the police station and out into freedom. I hazarded myself a small smile and thought of my bed. A most dangerous chapter of this whole situation had passed without any danger making its mark upon me.

Bethany however, had not been so fortunate.

14
VISIONS OF THE NEW BORN DEAD

I remember quite clearly the day that Mother died. The reason for this strong memory however, I shall not reveal in such an easy manner. She had been grossly unwell for a number of weeks, slowly losing her strength until she reached the stage where she could not even leave her bed. She was suffering from an affliction of the chest, a strength sapping poison, which drained the colour from her face and left her weakly gasping for breath. She lay all day and night in fever soaked sheets, which required regular changing to lessen the stench of coming death which staggered towards our home like a large but slow moving beast. Father had called a doctor to her after the sickness had been firmly in place for a full week with no sign of fading. The Doctor would not be drawn however and said nothing but;

"It is a powerful blight; if she is strong she will come through it."

By the third week, the fever burned so darkly within her that she lost all sense of time and place. She would cry out through the night according to Father and would spend her days rambling streams of words, which rarely made any sense. These confusion filled times slowly retreated and she became increasingly silent, the rank infection coursing through her body causing her to refuse all of the food which we attempted to feed her. In those final days she uttered no sounds at all other than the odd moan of pain and despair. We took turns to attend to her bedside and for some reason I found myself taking the majority of the responsibilities.

I would spend long hours by her side; studying her gaunt and deathly features, wondering how much longer this inner poison would torture her before delivering the final killing blow. I contemplated fate and of how one's behaviour and conduct could lead to the creation of our ends. I did not begin to believe in any sort of higher power, a single God or a collection of deities, whose games included ensuring that those who have led an unworthy or cruel life would be the ones whose ends would be the most painful or torturous. I did however wish to believe that good things happened to good people eventually, and if this were the case then there must be some element of the transverse where one paid for their wrongdoings.

    I watched her as she drifted in and out of sleep, trembling and coated in sweat, her long hair draped across the pillow like a shroud waiting to be wrapped around her dead face. I thought about the fire and anger with which she had dominated our family for so many years. I thought about the fear and the terror that she seemed so desperate to mete out upon Father, Niko and I. Her temper seemed unrestrained, unlimited to height or boundary, constant and unrelenting, ended now only by a poisonous curse which tore through her body from the inside with the lack of mercy that only a force of nature could display.

    I was with her in those final moments; I watched the final glimmer of light fade and die within her eyes as I laid my hands upon her. In pity, and out of a merciful act which none who had ever met her would believe she deserved, she was taken.

    I did not move from her side for a number of minutes after her passing. I sat and looked at her face, I studied the calm, and I noted the absence of tension's line or anger's hue. Her eyes, though dead and staring, were empty of the fire of accusation or the darkness of coming violence; she was finally at peace. I reached forwards and touched her for the last time, the tips of my fingers gently closing her eyelids, giving her the appearance of one who was asleep. How quiet the world was to me suddenly, how finally peaceful did I feel knowing that this dead, still body would never cause suffering from fist or curse again.

When finally I felt that this moment of peace between us had run its course, I stood, leaning forward to kiss my mother's forehead, something which I could never remember doing in all of my twenty-two years. Such sadness.

Mother's funeral was a small affair, attended only by Father, Niko and I. George Woodrow had been kind enough to provide the funeral services free of charge to Father, an act which I looked upon as both a sign of George's friendship and more cynically as being George's way of making sure that he played some part in putting the woman into the ground once and for all. A short service was held in St Mary's, nothing like the normal event which the church held so regularly. There was no one wishing to stand to give a eulogy, no tears or grief at loss, we did not even assist in the carrying of the coffin. We watched, not speaking or sharing. We observed respect for the sanctity of the church and followed the casket outside and to the hollow pit where she would be lowered. Throughout it all we were silent and distracted, lost within our own thoughts and memories.

As the diggers arrived and started to slowly fill the hole, the sound of the dirt hitting the wooden lid echoed through the grey drizzle of the day. Father and Niko departed to enter the church once again to see the clergyman, and I found myself standing alone watching each shovelful cover the box, burying her in the ground. Such was my unwavering occupation in this act that I did not notice the presence of another man by my side until he spoke.

"Finally at peace," he said, his voice a gravelly rasp. "I am glad for her."

I looked up from my thoughts and saw my fellow mourner. He was an aged man, all sweat and whiskers, his bush of grey hair barely restrained by the squat round hat which he wore on his head. His clothes were worn and bare in places, but gave the impression that it had been the man's best suit for many years.

"I'm sorry," I answered, observing him closely; "Did you know her?"

"Did."

"I do not know you."

"I knew her before your birth, before her marriage, before her descent."

"Descent?"

"Before she fell and lost the life she could have had. Before she chose over her family." He smiled wryly, an expression which showed the brown and black of his teeth, the rotten stumps sitting painfully in his raw gums.

"Oh," I said looking to the floor. "I understand she left her family to be with Father. It was ... unfortunate."

"Unfortunate was it? I would not say unfortunate, boy. No, that is not the word I would use to describe how she was taken from us." The rumble of his voice showed signs of a barely restrained growl and I could tell that this was a man prone to anger and violence, surely related to Mother. "Other words could be used. Bewitched is a good word, I would go as far as to say stolen."

I glanced up at him and saw that he had not taken his eyes from the hole which the gravedigger was continuing to fill. His whole body appeared to shake slightly, an almost imperceptible quiver, which I only noticed when looking at the clenched fists held at his sides. In a moment which reminded me of so many with my mother, I felt that danger was near and that this man, old though he was, could hold the potential for great violence.

"I am sorry for the loss," I said, slowly turning from him, "It is wrong for someone to become so separated from their family. She never spoke of you, although I am sure that she thought of you often." I began to walk away from the man, heading in the direction of the church and my family.

"Filthy, half-breed bastard!" he called after me as I strode onwards my head down; "If it hadn't been for you she wouldn't have left us! You killed her and you'll get yours." The sound of his voice and the words which he spat after me, stuck in my head long after I had made it to the safety of the church.

I told Father about the incident when we were alone later at The Princess Anne where we had gone for a rare social drink together. Niko was also with us, but was outside the pub talking to some friends, and I took the opportunity to find out more about the man.

"That would be her Father, James Hudson, a brutal man by all accounts," Father looked lost into his drink as he spoke. "I would think that he was where your Mother learned to use a fist rather than the tongue to deal with her problems."

"If he was brutal then I think Mother was better off away from him, do you not think?"

"I am sure you are right, Sib. I am sure you are, but she never forgave me for taking her away from her family. It was the root of her anger and I blame myself." Father had gone a little pale at the memory of those times.

"You were not to blame for her family abandoning her, Father. You have always said that they forced her from her home because of her plans to marry you. Their blindness to love is not a fault of yours, surely."

"You were not there and you do not know what you are talking about!" He snapped his face filling with a spite that I had not seen in him before. My alarm must have shown as he immediately apologised.

"I am sorry, Sibelius. I have kept the truth from you because I am not proud of my actions at that time." He looked lost again, caught up in the obviously shameful memories.

"No, Father, it is I who am sorry. I do not wish to make you more uncomfortable on today of all days. You have laid your wife to rest and I should not heighten your pain with my suppositions. Let us leave it there and I shall comment no more. Come; let us have one more drink before we leave." I stood and approached the bar where Tom poured us two more drinks. A shot of viina, a bottle of which I had procured from the docks from a Finnish ship six months earlier and given to Tom to keep behind the bar for Father, and a scotch whisky for myself, something which I had recently developed a taste for.

As I stood at the bar and looked back at Father's table, I struggled to understand fully how to approach discussing the subject of Mother's death with him. For someone who dealt with grieving families on a daily basis, my own business starting one year prior to Mother's death, I found it inordinately difficult to discuss such a matter with a member of my own family. I collected our drinks, paid Tom and returned to the table, vowing to myself to leave best alone. Father apparently did not share my fear.

"I blame myself because it *was* my fault, Sibelius."

"Father please?" I protested, hoping that he would not speak on.

"You see she was very young when we first met, very young and very vulnerable. She had been betrothed to a fine man, a local trader who was madly in love with her, and she him. I had seen her in the marketplace; she helped her family on their stall. I had seen her and I grew jealous of her man." He paused for a moment picking up his cup and taking a small sip. "I could be a charming man in my youth, Sib, full of confidence, swagger and the misguided notion that I knew everything. She was a good seven years younger than me and I made it my business to get to know her, to impress her and to make her mine. One evening as I accompanied her home after she finished work I persuaded her to come for a drink with me. As we sat and drank I realised that how much she was for her man and I grew angry. It was then that I did something that I am forever ashamed of. I laced her drink and got her drunk, so drunk that she was unable to stand without assistance. And then I took her home and I took advantage of her, a terrible deed which cursed me from that day onwards, for she fell pregnant." It was my turn to take a drink now.

"Father, stop."

"Her man rejected her," he continued ignoring my pleas, "her family disowned her and she was thrown onto the streets, carrying the child of a man who had abused her and who took her in guilt, carrying a child which she would forever resent. I am sorry, Sibelius, my act has caused pain to many, no more so than you."

I did not respond, I did not know how. My mind reeled with thoughts of Mother and of how she had meted out her spite and vehemence on all about her. Despite this new knowledge though, and the greater understanding of the actions which built such a powerful anger within her, I could not ever forgive her for the pain and the misery which she had forced upon our family. I now also understood why Father, racked with guilt, did not prevent her from venting such ire. Any normal person viewing this series of events from the outside would feel that any anger that I felt in return should be directed at Father, for planting the seed of the fury, but the simple fact was that I loved the man and he was not the one using fists, feet and heated objects upon me.

Two weeks following Father's confession to me, Mother's ghost returned to haunt me in the shape of three figures in the dark as I returned to my apartments from a card game in Bloomsbury. I had just paid the driver and was pulling my keys out of the pocket of my long coat when they jumped me.

At first I thought that they meant to rob me but, even though I held a fair amount of winnings in the breast of my coat, they did not attempt to raid my pockets at all. I was struck over the head with fists which came from all directions, and when I dropped to the floor from the blows with a shout, the assault did not lessen in the least. Hard boots with heavy soles were employed upon my torso, kicking and stamping until I moved no more and the only sound I could emit was the choking cough of blood. The battery only ceased when I heard the calls of others and cries for the police. My attackers fled then but one of them spat on me as he left and uttered two words which told me the reason for the assault.

"Half-breed Bastard!"

It was, I knew, the voice of James Hudson, my own grandfather. It seemed that Mother succeeded in obtaining one last beating in her name. I had no lasting damage other than some cracked ribs and a break to my left wrist which happened as I fell, injuries which healed over time. I did not report the assault and never told my Father or Niko who had orchestrated the deed, telling them that it was a simple robbing. Niko was still oblivious to the darker side of our family, and I thought that to tell Father the cause of my attack would only cause further shame and embarrassment to him.

I thought of how the shame I now felt regarding my role in Bethany's situation was as great as Father's although different in circumstance. Like Father I had ruined the life of a young girl through my own obsession, I had ploughed onwards, desperate to seek my goal and find revenge with little thought for how this may affect those around me. I remembered how keen she had been to become involved in my adventures and the stubbornness she had displayed when I made my pathetic attempts to keep her out of this horrid business. Perhaps it was the thought of having someone at my side during my exploits, and of that person being so fair and good that it gave me credence to take the law into my own hands. Whatever the reason for my lack of judgement and authority in preventing her involvement, the facts were simple; together we had found and stopped a killer, but one of us had fallen. I just wish that it had been me and not Beth, poor sweet, stubborn Bethany Finnan.

It was with this guilt hanging heavily upon my mind, combined with the physical tiredness of my efforts that I returned to Osborn Street with the night still and dark around me. I was glad in some way that the evening's incidents had closed one particular section of this situation. The beast had been vanquished once again, returning to Tuonela and to his rightful place as gatekeeper to the dead. However, I did not consider my work by any means complete as I had yet to find a way to deal with the members of the Dolorian Club who no doubt would only try to repeat the process. I knew that my involvement, in the investigation, discovery and subsequent death of Arthur Downing, would be grossly frowned upon by this grand order of fools and that it would not be long before they attempted to carry out an act of retribution as they had done with Father and Niko.

These thoughts I resolved to put to one side for a few short hours however as I felt the call of my bed and the need of sleep to reinvigorate both body and mind in preparation for the final moves in the game within which I had found myself a player.

As I slowly climbed the stairs however, I remembered that I had, in stupidity, agreed to carry out a photographic assignment in Knightsbridge this afternoon at three o'clock. I looked at my pocket watch and saw that it was twenty minutes short of four o'clock, there would be a little time for sleep if I were to keep the appointment. I let out a heavy sigh and turned descending the staircase again to gather the items that I would need to take with me.

Because the demand for my services often came at short notice, I kept a travel pack ready made up at all times should I require it. This pack was sizeable but, in order for me to carry out all the tasks required for assignments within the client's home, there were items which I needed with me. These included a locked wooden box containing the various developing chemicals required following the exposure. The reason for its extra security was because of the toxicity of said chemicals and their danger to the public if ingested, no more so than the fixative which I used, potassium cyanide. This chemical, which I had in liquid diluted form, was quite lethal if taken in and as such I upheld the utmost security when taking it out of the studio.

The other items in my mobile kit included, of course my camera and tripod as well as a piece of my own invention, the transportable darkroom. I will not bore you with the full details of this equipment but to say that it was to be easily constructed anywhere and was made of a piece of thick velvet cloth and a collection of tubular wooden rods which, when connected together made a frame large enough to enclose me within so that I could complete the photographic development.

With the tools of my trade collected into a cumbersome but neat pile by the doorway of my studio I went upstairs where I washed myself down and changed my clothing. I checked my watch again and saw that it was now half an hour past four in the morning and so, freshly cleaned and dressed, I laid upon my bed and slept for a few short hours until the time came for me to set out and arrange for my usual carriage driver to collect me and my mobile photography studio at a little after one o'clock.

The carriage journey was bumpy and rough enough to prevent me from slumber on my way to Knightsbridge. I hoped that the assignment could be completed with haste and efficiency, so that I would be able to return home to sleep and recuperate as I freely admit that I had never felt such tiredness. I concluded that my endeavours and exertions over the past few weeks both physical and emotional were finally beginning to overtake me, and it was a promised blessing that it would soon be coming to an end in one way or another.

The residence, in Lowndes Square, was a large townhouse of five storeys and was situated in a most desirable and well-kept area. Before this whole affair had started I had dreamt of one day living in such an area, those days were long since passed however. I stepped out of the carriage and admired the property, the only dream that I had left in my heart was to escape from my current situation alive. I thought of Earnshaw and the other members of the Dolorian club, they would probably know by now that their messenger of death had taken his own life, sending the spirit of Surma within him to flee back to the underworld. As I had been told in Earnshaw's carriage, the killings were only a small part of their long term plan; there would be no thought of surrender or retraction of their goals. There would be more organised terror to come, and mine and Bethany's part in the discovery and death of Arthur Downing would not go unpunished.

The offer of Earnshaw to join him was also playing on my mind and prodding gently at my unconscious. Bethany had already suffered a disturbance in her cognition and contact with reality, I had lost both my Father and Brother. Would it really be beyond me to concede defeat and take up a passive role within their ranks? It would surely be preferable to seeing any further hurt or pain coming to Beth or Tom. A decision clearly needed to be made, and quickly, before horror struck again.

As the driver and I began to unload my equipment from the roof of the carriage, the door of the Peckard's residence opened and I was shocked to see Mr Peckard himself stood at the door waiting to greet me.

He was a young man, probably no older than I. He had a round and ruddy face, which seemed to glow with kindness and which immediately endeared me to him.

"Mr Darke," he called, in a well-spoken but friendly tone. I climbed the steps to meet him, the driver following me, carrying my equipment.

"Just leave it at the door please, Sam, I will take it from there." I said and handed him five shillings. "I will be ready to be picked up in a little over an hour if you would be so kind." Sam nodded to me, he had been my driver on many such appointments before and, although I knew that he did not understand or agree with my work, he was always confident in my ability to pay him a little over the odds for his services and, as such, tried to be a flexible as he could. I turned to young man at my side and shook his hand warmly.

"Mr Peckard? I am so very sorry for your loss; I will try to be as discreet as possible in my work today and I promise that you will be left with a beautiful reminder of your dear family once I have left."

"Of course, of course," he muttered nervously, "please come in. I have heard so much about you and your work, all good of course." We entered the house and he led me, through the exquisitely decorated hallway, to the rear drawing room, where I found the two caskets that I had been expecting to see. "I was not quite sure how you wished the room to be arranged," he motioned to a softly furnished chair set next to a large houseplant in the corner. "I thought that maybe we could place them there, I do not know in truth, you are the expert in these matters."

I noted a reddening of the rims of his eyes and realised that his nervous and over friendly demeanour were due to the extremes of grief, which one can only imagine in a man who had lost both his love and his newly born infant. This was, of course, an odd situation for a man of his standing to force himself through, but I understood that it was the end product that he desired and, until this moment, had probably not given much thought to the actual process. This was an encounter which I had dealt with many times before and one which I was comfortable in dealing with.

"Mr Peckard, Benjamin. May I call you Benjamin?" he nodded as I raised my arm and placed my hand on his shoulder. "As you have quite rightly said, I am indeed the expert in these matters, and as such you can be quite confident in matters of discretion, respect for your loved one and my care for you as my employer for the day."

His body seemed to relax somewhat upon my touch and the sight of the warm, caring smile which I used for such an effect. The reddening in his eyes increased a little, which was to be expected, and I saw the soft wet glimmer of fluid in his eyes as he looked on me.

"I'm most sorry, Mr Darke. I fear that you have found me at a low time, I did not believe that such a thing would ever happen to me, to ..." his voice cracked a little, "to Louisa."

"Of course, Benjamin, it is a most unfortunate and sad occasion, but if you would like to leave me to complete my work, then I shall be as quick and efficient as possible. Why don't you take a stroll around the square for a time, get some air and think of the happy times that you and your lovely wife enjoyed? Take maybe, an hour? I promise to look after both Louisa and the babe, and when you return I will have finished my work and you will have a lasting memento of your dear family."

His shoulders shook beneath my touch and I could sense the relief that he would not have to remain in the house whilst I carried out my commission.

"Yes ... yes maybe that would be for the best. I will take a short stroll to the park perhaps." He began backing out of the door, obviously keen to get out of the room which housed his dead family. "I will have Mrs Godfrey bring you up some tea if you would like, or I have coffee if you prefer?"

The thought of coffee to help wake and stimulate me made me even more fond of the poor boy stood in front of me.

"A small pot of coffee would me most perfect, Benjamin." I left the room to bring in my equipment and, as the last of the items were brought into the drawing room, Mr Peckard stood at the doorway to the house seemingly in a rush to depart.

"One hour, Is that enough?"

"One hour will be more than enough for my task, Mr Peckard. Oh, one last thing would you like your wife to be covered or uncovered? It is a matter of choice for you entirely." He knew immediately what I meant.

"Covered please, I believe that this is the way it is done."

"Covered it is then, sir. Enjoy your stroll." He skipped down the steps looking to put distance between himself and the house. As he departed the smile left my face.

I got to work straight away setting up the tented darkroom facility, before turning my attentions to the caskets on the floor in front of me. The coffin holding Louisa Peckard was quite small, and I guessed that she would be a slight figure and easy to move into position. The other box however was so very tiny, of a size that you would have thought could contain a child's china doll. The photographing of small babies, dead with their first few months or more often at birth, was an area of my work which I really did not enjoy and usually dreaded such assignments. As I see it, there is no greater loss to the world than that of a babe who had not had any chance of living. The thoughts of what they could have been often prayed on my mind, more so than when photographing older children. For a baby is so new, so innocent to life, and within each tiny body there is such potential for greatness and love. It was my experiences with commissions where small babies were the focus that went someway into creating my feelings towards love and marriage. For I knew how delicate and beloved other people's babies were to me and so the thought of having one of my very own would bring about emotions within me that I feared I would not be able to control. And to lose that baby, to lose my own child? That is a place that I did not conceive ever being willing or strong enough to go to.

As I removed the lid from Louisa Peckard's coffin, I saw that she was indeed slight of body, and beautiful. She had long blond hair which wisped down across her shoulders, her eyes which were closed were large and, without attempting to open the lids I could imagine that they would have been her most outstanding feature. She wore the lightest of makeup; just enough to conceal death's cold pallor and the smallest amount of rouge upon her lips made them look fulsome yet demure. It would be such a shame that her face would not be evident in the final photograph.

I lifted her gently out of the casket and over to the chair. Her body was quite stiff, however this often worked in my favour as it made the models easier to pose. When I was quite sure that her position was adequate I turned my attentions to the small box. I unscrewed the fasteners and drew the lid to one side. There laid as if asleep was the most delicate of forms, a little girl.

My eyes immediately filled and I forced back the urge to let my emotions flood out. Such a beautiful tiny thing, so fragile and weak, never having a chance at survival. I paused for a short moment and looked down upon her, I thought of how she would have grown if she had lived. With a kind and loving Father and Mother, cherished by those around her and growing into a beautiful young woman, the very image of her mother. It was not to be.

I picked up the babe, so light in my arms that I hardly felt a weight at all, and carried her over to her mother's lap where I laid her in the arms of the woman who died trying to bring her into the world. The sadness ripped through me in a way that I had never experienced before. Was it my recent experiences which had stripped me of my cold professional demeanour? What had caused such a fall into outward warmth and care? A picture appeared in my mind as I questioned myself, a picture which revealed the key to my heart. Something now lost me.

The final piece of my preparation was to cover Louisa Peckard's head with a large black silk cloth, so that the whole of her face was obscured to the camera. This was a fashion which had become an almost unwritten rule when photographing mothers with their dead babes and only in the rarest of occasions was the head left uncovered. I did not know quite where this trend had appeared from but I followed the wishes of those who employed me and stuck to the fashion.

I withdrew my tripod from its sleeve and extended the legs, placing it in position on the other side of the room from the subjects. I then opened the large wooden case which contained the camera which I used for visiting assignments. It was not the best that I owned in terms of the quality of the portraits which it was able to produce, but it was sufficient to meet the standards of those who employed my services. I did not bring my best photographic equipment out with me on these visits for a number of reasons, size being one of them but also I found out, through a painful lesson, that a lone man carrying expensive items with him alone was a prime target for those who would be hardy enough of spirit to commit assaultive theft.

I paused briefly beginning to set up my camera. As a result of my tiredness and the events of the previous evening, I had not even begun to give thought to what I may see when I looked through the viewfinder at the subjects of today's assignment. Surely now that Surma's host had ended their own life and had returned the spirit of the guardian of Tuonela to his rightful place then there would be nothing amiss.

I took a moment to survey the room. I have been surrounded by the bodies of the dead since I was a babe and I had never suffered from any fear or dread of the spirit world. However there was something about this room, this setting, which filled me to near tipping point with tension and portent. The room itself was no different to many others that I had been in; that I had used as a setting and scenery for my photography, but a tiny knot of fear, a ball of nervous energy, felt as though it was developing deep within me. I could not pinpoint its origin, save for the presence of the dead on the cushioned chair. The room was ornately decorated with items of furniture and decoration, which ordinarily I would think were beautiful and fitting. At that exact moment however they oozed threat and menace of a kind which froze the marrow within me and sucked the breath from my lungs. The carved scrolling around the picture frame that suddenly resembled a mouth torn in terror, the large mirror above the mantle which hung tilted forward slightly at the top, giving the room a distorted and darkened reflection of what was contained within it, the slow ticking of the tall clock in the corner, each echoing click an exertion which grew seemingly louder and more resonant in nature.

The fire of tension within me sparked and crackled, threatening to burn a gaping and painful hole if it was not brought under control. The room felt cold and a chill crept about my skin like so many tiny insects. I shivered slightly at the feeling and found that this action threw some of the anxiety away from me. I shook myself a little more, trying to rid myself of the urge to run screaming from the room. All the while the form of the departed babe sat upon her mother's knee, her eyes open and watching my every move.

Did I open the eyes?

I did not remember doing so, maybe in my tiredness I had done it without thought. I glanced quickly at the eyes of the babe, they were milky and dead but I could swear that there was some focus within them. I crossed the room quickly and closed them once more, feeling the sharp claws of madness scratching at the door of my mind, and I once more shook myself in an attempt to shed the growing hysteria. Resolve and a demonstration of purpose were required at this time, the sooner that I completed the assignment and left this place the better for me as a whole.

As I nervously placed and secured my camera upon the tripod, I felt the cold sheen of perspiration upon the back of my neck, the exude of anxiety forming a bead which, although small, caused me to judder slightly as it ran down my collar and traced a line of fear down my spine. As I attempted to attach the winged nut, which held my camera in place, I found that my fingers trembled and were greasy with sweat. The nut slipped from my fingers to the floor and, as I bent down to retrieve it, I felt light headed and weak in the legs.

It took all of the concentration that I could muster to finally fit the camera and attach the large black velvet cloth, which I would be shortly placing over my head to take the focus on the subjects and take the exposure. Attempting to swallow the large, hard lump within my throat I drew the cloth over my head and looked through the viewfinder at the woman and her child.

There seemed to be no change in their appearance, they looked as dead as they had been a moment before. I withdrew my head from the velvet again and looked around the room, there was nothing out of the ordinary in its appearance, the portents of terror that had filled the room just moments before had gone and was replaced by the normal drawing room which I had entered.

Relief swept through me like a soothing tide as I realised that my visions of the dead were a thing of the past. Letting out a deep sigh, I placed my head under the cloth once more and began to focus the lens upon the subjects in readiness for the exposure onto the plate. I would take the picture quickly before developing it and leaving at the earliest opportunity.

As I readied myself to release the shutter, a cold breeze blew into the room quite suddenly and my first thought was that it would be the Peckard's maid entering the room with my coffee. The chill was so fresh however that it could not have been caused by a simple draught, it felt as though the area had been filled with ice, such was the extremity of the change in temperature. As I pressed the shutter release and took the exposure, I realised that the sudden loss of warmth had been a warning, for at that moment the features of the baby girl's face began to change in a most horrid manner.

The colour of her skin, previously pale and creamy, began to take on a darkened tone, grey in shade and becoming almost black around her tiny eyes. Her nose began to twitch, ever so slightly spreading throughout her face until each cheek flickered uncontrollably. The child's brow became dark with lined creases and my heart sank as I realised what was about to happen.

The baby began to shake, a quiver at first but the tremor appeared to become much more rigorous and increasingly violent as the seconds passed.

I was frozen to the spot, the ends of my legs lead weights which would take enormous strength to lift or move. It was as I stared helplessly at the scene before me that I noticed that it was not the child that shook at all but the mother upon whose legs it was sitting.

The child remained silent still, eyes closed, its face a bunched up knot of anguish and hatred. Sharp creases of torment were etched deep into the babe's pain filled features; its mouth open wide in a silent scream which, if made sound, would strip flesh from bone, such would be its shrill torture.

The mother had started to make a low moaning sound, monotonous and dire, full of foreboding and bloated with the dream of death. I thought to run from the room at that instant, but found that I was mesmerised by the view through the lens.

It was then that the babe's eyes shot open, a quick and violent action which exposed to me the very nature of hell in their glare. It was aware of my presence staring coldly at me, sneering in its hatred, like one would look at a louse ridden beggar. Its eyes hammered long sharp stakes through my stomach and I felt the urge to vomit, the acid bile sending burning shots to my throat, each lump stinging and tearing at the soft flesh of my gullet.

It opened its mouth to speak.

"There will be death to-night," the gravelled voice spat, its sharp, grating tone causing physical pain to my ears. The babe stretched its mouth wide, as if accustoming itself to the use of its tongue. "The beast will tear, the beast will rend, and the beast will feed. No child will survive".

"A ... child?" I stammered.

The monster responded with a smile. Its sight was not pleasant, but a cruel crack which split the face and exposed a toothless mouth with blackened gums.

"Not one," it laughed, "Not even two!" As it spoke blood began to seep from the corners of its mouth, a dark thick liquid which burnt the chin of the child with a hiss. "Better to be already dead than to be an orphan to-night. The son of Cyrene will weep tears of blood for the lost children of the faith he spurned."

"Cyrene? What do you mean?" I cried. "Who is the son of Cyrene? Explain yourself?"

The child did not respond to me but began to cry. It was not the cry of a baby, but of a banshee, sharp and angry. Its howl bristled with malevolence and pain, of torture and of unending torment. The sound brought agony to my ears and it was joined by the voice of the mother beneath the black velvet veil. The mother's cry was of sorrow however, it was the cry of a mother who had lost her child and together, the sounds of the dead, these wailing demons sent to taunt me, echoed in a volume which I could not believe was not heard throughout the house and even the streets outside.

The noise of the dead screaming and moaning in tandem was too much for me to bear any longer. I pulled my head from the cloth to stop the noise and horror, but the power of their spirit had become too strong and to my utter shock, although the bodies no longer moved, the noise and the tremors running through the room continued to increase.

Decorative china set upon the mantle were so shaken that they dropped to the floor, smashing into pieces, a glass lamp, thankfully not lit, tumbled over with a crashing noise which struggled to be heard over the cries of the ghost mother and her baby. I stood shaking in the middle of this tumult, my hands to my ears and my own cries adding to the din. Finally there was a deafening cracking noise and a split appeared in the wall above the mirror over the mantelpiece. The tear began to travel lower and lower until it reached the mirror's frame. Slowly a crack began to materialize on the glass, as if it were being pushed forcefully from behind. For a split second the darkened glass of the mirror seemed awash with a swarm of pale, ghostly faces, each one torn in anguish.

And then the mirror shattered outwards, sending glass flying from it, showering me with razor sharp needles which left slices and cuts upon my hands and face. It had ended.

The room was silent then and I knew that I had to leave, to warn others of the death and slaughter to come this evening. Taking one last look at the inanimate and cold mother and baby sat upon the chair I fled from the room crashing straight into a maid carrying a silver tray.

The tray carried a pot of coffee and crockery which smashed onto the polished wooden floor as she screamed in fright. Thankfully, for her, the hot coffee landed mostly on me and it was I that felt the burning on my legs as my trouser quickly soaked in the steaming liquid. I did not stop in my escape however. Shouting my apologies over my shoulder, I ran out of the house and was relieved to see Sam waiting outside, feeding his horses.

"Sam!" I called, pulling him to attention, "Sam I must get back to Whitechapel – immediately! We must go now!"

"But, Mr Darke," he stammered, "what about your equipment?"

"Equipment be damned!" I barked. "Let us go!" Sam leapt into action taking the reins in his hand and climbing to his seat atop the carriage as I jumped inside. "You will be paid handsomely for this, my friend!" I shouted to him through the window as we set off.

I have never known Sam drive as fast as he did that afternoon, it was probably due to the promise of money, but I would like to think that there was some element of honour and friendly assistance in the energy that he put into the effort of returning me to Whitechapel. I spent the journey trying to compose myself. My shirt clinging to me, drenched in terror's cold sweat. I shook uncontrollably, my hands a blur of tremor as I tried to contain the weight of horror that had been forced within me. My blood felt thick within my veins, depriving me of energy and causing me to struggle to gain breath.

I thought that I had a suitable level of bravery before this day. I had shown myself able to deal with the images of the talking dead with some degree of normality and lack of fear. Today however, I had seen into the cold abyss of death and I had realised that it was a terrifying sight to behold.

My mind was awash with thoughts of Cyrene. I knew it to be an ancient city in Libya of Greek origin, and something gnawed within me telling me that I knew the 'son'. In my tremulous state however, I could not control my mind enough to ascertain his identity. I stared blankly out of the window of the carriage, looking but not really seeing the grey face of London rumbling by. It was only when I heard the curses of Sam, in the driving seat above me that I realised that we had stopped at all. I pulled down the window and put my head out to see what the delay was.

"I'm sorry, Mr Darke," Sam called. "It looks like there's been some kind of accident up ahead. There's nowhere for us to go until it clears. Do you want me to run ahead and see how long it's going to take?"

"If you think you are able, Sam. Where are we? Have we got far to go?"

"We're not past Soho yet, sir," he said, stepping down to the cobbles. "I'll take a quick stroll down and see what the problem is."

He lit his pipe and set off down the road to where I, from my position leaning out of the window, could see a large crowd forming. Soho was still just over three miles away from Leman Road Police Station where I was heading, where I hoped to find and warn Inspector Draper before the killings took place.

After ten nervous minutes, sat shaking with frustration and anxiety, Sam returned. His face was grimly set and his eyes were cast downwards.

"Horrible business I'm afraid, Mr Darke, horrible." He shook his head as he spoke. "It's an accident involving two carriages and a young lad. The boy is dead, torn clean in half they are saying and one of the horses is dead and blocking the roadway. I reckon we are going to be here for another half an hour at least."

A young boy dead; how fitting this was on a day set to be flooded with the corpses of children. My anxiety could not be contained any longer and I jumped out of the carriage.

"I will make my own way from here, Sam. Thank you." I pulled some money out of my coat pocket and presented him with a guinea. "Thank you for your help today. Please, if you could return to Knightsbridge when you are able and collect my equipment, there will be another guinea for you when we next meet. Drop it off with Tom Finnan at the Alice."

I started heading off down the road before turning to Sam once more.

"Oh, and if you see Mr Peckard at the house. Do apologise on my behalf for any damage and assure him that I will have his picture delivered in due course." And with that I began to run.

The tiredness and exhaustion caused by my recent endeavours had taken a heavy toll upon my body and I found that I could hardly raise the strength to run with any real energy. The sweat ran down my face and dizziness overcame me on a few occasions. By the time I came within sight of Whitechapel Road, I had no idea of the time and checked my pocket watch during one of my brief pauses to reclaim my breath. It was after five o'clock and the night of London would soon be drawing in, bringing out all of its horrors and one beast in particular.

I burst in through the doors of Leman Road Police station shouting like a madman and calling Inspector Draper's name but found myself met by a wall of officers preventing my further entry into the station past the main desk. My arms and shoulders were held fast, and it was clear that my calls to see the Inspector would only be in vain. This thought was confirmed by the sudden presence of Sergeant Abe Thomas who appeared in front of me wearing a wide gap-toothed grin that gave the impression of a child whose birthday had been filled with every present imaginable.

"Good evening, Mr Darke. I find you in good spirits tonight. I'm afraid that the Inspector is not within the station at present, a situation which I am afraid for your sake, leaves me in charge."

I struggled to loose myself from those constricting my movements. The grip of the men on my arms was hard and deep. There would be no way of me exiting this situation of my own accord.

"Please, Sergeant, it is most important that I see the Inspector immediately!" I called, in desperation to the Sergeant's better nature. "It is a matter concerning the forthcoming deaths of a number of children at the hands of the killer of my family!"

Thomas laughed at this declaration. It would seem that his better nature was not to be accessed by one such as me.

"Good Lord, Darke," he crowed in mock concern, "Do you mean to tell me that this murderer has risen from the dead?" He turned to the police constable behind the desk. "Travers, round up the murder squad immediately, it would seem that this killer remains on our streets having climbed out of his grave. Tell me Mr Darke where will this terrible slaughter take place?"

"I do not know, Sergeant, it has something to do with a man born in Libya although I know that this sounds confused."

"Confused? Confused, Mr Darke? Why not at all, I shall telegram our Libya division immediately and request the names of every boy ever born in the country."

The surrounding policemen chuckled at this joke and I could see that my attempts to prevent the atrocity taking place with the help of the law would be wasted as long as Abe Thomas remained at the head of proceedings.

Within moments all semblance of humour dropped from his face leaving just harsh lines of bitterness and cruelty. He brought his face close to my own and I could smell the deep odour of stale whisky and tobacco.

"Well I am most pleased that you saw fit to warn us," his face was a contorted sneer, "I shall see to it that I give your portentous raving the full time and attention that it deserves ... none." He motioned to the corridor which led to the cells. "Gentlemen, it would seem that this man has come in off the streets with the express intention of wasting valuable police time. Take him to the cells and let us keep him until he calms."

The men around me laughed and began to drag me away, but I managed to free one of my arms. With all the strength within my body, I pulled myself away from the policemen and fell headlong into the doorway of the station. As I scrambled to my feet and pushed at the doors, they tried to grab at me but I launched myself out of the station and into the street. I began to run away from the building and heard the noise of laughter coming from behind me as Sergeant Thomas and his men stood in the doorway and gave no attempt at chase.

I ran around the corner before stopping to regain my breath. The darkness of night had fallen now and I knew that there would not be much time left before the killing began. I had failed, there would be no opportunity to prevent the massacre from occurring now as the only orphanage within any reachable distance of me was the Jews orphanage nearby on St Mark's Street.

It was at that moment that I realised that the answer had always been within my grasp and which fear and exhaustion had withheld from me. St Mark the Evangelist was born a Jew in northern Libya, before renouncing his faith and becoming a disciple of Christ. 'He will weep tears of blood for the children of the faith he spurned.' I ran to St Mark's Street and came to the doors of the orphanage.

The doors were locked and I hammered on them calling out for someone to answer, crying that they were in danger of attack. There was no response and I pressed my ear against the door. It was then that I heard the screams of the children. I was too late.

Again and again I threw my shoulder into the door in an attempt to force it open, but it was of no use. My body had neither weight nor strength to push it in and, as I continued in my desperation, each of my efforts became weaker and more pathetic in its fortitude.

All the while the thin, wavering screams of the children rang through me, making my endeavours feel ever more beyond my physical being. Finally, when I had not the strength left in my body to continue, I slid down the door, sobbing like a babe and crying for the help which I knew would not come in time to save them.

As I pressed my face against the wood in anguish, the sound filled my ears, muffled though it was from the other side of the door. The sound of the children crying, little boys, poor little orphan boys pleading for their pitiful and insignificant lives, lives which were being taken one by one in a slow and torturous fashion.

Why had I been cursed with knowing that these things would happen? I wished that I had been killed by the beast myself rather than being tortured in this fashion.

As the cries came to a sudden stop I realised that they were all dead. It was too much for me to bear and I ran away into the night, screaming and sobbing for the lives of the children and begging for my own death.

15
THE FEAR OF THE MOB

I do not know what happened to me for the rest of that evening. I sobbed and cried, wandered the streets like some itinerant madman, finally settling, not back at my apartments, but in the graveyard of St Mary Matfellon, lying curled in a ball and weeping at the grave of Grandfather until I fell into a fitful sleep.

I awoke as dawn broke around me, the birds in the trees chattered and chirped, a sound that I normally enjoyed, but on this morning, it felt as though they were taunting me, crying with laughter at my demise. My clothes glistened with dew, the cold dampness seeping through to stiffen my joints and chill my bones. Slowly, I rolled myself upright and tried to stand. My legs betrayed me somewhat and it was with a stagger and the aid of Grandfather's headstone that I straightened my back and faced the world.

The grim reality of last night's events sucked all semblance of life from my heart as I stumbled out of the graveyard and onto Whitechapel High Street. The market traders and costers were starting their day, busily shifting their handcarts and setting up stalls which would soon be laden with all manner of food, cloth and other wares. Loud voices would fill the air, calls to all within earshot of the goods on sale at the lowest prices. They paid no attention to me, appearing as I did to be a shambling drunk, a moucher; filthy and not worth casting an eye to. This suited me well as I did not wish to be seen or recognised by anyone I knew in this state.

I made my way back to Leman Road where I paused across the street from the police station, rallying my confidence to enter the building once more. I prayed inside that Sergeant Thomas was not on duty this morning and that I would find a policeman more sympathetic to my news.

As I crossed the road a constable stepped out of the station and onto the pavement. I remembered him from the previous evening; he had been one of the men holding my arms at Abe Thomas' behest. I decided to approach him in the hope that without the overbearing presence of Abe Thomas he would be more amenable.

"Excuse me, Constable!" I called as I approached him. He looked up and I could see the light of recognition in his eyes. His face remained firm, I am sure that he did not wish his early start to begin with any conversation with me.

"Mr Darke." He replied looking down at the floor.

"Constable, I trust you are well this morning, I have a request for you if you will humour me. I walked past St Mark's Orphanage last night and heard the most terrible screams coming from within. Please could you accompany me to check that all is well with them?" He looked at me with uncertainty for a moment before giving a wry smile.

"Why not, it is a pleasant enough morning and only around the corner. I know the matron; perhaps she will make me a drink to warm me up." He strode off, not waiting for me and I followed. My heart was not as bright as his and I feared that he would soon be brought crashing down to earth.

We approached the door that I had beaten with such a desperate fury the night before and the Constable tried to turn the handle to get in. It did not move.

"Strange." He said, gently rapping on the wood with his knuckles, "the place is usually full of life and activity by now."

"There is no life in there, trust me." I said in a flat tone. He waited a few moments before knocking again. "It is pointless, Constable, no one will come. You will have to break it in."

He continued to hammer upon the door. Each rap becoming more insistent.

"There will be no reply," I said in an almost lazy manner. "They are all dead inside." He ignored me and continued, this time beating his fists upon the doors.

"Open up!" He called, in his most authoritative tone. "Open this door immediately, this is the Police!"

"Do you not understand?" I sighed, leaning against the wall. "I came here last night, I did as you are doing, I struck the door with shoulder and fist until I could do no more. I heard the screams from within and the tears of the dying. Break down the door. It is the only way to know the truth."

The Constable turned and looked at me with an air of disgust and contempt. If there was one thing that I had learned in my years it was that Policemen did not like being told what to do any more than they enjoyed being proved wrong by a member of the public.

"You, Boy! Come here!" He shouted to a barrow boy carrying a small sack on his way to the market on Leman Road. "Go to the Police Station around the corner and tell them that Constable Townsend is about to break down the door of the Jews Orphanage on St Marks Street. Tell them to send a couple of men, either to help me or to arrest a man for wasting my time."

He shot me a furious glare as the lad ran off to the end of the street, before lowering his shoulder and charging at the door with a force which I could not have mustered. The door caved in under his weight and he flew inside. I remained leant against the wall not knowing whether to follow him and witness for myself the scene of devastation or to await the arrival of the other officers. It was when I heard his cries of horror that my inquisitive nature got the better of me.

"Oh God No! Oh dear God please no!" He cried.

As I stepped through the door, I could see nothing out of place. The hallway was darkened and the doors of each of the rooms downstairs, the laundry and the kitchen were open. One door remained closed and, had it not been for the sounds of disbelief and terror coming from the policeman upstairs, I would have opened it to look inside. I climbed the stairs slowly, following the sound of his voice, although in truth I could have been deaf and blind and found my way to where he was, due to the smell. I had once visited an abattoir a few years earlier, meeting the owner regarding a photography assignment where he wished to record the death of his eldest son. It was during this visit that I first experienced at first hand the intense smell of blood and the internal organs. During that visit the innards had belonged to cows and sheep, but the smell in the orphanage that morning was not so different. I had expected a scene of vile horror and depravity, but my imagination could never have been so base than to dream of the sight which I beheld that morning.

The room was red. Both from the blood which was sprayed upon the walls and floor, but mainly from the morning sun, which shone through the bloodstained windows and bathed the room in a glow, which would not have been out of place had it been a plane of hell itself. There were bodies laid, piled and hung around the room, both whole and eviscerated, emptied of all their insides and torn into lumps, which were scattered about the dormitory like so much discarded waste. Constable Townsend had dropped to his knees and was in prayer for the souls of those lost; I could not move but instead was frozen in disbelief. I did not even move when I heard the clatter of boots in the hall behind me and the cries of each of the other policemen as they entered this scene of horror.

This final outrage loosened something within my mind. It was the blade which slashed and which sliced the thin thread that had been frayed and gnawed at for so long. As the room slowly filled with men, their faces identical in their aspect, each one the very picture of abject disgust and disbelief, I turned and slowly made my way downstairs and out into the street once more. There I sat upon the pavement, not seeing or hearing the crowd, which had begun to assemble and throng outside trying to get a look inside the building. The speculation on the scene of carnage inside had started.

"I hear that a boy got murdered."

"They say the governess went mad and hanged herself."

"My brother said there was a man here last night, banging on the doors and demanding to be let in."

The word was out and into the streets, and it would not be long before rumours began that the killer had returned.

Over the next hour a great number of police arrived at the scene and slowly they managed to set out a cordon which held the crowd back and gave them space to work. I was ignored and left sat on the edge of the kerb, when one policeman tried to move me on, he was told to leave me as I was a witness.

Finally Inspector Draper arrived, followed closely by Sergeant Thomas who trailed at his heels like an angry bulldog. Draper walked straight past me not even looking down, although I knew that he was aware of my presence. Thomas, however, seemed unable to disregard my attendance at the scene and growled as he passed, barking at the officer stood at the door to not let me out of his sight.

I did not care, life for me was ended and I sat, filthy and broken, lost in thought. I was destined to be haunted and tormented by the dead. Bethany was lost also and there seemed to be no clean ending to the disaster which had befallen me. I decided at that point that there were three clear options available to me, all would bring an end to my involvement in this torment, but only one, the least likely to succeed, would be satisfactory. I sat in despair.

"And here you are, Mr Darke. Present at the scene of another terrible murder. One might say that you were either unlucky or the killer." I turned slightly, not raising my eyes and saw the highly polished brown brogues of Inspector Fred Draper shining up at me. I did not respond to him.

"Sergeant Thomas tells me that you led the police to the scene of the crime, is that so?"

"It is," I croaked.

"Then would you mind telling me how you came to be privy to this knowledge?"

"You would not believe me if I told you," I said, an edge of acid humour to my voice. I looked up at him. "Did the good sergeant also tell you that I came to warn you of the murders at the station last night and that he ridiculed me and would not hear my words?" A delicately disguised look of anger crossed his face and he replied, in truth.

"He did not, but I will ask you again. How did you know of the murders?"

I pushed myself to my feet and faced the man; it was time to tell Inspector Draper the truth of it all. This was the first of my three solutions to the issue.

"I was visited by the spirits of the dead, Inspector." I said. "The ghost of a child in fact. The ghost told me that there would be a massacre at the orphanage and that it was the killer of my family who would be responsible. The killer that was thought dead." I saw a look of quiet disbelief in his face; this was not the kind of man who leaned towards spiritualistic ideation, he was an accountant for God's sake. "I know that this sounds like madness, Inspector, and if I was in your position I think that I would agree with you. I can only tell you what I know however, there is more to it but I think that it would stretch the bounds of your imagination perhaps too far."

"I think that you will find that I am willing to listen to you, Sibelius." His voice was soft, comforting in fact. Quite different from the analytical and cold automaton that I had been used to. I looked to him and at that moment I fooled myself into thinking that he may yet believe me. "Tell me the truth, Mr Darke, tell me what you know?" I swallowed hard and began.

"In Finnish folklore, there is a place where the dead go to when they have passed from this world." I paused momentarily searching for any sign of ridicule in his face. There was none. "This world is known in Finland as Tuonela. Standing guard at the gateway to Tuonela is a mythical beast called Surma, the only people to have seen this beast and survived to tell the tale are long since gone from this world, for Surma's task is to prevent the dead from returning to the world of the living. Are you following me?"

Draper had begun to show small traces of discomfort and I could tell that I was losing him somewhat. He glanced over my shoulder and I turned quickly to see the broad face of Abe Thomas looking down at me. My heart sank.

"I am listening, Mr Darke please continue with your ... story."

I sighed a little and continued, knowing that each word I spoke worked towards confirming me a madman.

"A few weeks ago a group of gentlemen based at a club in the city, somehow drew Surma into this world, where he took possession of the body of a man of their choosing and was let loose upon the area to kill and feed upon children."

"But you think that he was also responsible for the deaths of your brother and father?"

"Surma is responsible for that deed but that was an exception to the rule and was carried out as a matter of vengeance."

"The guardian of hell had a grudge against your family? That makes sense," interjected Sergeant Thomas, with all the humour of a dying dog. I carried on regardless; I had nothing at all to lose any more.

"Yes, Sergeant, for it is not the first time that he has been summoned for such a task. The last time was twenty years ago when a man named Henry Holdsworth was responsible for the deaths of a number of children, my brother Johannes being the last of them. My father interrupted him about his business and beat him senseless. The beast Surma fled back to the underworld and Holdsworth, recognising his crimes handed himself to the police confessing all. You may check your records; you will find that I am correct."

Draper took a small leather bound notebook from his pocket and took a note of the name, whether he did this in seriousness or to humour me I shall never know.

"Holdsworth was never charged with any crimes however;" I continued. "There was not sufficient evidence and it was claimed that he was a lunatic. The gentleman's club behind the crimes used their power and influence to subdue the story and have Mr Holdsworth committed to an asylum."

"And how do you know this?"

"I tracked down the man himself and interviewed him, he told me all and I believed him."

"Ah, priceless, Darke," scoffed Thomas from behind me. "From one lunatic to another, how could we ever not believe you?" His laughter rang out loud and he was quietened by Draper who raised a hand in authority.

"Please, Sergeant. It is not our place to ridicule potential witnesses to crime." There was however the slightest indication that he had begun to tire of my tale and he turned to me in an attempt to bring a close to the discussion. "I have listened to your words, Mr Darke and I find that you have provided me with a most fantastical story of murder and wrongdoing. I have just two questions for you and then I think that I should leave you to be on your way so that I may continue with my investigations.'

"Of course," I sighed knowing that I had lost his ear, "What did you wish to know?"

"Two nights ago a man matching the description of a suspect witnessed at a crime scene was found hanged in his room in Love Lane. To all intents and purposes it was decided that these killings were over. You believe that it is the spirit of some underworld demon, possessing people and forcing them to kill. How then can the same person have committed these crimes? If you are correct then this 'demon' should have fled back to where he came from?"

"I do not know, sir. Perhaps the men behind this terrible scheme have called on him once more."

"The men? Of course and this would lead me to the next query that I have. Why would certain gentlemen of London wish to bring about such killings and outrage? Surely there is no sane purpose for such an action?"

"Of that I do know a little, Inspector. It would seem that this group are uncommonly worried about the social direction of our country. They see a world in which the poor will rise up against those in power, and they are scared. These killings are a means to an end, sir, and although I do not know the depth of their plans, I would say that they are men with grave purpose and that they must be stopped and immediately."

There was an edge of desperation in my voice now which, at the time I felt was required to press home this most important point to the Inspector but which, in afterthought, sounded like the crazed pleadings of a man on the verge of losing all of his senses. I was about to speak again, to insist that Draper acted on my warnings, when he looked to me again, raising his hand to my shoulder in a most informal manner.

"Mr Darke, I thank you for this most important information which I will include in my investigation and act upon at once. But for now you look tired and should rest, I am sure that you will appreciate my need to press on with matters straight away. Please go home now and I shall call on you when I require further information."

"But, Inspector you have not asked for the names of these men or of the place where they base their operations?"

"I shall, in good time, Sibelius. For now I need you to go back to your studio and rest. Take a couple of days to recuperate yourself and I will be in touch. Do you wish me to send an officer to escort you or will you manage?"

I was lost. I looked to the Inspector for the final time and, waving away his offer of support, I made my way back to Osborn Street. I knew that I was being followed and that my name was now marked as the main suspect in the slaughter at the orphanage, in fact I wondered why Draper had not had me arrested and dragged to a cell at the Leman Road station straight away. Was I that pathetic a figure that he did not fear that I would strike again?

As I stepped onto Whitechapel Road and the bustle of the morning markets, I could sense a feeling of tension and unease in the air. News of the massacre at the orphanage had spread wide already. The faces of people I passed were a mixture of worry and anger that such a terrible murder could have been committed so close to the Police Station, and under the very noses of those who were charged with catching murderers and child killers. Gossip and rumour abound and I overheard snippets of conversations, each of which filled me with a burning desire to return to my apartments as soon as possible and away from the eyes of the ignorant and accusing.

"Twenty-two boys dead I heard ..."

"... the matron was hung from the ceiling like a side of beef."

"Who could do such a deed,"

"... she said she saw a man running away from there."

"A pale man he was, hair as white as ..."

I pulled up my collar and lowered my face to the ground, pressing onwards to the safety of my home where I could lock my door behind me and try to think calmly about my next move. Anxiety welled within me like a gas flame, burning my insides and causing me to feel nauseous. I was fifty yards away from the Osborn Street turning now and what pale and withered religious belief remained within me prayed for the good fortune to let me reach home intact.

Thirty yards now and I felt the eyes of the world begin to fall on me. My head sank even further into the collar of my coat and my walking pace quickened to almost a run.

Ten yards, and my breathing had begun to reach a rapid level and I swear that I could hear my own heart beating to a frantic rhythm within my chest. I turned left at the corner and looked up briefly seeing the door to my studio beckoning me. I thought I could hear the heavy footsteps of the crowd behind me now but I admit to feeling too scared to turn and look at them. I reached the doorway and fumbled my keys from my coat pocket, desperately trying not to drop them from my shaking hands. I pushed the key into the first lock, turning it as quietly as I could so as not to attract attention. I moved to the second lock, selecting another key, inwardly cursing my levels of security which caused each entry and exit from the door to be such a chore. Forcing the second key in, I twisted it and pushed the door open in one fluid stroke. I stumbled in through the doorway as quickly as I could I slammed the door shut behind me, pushing across the cast iron deadbolts at the top and bottom before slumping to the floor.

How long before the crowds came for me? How long before they broke down my door and dragged me screaming into the street, imposing Lydford law upon me, hanging me for a murderer, convicted through rumour and supposition.

I do not know how long I sat there, breathing heavily and waiting for the mob to come to my door. They did not arrive however and I decided to move myself eventually and make the next move in this game that I seemed destined to lose. My first thought was to go to The Alice to see Tom and to retrieve my father's pistol from underneath the mattress of Bethany's bed. I pushed myself to my feet and looked to my stairs. I felt so tired as if every inch of energy had been sapped from me by the madness that was my life. Sluggishly I began to trudge up the stairs; perhaps a couple of hours sleep would help to refresh my mind and body enough to continue.

A hammering on the door made me jump to attention and I turned nervously hoping that whoever wanted my attention would leave straight away. There was silence for a few moments and then the hammering came again, I became convinced that the mob had come for me and a cold sweat once again appeared upon my brow.

"Sibelius, open up it's me Tom!" The relief was almost debilitating in itself, as I felt my legs weaken. "Sib, let me in, I know that you are there I saw you enter." I charged towards the door, pulling it open and dragging Tom inside by his collar before slamming it behind him.

"Oh, Tom, thank God it is you." I breathed, hugging him. As I have mentioned before I am not keen on bodily contact of any kind especially when it was of an emotional nature, but the action came naturally to me and I found that I did not want to let him go. He loosened himself from my grip however and broke away, taking hold of both of my shoulders. His eyes were red ringed and he looked deathly tired.

"Sib, I needed to see you," he said his voice cracked and broken. "I hear there was an awful murder at the orphanage last night; do you know anything of it?"

"I am afraid that I do, Tom. I was there both last night trying to warn the police and this morning when they found the bodies. I have never seen such horror as that which can be found in that accursed place this morning. The images will stay with me for all time."

Tom seemed nervous, jumpy and agitated it was as if he was scared at what I would say to him.

"You look worse than I do, Tom. How are things at the pub? Has Bethany made any recovery?" It was then that the tears poured from his eyes and he sank to his knees in front of me. In the twenty years that I had known this man, he had never acted such, not even when his wife died. I lowered myself to him and raised his chin so that I could look him in the eye. "What has happened? You must tell me!"

"Bethany ... began to come around a bit yesterday morning. She would not speak but she would eat a little of what we gave her and she drank well, as well as I've ever seen her drink. She must have consumed four or five pints of water which I put down to the length of time which she was not with us. By the afternoon she got up from her bed and began to move around the place, it was as if nothing had happened but for the fact that she did not speak. I took it that she was still in shock and chose to allow her freedom in the upstairs of the pub. She went about her normal chores, cleaning and tidying our living areas, taking clothes for washing, all the things that she would normally do but she was silent. It was only when she tried to go downstairs, to leave the pub that any trouble started."

"Trouble? What do you mean trouble? Is she well? Is she at home now?"

"Yes she is fine ... now. Tell me Sibelius, does the word Surma mean anything to you?" I could tell from the widening of his eyes that he could see how shocked I was. It felt as if all the blood had drained from my body and it was now I that sank to the floor.

"Yes ... yes, I know that word. Did she speak it?"

"She did. It was about an hour before she tried to leave that I first heard it. Quiet at first, more of a whispered mumble than anything else. I took it as further sign that she was coming through the worst of it, but as she went to go downstairs, As

Anne and I got in her way, she became louder; chanting the name as if in some kind of trance. It scared me, Sibelius, truly it did. We stood our ground however, telling her to stay in the safety of the house, telling her to rest some more. The last time she said the word it was a vicious scream as she lashed out at Anne, slapping her hard across the face and drawing her nails down Anne's cheek. I was so shocked that I did not move, not a footstep did I make as she pushed past us and downstairs. It was only when she entered the pub that I snapped out of my daze and chased her, but she was gone, out of the doors and into the street. Gone for three hours she was. I searched all around the area but did not see a sight of her, no one had seen her. When she returned she apologised for her actions, she even wept a little when she saw what she had done to Anne, my child had almost returned."

"Almost? Why almost?"

"I do not know, Sibelius, really I don't. I suppose what happened to her has changed her, seeing what she did would change anyone. Late in the evening Inspector Draper visited her, he had heard that she had awoken and had fled the pub and they wished to take a statement about Arthur Downing, about what she had seen. He would not let me be there when they spoke though; I do not know exactly what was said."

Cogs began to whirr and spring to life within my head. It was as if energy had suddenly been fired into my body.

"Tom, you must gather yourself and take me back to the Alice with you. I need to see Bethany for myself. Is she at the pub now?"

"Yes she is cleaning the pub ready for opening. Like I said it is as if nothing happened." He looked at me, confused by my sudden burst of gumption. "But, Surma? You never told me what Surma is. How is it important?" I looked at my friend for a moment. As much as I saw myself as being broken by these events, this man had been affected just as much.

I took my old friend by the arm and led him into my studio where we took a seat. We sat for the following hour and I told him, as best I could, of Surma, and of how the dead spoke to me, of Holdsworth and of Earnshaw and of how I had involved his daughter in affairs too dangerous to imagine. He listened, patiently and at times I thought that he would burst into anger and rage when he heard what his daughter had been doing and the peril she had faced. A lesser man would of, but not Tom. He listened quietly to what I had to say and at the end he took my hand and asked that we return to the Alice to see Bethany, so that I could see her for myself.

I quickly ran upstairs and changed my clothing; dressing in something which hid me better from the baying crowds who I felt sure would take me if they saw me, claiming me to be the killer. My outfit was completed by a hat which I had bought on a whim two years ago. I had only worn it once and had felt such a complete fool that it had gone to the back of my wardrobes. It was the tweed look that drew me to it, but I never felt that it could be worn seriously again. I did not plan to stalk many deer in my lifetime. Once in place however it perfectly masked my white hair and its brim came down low enough over my face to hide my features. I looked at myself in my mirror once dressed. Three weeks ago I would never have conceived leaving the house like this, but necessity can do cruel and heartless things to a man.

We set off quickly from my apartments and I kept my head down all the way, despite Tom's constant reassurances that I would not be the target of any local hate campaign. Tom held my arm and led me, as I could not bring myself to look up and catch someone's eye. I could hear the sounds of Whitechapel in full flow however, the cries of the traders selling their wares mixed with the bustle and hubbub of the locals about their business. One call sounded louder than all of the others to me however, it was the cry of the paper seller, a young lad calling out the same phrase over and over.

"Children murdered in their beds! The Pale Demon haunts London!"

It was enough to send chills through me and quicken my step even more. Thankfully, the journey from Osborn Street to the corner of Wentworth and Commercial streets was short and I pushed myself roughly through the doors, causing my hat to fall from my head.

As I entered I attracted the gaze of quite a few of the men in the pub, who stopped their chatter and stared at me as if they had never seen a man before. I suddenly realised that it was my hair that they were staring at and I briskly fastened the hat upon my head once more and crossed the bar to the door which led upstairs. Their eyes did not leave me.

The sweat dripped from my forehead as I made my way up the stairs. Tom had stayed in the bar and I hoped that his customers would have thought no more of me and carried on with their drinks. As I reached the top of the stairs I saw Bethany, she was in the kitchen washing dishes. I quickly removed the hat once more, stuffing it into my coat pocket. Straightening my hair, I walked to the kitchen doorway and softly called out to her.

"It is good to see you on your feet once more."

She ran over to me then and threw her arms around my neck holding me close. Such contact was both unusual and welcomed and I briefly took the opportunity to bring my arms around her back and hold her to me before removing myself from her closeness. I was embarrassed by her reaction to the sight of me and I tried to hide this from her.

"Oh Sibelius," she smiled so broadly and with such warmth that I felt a flood of emotion rising from within me. No one had ever responded to me as such and I admit that I struggled with the situation. "I thought I would never see you again, I thought that I had died and that you would be left to deal with everything by yourself. Tell me that you are well and that our troubles are over now. Tell me we are free."

"I regret, Beth, that I cannot say such things to you as yet. I am afraid that despite your finding of Downing and his subsequent death, further murder has taken place. Terrible, terrible murder of which I feel directly responsible." The shock on her face told me that she had not heard of the terror at the orphanage. "The root of the problem, the cause of this terror that has been brought upon us has been made clear to me though and I mean to deal with it."

I then told her of Earnshaw and of the activities of the Dolorian Club, activities which had brought death to our loved ones and fear to the world around us.

"I have, however, come to a decision on how to solve our problems."

"You have?"

"Yes I will visit the club to-morrow and confront them directly. I will threaten them with exposure if they do not desist. I hope that it will be enough."

To my surprise she pulled me close again and held me against her.

"I know I cannot stop you, but please be careful. You are ... dear to me." She spoke softly into my ear and I immediately pulled myself away from her again.

"I came here today. To see that you were well and in recovery. It would seem that your father is correct in that concern. I must leave here now and prepare myself for the confrontation to come. Before I go I must retrieve something which I left in your care, my revolver, it is under your mattress."

She looked shocked at this but did not speak, walking to her room and returning with the pistol and the box of shells, which I had placed there two nights earlier.

"When I return, we will speak, Bethany. I cannot talk of such matters whilst we are in danger however." I regretted any coldness in my voice. All who knew me would have thought it quite normal, but in this situation, at this time, I regretted it.

As I left her stood at the top of the stairs, I felt a warmth within me. Perhaps all was not lost. Perhaps there could be a future for me. These thoughts however dissipated quickly as I stepped back into the bar.

The pub was full.

Full of rough angry men. Men with murder in mind. On the far side of the room Tom was being held down by four men, he had a cut above his eye and blood streaming from his nose. One of the men stepped forward to face me.

"We've come here to take you to the police. The station is not so far away, although I would be surprised if you reached it." His voice was louder and showmanlike, he was obviously enjoying his time in the limelight. "Last night, when those poor boys were killed in their beds, people saw a man with white hair running from the scene." He stuck his thumbs in the pockets of his waistcoat and turned to the men behind him. "Now, I don't know of many young men with white hair around here! In fact the only ones anybody has ever seen are you and your brother. And he's dead already!"

There was a murmuring from the mob and I felt my hand tighten on the handle of the pistol in my pocket.

"In fact I reckon you may have killed him an' all! Done it as a warm up to your deeds in the Jew's home!" There was further grumble of assent and my arms were seized at my sides, held tightly by ignorant hands. "I say let's take 'im outside now and string 'im up. Let's not waste the police's time with the murderer!" There were cheers at this and I felt the sharpness of a blade at my throat. My thoughts were not for my immediate peril however, but were lost in vain hope that Bethany had not heard this mob court happening downstairs from her.

The arms began to pull at me and I felt the nick of the steel on the side of my neck as I was pulled forwards towards the doors of the pub. I once again thought of the pistol in my pocket, and if it had not been for the fact that my arms were seized I may have drawn it then.

The crowd dragged me outside, pulling my arms from my pockets, my hand losing my grip on the revolver contained within. As I looked up, I saw the terrible sight of a rope with a makeshift noose thrown over the gaslight outside the pub. So this is where it would end, I thought. Hanged by a crowd of scared men.

As the rope was put around my neck I began to feel the tightness as a gang of men began to pull at the other end, lifting me up until the tips of my shoes barely touched the floor. The strain of the hemp upon my windpipe began to cause me to begin to choke and my arms flapped in the air as I tried to reach into my pocket to retrieve my pistol.

I heard a screaming noise and saw that Bethany had appeared at the door of the pub, she ran towards me but was stopped when a large bald man stepped in front of her and struck her hard across the jaw, sending her sprawling to the floor. She was set upon by others who punched and kicked her as she lay motionless. I called out to her, I begged them to leave her be, but they were lost in their fear and anger and they continued to beat her mercilessly.

Still the rope tightened and I felt such pressure within my face that I thought my eyes would burst. My feet had left the floor now and I had begun to choke. Such fools would never make executioners, there was no drop, no instant breaking of the neck and death. Only hanging and struggling, slow strangulation, watched by a calling crowd, desperate to see a man die.

Suddenly a shot rang out and the noise of the mob stopped. Policemen appeared from all angles and the pressure on my neck was lessened, I fell to the floor. Some of the crowd ran, most stayed however, calling for my arrest, calling for my death. They were hushed when one man called out to them.

"You must desist from this at once! I will not have mob rule upon these streets!" Draper held a pistol aloft in his hand, it was him that had fired the shot. "There has been terrible killings here last night! Horrible, demonic killings which I had hoped never to see in my lifetime. But there is no proof, no evidence that this man is responsible for the murders of them children! None! It is my job to bring the killer of those boys to justice! Mine! And I will see justice and I will see the killer brought down. Let me do it!" He gestured to the other policemen now standing as a threatening presence in front of the mob. "Let us do it!"

I must admit that even in my desperate state I was shocked by the power and authority that Inspector Draper seemed to be able to exert over the crowd. They were silent as he spoke and I could see fear and shame begin to cross their faces as they realised that they were no longer in control.

Draper motioned to an officer to help Bethany to her feet. She was unconscious however and it took two men to lift her and carry her back inside the safety of the Alice.

The crowd began to back away, they knew that their opportunity for action was over, the mob had made their statement, and they had pointed their fingers, hoping that the police would take up the baton.

The noose was lifted from my head and my arms were held once more as I was brought to my feet. I looked up to thank the officer who had helped me and saw the face of Abe Thomas. He gave a nervous smile.

"That was a little close, Darke. Mighty close."

I was led into the now empty pub where I saw Tom hunched over on a stool, Anne tending to the wound above his eye. Bethany was still not responding to the policemen who were trying to rouse her and I heard talk of calling for a doctor. I took a seat at the bar and cursed myself for bringing such hurt to this poor family. This family who I looked upon as my own but whom I had senselessly destroyed through keeping them close.

"I would think that we arrived in time there, Mr Darke." I looked up and saw Draper standing over me.

"I did not do it, Inspector. You may take me in for questioning if you wish but I swear it was not me that did those awful things. They would have killed me; they would have killed Tom and Beth. I would not bring this upon them you must believe me."

"Why do you think I am here, Sibelius? To arrest you? If I thought that you had committed this crime I would have left you to the mob, I would have let them save me the paperwork. No, it was not you. I have no clear evidence of this but something inside me believes you, and you should be thankful for that.'

At that moment a man appeared at the door of the pub and was let through to see Bethany.

"I do not know what I will do if I have brought her any further harm. She has gone through so much already and it is all my fault."

"Nonsense, man." He said pulling a pipe out of his pocket and filling it with tobacco. "Is it your fault that a madman decided to kill and eat his victims? No, it is not. Is it your fault that your brother, her fiancé, was murdered? No it is not. We found that man and he is now dead. I do not believe the killer from the orphanage is the same man, there are hints of difference in the way the crime was committed." He struck a match and lit the pipe taking a large inhalation. "I think that it was just a cruel coincidence that these deaths have occurred in such a close period of time. They are not related, and if they are it is because somebody wishes to replicate Arthur Downing's crimes but on a larger scale."

We were joined by Tom who had come over to listen in on the conversation.

"I'm sorry, Tom." I said looking over at the prone Bethany who had still not awoken. The doctor sat by her side, pulling open her eyelids and examining her pupils. "I hope she will recover, I seem to have brought a curse to you."

Tom did not speak but placed his hand on my shoulder. He looked more broken than I had ever seen him.

"Mr Finnan, I suggest you do not reopen your public house for today but try to rest and recover from this ordeal. I will leave armed officers at the doors to protect you and your ladies. We will assess the long term damage to-morrow."

"What about me, Inspector?" I said, my voice piteous and weak. I was at an end.

"For you, Mr Darke I will provide the same courtesy, I shall make claim it is to keep a close eye on you. I am sure that you will not mind. It is not as if I could damage your reputation any further now is it?" I smiled at this, a last ironic humour to my downfall. I had wished for notoriety and success, I had gained the former but not as I had wished.

"Would it be possible for me to go to my club to-morrow, Inspector?" I asked in desperation. "There are rooms there I could board for a while and I would feel safer on the other side of town. You will be able to find me there if you feel it necessary."

"Feel free to come and go as you will, you are not a prisoner." He smiled and wandered out of the pub, puffing on his pipe.

I stayed at the Alice for the rest of the day, being told that it was best to let things settle for a while. Bethany was carried upstairs to her room and I suffered the ignominy of having a coat thrown over my head whilst being put into a waiting carriage outside and taken home.

The journey took moments but when I arrived my worst fears had been realised. Every one of my ground floor windows had been smashed and policemen were in the process of boarding them up as I stepped out of the carriage. As I approached the door I saw that the words CHILD KILLER had been scrawled countless times upon it. I had been defeated.

I left the policemen at my door and went inside. At their request I did not bother locking up, they would leave two officers stationed there overnight. If there was any hint of further trouble they would be forced to transfer me to Leman Road where they could protect me better.

I climbed the stairs and went to my room sitting on the edge of the bed. As I removed my overcoat, the box of shells fell to the floor. I removed the pistol, turning it in my hands. Just one bullet now and I could end all of this for me.

Just one bullet would be all it would take.

Thoughts of Bethany however prevented any further stupidity on this day. I placed the gun on the table beside my bed, lay down and dropped into a restless, tormented sleep. Tomorrow would come the end.

16
THE CLUB OF SORROWS

It is with great difficulty, that I will now attempt to convey to you some information regarding my inner thoughts and feelings, that I have never been able to express with any real confidence before. This is despite the fact that I feel as though I have opened myself up in a fashion that would have previously made me shudder with discomfort and shame. With regards to confessions of the soul I feel that I have nothing left to lose. What can be taken from me that I have not already endeavoured to free myself of already?

The matter in which I wish to momentarily divert attentions to I hope will allow my actions to be fully understood and convey the truth of the legacy that I have bestowed with such apparent abandon.

This matter is love.

The attainment of love; the inner feelings which come as a result of finding it and most of all how it is able to be expressed, or in my case not.

I have given this subject much thought during my life. This is partly because of its maddening effect on how I interact with the wider world, but also so that I can try to unravel and understand just how I turned into the man that I became. A man so afraid of sharing his thoughts and feelings with another that he developed a reputation as one that is cold, rude, unfeeling even.

It is not a lack of feelings that cause me to act in this way, quite the opposite in fact. It is the constant flood of thoughts and emotions, of instincts and of pain, that I have to endeavour to keep contained to such a degree that I am forced to hide myself away from the world. This is in both mind and body, and is crucial to how I manage to survive and go about my business in the most ordinary sense.

If I acted on all urges, feelings and thinking which pass through my mind, like so many speeding carriages, then I am sure that I would have long ago become a permanent resident of some such asylum similar to the one which previously housed poor Henry Holdsworth. It is the reason why I lived such a solitary life as soon as I could after reaching maturity. It is why I chose not to continue within the family business and also why I sometimes kept myself apart from those few that were close to me. I set up my own business within my own premises, so that I was able to lock myself away for days on end, when either the midnight of doom or the bright light of hysteria struck me.

It is not that I am incapable of feeling love, I am. I felt great love for my family, while they were alive and in matters of love of the more romantic kind there have only ever been two occasions when this has become a shuddering reality within my mind.

I have given much thought to these romantic wishes and long ago decided that they were immoral and would lead only to further madness and misery. The first of these feelings was an impossible one from the start and quickly became something which would only stay within the darkest recesses of my thoughts, creating an 'ideal' which would be most difficult to attain.

That feeling was for Tom's wife, Beth Finnan.

To me she was the light of my life, the image to which I was drawn and which pulled me out of the blackness when I became enveloped. Although I only knew her for such a short time and at an early age, I can bring to my mind a clear, photographic image whenever I think of her, every part of her smooth and perfect face, and every dark curled lock of beautiful hair.

I am aware that this lifelong obsession is linked to the damage meted out on me by my own mother and the desperate need that I had as a child for a positive image of womanhood. It could be said even that I wished for her to be a replacement for my mother, but as I grew older it became so much more than that. For me she was the embodiment of perfection and the ideal which I held myself alone for, an impossible dream which created the impossibility of true love within my life.

That was until I first noticed her daughter, Bethany. Of course I had always been aware of her; I had been at the pub on the day that she was born upstairs. As a small child I had resented her greatly. It was through her birth that my image of perfection had been taken away, she had killed the woman I loved. As she grew up, I learnt to tolerate her as she appeared at the door of our parlour on a regular basis asking if she could spend time with Niko and I. Over the last couple of years as her romance with Niko began to blossom, I was pleased for Niko that he had found love from such a good source, Tom being such a close friend to me. This happiness for Niko was tarnished internally for me however as her striking resemblance to her mother developed.

I had to block such thoughts from my mind every time that I saw her. It caused such torment within me, both through seeing so much of her mother in her and the subsequent familiarity and care which I developed for her as a woman in her own right when she became betrothed to my brother.

The tragic events that brought us closer still, brought clear to me the truth that I had long fought against within my soul; that I loved her deeply and that I had finally found the woman to whom I could open myself up and allow my inner feelings to run free with no fear of rejection or distress.

Love had finally found me, long waiting for its call, but it had come at a time where it would be destined to suffer and die; to be cast away and forgotten, lost for all time. Bethany Finnan lay in a comatose state, thrust there by the hands of a killer, whom I stupidly set her on the path to find.

It was a cold October morning as I left my apartments, and asked the policemen guarding my door to hail a cab to take me to the safety of my club. He obliged quickly stating that he would remain at my door until his relief arrived and he could let Inspector Draper know that I had left.

As I got into the carriage I was intent on my decided purpose. I had resigned myself to the thought that there was only a slim hope left that any lasting good could come of this. I had thought long and hard into the night, staring into the oblivion that I had become a part of. I had thought of the offer that Earnshaw made me and, in the depths of my despair, I had wondered whether this deal with the devil would still be available to me.

There would be worse things than to be alive and working again, to be free of the fear and terror affecting me as it had done. Yes, they had been responsible for the deaths of the last remaining members of my family, but this was indirectly. Of course they had unleashed the beast, but they had no direct control over where he went or who he preyed on. I thought about how easy it would be to fool myself into thinking that their cause was just and that I was part of something greater.

I even considered that they may be able to assist in the restoration of Bethany to her former self. They obviously had some degree of knowledge and ability to access and manipulate powers beyond the normal world. Earnshaw himself specialised in matters of the brain, who better could there be to aid her recuperation. I continued to toss these thoughts around my tired mind as I sat within the carriage which took me to my destination in Pall Mall. In fact my thoughts were still addled as it drew up outside The Dolorian Club.

I approached the doorway of the club; it was large, dark red in colour and highly polished. It was of such a size and height that it towered menacingly over anyone who stood on its step. I had not noticed its threatening nature before, but had seemed so entirely pleased with myself for being accepted as a member that I am sure that it could have bore the sign 'Entrance to Hell' and I would never had spotted it. I pushed at the door to open it. It did not move. This was most odd as I had never known the club's entrance to be locked, no matter what time of day or night I had been there. I tried it again without success and began looking to the frame for sign of a bell. There was a brass handle in the shape of a ring hanging from the mouth of a stag, and I marvelled at its intricate design before pulling on it. Hearing the sound of a distant muffled bell from inside the club and I stood back on the step and waited to be received. I looked to the windows of the club each of which had the backs of thick velvet curtains within them and I remembered there being a distinct lack of light within the building on my previous visits no matter what time of day or night it was. This was obviously not a place where natural light and the glow and warmth of the day's sun were welcomed.

Eventually a tall, dark man, who I had never seen before on any of my previous visits, opened the door and stared blankly at me. He stood in the doorway, clearly barring my way in and as I made a step to enter the building, he moved forwards so as to prevent me.

"Excuse me," I said in almost mock annoyance. "I am a member here and would like to come in. My name is Sibelius Darke; you will find my name on your roster."

The man continued to stare at me in a most curious way, but did not respond at all. I had contemplated the idea that Charles Earnshaw would make moves to rescind my membership to the club, but I had always thought that I would at least be able to enter the building first before being made aware of this fact.

I was about to turn upon my heel and leave to plot another way of gaining access to Earnshaw and his associates, when a short round man bustled into the doorway from the inner hall, pushing the taller man to one side as if he were a mannequin. I recognised him immediately as Gerald Hopple, the club's superintendent, a man who I had acquaintance with on many occasions since my membership began.

"Mr Darke, sir?" he grinned. "I am so sorry for the behaviour of Osman; he is new here and does not as yet speak a word of English. He came to me with the highest of recommendations from a friend in India, but he has been nothing but trouble since his arrival two weeks ago. He hears the doorbell and answers but has no idea what to say or do after that. Please do come in."

He pulled the door open so that I could enter; the tall foreigner however did not move and had yet to move his eyes from me. I had almost believed Hopple's story but, knowing what I did about the club now, I could only see this supposed new employee as a sinister presence. In fact, I was unsure of the validity of any of the staff and members of this foul institution. Every one of them was a potential accomplice to their delusional scheme which used murder and fear to meet its ends. I decided to play along with the charade until its conclusion, if they were acting then I could play my part also.

I stepped into the hallway, looking up at the broad staircase which dominated the entrance to the club. I eyed the walls suspiciously, looking for some sign of malevolence and wrongdoing. I do not know what I expected to suddenly see that had not been evident before, there were no grand paintings of the devil on show, no tapestries showing the rich upper classes tearing the poor to shreds in a ritualistic fashion. In fact the decor was well adjusted, classical in its appearance and not dissimilar to a hundred other gentlemen's clubs throughout the civilised world. The walls were neatly painted in a deep crimson colour and bore upon them gold framed pieces of art containing the portraits of previous members as well as delicately painted city scenes showing studious and hard working gentlemen going about their business and creating a better world for us all. In previous visits I had noted these pictures and aspired myself to be one of these gentlemen of the future, leading the way in the name of the British Empire and taking our resolve and imagination to the masses for the greater good. I now saw that this 'greater good' came at an awful price, a price which I had been given the opportunity to be part of, forcing society's salvation upon an unknowing public.

"I had hoped to see Charles Earnshaw if he was here." I said, as I turned back to Hopple and removed my hat, giving it to the waiting Osman. He took it from me with a quiet gentleness, which belied his stature; however, I noted that his hands were of a massive size, each one heavily marked with scars, which showed me that he was no stranger to the use of a blade. I had seen similar markings upon other men and each of these had received their scarring from either practice or melee. Osman looked at me in a confused manner momentarily and I realised that he hoped to take my heavy woollen overcoat also. I took hold of the collars and pulled it around me a little tighter to let him know that I did not wish to be relieved of it and he must of understood as he turned briskly and walked away.

"You are very lucky, Mr Darke. Mr Earnshaw is in the second floor study as we speak. It is very rare that we are honoured with his company these days. He is such a busy and important man."

"Would he be available for visits? I do not mean to keep him long, I just wish to speak to him regarding a business opportunity which he made known to me."

"I shall go and enquire immediately, please take a seat in the library and make yourself comfortable. Would you like Osman to bring you a drink while you wait?"

"A whisky would be most welcome," I answered, walking into the library. On my previous visits to the club the library had been my most favourite room of the building, holding within it a multitude of books all of which were available to read or borrow. I did not sit upon entering but walked slowly besides the shelves taking in the titles and authors on display. It had been the fulfilment of a childhood dream for me when I had first seen it. Now I found it a suspicious place and wondered where the dark volumes containing instructions for magic of the foulest kind were kept and where the source of the summoning rituals were to be found. Thankfully for me, my stay within this accursed place was to be short-lived as the door opened and Hopple bumbled in.

"Mr Darke? So sorry to keep you. I have spoken to Mr Earnshaw and, although he looked a little surprised at your arrival, he said that he would be very pleased to meet with you, if you would like to follow me up to the second floor drawing room." I nodded my assent and followed the small man out of the library and up the staircase.

The second floor drawing room was somewhere that I had not visited since my acceptance into the club, although it had been pointed out to me in passing by Hopple himself during my initial visit and tour of the clubs facilities. I had been told that entry this room was restricted to only the most venerated and esteemed club members, something of an 'inner sanctum' where one could only hope to enter after many years of membership.

As we approached the door, Hopple gave a nervous cough and tapped lightly upon the door panel with the back of his knuckles. I did not hear any reply or signal to enter, but he carefully turned the brass handle and, pushing the door ajar, ushered me inside.

The room was panelled in dark polished mahogany, the gloss of which reflected what little excuse there was for light permeating the dusty gloom. Broad, high backed chairs were dispersed about the room in twos or threes, creating individual seating areas for quiet assignations and whispered words. Each seating area had one or two tall wooden tables upon which sat polished brass paraffin lamps with green frosted glass shades. The light coming through these shades was so diffused that it was a wonder that they were ever lit at all for all the brightness that they had the capacity to create. Silver plated coasters were also scattered on the tables, left to protect the tables and bear the weight of the thick crystal goblets which the club supplied filled with the member's liquor of choice.

A large fireplace stood as the centrepiece of the room, dominating all within its sight. The logs which sat upon the iron grate, although lit, gave off very little in the way of light or life, indeed if it had not been for the slow clockwork crackle of the indistinct flame, it would have been impossible to ascertain whether the fire was even alight or not. The fireplace's surround was of grand but disturbing design, intricately carved from rough, blackened stone and upon each side were carved scenes of figures surrounded and burned within the midst of some uncontrollable holy or unholy flame. The black pyre was awash with flicking whips of fire which licked at the bodies of the victims and caused their faces to be etched in torment as they screamed for forgiveness and death from the unidentified master who brandished the blaze.

The mantle of the fireplace was deep and long, perhaps the length of two grown men and upon this shelf were sat an array of objects of curiosity which, despite the diversity of their character, each held one common theme obvious to all who examined it.

Death.

There were small stuffed animals; weasel, fox and water rat, wild when they were alive and now moulded and posed to reflect this same ferality in death. Their mouths were open as if in cry and each small, sharp tooth was bared in a display of the anger of the murdered and the threat of the wilderness. The glass eyes of each, carefully inserted after their natural orbs were scooped from their heads, seemed to stare straight back at those who looked upon them, showing no sense of sadness as is often the case with those poor creatures that fall victim to the hunter and the taxidermist's tools. These were eyes that threw warnings to any that came near, promises of blood and pain through tooth and claw to any foolish enough to be tempted to touch them.

Other items upon the mantle included skulls, such as would normally be found in the studies of those who were enraptured by gruesome and deathly form. As I glanced at them, it seemed impossible to identify which poor beasts they came from, although some were so alike to human that I shuddered to contemplate their origin too deeply.

"I should advertise myself as a medium, Mr Darke." Came the voice of Earnshaw who sat alone on the other side of the room. I admit to some shock in seeing him, as he had been so quiet since my entry that he had obviously been observing me like a hunter studies its prey before the kill. I glanced quickly around the other chairs in the room and saw that we were alone. The tension immediately rose within me.

He was dressed in a well-tailored charcoal grey suit and held a carved crystal glass in one hand and a cigar in the other. The smoke from the cigar swam around his head, partially obscuring his face, although I was able to see his shrewd eyes smiling at me through the blue-grey haze. He gestured towards the seat opposite him, a high backed red leather chair. Besides the seat was a small table, upon which I saw a glass of whisky placed waiting for me. I thought of Holdsworth's words and the drink that he had been offered and decided to resist any temptation to taste it.

"Do you believe in ghosts, Sibelius? Do you believe that the spirits hover over us watching our every move?"

"To be honest, sir, I do not know what to believe any more."

"Of course, you have had a most traumatic time I believe. Tell me of your adventures and why you have come to me as I predicted." I sat slowly, keeping my eyes lowered in a sign of deference and respect.

"I come to you in penitence, Mr Earnshaw. I feel that I judged your purpose too harshly and wish to submit myself to your cause. I was foolish to refuse the offer to join you and your friends."

"Yes, you were, Sibelius. You were very foolish indeed, but thankfully I believe in second chances for those who show aptitude for success. I think you may have this, Darke, but first you must tell me; do you see the bravery of what we mean to do here? Do you see the greater view that we are trying to prevent in the future?"

"I see that you are assisting this great country to remain strong and in control of its affairs. Through chaos and destruction will come peace and power." He smiled at me broadly; I had obviously managed to capture the task in hand successfully.

"So true, Darke, so very true. Injury and death are but small prices to pay for the benefit of many. I understand that you have suffered losses through this affair, but it is of great credit to you that you are able to take a more rational view, rather than sink into emotion and despair." He looked down towards the green glass ashtray on his table carefully dropping the growing ash from the end of his cigar. Without looking back to me he continued. "And do you now see the purpose of the beast, Mr Darke?"

"Yes, yes I do. It is to cause a social change in this country, to encourage the poor to remain in their place and to keep them, through fear of the unknown, from seeing the potential of their power and the need to rise up against the ruling classes."

Earnshaw laughed aloud at my supposition. It was a laughter filled with warmth and love, like one would make when finding humour at the poor jokes of a dear nephew.

"Heavens, Darke. You really do have a taste for the serious don't you? All that waffle I gave you in the carriage about revolution and a war between the classes. Yes, there is an element of that to the beast's good work, but he is merely a blunt tool to start the gears in motion. Did you not think that there were other, more peaceful and less horrific methods in which we could instigate our vision? Did you not feel that there was an element of the dramatic about our ways?"

"Well, of course but ..."

"We used the beast, Surma for one main reason, the reason that has kept us interested and enthralled at his actions. We used him because it was ... fun." I choked slightly as he said it, an action which appeared to delight him. "It is fun to hear of his exploits, Sibelius. It is fun to see the panic in the eyes of the ignorant. We used the beast for one purpose alone, to tear the heads off of small children with gusto and verve; to feed on their flesh with all the tempestuous ferocity of a lion in the wild. Have you not seen the love that London has had for the beast? Surely there is nothing more enlivening and stimulating to the mind and body than the thought of a killer on the loose."

"But the beast is gone now, he left when Downing died."

"Did he? What about the Jew boys? Was that not the beast?"

"Well of course not, the police say that it displayed the hand of a different killer, a pretender."

"Sibelius Darke you are nothing but a disappointment to me. Had it not occurred to you that it was the same creature but held in a different host? I thought that there was more fire in your mind, young man."

"I think you will find that there is more fire to me than you give credit, sir." I snapped angrily. He chuckled at this statement and absent mindedly flicked the ash from his cigar once again. "Tell me, Mr Earnshaw, was it you or one of your associates that entered my property and found my notes and records that I keep?"

"I take it you are referring to your little library of secrets, the catalogue of lives that you hold so dear and use to your advantage?"

"I am."

"It was not I who discovered them, but when I heard of its existence I could not keep myself away. I have always been fascinated by eccentricity and obsession and I found your lust for knowledge on the lives of others too exciting to resist. Why do you wish to know?"

"Did you care to read any of my records?"

"I am afraid that time was limited, I glanced over a few pages, to be brutally honest, Sibelius, I could not decipher any competent system of filing in use and I bored quickly. I would have thought that a practical businessman such as yourself would have kept documents like that in some semblance of order, yet another reason for me to feel let down the more I discovered of you."

"It would seem that I am destined to disappoint. I take it in your 'glancing' that you did not see my notes on a Mr Archibald Kemp?"

"No, I have never heard of the man. Who is he?"

"It is a most interesting story; would you humour me to tell you of him?" Earnshaw put his glass on a coaster and his cigar in the glass tray. He carefully placed his hands on the armrests of his leather chair and pushed himself back making himself comfortable.

"Oh, I do love a good story, Mr Darke." He said in a boyish manner, his eyes widening with mock delight. "I would like nothing better than to hear you tell the tale." He was humouring me indeed.

"Archibald Kemp was a man that you would refer to Mr Earnshaw, as a contradiction, much the same as you called me when last we met. In fact, I am most surprised that you have not heard of him before, as his story is one that you would have found most diverting.

"A pleasant and agreeable man, by all accounts, Archibald was born into a well respected and financially secure family which boasted a line of medical men dating back as far as the 1500's. The Kemps were born and bred to be doctors, it was in their very nature, and to be anything else would be against the fabric of their being. The extent of the family's medical experiences were too numerous to mention and included royal physicians, army doctors, surgeons and even men who, like yourself, are committed to the function and workings of the human brain.

"Archibald, however, was not so keen to follow in the learned footsteps of the generations of Kemps before him. He had no wish to keep to his family's noble traditions and to join the military, as he was full of cowardice and fear. He knew this within himself from an early age and tried hard to cover the fact through the demonstration to all who saw him that he was not fit for a medical life. He was a sharp and intelligent young man but feigned stupidity and intentionally sabotaged all attempts by his poor family to steer and direct him. He would turn up late for lessons and examinations and would fake illness and disease in his endeavours to prevent his destiny.

"His father, Henry Kemp, during a fit of pique at his son's insubordination, made it his business to take control.

Within the space of one day, and a large sum of the family's money, Henry arranged for Archibald to not only pass all of his medical examinations but to be enlisted as an officer in the 32nd Regiment of Foot, just in time to catch the outbound troop ship as it sailed to India for the regiment's instalment at Cawnpore.

"Archibald Kemp maintained his position within the regiment, acting as the regimental doctor during it's time in Cawnpore. He was not a popular man, well known for shirking in his duties and using his family's name to endear himself to the senior officers, often at the expense of his colleagues, both in his and the other regiments stationed in the city. This disregard for the personal standing, which he held with his fellow soldiers in order to avoid his duties, caused a great deal of anger within the barracks. Threats were made, one officer, Lieutenant Cox was even noted to remark;

"When the next action comes and the rifles are raised in anger, the first bullet I fire will be at that snivelling coward Kemp.'

"When Archibald himself heard this threat he was not scared as it was nothing compared to the fear he held for involvement in open battle.

"The city itself was said to be safe under the command of General Wheeler, and, although there were also questions raised on occasion regarding the medical abilities of Kemp, this was a time of peace and the man himself felt relatively safe there and free from danger.

"In June 1857 however, the Indian rebellion began and spread to areas close to Cawnpore. Feeling that those Indians living within Cawnpore were not a potential risk of rebellion, General Wheeler ordered the 32nd and 8th regiments out of the city to provide reinforcement for the besieged British forces at Lucknow.

"The thought of coming battle was too distressing for Kemp to take and so, reverting back to the actions of his youth, he feigned illness and avoided leaving the city with the rest of the troops. His previous hard work at ingratiating himself with his superiors led to him being requested to act as the medical authority for the remaining British contingent in Cawnpore, which numbered nine hundred souls, and consisted of around three hundred military men, three hundred women and children with the rest of the numbers made up of merchants, engineers and servants.

"In charge of a small team of medical staff, Kemp felt secure in his role as it put him in a position of authority, where direct medical practice tasks, of which his skills and knowledge were very poor, could be delegated to lesser, more able staff. Besides, Cawnpore was safely removed from the rebellion and as such any risk of coming into contact with the hostile forces.

"This remained the case until Lieutenant Cox returned to Cawnpore from action at Lucknow with an injury to his leg. On the night of 2nd June 1857, Cox was drunk and decided to act upon his previous threat to Kemp, searching him out in the medical buildings. Upon finding his quarry he fired on him shouting,

"You cowardly blackguard, I'll see you dead!"

"He missed Kemp completely but, more importantly he also narrowly missed an Indian guard who had been trying to bring him under control. Cox was arrested and thrown into gaol for the night.

"By morning, news of the incident had spread through the barracks and had gained particular attention of the Indian soldiers. Rumours spread that the Indian guard had in fact been the target of Cox's drunken rage and that his exact words were,

"You cowardly *black*, I'll see you dead.'

"The ripples of unrest grew when a hastily convened court acquitted Cox of all charges and he was sent the following day back to Lucknow to resume front line action.

"Within three days there was rebellion at Cawnpore, one which resulted in a siege of General Wheeler's scant forces and the deaths of many British soldiers.

"After twenty days of bloody siege, during which Kemp was quite notable by his absence in the hospital buildings, General Wheeler finally sent a note of surrender to the Indian regiments. They were told that they would be allowed safe passage out of Cawnpore from boats at the nearby Ganges which would take them to British held Allahabad. For Kemp, who had spent most of the siege hidden in a medical store cupboard, this was the best result he could have wished for.

"What happened on the morning of June 27th 1857 has now been carved into the annals of military atrocity. As the soldiers, women and children boarded the boats to safety, shots were fired, from which side it is not known. What is known is that the massively outnumbered British soldiers were slain in a most brutal fashion by the Indian regiments. It was a massacre of the most disgusting nature, the British men overpowered and hacked to pieces in anger.

"As the dust cleared only 120 British women and children remained, together with a small medical staff led by a cowering Archibald Kemp. They were taken as captives and returned to the heart of the city.

"The British army, upon hearing of the atrocity, immediately sent a large force to retake Cawnpore and avenge the massacre. Some say, that the methods they used upon rebels, as they advanced upon the city, were as brutal, if not more so, than those meted out upon those poor massacred soldiers, and news of atrocities committed as revenge spread to the Indian Regiments as they awaited the storm of British anger.

"They tried to use their prisoners as bargaining pieces to lessen the coming violence but were unsuccessful in every attempt. Finally, on July 15th 1857, as the British neared the city, the order was given to kill every British woman and child held prisoner within the city.

"The prisoners were being kept in an assembly room in the city and when they saw the armed Indian troops advancing upon them with purpose they locked the doors and barricaded themselves inside. Kemp, until this point had remained quiet and hopeful of their value as barter. As he looked through the shuttered windows and foresaw the coming slaughter he realised that his death, as well as the deaths of everyone within the building, was inevitable.

"Archibald Kemp; idler, sneak and coward stood up in front of the prisoners and ordered the doors open so that he may face his killers. He asked the other men from his medical team to join him but they refused, and so he stepped out of the assembly rooms alone. As the doors banged shut behind him, he charged at the massed Indian soldiers, armed only with a knife and a piece of wood.

"It is said, by Indian witnesses to the event, that he killed seven men before he finally fell and that he fought as bravely as they had ever seen a British Soldier in battle. Eventually he fell to his knees in the dust as the blades pierced him and ran him through, the multiple wounds bringing a quick but painful death. His body was dragged off into the streets of Cawnpore and held aloft as a trophy, a testament to the strength of Indian will and power over the British Empire.

"The doors of the assembly hall were broken down and the resulting massacre saw every woman and child hacked to pieces with cleavers and thrown down a dry well in the city. Those that feigned death and hid under the corpses hoping for mercy were heartlessly flung down with the rest of them, buried alive under a mass of bodies.

"When the British forces arrived and recaptured the city a day later they found a scene of devastation. The streets were strewn with the clothes of children, stripped as their bodies were dumped; long clumps of hair, cut from British women were seen caught in the branches of the trees surrounding the assembly hall, fluttering in the dry wind.

"They interrogated and tortured the Indian rebels in a most brutal and atrocious manner, none were spared and tales came out of the city of Muslim rebels being sewn into pigskins before being hung. Those that spoke before they died told the story of the massacre and of how one brave British soldier had strode out from the assembly hall to fight to the death.

"Archibald Kemp did not save any lives when he strode out of those doors to meet his death and those who knew him in life would not believe the tale when they were told it. On that day in Cawnpore he had found something within himself, something that some would call bravery but I like to think of a fire that had sparked. He had gone against every instinct to run away and he had died a gallant and brave man."

Earnshaw had been utterly silent throughout the telling of my tale. I do not know why it had come to me at this time, or why I felt the need to tell it, but suddenly I understood the tale. It was important to me. Earnshaw took a sip of his drink and drew deeply on his cigar before he spoke.

"So are you telling me that I should not judge you so quickly, Sibelius? That you could be another Archibald Kemp? A hidden hero destined to demonstrate will and fortitude previously thought beyond you? Am I to believe that deep within you is a fire powerful enough to drive you to anger and violence if required?"

He paused momentarily but it was more for effect than to give me the opportunity to respond, which I did not.

"Do you remember what I told you when last we met, Sibelius? I told you that you would come to me beaten and lost. That is how I find you. You come to me with claims of deference and you appear to have not slept for a week." I looked down at myself; it was true I cut a most shabby form, something that just a few short weeks ago I would have had nightmares about. I had discovered since then, however, that there were more important nightmares to contend with.

"It is true, I could do with a period of rest and a change of clothes, but that is not something that is beyond me, if given the right sort of encouragement. I think you will find that I have the power to surprise, sir. Do you still feel that I have a part to play in your plans, Mr Earnshaw?"

"A part to play?" he pondered that query for a moment, "I would remind you of my final words to you in the carriage, Sibelius. I told you that you would ask for redemption and that you would not find it. Do you really wish me to go back on my word? That is something that I am afraid, I would struggle to do. How would I ever live with myself if we both knew that my word was not worth a thing?"

"So true, Mr Earnshaw. So true. You could not live with yourself." I broke his gaze momentarily, now was the time.

Quickly pulling the pistol from the pocket of my overcoat and, pointing the barrel at his head, I pulled back the hammer with a loud click. He smiled at me once more and took a small sip from his brandy glass.

"Sibelius, my boy. I have told you before, I know you better than you know yourself. You are not a killer; you don't have it within you." He gave a small chuckle, one which made him choke a little with hilarity. "I know men who kill, Darke. I am surrounded by them here in this grand establishment. Each man here has shown that they are willing to make sacrifices and do the unthinkable. I thought once that you had the potential but now I see you for who you really are, Sibelius. You are emotionally weak and clinging to your sanity with well-bitten nails. You do not have what it takes man!" He had raised his voice a little now in an attempt to demonstrate his dominance. "Do you know what I did to show my commitment to the cause, Mr Darke? Do you know of the sacrifices I have made to be where I am?"

I did not answer, but stood staring at him, the barrel of my pistol quavering slightly. He saw the edge of fear within me and continued.

"Seven years ago I was approached by a gentleman within the club. He told me of their endeavour and said that if I wished to join them that I should give them something, a small token of my faith. Do you know what I gave, Sibelius? I gave the life of my newborn son. You saw the babe yourself, photographed him when we first met. Do you not remember?"

"I do," I replied, my voice shaking in disbelief.

"The child was of no matter to me, he had only just been born. But it was the strength of my decision, Sibelius. The strength of the sign that I gave which put them in no doubt that I was for them. How do you think that the beast was brought to this world? It takes a great deal of power and sacrifice to draw out such a monster. You will of course remember my daughter Marie, lovely girl, so sweet, so pure at only fourteen. I will not tell you what acts were committed to her before her death; I will leave your imagination to fire a little as I tell you that such a monster can only be summoned through the death of an innocent at the heights of terror and pain. As a means to an end, she was a daughter to be proud of and my decision to use her as a tool for summoning I see as one of love of the greatest kind; she performed beautifully as I knew she would, creating a perfect monster for us."

"I did not believe in monsters before three weeks ago, Mr Earnshaw. I always thought that they were myth and tale, created to bring fear to small children. These past few weeks however, have proven to me their existence. I have spoken to mad men who have been possessed to kill children, men who have experienced the taste of murder, but I believe that there is no greater monster than you. You are a curse upon the world, you and your gentleman associates. You are vermin to be exterminated." I steadied my hand and shifted my finger on the trigger slightly. He continued to smile at me.

"Do you think that you could shoot me and just walk out of here? You would not make it to the door alive."

"Mr Earnshaw," I spat, "I do not mean to leave at all." My hand tensed upon the gun and my finger began to move upon the trigger. In that moment I saw a flash of fear in his eyes and he opened his mouth to call for help. He did not manage to make a sound.

I pulled the trigger, the noise echoed around the room ringing within my ears. Instantly he was gone, a hole appearing in his chest, a hole which instantly began to leak blood. His body slumped forwards, falling from the chair and onto the table by his side bringing it crashing over in a crescendo of broken glass and snapping wood.

As the brass lamp broke upon the floor, flames fed by paraffin shot out onto the floor setting it alight. The body of Earnshaw was immediately consumed by the fire and I took a moment to take a decanter of brandy from the wooden sideboard and tipped its contents around the carpet causing the blaze to roar and expand. The fire quickly took hold of the room and I moved towards the doorway to escape from the area. I knew that there would be little hope of leaving the building alive but it was with thoughts of Bethany and seeing her again that I threw open the door and charged out into the corridor.

I looked down the hallway towards the stairs and saw the running figure of Osman, who must have heard the gunshot. He had a large curved blade drawn which he held above his head as he gave a terrifying cry in his native tongue. I raised my pistol to shoulder height as he sped towards me at frightening speed. I flinched as I pulled the trigger and the large man was stopped briefly by a bullet in his shoulder, a large hole appearing in the white silken shirt which exploded in a bright red hue. Unfortunately for me however he continued his charge and within a second he was upon me.

The large blade slashed down towards my head and I threw myself to one side in an attempt to avoid the steel. The sword caught the top of my left ear, slicing through and embedding itself in my shoulder. I awaited death but it did not come and I blessed my love of good tailoring for wearing such a heavily woven top-coat. Through instinct for survival I pushed the barrel of the pistol into his chest as he ran into me pushing me over. The gun went off as I fell backwards and I found myself laid upon the floor of the corridor with the heavy body of the Indian laying upon me, blood pumping from a large hole just below where his heart would be. The weight of the man was immense and I struggled to push him away from me as the flames from the drawing room crept towards my head.

I felt the thud of footsteps drumming upon the floorboards as more men approached and in desperation I found some hidden strength within me to throw off my weighty oppressor. Scrambling to my feet, I ran towards the stairs, my neck wet with the blood pouring profusely from my ear.

As I reached the end of the corridor I stopped to peer around the corner and saw two men scrambling up the stairs towards me. I fired twice upon the first man, a dark haired youth with cold eyes, missing him with the first bullet but striking him in the side of the head with the second, causing the rear of his skull to shatter as he tumbled backwards. The second man raised his own gun and it was only through my quick actions, throwing myself back into the safety of the corridor, that I avoided a bullet from hitting my own head, the lead embedding itself in the wall opposite.

I took a breath before swinging outwards once again and pulling the trigger twice, the first shot flew narrowly above the man's head causing him to duck. My second shot, fired quickly after a slight lowering of my pistol's barrel, did not send a bullet into the man, the only noise was the dull click as I quickly realised that I had already fired six shots. I thrust my hand into the pocket of my overcoat as I emptied the spent shells onto the carpeted floor. With nervous fingers I hastily attempted to replace the shells only managing to replace two as the man ran around the corner. As he saw me he raised his gun aiming it at my forehead. He stopped running and slowly approached me, keeping the gun still in his hand.

"Drop your weapon or I will kill you where you stand," he said the authority in his voice burgeoned by the knowledge that he had me. I held my arms outward. The game was up and my end had arrived as I felt the cold iron of the barrel touch my forehead.

It was as I began to drop my gun that I saw his eyes widen incredulously as he saw something behind me. I quickly turned my head and was shocked to see the flaming, stumbling body of Charles Earnshaw struggling out of the drawing room and bringing the flames from the room with him.

This horrifying distraction gave me all the time I needed as I raised my pistol bringing it up under the chin of my captor and pushing the end of the barrel into the soft flesh. I pulled the trigger twice sending the top of the man's head upwards onto the white painted ceiling above us.

With one final glance back at Earnshaw, who had now dropped to his knees consumed by the spreading fire, I reloaded my weapon and ran down the stairs, closely followed by the blaze which had taken hold of the corridor.

I flew down the stairs calling at the top of my voice,
"Fire! Fire!"

My panicked shouting had the desired effect as men appeared to forget the sounds of the gun battle which had ensued above them, and instead ran down the stairs desperate to escape the flames which now shot along the walls at alarming speed. Smoke filled the building, surrounding me as I ran, burning my eyes, causing them to stream and obscuring my vision. As I ran I occasionally saw others appearing in my path and in my own panic I fired upon them, not knowing if I was hitting my intended targets or not.

As I neared the bottom of the stairs I turned to see that the flames had overtaken me and the ground floor library was quickly becoming engulfed. I looked towards the entrance to the building, the doors had been flung open as men tried to escape. Each of these men were potentially guilty of sending the beast onto the streets of London. With a cold anger, which I do not regret, I raised my pistol and shot them in the back as they tried to escape the blaze. I fired on them until I heard the dull click of the hammer, upon which I searched my pockets and found that I only had five shells remaining. Loading these into my pistol I stood at the side of the door and waited until I saw the shadows of those fleeing from the smoke, shooting them as they neared freedom. When my pistol was empty once more I threw it into the flames and ran out of the door, tripping over the bodies of those I had killed.

As I fell out of the club, the clean air hit the back of my throat causing me to cough and choke. A crowd had begun to arrive and I heard the sound of bells and whistles that told me that the alarm had been sent calling for men to douse the flames. I hoped they would not arrive in time. I hoped that the building would burn to the ground, taking with it all the twisted ideals and assignations of evil that had happened within it. These men had called on a beast from hell as a tool to cleanse their world. Their actions had brought with it a fire that would finally destroy the devilish organisation also.

As the windows of the club exploded outwards above me, I stumbled into the crowd and away, drenched in the blood of both myself and the men I had killed. There was one final grim task to undertake before I could be rid of this curse.

17
THE SWAN OF TUONELA

I do not like people. I never have. To me they are a stain upon the world, cold and rude, ignorant and self serving. I know this because I know myself; I am one of the 'people'. I know what I am like on the inside, how I scheme and plot to get my own way, how every action that I take is with my own interests in mind. I am sure that there are some good people in the world; I just have never seen enough evidence of their existence to show me that our species deserves its position upon the world.

When I think of everyone that I have ever met in my lifetime, I can name only a handful, no greater than seven, that I would ever say were those that I cared about or loved. Perhaps this says more about me and my inability to interact with people and develop relationships, but I know that somewhere in this supposition of mine I am right. I must be.

My abhorrence of others, my desire to stay away from their company and to keep myself in solitude for as much of my life as I can, has directed my life since a child. My happiest times were when I was shut in my room reading in peace, oblivious of the world around me and lost within some other reality. Even when these times were untenable and I was forced by Mother or Father to go out and run errands for them, I developed a state of mind where I could be singularly alone whilst surrounded by others. I could be so preoccupied, so caught up in the myriad of thoughts and ideas rushing through my mind that the physical world around me was merely an afterthought. It was an intentional state, which I forced myself into just to block out what I did not want to see, what I could not deal with. Real life.

I blame the development of this ability, to fill my mind with such a rush of thoughts that I am unable to function in what others would call a normal way, on my dislike of people. It was an ever increasing circle of destruction however, a cycle which I have now become entrenched in for all of my short life. My thoughts could take me to the edge of mania, where I would be so full of ideas, so ready to change the world, that I would see myself as above everything and everybody else. Nothing solid ever materialised from these 'heights' however as I had not developed the skills socially to put them into action, to make them work. The effect of this were the 'depths', those dark times when I would retreat so far into myself that sometimes I felt the only escape would be to take my own life.

Ever present throughout this journey of elation and misery would be one force, one truth which never left my mind.

Death.

I suppose even my choice of business was the result of my fluctuating mental state. My interactions with the living were minimal, simply there for the function of creating work for me, for this purpose I created a mask, the facade of a confident and sociable young man which I was able to don when required, and when I did work, when I did have to interact with others for any length of time; they were corpses, empty shells of the living which I could manipulate, speak to and ignore without any fear of making a fool of myself.

Death has always been there for me, both as a child in the family business, in my own work enterprises and of course within my own mind; constant.

There is a Latin phrase which is often linked to my profession and the photographs that I take, 'Memento Mori'; it is roughly translated as 'Remember your Mortality' or 'Remember that you are going to die'. My own mortality is something which has weighed heavily with me since early childhood, whether wondering if my next beating from Mother would be my last, to sitting awake for nights on end dreading the thought of Surma coming for me in the night. As I grew older there were times when I even wished for it all to end, but was too cowardly to act on my impulses.

The reason that I am stating this now however, the need for me to impart my true feelings on death are because, as I left the Dolorian Club burning behind me and as I boarded a carriage to take me back to Whitechapel, I was happy to finally embrace my mortality, to realise that the end was coming and that the time had come to bring my torment to a close.

I stepped into The Alice for the last time with a heavy but committed heart. The darkness of the pub was a shock to my eyes after entering from such bright sunlight outside, however, the blackness of the environment felt suitable to my mood and demeanour. Shafts of light attempted to break in through the dusty window panes, but their attempt to brighten the atmosphere of the pub only appeared to reach a few yards in and, if anything, only accentuated the surrounding dusty gloom. Despite the time of day, the pub was strangely empty, just a few old men sat nursing their drinks in silence, the stillness of the room acting like a thick blanket muffling any sound.

Tom stood behind the bar, mindlessly polishing a glass whilst staring into the space before him with lost and empty eyes. He hadn't even noticed me enter and so I stood for a moment and thought about my great friend. The rock within my chest weighed heavy as thought of the loss and despair which I had brought into his life. I should never have let Bethany become involved in my mad schemes for revenge; her attachment to me had only brought her to lunacy and confined her within a solitary cell of my making.

I thought back even further and began to regret even meeting Tom and his wife twenty years ago. Who knows what paths their lives may have taken if I had not clung to them like a small leech in an effort to find respite from the terror of life with my mother.

I approached the bar and pulled a stool towards me, the sound of its wooden leg scraping on the floor made a noise, which, in the silence of the room, sounded deafening. The sound sparked Tom into life and he shook his head slightly as if throwing himself free from the dreamlike state in which he was trapped.

"Sib, I'm sorry I was away then. I am so tired I feel like I could sleep for a week. So much has happened lately, so many terrible things. I just wish I could get away, take Bethany and leave this place." I could tell that his mind was on other places as it took this long for him to really notice the state of me. "Good God's man, what happened to you? You are covered in blood?"

I looked down at my clothes, the blood had dried and darkened on them now and as such the cloth had disguised their covering somewhat, but my hands and neck had dried bright red.

"Do not worry, my friend. Most of it is not mine." I forced a smile and touched a tentative hand to my ear. It felt crusted and I drew my hand away quickly so as not to restart the bleeding. "I have been to my club uptown. They were not pleased to see me and I will not return there. Their threat is gone. Could I have a whisky?"

Tom said nothing but reached under the bar for my bottle. He poured a glass and carefully placed the bottle next to it.

"Just help yourself," he muttered, still staring at the mess of me. "You look like you have earned it."

I took a small sip, the urge to throw it down my throat was strong but I needed to be clear of head for the task in front of me.

"How is Bethany today?"

"A little improved. When she finally woke she cried hysterically thinking that you had been killed. I told her what happened; of how the police saved us, but she does not know that you told me everything, she thinks that I do not know. I almost do not want to tell her, I need to keep things normal for her, as normal as they could be anyway." He paused briefly, his eyes looking deep into the distance. "I have some money saved, Sibelius. I thought that now this was over I could sell up and take Beth and Anne out into the country. Find a quiet pub to run, away from London and its fear. You could come too ... if you like, we could be happy again, a fresh start. Do you understand, Sib?"

"I do, Tom, I do. A fresh start I think would be good for all of us, Bethany in particular. Can I go up and visit her? I wish to tell her that she is safe now, that the men who brought this terror to us are gone." He nodded his assent and I supped the rest of my drink, getting up off the stool and walking towards the door to the stairs. As I reached it I turned around. "You deserve a new beginning, Tom, you all do." I stepped through the door and heard Tom shout after me.

"With you, Sib. With you as well." He called. I did not reply, but continued to walk up the stairs, the ache of tears burning the back of my eyes.

As I reached the top of the stairs I looked into the doorway of Bethany's room, she was asleep on her bed, curled up and facing the wall. Quietly I walked into the room and sat upon the chair besides her bed. She looked so at peace, that I did not wake her. For half an hour I sat and watched her, there were bruises upon her face, cuts about her cheeks and her eyes were red and swollen but it did nothing to assuage her beauty. I could have sat there forever gazing at her but she turned in her sleep, rolling over to face me. Her eyes opened briefly and she smiled before drifting back into her slumber.

"Bethany?" I whispered. She groaned a little but her eyes remained closed. "Bethany, it is over now. I have killed the men who caused this. They will not bring danger to your door again." She did not respond and I could not tell if she heard me or if she slept still. "Bethany?" I called quietly, "there is one more task I must carry out, one more thing to make you safe forever." Her face twitched a little but she did not stir. "I know where the beast hides, Bethany. I know where he is and I know how to send him home for good." Another slight twitch of her cheek and she rolled over once more to face the wall.

Slowly I stood up, looking down on the sleeping girl. I would miss her. I bent down and laid a light kiss upon her brow.

"I love you, Bethany Finnan. I always have. Goodbye."

She did not stir and I left the room. As I reached the bottom of the stairs I decided to leave the Princess Alice by the back door, I could not bear to see Tom again.

My short walk home was heavy with emotion, as I looked at these filthy, beautiful streets that I had known all of my life. I thought of how I ran through them as a child, skipping through the alleyways and in and out of the bustling crowds, always with intent, always with an errand to run for Mother in fear of a beating if I did not complete it quickly.

As I turned the corner into Osborn Street I saw the broken remnants of my studios, boarded up and shattered the object of so much hatred. There was no police presence and I was thankful for that. It would make matters easier.

I walked through my front door, briefly looking over my shoulder. People carried on their evening business without a second glance at me. Yesterday I was the pariah of the neighbourhood, as good as convicted in their scared eyes. Today I was forgotten.

Making sure that I left my front door ajar, I entered my hallway and made my way into the studio. This was the place where horror began when, through the lens of my camera, the fourteen year old daughter of a monster tried to warn me of the return of a demon.

I picked up the tripod to my camera and, folding the legs together, I carried it over to the darkroom. Withdrawing the keys from my coat pocket, I unlocked the padlock which held the door to my darkroom secure. As I pushed the door open I tossed the keys to the floor at the side of me, I would not need them anymore. The familiar smell of chemicals wafted out of the room and into my senses reminding me of the many hours that I had spent shut away in the dim red light developing my pictures, creating my art. I entered slowly, pulling the door closed behind me and leaving just a small opening so that I could see out into the studio. I had a few moments left to commit myself to this course of action and carried out my final act in the darkroom. I had thought of nothing else for a number of hours and as such any hint of hesitation on my part was lessened considerably.

A sweet but sickly feeling caught in my throat, it would only be a matter of time before I destroyed my reputation forever in the cause of safety for the area.

I heard the soft click of the outer door as my follower entered the building. The door to the studio creaked open and I peered cautiously through the crack in the darkroom door as they walked in.

There was a look of confusion on their face as they found that I was not immediately visible, they walked three yards into the room and glanced suspiciously around, looking for any sign of me. Thankfully they had not considered my place of hiding and so turned to leave, presumably to search upstairs. It was at that moment that I leapt from my hiding place and swung the tripod hard, aiming to strike my intruder about the head.

I had thought that it would be easy to bring them down but they turned with such speed, such inhuman speed. I had been aiming for the back of the head but my target turned and, instead of connecting with a ferociously hard blow, I struck a glancing blow to the forehead. Luckily for me it was enough to send them sprawling to the floor, giving me the time to leap upon them and place my hands around their slim throat.

Bethany looked up at me, her eyes full of hatred and anger. She struggled to throw me from her, but my weight was too much. Her hands clenched into fists and swung maddeningly at me, striking around my shoulders and sides. These blows hurt, they stung with an aching ferocity, but I did not falter from my task and kept my fingers securely around her pale neck, squeezing ever tighter and pressing the life from her. She screamed obscenities at me, the words spitting forth with all the bile and wrath that she could manage from her constricted throat. I pressed harder, the tears running down my face as I tried to desperately control my emotions. Her hands flashed to my wrists, sharp nails digging hard into the flesh of my forearms, drawing blood which ran down onto her throat, but I did not feel any pain, I had passed that point now. I could smell burning coming from behind me and I knew that the fire which I had set in the darkroom had taken hold, slowly making its way through the many flammable chemicals enclosed within the room, each one spurring the flames on to greater heat and energy.

My eyes struggled to see her through the tears, as the smoke and my emotions assaulted my body, but I blindly continued squeezing at her soft throat. Stiff and tense, unbreakable in their task; the muscles within my arms strained to bursting point in pursuit of the death of the woman I loved.

I could see the life draining from her as she struggled less and less, she was dying by my hand, her neck crushed, the air prevented from entering her body. For a brief moment I saw the image in my mind of my mother, a reminder of actions past, her pale eyes imploring me as the light died within them. I thought then of Lemminkäinen and of the swan which passed within his sights and of Grandfather's dying words to me. Still the doubt lurked though, still the fear of what I was doing to this poor girl.

Suddenly Bethany's face changed before me and she fell peaceful; she looked at me softly as those last embers of life began to die within her. Such a beautiful girl, how could I do this to her? How could I kill what I desired most in the world?

As if in answer to my question, a paleness came over her then, a shade which, whilst turning her skin a deathly white, accentuated the darkened grey lines around her eyes as they squeezed shut in a final show of anger. When her eyes flashed open again they were not the eyes of Bethany, but of Surma. They were fire white and flecked with red, the eyes of a demon, the demon that was rampant within this poor girl. The beast smiled at me.

It was at this point that I felt a burning within my fingers. It was a burning not of heat but of ice, a coldness which spread through my hands and began to rise up my forearms, enveloping me in the touch of death. I lost all feeling and my hands loosened from Bethany's neck as the demon's spirit began to claim me.

As it reached my shoulders and rose up my neck into my head, I began to feel the presence of Surma within me. He entered my head at the base of my skull and I knew that I had succeeded in my goal.

I was the beast and the beast was me.

Bethany lost consciousness and I fell sideways, landing on the dusty wooden floor, rigid with the spectre slowly taking control of my body. I lay staring up at the ceiling, unable to move or feel any part of myself. Images flooded into my mind; memories of the beast which had taken me for its own, rushed at high speed, it was like seeing a hundred vivid lifelike photographs one after the other.

I saw Bethany's bedroom through her eyes, I saw Tom, Anne and I visiting her/me, each of us stood over and speaking in a language that I did not understand. I saw children, who ran screaming from me as I picked them up and tore through their throats with my teeth, I could even taste their blood as it ran down my throat, sating an unspeakable hunger.

I saw Bethany charging towards me, her eyes wild with anger, her nails flashing in the gas lit street, distracting me from the broken form of a small boy who lay dead at my feet.

I was forced to watch the death of James Flint, who bravely tried to fight for his life, but whose arms I snapped from his shoulders, his last cries ending as his head was torn from his body, my feeding only interrupted by the screams of a drunken Mary Tanner as she fell down the stone steps towards me.

I saw the murder of my Father and my brother, Niko's death quick and grotesque as my hand thrust through his neck, taking hold of the top of his spine and pulling the head free. Father's death was not so hasty; I took my time over his demise. He was hung by his ankles from the bannisters of the house, unable to cry for help as his tongue had been ripped out, slowly he had been tortured by me until death; his misery only ended when his arteries were sliced and he sprayed the walls a deep, thick red.

Finally, I saw a cold stone altar, upon which I lay, surrounded by tall men in dark grey, cloth hoods which covered their faces. I screamed in pain as I was pulled from my own world and forced into the body of a man, forced to suffer with an intolerable hunger which could never be sated.

The flames had spread from the darkroom now and were beginning to engulf my studio; they shot up the linen backdrops on the walls, enclosing the room with fire and destroying the business that I had spent years building. Even if I had wished to escape I could not have, I was no longer in control of my body and I waited for the beast within me to attempt to move me away from danger. No movement came.

Bethany began to wake next to me, she was oblivious to the fire in the room at first and looked like a child waking from a long and much needed sleep. She saw the flames spreading around her and panic shot across her face. She tried to stand, at first unsteady but the fear of the burning room overcame her lethargy and dizziness. As she stood and started towards the door she looked down and saw me lying on the floor rigid and dying, doomed to burn within a fire of my own making. I could not speak to her, to tell her how I felt and why I had acted how I did. My body would not work though, and all I could do was to look at her for the last time. A single tear ran down my cheek, the only means I had left to express my feelings. She understood, I know that she did. With a last glance at me, she ran from the room. Bethany was safe, I had succeeded.

"Why will this body not work?" Came a soft singing voice within my mind. "This form is mine and yet it will not move as I wish."

"This body is dying," I answered with all the effort I could muster. "There is a poison running through its veins and soon it will cease to function."

"Poison?" Its voice was smooth and warm, it felt comfortable and soothing to my ears, I wondered whether this was the true voice of Surma or whether the soporific nature of the chemical I had ingested had begun to take effect and cause me to hallucinate.

"Potassium cyanide; I put poison in my body to end my life, and in doing so I have finished your time upon this earth. If you stay with me you will die with me. Return to Tuonela, you will not be pulled from your home again."

"Thank you." Spoke the voice, and with that I felt the beast leave my body. As he slowly withdrew from me I began to regain feeling and control. I felt the heat of the flames and I felt the bitter poison slowly destroying my body from the inside. There was no hope for me now and I let the fire engulf my body and burn me to ash.

I would see Surma again soon, but I would not fear him. I would travel to Tuonela and I would find my family once more. We would embrace and tell tales to each other, tales of bravery and honour, of good men overcoming terrible evil. We will tell the stories that we have told time and again. I may even attempt to tell them of the circumstances that led to my death, of how I found love and lost it, and of how I stopped a killer and the men behind him.

I would tell it as best I could and I would try to make it as exciting as those wonderful tales told to me when I was a boy.

But of course, I was never a good storyteller, not like Grandfather.

Printed in Great Britain
by Amazon